JUSTICE FOR MARY (SPECIAL FORCES: OPERATION ALPHA)

HELLFORCE SECURITY: ALPHA TEAM, BOOK 1

RAYNE LEWIS

Editing by Rebecca Hodgkins
Cover by Lori Jackson

Dear Readers,

Welcome to the Special Forces: Operation Alpha Fan-Fiction world!

If you are new to this amazing world, in a nutshell the author wrote a story using one or more of my characters in it. Sometimes that character has a major role in the story, and other times they are only mentioned briefly. This is perfectly legal and allowable because they are going through Aces Press to publish the story.

This book is entirely the work of the author who wrote it. While I might have assisted with brainstorming and other ideas about which of my characters to use, I didn't have any part in the process or writing or editing the story.

I'm proud and excited that so many authors loved my characters enough that they wanted to write them into their own story. Thank you for supporting them, and me!

READ ON!
    Xoxo
    Susan Stoker

To J, my very own Alpha hero, who believed in me way before I believed in myself. You are my rock when I need to stand, my shoulder when I need to cry, and my wings when you lift me to soar to heights greater than I ever imagined.
Loves.

PROLOGUE

He felt the searing heat before he felt the pain. His head clouded in confusion as his ears rang with a high-pitched tone. He bit with crushing force against his molars, wincing at the pressure. Even though the ringing was piercing, it was nothing compared to the burning flesh of his arm. He tried to lift it but his mind was disconnected from his muscles. Agony ensued.

Fuck! He tried to bark out the word, but his voice was silent as were his screams. He needed to get up. *Why can't I move? What the fuck just happened?* He commanded his body: *Move. Get up. Stand.* It betrayed him. The pebbled dirt below his cheek dug into his face. A growing pool of crimson melded with the dirt beneath him. His breath became labored. He was going into shock.

He closed his eyes, searching his memory. *A baby. Mother. Teammates.* The unbearable, excruciating pain made it impossible to think. *Driving. Arctic. Brother.* The smell jolted his memory. *Fuel. Burning fuel. The Humvee. My team.*

They were driving to the village when the explosion erupted. *His team. Where was his team?* Shivering cold came over his body and he watched as the growing pool widened, blood leaching from his body. He was dying. He knew it. He would die in the foothills of Afghanistan at the age of thirty-four. His momma and daddy would be visited by the Casualty Assistance Officers. The last thing he'd do on this earth was break his momma's heart. That truth was worse than the pain of his dying body.

His life played through his mind as if on fast forward. Joy, happiness, sadness, pride, regret. *Regret.* He would leave no legacy. Just a name carved into a cold slab of granite. Name. Rank. Date. He would leave no wife. He would leave no children. Pain hit again at the thought. *Regret.* He couldn't keep his eyes open. They fluttered as his body fought for every bit of life to which it could cling. The whitest of white light encompassed him, enveloped him. All the demons he fought that haunted his dreams—and his days—melted away.

Peace. Eternal peace. Eternal peace without a legacy. That would be King's eternal hell. His last regret.

CHAPTER 1

FOUR YEARS LATER

Mary sighed in frustration. "Get your ass up off the couch!" Her voice didn't begin to express the eruption of anger flowing in her veins.

"Busy." He replied without even looking at her. "No, No, bro. Get the guy on the left, then we'll flank to get the dude in the black gear." He spoke into the mic attached to the headset.

Mary couldn't hold her anger in any longer. Her brother, Trent, was a grown man, thirty-two, acting like an immature, adolescent child. She was sick of doing everything on her own. Exhausted and plain fed up. Things were falling apart and she couldn't hold them together much longer.

She'd been working the graveyard shift, waiting tables at a sleazy dive of a diner, which even though it was full-time didn't pay shit, and the tips were minimal during the night shifts. If she had to have her ass groped one more time, someone was going to have to post bail for her. Add to that she worked part-time as a day activity director at Rebecca's Hope, a shelter for abused women.

And, if that wasn't enough to run her ragged, she visited her mother every evening between jobs at the senior living center. The days her mother recognized her were waning, and Mary felt terrible for wanting to skip today. She was tired, barely waking this afternoon after last night's shift, and having had a crappy sleep this morning before she needed to be at the women's shelter.

So, she was contemplating skipping her ritual evening visit. Her mother wouldn't know if she skipped a day, but it may just be the day she had a moment of clarity, and if that happened, Mary wanted to be there.

"Trent, listen to me. I need you to run to the bank and deposit this check."

Her brother ignored her, zoned into the battlefield, wannabe soldier, combat game.

"Trent!" She kept her voice just below a scream and stepped between him and the tv.

"Busy. God...Get out of the way Mary! I'm almost to the check-point." He craned his head, looking around her, and continued to play. "No, dude...just my bitch of a sister."

What was he doing? Wanting to be a soldier, a hero, but not wanting to give the sacrifice required, so he found his hero status in a video game? *If only he was a real man and actually served his country! That's it.* She walked over to the gaming console, reached down, and yanked the plug out of the wall socket.

"What the hell! What are you doing! You fucking bitch!" Trent jumped off the couch, ran to the console, and shoved the plug back into the wall.

Mary stood with her arms crossed.

Trent glared at his sister, seeing that the game was lost. "You're a fucking cunt!" He pulled the headset off. "Shouldn't you be at work or something?"

Mary's rage boiled over. "Yes, Trent, I am on my way to work. To my *second* job after working all night. Which is why I need you to deposit this check at the bank. It has to go into my account to cover the check I wrote for the electricity. She handed it to him.

"Can't you do it? Why don't you get a direct deposit like every other normal person."

"The diner doesn't offer direct deposit. I need you to do this. It absolutely has to be in my account, toooday." She stretched and held the syllables of the word.

"So, then you should do it. Stop trying to pawn your shit off on me. Do it yourself."

God, she couldn't believe his arrogance. Actually, yes, she could because Trent had always been selfish. "I can't. I don't have time. I have a long shift at the shelter, and then I have to sneak in a quick visit with Mom before going straight to the diner." Even just hearing herself list off her to-do list made her exhausted.

"Why do you even go there? Not like the old crow's going to know you. Save yourself the time and trouble and leave her there. No one needs to visit her."

How could he be so cold and calloused? What happened to the boy she grew up with? Where did the fun-loving, wholehearted brother go? When did he turn into a deviant adolescent, always finding trouble when trouble was finding him, and when did he turn into a cold-hearted man-child?

He'd always been in trouble...with the law, with her parents, but he never showed the arrogance and anger outbursts as he had lately. She'd become scared of her own brother. Many times she questioned why she'd allowed him to stay.

The answer: because that's what her Mom would want.

Even through the years of Trent raising hell and disrespecting her mom and dad, they always coddled him, hoping that tomorrow would be a new day. That, *tomorrow*, things would change; he would change.

She should have kicked him out or called the police many times before, but her mother's words, the words she said during one of her rare lucid moments, haunted her. "Take care of my little boy. He has a good heart." Her heart hurt and her eyes watered at the thought of her mother being there alone. "You're cold, Trent."

"And, you're ridiculous, Mary." He mimicked her tone. "If you think it even matters that you go there each day, sitting next to an old, brain-damaged lady, you're a moron. But then, it's not like you have anyone else who wants to spend time with you." He laughed, "You're thirty and don't even have a boyfriend. You're so pathetic."

"She's not brain-damaged; she has early-onset dementia." Tears welled in her eyes and she willed them not to fall. She knew it would only spur him on to see his words hurt her. He'd become so hurtful and cruel. It was as if he tried to throw barbs at her just to see them stick.

Trent wasn't the same fun-loving, protective big brother she grew up with. He hung out with a bunch of hoodlums; a shady gang of friends doing God only knew what, and trouble always followed them. Theft, public intoxication, fights, bar brawls, and too many arrests to count. And, when he wasn't with them, he was playing video games with them or sleeping the day away.

"FYI, boyfriends don't like when chicks cry," he flicked the lone tear running down her cheek that betrayed her before she could wipe it.

She flinched away from his touch as he went back to the couch, put his headset back on, and grabbed the controller now that the console was back to life.

Her heart stung at his words. It's not that she didn't want a boyfriend. She would love to find someone who loved her. She dreamt of it each time she fell asleep. But, she didn't have time for a boyfriend. Even if she had time, truth be told, she wasn't girlfriend material.

She was too shy and too plain to attract a man. She knew she wasn't a dog, she had pretty features, but she just wasn't what guys wanted. She didn't do a slathering of makeup like she'd seen other women do. She only put a hint of makeup on to accentuate her natural features and bring out her green eyes. Her hair was long, but just plain brown, and fell below her boobs with a natural curl to it.

Because of her lack of time, she wore it up in a messy bun, one: because the restaurant required it; and two: there was no sense in styling it for her first job and then wrecking the style, throwing it up for the restaurant gig.

"Yo, Chet. You there? I'm back at your six."

Her brother's voice startled her from her thoughts of her non-existent love life, and his use of military lingo was just atrocious. She mentally rolled her eyes.

"Trent, I'm not done speaking to you."

Her brother's annoyance was palpable. "Fuck off, Mary. I'm not going to be your errand boy. Not my responsibility to do your shit."

"That's 'cuz you have *no* responsibility, Trent." She set her hands on her hips as she laid it on the line. "You do nothing. Absolutely nothing besides sitting on your ass, playing video games, and eating the food that *I* buy. You don't pay rent. You don't do any chores. You don't have a job. You've mooched off Mom, and now me. God, Trent, you barely even bathe."

She was getting worked up, feeling her heartbeat in her temples, a sign a migraine was just around the corner. That's all she needed, a headache to make her bad day into a shit day. "You do nothing. Not even visit your own mother. You're thirty-two, Trent, time to grow up."

Trent ignored her, getting back into his game with his buddies.

"I'm talking to you!" She attempted to pull the controller from his hands, needing him to give her his attention. She almost grasped it, but he pulled it to the side, out of her reach.

"Bitch! What are you doing? Fucking psycho!" He didn't take his eyes from the game as he yelled at her.

"Trent! Look. At. Me. I need your help! Enough with the stupid game." This time she got a hold of it and yanked the controller from his hands.

Trent stood lightning-fast and threw a punch. He connected with her jaw and knocked her backwards over the coffee table and onto her back.

Instant pain radiated along her side where she caught the long edge of the overturned table. The punch and fall hurt, and she let out a scream. She cradled her side but her brother wasn't done. He leaped over the table and grabbed a handful of her blouse. He cocked an elbow back and made a fist.

Mary threw her hands up, crossed them over her face, and waited for him to throw another blow.

"You fucking dumb cunt!" He shook her and grasped her around her throat. "Don't you ever, and I mean *ever*, touch my shit again, you hear me! Next time it'll be much worse than a fall!" He pulled her forward with her blouse and pushed her back with such force her head ricocheted off the concrete basement floor. That would definitely be bringing on a migraine.

She looked up into his eyes, burning with fury, and didn't recognize her own brother. *Who has he become?* Her lips tightened, holding back her sobs, but she began to cry anyway.

Her brother paid no attention, just picked up his controller and went back to his game.

She lay on the ground, scared to death that he would lay another hand on her. Her jaw throbbed in excruciating pain when she worked it from left to right. She wanted this day to end, but seeing it was still morning, she'd be facing it with a busted jaw and a busted heart.

This wasn't the first time Trent had hit her. She'd lived in denial long enough. Her brother had changed beyond recognition and he wouldn't get any better. So she needed to change her life too, find a way out, get away from her asshole of a brother.

CHAPTER 2

King muttered under his breath at the stacks of paper littering his desk. Things had gotten out of control with his office skills, and he needed to fix it, pronto! But, he and the guys had been on back, to back, to back missions. There was no break in downtime, not even a lull, to give him time to find an assistant, but he needed to find one, and he wasn't dicking around any longer.

"Whoa! Looks like you need a maid," Trip mused, knowing King had no time to get the paperwork squared away. "Maybe one of those women that wear those sexy French maid costumes." He didn't wait for King to reply, just continued on. "Speaking of maid costumes, I was with this chick last night, and you should have seen what she could do with a feather duster! I could've shot a game of pool with my dic—"

"No one but you was talking about maid costumes." King didn't look up from his desk, just continued to shuffle and haphazardly organize papers.

Trip laughed, "Yeah, I know, but I needed a segue into what a wild night I had. Best lay I've ever had in my life. And, she could suck the chrome off a bumper."

King looked up, stilled in his task, "Is there a reason you're in my office?"

"Oh, yeah, there's a man, Tillman, waiting in the entrance. Says you have an appointment with him. Lots of stars on his shoulders. Big brass."

"Fuck!" King bit out the word like venom. "Why didn't you say that right away, instead of telling me that ridiculous story of a French maid?" He pulled his phone from his pocket and checked his calendar app. "Shit. General Tillman's today." Not that he would think a four-star General would show up on the wrong date, but he was hoping so. "Put him in the conference room, get him something to drink, and I'll be there in five." King opened his laptop and began clicking and typing away.

"Sure can do, boss." Trip turned on his heels and beelined it to meet the general.

Shit! This was the third time this month he'd messed up his schedule. Once with a Hollywood B-list celebrity's agent looking for a security detail for his not-so-famous client, which made King anything but disappointed he didn't get the gig because of his faux pas.

But, the other two meant he almost missed money. The clientele Hellforce held weren't run-of-the-mill customers. No. Most of his clientele came from the DOD, and the Department of Defense did not like to be kept waiting. Luckily, he was able to salvage the contracts and secure them, but he had a hard time negotiating because he almost missed the meeting and didn't have the leverage to get the amount of money he knew his guys were worth.

He needed an assistant ASAP and would put an ad out as soon as he got done with the brass in the conference room.

≈

I actually quit my job! Mary couldn't believe it all came down to defending herself. So what if it involved scalding burns? The creep deserved it when he slid his palm over her ass and tried to cop a feel under the hem of her dress. A cup of coffee to his crotch sent him screaming and also got him a ride to the hospital when the ambulance showed up. *Ooops, I slipped when you grabbed my ass. Oh, well.* Her boss was there, saw the entire confrontation, and before he could fire her, she told him she quit. *A girl's gotta do what she's gotta do.*

Back at home, Mary balled up the seafoam green, out-of-date, out-of-style waitress uniform and pitched it in the bathroom trash can. The hell if she was going to wash it and return it to her asshole boss.

She reached into the shower and turned the handle all the way to HOT. The water heater was on its last leg, and she couldn't afford to call a repair service, so she knew the water would be lukewarm at best, and the five-minute shower would be anything but relaxing, but she had to get the stench and retch of the diner off her.

Already undressed, she studied herself in the full-length mirror. Her side was bruised a deep purple and was beyond tender to the touch. She winced at every turn and touch. She pulled her hair tie and watched as her hair cascaded over her shoulders and down around her breasts, the shorter wisps framing her face.

Was she that plain? Did her looks repel men like some sort of plague? She stared at her reflection, steam barely condensing on the outer edges of the mirror. She leaned closer examining her face.

Her normally bright, green eyes had dulled over the last few months, not having much to shine about. She was pretty, in a plain, uninteresting way. No wonder she didn't get a second glance. She was ordinary and uninteresting. She let out a sigh. *No sense in agonizing over something that can't be changed.*

Checking that the water hadn't run cold, she stepped in, leaned her head back, and let the flood of water slick her hair.

It felt great to get the day washed off her body. She reached for her loofa and poured a generous glob of body wash on it then began to lather her body. It felt amazing gliding across her skin and over her breasts, and it teased her nipples to erection. She'd always had sensitive nipples, but she chalked that up to them being rather large nubs.

Looking down, she assessed her breasts. They weren't huge, but they were large and heavy. Large for her slender, five-foot-seven, one-hundred-forty-pound frame. Without a bra, her cleavage parted naturally but stood high on her chest, her breasts were firm and didn't sag or hang to the sides. She ran the cherry blossom suds over them, the scent filling the air, then assessed them again.

They were boobs.

She mentally shrugged. They were more than a handful, but nothing pornstar-worthy.

She closed her eyes and let the caresses of the sponge work its way down her body. What would it feel like if the sponge were a man's hands? Would it feel this sensual, or would she feel every callus on his roughened hands? Working hands. *Mmmm.* She imagined those hands roaming her body. Her breathing increased as she rubbed the lather over her mound of lightly trimmed curls. She brought a hand to her erect nipple and gently rolled the swollen, lathered nub between her fingers. Would a man find her attractive enough to want to explore her body? She pulled slightly feeling the jolt radiate through her chest.

Dropping the loofa, she brought her hand to her virgin lips and caressed the pouty folds. It felt so good, but it felt even better when she imagined the caresses to be a man's. She pushed her middle finger into the folds and felt the tight muscles envelop her.

Oh, the erotic things she would let a man do to her. Her breath hitched when she added a second. She pumped them slowly, in and out, and tugged at her nipple in tandem, pulling until her moan echoed off the shower walls. She did the same to the other bud starving for attention. Her core refused when she tried to add a third. She winced when she didn't stretch to accommodate. Her second finger pushed deeper, along with the first, and it curled to match the other, vigorously rubbing against the ribbed walls.

Damn! The sensation was incredible and piquing. She let out another moan and kept her fingers curled as she frantically rubbed at the roughened spot. His fingers would be much larger than hers and would fill her, stretch her, bringing her to orgasm a hell of a lot faster.

She imagined him kissing her neck, down to her aching breasts, biting a nipple or two. *Oh, God!* The pressure was building, and she was on the verge of losing it. *Faster. Faster. Rub faster.* His imaginary fingers worked her over the edge. She felt herself beginning to tremble, and leaned her back against the shower wall. *Fuck me.* She crooned to the alpha male in her mind. She used her thumb to press hard against her clit, tugging hard on her swollen nipples at the bud's tight end, and she went off like a rocket.

"Fuck me!" She shrilled, as she came with such force she slumped onto the shower floor. Her inner muscles spasmed while she held her fingers deep, not wanting to move them and lose the monstrous orgasm, and were crushed by the convulsing contractions, while her breasts heaved high on her chest, her breathing shuttering and erratic. She was coming down from the rush. The slick wetness of her cum let her fingers continue to glide in and out of herself, while her orgasm diminished.

The shower ran cold, but she didn't notice until the bliss of ecstasy waned. *Fuck.* The rapture of her five-minute finger session wasn't nearly what she imagined would be a night with an incredible man.

She pulled her fingers free from her core and washed them off in the cooling water. She stood and cleaned the wetness from her thighs. The water was brisk and she shivered, but not from her erotic euphoria.

If only there were a man who could fill her heart, as well as her body, with pure bliss. But, if she found him, would he want her? Her heart fell. Who would want a plain Jane?

She was merely Mary.

~

"Where in the hell is the Woodman file?" King's booming bellow reached the closed doors of the weight room.

"Sounds like he's pissed." Cy curled his bicep, watching his form in the mirror.

"Not going to be the one to help him clean that hellhole of an office." Slate strained out the words as he pushed the bar of weights up, T-BAR spotting him when his arms began to tremble.

The guys worked out, listening to King rant down the hallway, all of them hoping he found whatever he was looking for before their workout was over.

"He thinks he has to do everything himself. Doesn't trust anyone to help him. I stayed last week to give him a hand, thinking if we could get the files into piles, and even better into the filing cabinet, he'd be more organized. Nope, he just chewed my ass, called me an asshole, and kicked me out of his office." Trip put the free-weights back on the rack and wiped his face with a towel. "Think he needs to have an intervention."

Arctic chimed in next. "When he and I first started this place, Hellforce was a fraction of what it is now, and he could handle the paperwork, books, payroll, and scheduling *and* run missions. Now, he's too stubborn to admit he needs to bring someone in, someone that can keep him out of the administration part, keep him up-to-date and functioning to allow him to focus on what matters...saving our asses on missions and not worrying where his files are hiding."

The guys continued their workout, hoping King would cool off before they returned to their offices.

CHAPTER 3

It was the sixth interview Mary sat through in a seven-day stretch, and she was no closer to being employed than she was from day one. She had one more to go, and if she was given the pleasant smile and the "Don't call us, we'll call you," bullshit, then eagerly escorted to the door again, she was going to go ballistic. She couldn't afford to not get the next job. *Ugh!* She hated the interview process. She hated to have to sell herself, pimp herself out to the interviewer, hoping she could turn a trick better than the other bazillion candidates that applied and pimped themselves out before her.

She needed caffeine.

Mary was unfamiliar with this side of town and had no idea if a Starbucks was in the area. She dug through her purse and retrieved her phone. Her trusty app would lead her to the closest coffee joint. She didn't care which cafe, just as long as they brewed beans and had scones, she was golden!

Tapping the app, she headed to the cafe around the corner, a coffee and bookstore called, *Brews & Books*. She hoped it wasn't a dive, because she would at least like a brew that didn't eat the metal off a spoon.

The cafe had a cute storefront with a green and white awning overhanging three sets of chairs and tables on the walkway. Pulling open the door, she was pleasantly surprised at the quaint and relaxing atmosphere. It wasn't stuffy or snooty like the big chain conglomerates. It had a "homey" vibe to it. Lining the front window were racks of books, some for sale, while others were for the customers to read while they sipped their brew. *Books and Brews*, clever and catchy.

She walked to the counter and noticed even the warm tan color on the walls was inviting. She knew she was going to like this coffee just by how much attention the owner put into making the cafe welcoming.

A very short, mid-twenties, cute-as-a-button woman stood behind the counter, tucking a strand of strawberry-blond hair behind her ear. Her name tag read, Imogen. "Welcome to Brews & Books, what can I get 'cha?"

Mary's eyes fell from the menu board, written in chalk with names of authors next to their favorite coffee brew of choice. She didn't know half the crap listed on the board, but she did recognize some of the authors.

She went with something safe. "Um...could I get...a," she perused the menu one last time, "a peppermint latte, please?" Mary second-guessed her order, but changed her mind about changing her mind.

"Good choice. We make the best latte. Can I get a name?"

"Mary."

"M-a-r-y." The woman spoke as she wrote on the cup. "A name I can actually spell...and pronounce. Can't get any plainer than that." The woman chuckled, and Mary did as well though she was anything but happy with the innocent statement.

A plain name for a plain girl. *Good God, even my name is boring. Why couldn't I have a name like Jasmine or Harley, something that's sassy or original? Nope. Just plain Mary. Heaven help me, I was doomed from birth.*

The petite woman pointed to a rack of books over by a large sideboard with books standing open and upright, for customers to notice the titles. "There's some of our newest books. If you want to nestle down with a hunky alpha-male and sip your drink, those are the go-to books!" The woman winked at her, "Be back with your latte."

Just as Mary was going to tell her that alpha males were not her thing, the woman scampered away, humming a tune Mary wasn't familiar with. Instead of standing there deftly, she strode over to the sideboard. Mary picked up the book closest to her and sucked in a breath. *Oh, my God! Wowza!* There was more meat on that cover than she'd find in a butcher's market. *Maybe I could go for a little alpha after all.*

"Edwards," Mary said the author's name, committing it to

memory. She had no extra cash, barely able to splurge on coffee. She put the book back and picked up the one next to it. It, too, was as tantalizing as the first. The ripped, sculpted man on the cover was gorgeous! His six-pack abs and toned muscles made Mary tingle and zing. *What was that?* She noted the author's name and traced the intricate design of a black spade and red heart overlaid by the single letter S.

"Intriguing," she said to no one in particular. Mary thought the books were appealing, but there was a reason they only existed in a fictional world, because no real alpha-males existed in the real world.

They were like unicorns. If they existed, she didn't know where they were hiding, but if she could live in their world for a few hours...count her in.

She noted the author's name, then she heard her name called. She put the book down and went to retrieve her drink. She couldn't wait to get the pick-me-up from the brew.

"Here you go, hun. Careful, it's hot. Not that you wouldn't know that already, but we have to warn each customer. Liability and all."

Mary smiled at Imogen. She was as notable as her name. The design poured into the brown foam was a ribbon of small hearts. Nothing fancy like others she'd seen before. Just a simple design as plain as her. She lifted the cup to her nose and inhaled the scent. The peppermint infused her nostrils and embedded deep within her. "This smells like heaven." As plain as her milk design was, the scent of the coffee made up for it ten-fold.

Imogen laughed and took a sip from the cup in her hand. "If you think the smell is great, wait until you taste it."

Mary brought the drink to her lips, careful of the steam rising, and took a small sip. Her taste buds jumped to life. The contrast between the hot coffee and the chill of the peppermint was invigorating.

Imogen sipped her own coffee and smiled from behind her cup. "Good, hmm?"

"This is the best latte I've ever had." Mary took another sip, this one a little bigger than the last. "If I could marry this coffee, I would." She took a third sip then put the coffee down on the counter. "What are you drinking?" Mary motioned to Imogen's cup.

"Good ol' plain black. No cream. No sugar. No fluff. No stuff." She took a satisfying pull, "Only way to drink it."

Mary had no poker face and knew the stunned look was clearly readable. "You own a coffee shop," she paused, "but you only drink black coffee. How is that possible? You have every conceivable flavor. There has to be something else you drink?"

"Nope," Imogene popped the *P* and took another sip, "drinking the O.G."

Mary just shook her head, "To each their own," then raised her cup, and Imogen tapped her cup to Mary's.

"If you don't mind me saying, you're awfully dressed up for a mid-morning coffee."

Mary looked down and ran a hand over her silky blouse and absently flattened the front of her pants.

"You look fine, hun, I'm just curious as to where you're going...or where you've been."

Mary suddenly felt self-conscious, because she knew her clothes weren't the best and definitely not designer. *Is that the reason I was turned away at so many interviews?* She mentally chastised herself, wishing she would have bought a new outfit, but her bank account was tapped out. Even the check she wrote for the electricity "technically" was made of rubber, until Trent deposited it into the bank. *Fuck!* Would he remember to deposit it? After he hit her, she was in such a hurry to get away from him, she didn't even think to grab the check off the table. *Damn it.*

"Well, it doesn't matter. None of my beeswax, anyway."

Mary realized she'd been silent, stuck in her own mind. "Interviews," Mary blurted the word fast and forcefully, causing Imogen to startle. "I'm going to...I've been to some...I had interviews earlier, and now...I have one to...go to." *Which is pointless, 'cuz I most likely won't get it anyway.* She chastised herself, again, for the thought.

Imogen motioned to a small table close to the counter, and Mary took the cue and sat down, placing her drink on the glass tabletop.

"You look like you're drowning, sweet. Anything you care to get off your chest?" She patted Mary's hand, then sat back in the chair, as if expecting Mary to talk.

Imogene was younger than Mary. She guessed mid-twenties, but she had soulful eyes. Still young and vibrant, but windows of wisdom, even for her young age.

"You don't want to hear me babble, I'll ha—"

"Nonsense. I wouldn't have asked if I didn't want to hear. The shop usually won't get busy until afternoon, so I'm an open ear."

Mary didn't know if she wanted to unload on a stranger, but if she had an open and willing ear, why not? She could be straight and honest, not hold back, because she probably wouldn't be back to this shop with it being on the opposite side of town from where she lived.

"I'm never going to find a job. I've been to six interviews in seven days, and no one's called me back." Mary sipped from her mug, "I've been waitressing, and I have minimal office skills, but I know if someone just gives me a chance, I can prove that I am fit for the job. All I need is a chance."

"Sounds like you may be getting burnt out, all those interviews in a row, probably makes your responses sound robotic."

She thought about it, and Imogen was right. She repeated the same dialogue at each interview, never thinking it may sound rehearsed, or as Imogen said, "robotic."

"Looks like you need a new approach."

"I'm sick of trying to sell myself." Her words were soft before she pulled a sip from her cooling latte. "I'm not prostituting my body, but I am my soul, and it's just as disgusting." She felt overwhelmed at the thought of another interview. She didn't want to go through the humiliation of getting rejected, again.

"Hun, listen to me." Imogen leaned in, folding her arms on the tabletop, waiting to get Mary's undivided attention. "Are you listening?"

Mary nodded.

"Okay, at this next interview, you're going to put yourself out there."

"I always do."

"No, sweet," Imogen shook her head, over-exaggerating the motion, "I mean you're going to walk into that interview, and you are going to own it!"

Mary highly doubted that.

"Don't you doubt me...I can see it in your eyes, it's all over your face."

Damn my non-poker face! Mary was thankful that the next job wasn't for Imogen.

"You go into this next interview, and *you* interview *them.*"

"What?"

"You. Interview. Them."

Mary wasn't tracking. "I interview them," she deadpanned.

"Mmm-hhmmmm." Imogen got a snarky little smirk on her face and leaned back in the chair, arms crossed over her chest.

For as small as this half-pint woman was, she sure packed a

punch. She oozed confidence and probably shit rainbows. It was an odd combination to see this happy, jubilant, sunshine-y woman morph into a fierce, confident, take-no-shit attitude in the next turn. Mary envied her.

Mary didn't lack confidence—she was just shy, which was mistaken for no confidence. Imogen's confidence and straight attitude must have been contagious because Mary started to feel like she could take on the next interview.

"The next company, what did you say it was?"

Mary didn't say, but she offered up the information. "It's some kind of security company, I think? Like they must install home security systems or something? To tell you the truth, I really didn't pay attention or care. I just saw Help Wanted: secretary and personal assistant. Probably going to be answering phones and doing coffee runs." Mary chuckled, "And, I know just the place that sells the best lattes."

Imogene winked at her and they both fell into laughter.

"See, I can tell your confidence is already rising, so when you go to the next interview, you be the interviewer. You make them answer your concerns and questions. You make them want you and no one but you. Let them be interviewed to be the lucky company that gets you as their next employee. Do you hear me?"

"Yeah."

"Phhht, come on, that was pitiful. You going to get a job with pitiful?"

"No."

"Then let me hear you. Are you going to get the next job?"

Mary blurted out the word, "Yeah."

"Not with that confidence. I want you to dig down deep, feel it in your soul. Dig. Deep."

Mary felt her adrenaline kick in. She was going to nail the next interview; knock it outta the park. Wasn't going to take no for an answer. No more rejections. She was going to own it!

"Are you going to get the next job?"

"*Yeah!* Fuck the next interviewer! They can kiss my ass. I'm not taking no for an answer!" The words were freeing. Mary felt like floating and not coming down.

That was, until she saw a group of customers had walked in and stood at the counter.

Mary's confidence deflated like a carnival balloon. As she shrunk into herself, five shades of embarrassment crossed her face. Her exuberance was a bit over the top and she hoped they didn't hear the profanity spew from her mouth.

A few in the group were holding back their laughter, trying to keep it inconspicuous behind their hands and smiles, but the customer who entered first must have gotten an earful, because he stood in shock and utter disbelief, locking eyes with her. To top it off, he was drop-dead gorgeous. *Fuck!* That meant he'd heard her war cry. So much for her confidence with the next interview. This group just shattered her new-found confidence.

Damn it!

CHAPTER 4

King felt better. Getting out of the office with the guys was what he needed. Just stepping away from the office where the walls were closing in on him and getting a cup of java had him feeling centered. Now, back at Hellforce, he was ready to dive back into getting his office organized.

"Yo, King," T-BAR knocked on the door jamb and stuck his head into the office, "—chick's here to see you."

"Chick?" King quizzically raised a questioning eyebrow.

"Yeah, hot one too! Says she's here for an interview?"

King looked at his watch, *Fuck!* He forgot about the appointment.

T continued, not paying attention to King quickening his pace and frantically cleaning. "You gonna put a chick on the team? She doesn't look military, but she's hot! So, maybe we could—"

"She's not for the team." King started stacking the files he'd organized onto stacks again, clearing his desk so he could have at least one clear spot to have the interview. "And, stop referring to her as a 'chick'."

"Not a team girl?" T looked disappointed. "What's she here for?"

King was resigned, not wanting to admit he needed help.

"Well?"

King cleared his throat. "I'm looking to hire an administrative assistant."

T let the grin lift his face, not hiding his glee. "So...you need a secretary?"

"*Administrative assistant*," King corrected him, hoping the more professional title would lessen the blow of having to admit he needed help. He continued stacking papers, lifting folders from the chair in front of his desk so the interviewee would have a place to sit.

"Well, this secretary's hot." T crossed his arms over his chest and settled against the doorframe. "So, she gonna take dictation for you, maybe wear her hair in a bun, pull her glasses down low, and stare at you over the rims while she bites the tip of a pencil eraser? That type of secretary?"

King stilled.

"Gonna give her the beef bayonet on your desk or the copy machine? That kinda secretary?" T waggled his eyebrows, setting a mental image.

King shook the thought T planted from his head and reprimanded him. "You're the reason places need an HR department."

T shrugged his shoulders.

"You need to get out more and stop watching so much porn. My god, T!"

"Well, once you see the hot chick—woman—here for the interview, you're going to be begging her to—"

"Not another word!" King stopped him with a stern look. He knew the guys were crude—hell, he was crude, too—but now, being close to forty, and the boss, he tried to curb the habit of objectifying women.

When he was enlisted, he was the same horn-dog as T and the guys. Used his soldier and Delta status to notch many bedposts, but he was just coming into a new phase in life. Not that he was looking to settle down, it just didn't seem right to look at every hot woman as an opportunity to get a piece of ass.

"So... if you don't hire her, can *I* give her the beef bayonet?"

King closed his eyes and shook his head. If he did hire this woman, he was going to have to sit down with the team and go over office protocol and what constituted sexual harassment. Maybe he didn't want a woman in the office. Shit, he could be looking at a lawsuit within the first week if he didn't steer T clear.

"So, you aren't saying no to the bayonet...or are you thinking about it, 'cuz I gotta know if I can get her digits."

"Fuck, T! Stop thinking with your dick. Nobody will be sleeping with this woman, whether she gets the job or not. I'd feel sorry for her if she had to beat you off with a broom."

T opened his mouth.

"And, don't even make one remark about being beat off."

T closed his mouth, pursing his lips into a straight line.

"T-BAR, you're almost the same age as me. When are you going to get it out of your head that every girl wants a piece of you?"

"Everyone...wants a piece...of the T-bone." His overconfidence only made the statement that much worse.

"Ew, that's disgusting." Ember, Slate's longtime friend, made her way into King's office. "That's not only, not true, but it's disgusting how many dog houses that bone has actually been in." She shivered for full effect.

"Bitches like it."

"You're juvenile, T."

He shot her a wink and she rolled her eyes. T and Ember were close friends, both being former snipers, and she knew the stories of his bed-jumping habits. With his sultry English accent, T had women dropping panties and lining up to be the next one-night stand, or UAL as T called it. Use it. Abuse it. Lose it.

Though he knew true love existed, it wasn't for him. His accent wooed the ladies straight to his zipper. Hell, T reading the phone book would come off as sexy.

Ember addressed King, who was still clearing his desk. "Got those tactical flak vests you wanted, and I bought a few new canisters from the range. Where'd you want me to put 'em?"

"Put them in the holding room upstairs."

Ember handed him an invoice and then eyed his office. "Whoa, King, you need a secretary."

T laughed and said, "Administrative assistant. God, Em, don't be so crude...get with the times, PC."

Ember looked at him with confusion. "Anyway, King, there's a hot chick in the entryway, says she's waiting to meet with you." Ember widened her eyes to punctuate, "And, I mean, *damn*...she's really hot."

T busted out laughing, turned, and walked out of the office. King hung his head and let out a breath.

"Can you send her back on your way out, please?" He scrubbed his hands down his face and stroked his short beard, then gave Ember a flattened smile.

Ember shot him a thumbs up.

Hell, his day couldn't get any worse.

≈

Mary steeled herself before entering the office of her next interviewer. *Tamp down the nerves, you got this. You're here to interview them, they're not here to interview you.* She closed her eyes and took in a deep cleansing breath.

"Don't let him scare you, he's a teddy bear," said the woman who escorted her to the office. Mary opened her eyes and caught the woman's smile.

"You work here, too?" Mary could hear her own nerves.

"Nope. Just a friend of the guys. I own a gun range in town."

Mary nodded. "So, do they install security systems, like cameras and house alarms? Or, supply security help, like bodyguards, or something like that?"

Ember let out a chuckle and threw a chin lift, "Something like that." She touched Mary's elbow, "Don't worry, you got this!"

Not understanding what was so funny, Mary once again mentally prepared herself, ginning up the confidence Imogen instilled in her. She did have this. She was going to nail this interview! Nothing was going to stop her.

Ember knocked on King's closed door, then stepped to the side, throwing Mary a thumbs up, and walked down the corridor.

The door opened, and Mary froze. All the confidence she felt a second ago plummeted when she saw the man on the other side of the door. Not because he was over six-feet tall and menacing-looking, or the fact he was as big as a brick shithouse and his shoulders spanned from each side of the door jambs. No, Mary's confidence shattered, because the man standing in front of her was the same man, the customer, who stood staring and horrified, as she yelled and ranted at the coffee house.

If her memory served her right, her exact words were, *"Fuck the next interviewer! They can kiss my ass, I'm not taking no for an answer!"*

Fuck! She wanted to make a run for the front door.

~

Holy hell, she's hot!

That was the first thought entering King's mind when he opened his office door. Miles of sun-kissed, caramel-brown hair pulled up into a bun with tendrils escaping from its confines, and the black-rimmed glasses sliding down her nose had his libido ratcheting up. He was caught speechless, which was odd because King was never short on words. But, the look of terror and fright flaming in her green eyes had him on alert. Then, realization dawned. *The coffee house.* She was the girl from the coffee house. His interviewee.

"You're from the coffee house." King's statement fell from his lips before he could call it back.

Oh, fuck no! Mary's mind reeled at the massive man standing before her. This had to be some cosmic joke! Karma couldn't be this cruel. She wanted to bolt, but she stood rooted in place.

"Um...I... I..." Mary stammered, not even quite sure what she was trying to say. "I'm sorry...I need to...I have to leave." She uprooted her feet, turned, and moved at a fast-clipped pace towards the front doors.

"Hey, wait!" His deep, gruff voice called from the open doorway.

She reached to push open the glass door when a heavy hand landed on her shoulder, halting her in her tracks. Mary stopped only feet from her getaway.

"Where're you going, Sugar?"

King's eyes widened. *Sugar? Did I just call her, Sugar?* King had never used an endearment in his life. It was definitely inappropriate to say it to a stranger, let alone a person he was about to interview.

Did he just call me Sugar? Mary knew she should be angry. She didn't know this man! But, for some strange reason, hearing this hulk of a man call her Sugar brought a tingle to her heart.

"Um, sorry, ma'am...miss, um..." King was stammering now. His hand remained outstretched, as she faced the door. All King could see was her partial profile and the nape of her slender neck.

"Please, let me go."

He heard her whispered plea but kept his hand planted in place.

"I need to leave."

The moment settled between them.

"Sure that's what you want?"

No. That's not what she wanted. She wanted to stay for the interview. Correction, she *needed* to stay for the interview. She had to land a job. Any job. The second notice had come from the bank that morning, saying the mortgage payment needed to be paid within fourteen days, or the foreclosure process would proceed. *God. Can I let my pride and embarrassment keep me from this interview?* Simple answer, *Yes!* But, would she let it? *No!*

"May I ask one question before you bolt, Sugar?" *Sugar! Damn it!* He winced.

Her heart skittered at the Texas twang in his baritone voice. She felt it reverberate in her chest. His heavy hand resting on her shoulder should have made her feel trapped, but it was just the opposite, it brought a comforting calm over her. A sense of security she had long missed and yearned for, but hadn't found. She stayed rooted in place. His hand slid from her shoulder, giving her the freedom to take the few steps needed to clear the door, but with his hand gone, she mourned the loss of his touch.

She was facing away from him. He wanted one question. She could handle one question. "Ask."

Silence fell before King spoke. "Are you leaving because you've changed your mind about the position, or are you leaving because of the coffee house?"

"That's two questions." Only three words. She tried to keep her voice steady, but even she could hear her own unease.

King waited, letting the silence determine the next point of action.

Neither broke.

Mary heard King step back.

Her breathing increased.

Another step.

She closed her eyes.

A third step of retreat in the deafening silence.

Her mind said, "fight," but her nerves said, "flight." She stepped forward, her palm met the coolness of the door. Just two more steps and she'd escape from facing her humiliation. Should she at least face him, thank him for calling her for the interview, but tell him she would have to politely decline? She at least owed him that much. When she turned, she was stunned. He was gone. *How did he leave without being heard? No man that huge could move that silently.*

She looked down the corridor but didn't see him. She glanced at his office, but the door was now shut. *Probably for the best.* She didn't feel like being battered through another interview and then getting the brush-off short of, "Don't let the door hit you in the ass on the way out."

She warred with her conscience. If she didn't get a job, she would lose her mother's house. She would be out on her ass. She had given up her apartment over a year-and-a-half ago to take care of her mom. When it got beyond her capabilities, Mary reluctantly had to move her to the living center where she could get 24/7 care. Tears pricked Mary's eyes.

"Interview done already?" The woman she met earlier asked from behind her. "That didn't take long. When do you start?"

Mary didn't answer. Tears still brimmed her eyes with the thought of her mother.

"I didn't get to introduce myself, I'm Ember."

Mary's shyness tried to make her shrink, but she forged ahead. "I'm Mary."

Ember read her face. "King didn't scare you, did he?" Ember threw a cursory glance back towards the office door. "He comes off as overpowering, but underneath, he's got a big heart. He needed a secretary, like, yesterday. Needs someone that can keep him on track. Someone who isn't afraid to go toe-to-toe with him and won't back down. Someone that'll push back. He's stubborn and set in his ways, and he knows what he likes, so he'll be a bear. Comes off as a grizzly but is really a teddy." Ember laughed at the image of huge, strapping King being all soft and cuddly. "He thinks he has claws, but he really has paws."

"King?" Mary held a puzzled look.

"Um...yeah," she turned and pointed to his office door, "King."

Mary figured it must be his last name.

"He *did* hire you?" Ember's question matched her confused look.

Mary must've hesitated a bit too long.

"That son of a bitch!" Ember started towards King's office, when Mary stopped her.

"Wait, wait, no, I didn't take the interview."

Ember whirled around. "What?"

She was just about to tell the story of why she couldn't interview, but of all the stupid things to do, Mary started to laugh. The thought of this barely five-foot-three woman barging into King's office and dressing him down had her laughing. She hadn't laughed in so long. It felt freeing.

She spoke between bouts. "Oh, god," she laughed a bit more, "don't go in there."

Her laughter was contagious. Ember started to chuckle, which turned it into a laugh, and pretty soon neither knew why they were laughing.

"So, why didn't you interview?" Ember was trying to settle herself.

Mary wiped the laughter-tears from her eyes, then proceeded to tell Ember about the whole coffeehouse fiasco. How King and the guys entered the coffee house during her tirade and final war cry. By the end of the story, it was Ember who was wiping her own tears, crying at the image of King standing shocked, as Mary belted out her defiance.

"So, you see, there's no way I can go in there and face him, and even if I do, there's no way I'd be hired."

Ember took Mary by the hand and led her back to King's closed office door.

"What are you doing?" Mary whispered as Ember pulled her along. "I can't do this."

"Sure you can." Ember seemed determined to get her to interview. "Listen, King is huge, overpowering, gruff, ornery and a lion with a thorn in his paw—"

"Not making this any more appealing."

Ember rolled her eyes. "He's also a big ol' softy, though he'd never let anyone know it. He's generous and kind, and most of all, he's forgiving."

"How do *you* know this if he doesn't let anyone know."

"I've known him a while, and he helped me when I really needed it." Ember sobered, and Mary sensed there was a story behind the sadness she saw in the woman's eyes. "Because he's all these things, but if called out, he'd deny it until his dying breath."

"Why?"

"One, 'cuz he's a guy, and two, if he'd admit it, he'd think no one would fear him."

"Fear him?"

"Yeah, alpha male bullshit. Give him a chance. What's the worst that could happen?"

"I could be humiliated and die on the spot."

Ember let out a light chuckle. "No, the worst that could happen is you don't get the job, and you're no worse off than you are right now."

Mary thought about that.

"Plus, if you get the job, I could gain a friend. God knows these lugs could use some estrogen around here. So much testosterone running through this place, even I get a girl-boner walking in through these doors."

Mary belted out a laugh, and Ember joined in alongside her.

"Ladies?" King was standing in his office doorway, hands leaning against the jambs, making his six-foot-two frame look larger than normal. "May I help you?"

He crossed his arms over his chest, making his biceps bulge and his rolled sleeves stretch like a tourniquet around each crafted muscle. He was nothing but one-hundred-percent pure, male deliciousness. Mary felt herself weaken in the knees, this time not because of fear or embarrassment, but because the zinging in her female region was unexpected and downright earth-shattering.

"See, girl-boner," Ember whispered, matter-of-factly.

Mary held back her laugh and stepped up, addressing King. "Um, Mr. King, I was hoping, if possible, that I may still...be able to get that interview."

King took her in, and Mary wanted a second chance. She stood a little straighter, summoning her courage, trying not to let her shyness get the best of her.

"King." Ember used a mom voice, warning him to behave and get in line. A voice her mother, Susan, used on her and her sister, Rhys, growing up.

He ignored Ember's warning and addressed Mary directly, "Of course, Sug'— Mrs. ...." He caught himself before he slipped, again.

"Jones. And, it's Miss." She tried keeping the blush from spreading across her face.

"Come in; take a seat."

"Good luck with that!" Another sexy, muscled man walked up behind Ember, chuckling. "You can take a seat, *if* you can find a seat in that hellhole." Both he and Ember laughed.

King glared at the newcomer, but he ignored the glare and put his hand on the small of Ember's back in a comforting, protective manner. Mary didn't know who he was, but he was gorgeous! He had the most stunning, beautiful slate-blue eyes. Mary thought a girl could get lost in them for hours. He pulled Ember close and placed a kiss on her temple. *They must be a couple.* Mary thought they seemed fit for each other.

"Ready to go, Red?" The blue-eyed man directed Ember towards the front door.

"It was nice to meet you," Mary said.

"You too. Maybe we can catch lunch once you start work here." Ember tossed King a knowing smile, one that he didn't return.

Man, he has the gruff grizzly vibe down pat. Mary didn't see the teddy bear that Ember spoke of anywhere in sight.

"Be back after lunch." Blue eyes said, "Later, King."

"Later, Slate."

Slate. That name seemed to fit 'Blue Eyes' perfectly.

King sidestepped out of the doorway and motioned for Mary to precede him into the office. Mary wasn't sure if he was chivalrous, or if he didn't want anyone at his back. He gave off the vibe of being alert and aware of his surroundings at all times. She assumed he may have a military background considering he was in security, and after seeing King and Slate's bulk, she was leaning towards this business being personal security instead of installing home security systems.

∾

Hellhole.

Mary thought that description was quite accurate. King's office resembled a whirlwind, category 5 hurricane or tornado from the number of papers and files strewn haphazardly around the office and on every available surface. Not only was his desk partially overtaken, but things were also littered, well...everywhere.

The desk, the chair, stacks on the floor, against the floorboards lining the wall. Even the leather couch against the far wall was buried along with the table in front of it. *Who in this day and age still has paper files? Has he ever heard of going paperless?* He had a laptop on his desk, although it too was buried beneath file folders. Ember was right when she said he needed a secretary "like, a week ago."

"Please, have a seat." King placed his hand on the back of a chair, the only one that was clutter-free, pulling it back slightly and motioned for her to sit. He stood behind it until she was seated—again—a chivalrous move, then walked around the handcrafted mahogany desk that definitely made a statement. It was an impressive piece of furniture for an impressive man. It wasn't pompous or pretentious. On the contrary, it afforded him nicely. With his size and presence, a sleek, modern, glass-and-chrome-style desk would be ill-suited and unbecoming.

He took a seat in his leather office chair, settling his weight. Mary didn't know how the chair held his large frame. She was expecting the chair to collapse any second.

He leaned forward, elbows apart, hands folded atop his blotter where it wasn't covered in papers, and scrutinized her. She felt herself shrink in the sight of his gaze.

"Why should I hire you, Ms. Jones?" His deep sapphire-blue eyes burrowed into her, reaching down to her soul. He was intense and intimidating, but Mary discerned a depth to this man—pain, hurt, anguish, a side he most likely kept hidden and never revealed to anyone. His bearded face hid the lines not of age but of worry, set there by burdensome responsibility. She sensed he was younger than his facade afforded him.

Why should he hire me? It was a damn good question. One Mary wasn't prepared for. She had a list, though a very short list, of her attributes: organized; timely; efficient; multi-tasker; all the things one would list when trying to pimp themselves out to a potential future employer. Her list was nothing impressive. Why should, or would, he hire her? She was most likely a carbon copy of the other applicants he interviewed. She felt herself begin to shrink and fold into herself, but then the words of the spitfire, Imogen, resounded in her mind, *"When you go to the next interview, you be the interviewer."* Yes. She could be the interviewer.

"Why do you want to hire me, Mr. King?" She sat upright, projecting herself. She felt bold and daring. This was way outside her wheelhouse. She was anything but bold and brash, but her shyness wasn't going to rule the interview.

King didn't shock or recoil from her question—just the opposite. A sly grin worked the edges of his mouth and then pulled across his face. He leaned back carelessly into his chair, stroked his graying beard, and folded his arms. His tats didn't hide the sculpted tone of his forearms, though his left arm didn't quite match his right. His reclined position made Mary slightly regret her line of questioning, and she figured she had crossed a line beyond that of any inter-viewer, though she stayed impassive, straight-faced, and out of char-acter. She felt a pit in her stomach grow and churn with her conflicting emotions. The ball was in her court. She would either nail this interview, or she had just fucked herself out of another job.

Either way, she was in charge.

CHAPTER 5

Mary thought she was going to keel over right in front of this man. She hadn't known she was holding her breath until the burn of her lungs screamed to be released. Not to be found out, she released it in a slow, steady, discrete, even flow, letting the exhale calm her nerves. *What am I doing?* She needed this job, and she was blowing it. Why was she embracing the whole, 'Fake it till you Make it' schtick?

She wasn't assertive or aggressive. She was quite the opposite...passive; meek; submissive. Nowadays, she wasn't a "take-the-bull-by-the-horns," type of person. She found herself dutiful in most of her ways, a lot stemming from caring for her mother for the last year-and-a-half. There was a point in time when she was confident and feisty. Even cheeky. She had an in-your-face, take-no-shit attitude and wasn't afraid to make it known. She was bold and self-assured in her decisions. In her college heyday, she was always the one to speak up and take charge. But, the bubble of college came face-to-face with reality and imploded, and life had beat that trait out of her. She missed that girl.

Mary wasn't sure how long she was lost in her head, but when she looked up, King was no longer reclined in his chair. He was now leaning forward on his desk, elbows propped, hands interlaced with his index fingers steepled. Observant. His features hard, with his steel eyes trained on her.

"Just to clarify *your* position, I'll be conducting this interview." His voice was low and assured, leaving no doubt he was the one in charge, "And you, Ms. Jones, will be the one interviewing for the position. So once again, I will ask you, 'Why should I hire you?'"

The sight and sound made her visceral swallow prominent, and her confident guise waned. Mary closed her eyes and mustered up what confidence she had left. She steeled herself, letting a bit of the "heyday Mary" peek through.

"Mr. King, I can assure you, I'm—"

"Just King."

"What?"

"Not Mr. King. Just King."

For a moment she was baffled. *Does he have some type of God complex that he wants to be called King? Is he conceited?* He didn't seem to carry arrogance.

Sensing her questions, King explained, "It's my nic. Got it on my first deployment to Iraq, and it's stuck ever since."

So, he *was* military. Mary knew it. He oozed that military vibe.

Before she could ask, King continued, "My name is Henry Edward Clark, but everyone calls me King. I'd prefer it if you would as well."

Henry. She liked it. He looked like a 'Henry,' though the name King suited him to a T. She wondered about the significance the moniker held.

Sensing yet another of her questions he said, "King Henry...King Edward. Henry was a ruthless ruler, and Edward was the people's king, loved by all. I guess I exude both traits, so guys started calling me King."

Mary understood what Ember had meant. Claws or paws...Henry or Edward. There was no name for him other than King.

King liked her tenacity. She showed an utter defiance he found endearing. He pegged her as insecure, unconfident, a shrinking-violet. Her self-assured, take-charge facade had King's bull-shit meter piqued at one-hundred. If there was one skill he mastered in the Army as a Delta, it was ferreting out the truth, whether it be by interrogation or observation. There was no need to interrogate, but King sat back and let her charade continue. A person could learn more by staying silent and letting a scene play out than by inserting themselves and demanding answers. No, King rather enjoyed the stage she set herself upon.

"Now, Ms. Jones, do you have your resume with you?" King assumed she didn't have one, because she entered the office bare-handed, but he waited for her reply. How would she play out the scenario? Lie? Make an excuse? Tell the truth? The stage was set, how would she dance?

King leaned into his steepled fingers and watched, knowing the stages of discovery to come. He was masterful at reading people and knew the predictable response and reactions to follow. *Showtime!*

Mary looked at her hands as if she would miraculously find her resume there. Follow that with a widening of her eyes as she real-ized that she was, in fact, without said resume. Next, came the predictable tilt of the head and side-eyeing, coupled with memory recall, a searching for the sequence of events. King waited patiently, waiting for the "Eureka" moment.

Three…Two…One…

Mary closed her eyes and dropped her head.

Eureka! There it was. King inwardly smiled.

"Fuck," Mary muttered.

The subtle curse surprised him. She had an innocence about her and didn't seem like the type to swear. But then, the coffeehouse came to mind and her innocent demeanor went out the window. He looked her over again. Maybe she was spunky, and her innocence had a badass streak lying beneath the surface. He liked her, enough to have surprised himself by calling her "Sugar" earlier.

"Mr. Clark, King…fuck…" She spoke as she met his eyes, "I swear I had a resume, but I think I left it at the coffeehouse." She let out a breath which came out more as a huff.

"That's unfortunate." King resumed the position from earlier, reclined in his chair, arms crossed over his barrel chest.

Mary mentally cursed herself. How was she supposed to prove she could handle menial office tasks and organizational skills when she couldn't even keep track of her resume? Once again, she humiliated herself in front of her potential, could-be boss. She surrendered in defeat. Life had a way of kicking you when you were down, and she was down.

She stood and ran her hands atop her thighs, pressing the non-existent wrinkles from her pants. "Thank you for your time, King." She held out her hand to offer a handshake, waiting for him to dismiss her. He eyed her for a brief moment, then leaned forward and took her slender hand in his. God, the size of his hand was astonishing! Her hand looked like a child's cradled within his paw. Maybe he was a bear after all.

Mary swore his hand electrified hers. *It must be my nerves.* He gave her a curt nod, not shaking her hand, but she sensed it was his dismissal. She turned, hating herself for being so careless, berating herself for fucking up one more interview. *God.*

Seven interviews, seven days. How pathetic am I?

Her vile vitriol swam in her head. She was almost to the door, hand on the knob, when she had a moment of reckoning. She was a good person, damn it! Sure, she outwardly didn't display the true Mary that she was below the surface, below all the baggage that life had piled on top of her. She wasn't going to go down without a fight —not a physical fight, but a fight nonetheless.

"You know, King," she spoke softly, slowly, and calmly to the door in front of her, looking inward and searching her mind, mentally living out the words as she spoke them. "I'm a good person. I'm kind. I'm caring, compassionate. I wear my heart on my sleeve. I give too much and take too little." She paused. "I juggle a thousand things at once and just keep juggling when a thousand more are tossed into the mix. I'm competent, and I'm trustworthy."

Her tone became a bit more poised. "I'm a fighter." Images of all the times she wanted to give up, not sure she could take on one more day of her mother's care, wanting to leave the burden in someone else's hands, but somehow finding the courage to take one more step, one more day, one more piece of herself, her soul, and give it to the woman she loved more than anyone on earth. Her eyes pricked, but she wasn't giving in.

"I can lead. I can organize. I'm capable. I can handle just about any task given to me and give back ten-times what's expected. I have a management degree, for Christ's sake. I'm more than qualified to field phone calls, sort papers, keep appointments, and make a fucking pot of coffee." She didn't realize the boldness that was encroaching on her soliloquy. Her mind swirled with the woman she knew she could be, not the woman who was washed up, beaten down, and worn out. She was burnt out, and she was pissed. She missed the woman she left behind, the feisty, take-no-shit, in-your-face, tell-you-like-it-is girl. *Where did she go? Why was she hiding? And how long can I hang onto her right now?*

Her candor prevailed. "I'm a damn good person, King. I'm shy but bold. I'm underestimated. I don't sugarcoat. And, I'm damn sure not going to be taken advantage of." She shook her head, gazing into her memories, ramping herself up. "You want honesty? Be careful what you ask for, 'cuz I'm done with the bullshit. I don't do drama. I'm done being a pushover. If you're looking for a 'Yes, man' that'll kiss your ass while blowing smoke up it too, then I'm not your person. Move on.

"I've been to seven interviews in seven days, and I can do seven more, 'cuz I know somewhere, somehow, someone's going to find me worthy. I've been chewed up and spit out, but I'm still here. Ready for another round. I'll most likely get knocked down again, but it doesn't matter. I'm a fighter. I'm determined, and in the end, I'm going to win.

"Maybe it won't be here, maybe it won't be at the next five, six, ten, twelve interviews I go to, but I. Will. Overcome. I will win."

She came to. She arrived, not knowing she was gone. Her chest was heaving, and her hand was crushing the knob in her grasp. The sudden realization that she was in King's office sent a flood of fear from head to toe, stunning her like an ice-cold bucket of water raining over her body. She squeezed her eyes shut, hoping it was a dream. *Did I really just vomit an emotional tirade?* God, she was an idiot. She should just open the door and walk out. Straight out, cut ties. Skip the embarrassment. But, it was a losing battle when she turned her head, and her eyes landed on the one person she hoped had somehow magically disappeared.

King.

He sat in his chair, one arm bent and resting slack on the desk, tucked under the elbow of the other. He propped his fist against his lips and his thumb on his bearded chin. He sat motionlessly. Emotionless. A deadpan stare looked back at her. *Shit!*

King felt his smile build. God, she was cute. Flustered and honest. King didn't think he'd ever had a more honest interview. She bore her soul, held nothing back. Laid herself out. It was refreshing and, for damn sure, freeing.

The other interviews he sat through the previous day had him cringing before they even sat down. He spotted the bullshit from the onset of each interview. People lying, trying to portray themselves in the best light, telling him what they thought he wanted to hear, hoping he wouldn't see their true nature until after they were hired. Mary was brilliant...Mary was a breath of fresh air.

King rose and motioned to the vacant chair in front of him. "Ms. Jones, I believe we need to discuss the date you will be starting."

CHAPTER 6

I did it! I got the job.

Mary was on cloud nine. Who knew verbal diarrhea would land her a job? After her tirade, she didn't want to face King. She couldn't handle the humiliation and rejection. But, when Mary took the seat across from him, behind his rough and hardened facade, King was relaxed and kind but still straightforward. She could see why Ember had referred to him as a teddy bear, though she doubted he would *ever* let anyone see that part of him. He was all growl.

He kept her guessing—one minute he was kind, nice, and a teddy, and the next, he was straightforward, all grumpy and growly. It seemed when he spoke business, grizzly. When he asked personal questions, the tender, softhearted teddy peeked through. He was an enigma.

Now, she was driving home. She made a mental note to call the director at Rebecca's Hope and see if she could switch hours to accommodate her new job.

My new job!

Mary let out a giddy, little girl squeal. This was exactly what she needed. The pay was amazing, and the hours were great. Mary's mouth dropped when King went over the salary and benefits package. She had never had a salary or benefits before...ever!

The pay would increase to full salary after her probation period, but even at starting pay, it was unbelievable. She tried not to show her surprise, but King didn't miss much. He smiled throughout the interview when he raised certain points and she tried to hide her glee.

The pay would be more than she made at the center and the restaurant combined. But, she didn't want to quit the center quite yet.

First, she loved the people she worked with, and helping those who lost hope, or were in dire situations, made her feel she was making a difference. Second, she needed to keep a backup in case this dream job was just that, a dream, and it didn't pan out. And third, even though Hellforce paid a lot, she needed the second job to catch up on past-due bills and the last four missed mortgage payments.

But, the ultimate reason she needed to keep two jobs was her mother. The cost of the private living center was outrageous. 24/7, around-the-clock care was not cheap. She could put her mother in a public, community home, but she wouldn't get the individual specialized care and attention she required. Trent was no help at all, so the burden of payment was put on Mary's shoulders. If she could catch up on the past-due mortgage, she could stay in the house and not have to sell it. If she did sell, she could get a small one-bedroom apartment and put the sale's money towards her mother's care.

Trent would have to fend for himself. It wasn't Mary's problem to take care of her older brother, though that is exactly what she was currently doing. He had sponged off their mother, and once she went to the living center, Trent was supposed to do the responsible thing and take care of himself. But, that was yet to happen.

If she were forced to sell the house, he would have no choice but to become an adult at the age of thirty-two.

After all, the house was her mother's, even though Mary had control of the estate. Her mother and father worked their asses off to buy the house. It wasn't until her father died that her mother had to remortgage it, which put her in the current predicament of monthly payments to the bank.

Mary's mind kept returning to the interview...and, the interviewer.

King. Was. *Fine*!

She shivered and goosebumps rose on her arms just thinking about him. He was older than her, but that made him all the more appealing. Guys Mary's age seemed immature and most were self-centered arrogant assholes.

It was pitiful to admit, but Mary didn't date. At the age of thirty, she could count on one hand the number of dates she had gone on and still have fingers left over. Not that she didn't want to date, but with working two jobs and taking care of her mother, she didn't have the time. And, sad to say, even if she did have the time, guys never gave her a second glance.

Maybe she was too plain, or not Kardashian enough, to attract a man.

But, King was *all man*! She found herself being drawn to him. Her mind drifted back to the interview.

~

After King had basically told her she had the job, she pulled out a small pad of paper and a yellow number two pencil from her bag. She wiped absently at the dangling strand of hair that had come loose from her bun.

Pushing up her glasses, she asked, "I understand I am interviewing for an administrative position, but...what exactly is Hellforce?"

It was her first question. Seemed kinda silly to be interviewing at a place where she had no idea what the business actually did, but she was desperate and would work just about anywhere. Seeing the size and brawn of King, and then Slate, had her interest piqued.

"I mean, I don't think it's home security systems, and my god, the size of you, you have to be doing something with all those muscles...not that I'm looking, or admiring...I just, ah...fuck...I mean..."

~

King couldn't keep his grin suppressed. Damn, she was cute. And attractive as hell! She had the whole naughty secretary vibe going that T had joked about earlier. King couldn't deny that he could picture her in the naughty role. *Be professional.* He shook the thought from his head. "No, we don't do home security."

The thought of him and the team wiring up someone's house with a security system instead of hunting down and putting away the earth's scum had him internally laughing. "We provide security for outside interests." King tried to be as vague as possible. "We provide most of our security out of town."

"Out of town" wasn't *exactly* lying. Just usually, three-thousand miles, give or take a thousand or so, wasn't what most considered, "out of town," but in all fairness, it *was* accurate.

"Oh." Mary bit the corner of her lip. "So, like, bodyguard stuff?"

King felt himself twitch in his boxers when she bit her lip.

Fuck! He would love to be that lip.

"We provide protection for those requesting security." King didn't want to get into specifics. If she made it past the sixty-day probation period, and he could gauge if she was going to be a fit for the company, then he would reevaluate her and let her know the true workings of Hellforce and see if she would like to continue with the company. Until then, keeping the company's secrecy was in his benefit, and hers, as well.

She frantically jotted down notes as King spoke.

"Will I be required to travel with you...I mean, with the company?" Mary corrected herself but could feel her face heat. She would travel if needed, but she didn't want to be far from her mother for too long.

"No. Travel isn't required. You will be manning the office even when we are on the job site."*Job site. How ridiculous was that?*

Then, again, not a complete lie. Just not the type of "job site," most would picture.

Mary readjusted herself in her seat. She lost King's gaze and focused on the gloss finish of his mahogany desk. She had a feeling that there was more to the job than what King was putting forward.

Is this job too good to be true? Am I thinking too much into this? It had to be a legitimate job, right? Maybe she should decline and find something where she could work closer to home? The commute across town would be something she could get used to, but saving every penny meant she walked to the center and the diner, but she couldn't walk across town and into the rural area. God knew her twenty-year-old VW Beetle was on its last leg. What if her car finally died and she wasn't able to commute? Did the city bus have a route that was near here? Probably not. The route most likely ended at the edge of town. Hellforce was out of town and then some.

King leaned forward, relaxed and casual, then reached across the desk and pulled her lip from between her teeth. His thumb grazed the pouty flesh and wetness dampened the pad. The feeling of her wetness, her saliva on his flesh, aroused him, awakening his libido. What wouldn't he do to feel her wetness with all his fingers, not just his thumb? Christ! It had been months since he'd been with a woman, and now all he wanted to do was see how much saliva she could spread on his—

"Sorry." Mary's shoulders came up and she reddened. Her right hand nervously fingered the gold cross necklace that lay above her full, rounded left breast. "I didn't realize I was doing that." Her hand came to her mouth and she touched her lip. Without realizing it, she bit it once more, this time letting her teeth graze the abused area, sliding it slowly between her teeth. Her tongue darted out and caressed the swollen flesh, making it glisten with additional wetness, and she rolled her lips like she was smoothing out her lipstick.

Pushing up her glasses once more and tucking a stray tendril behind her ear, she tapped the pink eraser to her lip and gently bit the tip, then tapped it a few times on her bottom lip.

King thought he was going to lose his mind.

Naughty!

He felt the strain of himself lengthening beneath the desk and he hoped he wouldn't have to contend with wearing wet boxers the rest of the day. He knew he was leaking and he mentally fought the urge to control himself from blowing, exploding like a prepubescent teen. *Good God!*

How long had it been since just the sight of a woman, unconsciously hinting at sexual innuendos, aroused him? King never had to push to find a woman to go with him for a night. Hell, women practically threw themselves at him, and his team, when they were out at the bar. Bar, grocery store, gas station, King had picked up women in the most common of places.

Not that he was a man-whore, but he had notched a fair share of bedposts. All with women who wanted to notch his, as well. He'd never had an innocent woman under him, so the fact that they wanted to notch each other was fine with him. Things would never progress beyond a single night. He wasn't a man to settle down.

He once had dreams of a family, a large family, but with his line of work, he could never leave a wife and kids at home, not sure if he would return home to them. He had too many close calls with the Reaper—they were on a first-name basis, so the thought of having a wife and kids was off the table.

"Henry?"

His given name sprouting from Mary's lips stunned him back to her attention. *Holy. Fuck. Do. Not. Cum!* He felt his balls tighten and his spine tingle. *Fuck! Fuck! FFF...* He held his breath, God, Almighty, he willed himself not to cum.

"Are you all right?" Mary's voice held a hint of concern tinged with panic. She stood from her seat, ready to come around the desk to his aid.

You've fought in war. You've withstood torture. Control. Yourself. The mental pep talk calmed him, but he was on the precipice of exploding. "No. No... I'm fine," he brought his fist to his chest and feigned indigestion. "Just felt a rise of heartburn come on. I'm okay." What a sad excuse of a lie. It was barely believable, even to him. And, it wasn't bile that was rising.

Mary bent to grab her purse at her feet and King felt a flame of heat travel up his chest when her blouse dipped open and she unwittingly exposed a voluptuous mound of her breast.

Christ on a cracker! He swallowed and mentally meditated to keep his breathing even.

She scrambled around in her purse and pulled out a roll of antacids. "Here, these will help." She unrolled two of the dime-sized disks and handed them to him.

He thanked her and popped them in his mouth, chewed them, and swallowed. He didn't need them, and King hated to take any kind of medicine, prescription or over the counter, didn't matter, but he'd painted himself into a corner so he had no choice but to take them. After chewing them, he washed them down with the bottle of water that was sitting on his desk.

"You aren't supposed to drink any fluid after taking them," Mary said, handing him the rest of the roll, "it renders them useless. If you get another reflux, take two more."

King picked up the roll, folding the paper on the end, "Thanks." He put them in his top drawer for safekeeping. He wasn't even going to venture putting them in his front pocket. With his manhood on a hair-trigger, he wasn't going to chance brushing up against himself and game over. He was getting himself under control. As long as she didn't bite or lick her lips, or expose any more flesh, he would be good.

~

As the interview progressed, King spoke about the salary and the benefits package. It was a salaried position because although she would have set hours, King knew that things got harried around the office, especially once she would be in the loop of what the team's real objective was. She may be needed occasionally at odd times or may be needed to stay late, so it was more beneficial for her sake that he pay her a guaranteed wage.

Mary swallowed her excitement down, not wanting to seem too eager. "So, that's a yearly income? All of that?" She wanted to clarify in case she misheard or misunderstood. "I would be making that much, *each* week?"

She'd never had a guaranteed wage. *Never.* She made a measly hourly wage and crappy tips at the diner. And the nightshift tips were crap.

No, they were worse than crap. They were an all-you-can-eat-taco-Tuesday buffet with an injection of Ex-Lax and food poisoning...rolled up with gut rot. Yup, definitely worse than crap.

"Yes," King knew she wasn't expecting the job to pay what he was offering. Once she learned the workings of Hellforce, she would understand why he paid his team handsomely. And Mary would be considered part of the team as well. "You'll start at an average base pay until you reach your thirty-day probation period. Then, we'll reevaluate and see if you're a fit for us, not if we're a fit for you. I'll be frank," Mary swallowed as King continued, "for this to work, we both need to be able to work together. I'm stubborn, overbearing, and mean, and most of the time, a son-of-a-bitch." Mary was surprised at his candor. "I want things done a certain way. I *need* things done a certain way. I won't accept them done any other way. This isn't a democracy. We don't take votes on the way things are run. We don't have safe spaces, and there are no participation trophies. I'm the boss."

Mary found her eyes widening. He was seriously frightening as he laid it out before her.

"This is a high-pressure job. I won't lie to you, Mary. I need someone to be at my beck and call. I won't overuse you, but there will be times I will need you. I need to know if that will work for you?"

Mary felt sweat form on her palms. *Whoa! Why does he look so lethal? Is it my imagination or did he transform before my eyes? He doesn't seem like the teddy bear right now.*

"Are you comfortable working beyond your set hours?" This was a pivotal question. King would need her to be flexible. "It won't be an everyday thing, but there will be times I will absolutely need you here."

Mary thought about the question, biting her lip once more. She thought about her mother at the care center. Though Mary didn't know if her mother even knew she was there, it was meaningful that her mother had someone familiar with her, in case she would have a moment of lucidity. It wasn't crucial in any sense, but Mary's stomach churned with the thought of not being there every day with her. But, she'd need to suck it up. She needed this job.

"Yup, that works for me. I can be here when you need me." Rebecca's Hope popped into her head. She would have to quit the center. She'd make the phone call after her interview was done. She hoped she could keep the center job for at least a couple more months until she passed her probationary period. Hopefully, the center would rehire her if this Hellforce thing didn't work out.

King caught the slight hesitation in her response. The hitch of her breathing, and the overemphasized enthusiasm in her voice. *What is she hiding?* He was about to call her out when there was a knock on his door. Irritated, he paused to see who it was. He had an open-door policy, but the knuckleheaded teammates didn't realize when the door wasn't open, it meant the policy was closed.

T-BAR opened the door and strode in, followed by Trip. "Hey, boss, we need to know if we—" T's eyes rose above his hairline when he saw Mary sitting in front of King's desk, half turned to get a look at who was coming in the door. Cue T-Dog in three...two...one... "Helllooo, again." T cocked a single eyebrow and swaggered into the office and over to Mary, propping one arm on the back of her chair and the other on the armrest. He leaned down to eye level with her. "Did it hurt when you fell from heaven, 'cuz baby, you must be an angel." He added a wink and readjusted his stance.

"Nope, that's it, nope. Out! Get the fuck out!" King rounded his desk before T dropped the last word of the sentence, bulldozing him into Trip and corralling him with his broad chest, pushing the duo out the door, shutting it, and locking the knob. Mary stifled a giggle at the frantic pace King pushed them out of his office.

King leaned against the door, sighing heavily. "I am going to deeply apologize for their behavior."

"*Their* behavior? Wasn't it just one guy's behavior?"

"Unfortunately, no. I am going to apologize on behalf of the entire team." King walked back behind his desk and took his seat. "See, my men have walked through hell. They have seen pure evil. They are seasoned veterans. They don't mince words, and they are raw. They are crude, rude, uncouth, don't think before they speak, inappropriate, and they are overall male pigs. They tell off-color jokes, are foul-mouthed, and don't do political correctness. They don't know how to act around a lady, as you can clearly tell," he motioned to the now-locked door, "and are all in dire need of an intervention, a course of office etiquette." King stroked his slightly graying beard, scrubbing his face trying to ward off his frustration. "Ms. Jones, I apologize for T's rude and unethical treatment of you in this office. Please," he huffed out a breath, "please accept my apology on his behalf."

Mary couldn't hold back her laughter. It burst out of her gut and was so unladylike it made her laugh even harder. King looked absolutely devastated, offering the apology. His yearning plea seemed to scream, *Please don't sue me!*

"Mr. King." She smiled, using the title she mistook at the onset of the interview, "I'm a big girl. I wear big girl panties, and I have very thick skin." She held back her laugh when she mentioned the word panties and saw the unsubtle flare in his eyes. "I understand you are not responsible for the actions of your men—" She stopped King before he was about to butt in, "I know you are the boss, and the buck stops with you, but I understand your men must be used to a military atmosphere and political correctness is not their forte. I am not going to sue your company. I am not going to play the victim card. If something is too inappropriate, or something becomes a problem, I will come to you and not a lawyer. I can take an off-color joke; hell, I may tell a few of my own. I'm not going to faint at the first outburst of a swear word. Rile me up, and I can make a sailor blush. I roll with the punches. I ask that I be treated with respect but not kid gloves. I don't have personal sensitivity issues that people need to strive to avoid. Your guy's boldness was actually pretty funny. Hell, I'm flattered."

King let out a breath he didn't know he was holding. *God, she was a breath of fresh air.* "Do *not* tell T that. He will 'flatter' you until you can't take it anymore."

Mary flung her head back and laughed so hard, King could count her molars. "Okay, mum's the word."

King went on, "I can promise you this, Mary," it was the first time he addressed her by her first name and not Ms. Jones, "I won't let anyone disrespect you. A joke is one thing, but blatant disrespect *will not* be tolerated. I will ask them to tone themselves down." He scrubbed his face with both hands, then crossed his arms in front of himself and hung his head. "They will try, I'm sure of that. Although, some," Mary knew he was most likely referring to T, "will need a little more time and reminding than others."

"Henry," Mary reached out and laid her hand on his tattooed forearm, and he swore he felt a jolt electrifying his body, something he'd never experienced before. "I don't expect your men to change their stripes. As you said, we need to be able to work together, and if they need to walk on eggshells just to try to not offend me, that'll throw a wrench into the works, and you won't have the same cohesion as a whole."

King was stunned. Not at the fact that she wasn't expecting them to change, but at the fact that she was so nonchalant and straightforward in her explanation. At that moment, King knew two things. One: she was going to work out just fine, be one with the team, and was perfect for the job. And, two: he was in deep shit because he knew he was teetering on the edge of falling for this woman. This gorgeous, shy, bold, funny, strong woman. If anyone had to watch themselves around her, it was him. Yup, he was fucked.

$\sim$

She'd emailed him with a barrage of questions after she was hired. They were random in nature. What office attire was required? Would she have a lunch break where she would be able to leave the building or should she pack a lunch? Wondering if she had a certain place she would need to park, or if she should just park anywhere in the lot?

King replied to her, letting her know she would have her own reserved spot next to the lot by the building. She'd never been important enough to warrant her own...well, anything, but for some weird, idiotic reason it made her feel important. Like she *mattered*. She emailed him a few more times, but King wasn't big on email. Only time he used it was for official channels per se. After the fifth email, King threw her a text.

KING: *Use text to message me any further questions. Easier to respond and quicker than emails. Phone's always on me.*

MARY: *Are you sure you want me clogging up your text messages? The constant chiming of your phone may be distracting. :) *smiley emoji**

King liked he could sense her humor in her text and could actually feel her smile. He wasn't big on emojis, but he liked that she added one onto her message.

MARY: *Do any of the guys have food allergies?*

KING: *No. Why?*

MARY: *Made a batch of homemade chocolate chip cookies, and they contain nuts. Don't need any of the guys going into anaphylactic shock on my first day. *cookie and skull & crossbones emoji**

King laughed out loud, holding the sound of her voice, through text, in his mind.

KING: *You didn't need to make any treats for your first day. Tomorrow will be hectic, there may not be time for sweets.*

MARY: *Are you refusing my gift?*

KING: *No.*

MARY: *I think you are. *crying emoji**

MARY: *Maybe I won't bring them then. *Pissed, cursing emoji**

KING: *Please bring them.*

MARY: *I don't know.*

KING: *Are you going to make me beg?*

MARY: *So, you're that kind of role player? Didn't take you as a submissive. *bullwhip emoji followed by an eggplant and tongue**

Holy shit! Did she just send an erotic BDSM toy and penis emoji to her new boss? OH, FUCK! She couldn't unsend it. *Oh, God, you've pushed the envelope too far, not thinking, caught up in the text exchange.* Mary bit the corner of her lip.

There was no reply.

She waited.

Nada. Zip. Zilch. No reply. No comeback.

Mary hung her head. *Why did she send that? AAHHR!* She mentally kicked herself a million different ways.

Then, her phone chimed.

KING: *As your boss, I have no comments or thoughts on the matter of submissiveness.*

That was it. Pure, straight, and to the point. No banter. She could sense the authoritarian in his words. King Grizzly.

She wallowed in her humility.

Ding!

KING: *But, as a male, I DO NOT have a submissive bone in my body. I'm the tamer, not the tamee. I'm not to be tamed.*

Mary felt the heat overtake her body. *Holy crap!* His words made her tingle, and she wanted to be the tamee.

KING: *So...about those cookies...*

What? How does he go from talking about submissiveness, back to cookies? Mary waited.

KING: *No takesie-backsies. You said you were bringing them. I WILL be expecting them tomorrow.*

Takesie-Backsies. WTF was that? King shook his head in astonishment, and embarrassment, that he would actually utter, let alone, type those two words.

Ding!

MARY: *Did you really just type those words?*

KING: *Unfortunately, yes. You can delete it now.*

MARY: *No way! Are you kidding me? Maybe I'll keep 'em, screenshot it as blackmail and use it to my advantage.*

King replied before he thought better of himself.

KING: *You want to take advantage of me?*

Mary took a shuddering breath when she read his response. *Is he flirting with me? Is* this *how you flirt?* She was ill-informed of the whole flirtatious process. This was her boss, well, soon-to-be boss. *Was this ethical? Was this a bad idea? Should I just go for it?* She bit her thumbnail, contemplating her next move. Curling her lip beneath her teeth, she replied.

MARY: *Are you offering?*

She waited.

KING: *As your boss, No. As the aforementioned male, maybe? We should wait to see how the workplace relationship works before we explore how other relations will work.*

Mary didn't respond. She didn't know how to respond. This was probably a bad idea. Correction, this was a *terrible* idea. It would only make things more complicated than they needed to be. She needed this job and to have anything but a professional relationship would cause nothing but *doom*. Her phone chimed.

KING: *Thinking better of it, we can ixnay this whole conversation. Disregard the entire thing.*

KING: *Except the cookies. I expect cookies.*

King's last response lightened the tension and anxiety flowing through her.

MARY: *I think it would be for the best, Mr. Clark *cute smile emoji followed by a thumbs up**

CHAPTER 7

King looked over the background check again that Cypher had run on Mary.

Mary Peyton Jones, DOB: December 16th; age 30. No priors; clean record, not even as much as a parking or speeding ticket. High school diploma graduated with honors; Management bachelor's degree. Work history: unskilled laborer: Pete's Diner; current employment: Rebecca's Hope.

As far as he could tell, she looked stellar on paper. Would that translate into the office setting at Hellforce? He damn well hoped so. Today was her first day and she would be arriving at nine a.m. And King couldn't wait for her to show.

He walked over to the file cabinet and grabbed a folder from the top. Labeling the tab: JONES, MARY PEYTON, he slipped the paper inside. He also added the copy of the NDA she signed.

The Non-Disclosure Agreement was a must. Any employee would have to sign one including his current team, the men he trusted more than anyone on the planet. Yes, even the men he entrusted with his life had an NDA in each of their files. Each man retained a security clearance from the DOD, due to their government assignments. King pulled the paper out of the printer where he had a fresh copy of the resume Mary emailed him. He checked her references, and at this juncture, he found nothing but glowing recommendations and exemplary reviews.

Placing the file on his desk, King looked around his office.

Ember was right, it was a Grade A hellhole. Papers littered every surface and square inch.

The fact of it being, King trusted no one.

Cy told him he could trust the security firewalls on his computer since they were, after all, in the security business. Cypher had the network impenetrable. King remembered the back-and-forth argument he had with Cy when he last updated the software on his laptop.

"Why take the chance? We have enemies that would die trying everything to break into our systems. The information we have from the DOD alone would be worth millions on the black market, and any terrorist hack would love to get their hands on ANY of our information." King knew he had enemies. Hell, he had enemies of enemies that would love to take down Hellforce and any member of the team. "The Enemy of my Enemy is my Friend," was not a chance King was willing to take.

"Not going to happen, King." Cy looked insulted to even be having this conversation. "I have so many breaks, walls, encrypted code, and planted viruses in place, that even if we were to be hacked, which is impossible, the hacker would kill his own system before any walls were penetrated or any information was captured. No one can get into our network."

"I don't trust anyone farther than I can throw them, and if I can't see them, I can't throw them."

Cy shook his head, irritated with King's distrust of his ability to keep the company safe and impenetrable from cyber hacks. "What the hell does that even have to do with system files. Just use your damn laptop and ditch the papermill permeating in this office. My God, King. You're a fucking Luddite!"

King didn't know all the fancy bells and whistles Cy had in place, but he knew one thing: paper didn't crash, didn't get corrupted or infected, and paper didn't get hacked. And, for someone to steal his files, they would have to penetrate Hellforce, and that was an absolute impossibility. No one could pass through the security system, and all the checks and balances, to get into his fortress. Just as when Mary arrived for her interview, the three-story nondescript building had four levels of security before someone could even get to the lobby. Anyone wishing to get into the building must be escorted by an armed guard. To say King was paranoid was an uneducated guess. King was astutely aware of the plethora of what he possessed and was not naive as to what extent people would go to get it.

And, if anyone was lucky enough—or stupid enough—to break in and get that far into the building, the offices were locked tighter than Fort Knox. The security team that patrolled the grounds of Hellforce were all former military veterans mostly from Special Forces. A lot of them were medically discharged, so keeping them in the security realm was an easy transition for them.

At the beginning of each shift, each security detail was assigned at random, so not even the supervisor was in-the-know of what guard would be patrolling which sector. They rotated in three-round shifts and patrolled a different area each day. Number one: to break up the monotony, and number two: it was a way to prevent a possible rogue player within the security force from turning traitorous.

King looked around his office and knew he had to get it organized. But, in a strange, peculiar way, it was already organized—just in King's irrational way of organizing. He had a system and he could locate almost any file...except on the rare occasion it was misplaced...which, okay, happened more than he wished to admit. Yes, he needed to get organized. He needed Mary.

Mary felt the lump forming behind her ear before she even found her bearings. She felt like throwing up. *What the hell happened and why am I on the floor of Trent's room?* She felt the lump and her fingertips were tinged with blood. Her head beat out a rhythm that churned her nausea. Her hands began to shake. *Fuck!*

She pulled herself up to her knees feeling the room sway and tip. *Oh, God, she was going to throw up.* She held back the bile creeping up her throat, but it was no use. She retched once, spilling bile onto the thinly woven carpet overlaying the basement concrete. Her mother's house was a rarity in Texas, as hardly any homes had basements. Right now, she was wishing her house didn't have one.

What was going on? *Arguing.* She heard yelling coming from upstairs on the main level of the house. *Male voices.* She needed to get upstairs to see who was up there. She staggered to her feet, the room still tipsy.

Looking around, she saw her brother's room was ransacked. Not that Trent's room was ever clean, but the mattress was tossed off the bed frame, dresser drawers pulled out, tipped on end, and emptied of their contents. Even the dresser itself was tipped onto its side. The three shelves that lined the wall were swept clean, and one was pushed over, blocking her exit.

She stumbled forward, crashing to her knees, but caught herself from face planting on the laundry basket. *The laundry. Trent's laundry.*

Her memory swirled. *Think!*

She was bringing Trent's laundry to his bedroom before she was leaving for work. Her first day of work at Hellforce. Images flashed in intervals. She willed her brain to fit them together in sequence. *A man. In Trent's room. Startled. Yes.*

She found someone going through her brother's dresser. *Struggle. Scratching. A fist to her cheek.*

She brought her hand to her cheekbone. It was tender but not split open. She checked her fingers for additional blood but there was none. Her mind swirled and whirled some more. *Her scream. Then, stars. Blackness.*

She must have hit her head after she fell. *Was I pushed? Was I punched?* Her memory was absent. Who was the man, and where was Trent?

The male voices got distant. She could hear rustling, heavy feet, boots on the hardwood, and something being dragged. Something heavy by the sound of it.

Again, arguing. *Are they leaving? Should I stay here until they leave?*

She checked her back pocket for her phone to call the police, but it wasn't there. It must've fallen out when she fell, because she was never without it, even in the house. She searched the ground but every time she bent over, a wall of nausea welled in her throat and the room tipped. She must have hit her head harder than she thought.

Again, she felt the swelling lump. It was wetter now and she felt blood trickling down her neck. Looking down at her shoulder, she saw a stain of crimson growing on her blouse. *Fuck!* She needed to stop the bleeding. She picked up one of Trent's t-shirts, willing the spin to stop, and applied pressure to her head.

"Sssswwwsss!" She winced and sucked in a breath at the sting and the pain. Damn! She must have one hell of a wound.

She needed to get upstairs. She had a gun and money, other important documents in her parents' bedroom safe, irreplaceable sentimental jewelry, and she would guess whoever was in the house would head there next.

Mary held onto the wall, letting it guide her and prop her up as she made her way to the stairs. Items blocked her path to the bedroom doorway. Shaking, she climbed over the strewn items, and atop the overturned bookshelf, out of her brother's room.

By the time she crawled to the top of the basement stairs, she heard the garage door shut.

Silence. Eerie silence.

Pulling herself up the last riser, she used the handrail to stand upright. The room stayed steady, though her stomach churned.

Staggering her way through the kitchen and down the short hallway that led to her parents' room, Mary froze at the sight of her mother's pristine, cherished room, ransacked. Tossed. Looted. Nothing was left untouched. Pillaged. Tears filled her eyes at the sight of broken tchotchkes and knickknacks, broken and crushed on the hardwood floor. The perfume bottles her mother had neatly lined atop her dresser were smashed.

But, the sight of the broken picture frame, glass shattered and piercing the beloved picture of her father standing tall and proud in his Army uniform, holding his new bride in his arms, made Mary weep. It was her mother's favorite picture that sat on her bedside table. Her mother said it was the last thing she saw before falling asleep, and the first thing she saw in the dawn of a new day. Her beloved husband. He may be gone, but never forgotten.

She bent to pick it up, but the room swayed and she felt blackness encroach in her sight. She beat the darkness back, picked up the picture, and laid it reverently on the chest dresser, the one thing that was still standing upright.

She made her way to the closet. She had to get to the safe. The closet door was open, and even though she hadn't entered it, she knew someone else had. The pull string light was on, the lone, bare bulb lit, shining like a beacon telling her someone had violated this room as well. Her heart dropped.

She looked to the back of the closet, back behind where the suitcases once hid the hole in the wall. The hole that held a small three-foot by two-foot safe. The safe that was no longer in the hole, in the wall, in the closet, in her mother's room.

Gone.

Someone knew exactly what they were looking for.

King paced his office from the window to the door, getting angrier and more pissed with every step he took. *Where the fuck is she?* It was Mary's first day on the job, and she was already an hour late. *Unacceptable.* She didn't even call to say she was running behind. On top of that, King called her cell three times and each time left a voicemail. *Is she ghosting me?* The first voicemail started with concern, wondering if she was ok. The second held a bit more of a stern, "Where are you?" And, the third ended with him questioning his judgment of hiring her.

He needed to busy himself somewhere other than his office. *The range. Yes!* That was always a good way for him to blow off steam.

He took the stairs to the basement, always the stairs, where the team's armory and the indoor range were located. He wasn't going to shoot the big guys today—it would be pistols, tactical force focus, randomized targets. He didn't really care what he was shooting at, just as long as he could fire off a few hundred rounds, settling his nerves, hoping Mary had a *damn* good excuse for being late, or possibly missing the first day on the job because otherwise, it would be her last.

"Is there anything else you can think of that's missing?"

Mary stared blankly at the officer taking her statement and wanted to laugh. Did he see the state of the disaster they were standing in? If anything other than the safe was missing, it wouldn't be discovered until she was able to put the house back in order, which she knew wouldn't be anytime soon. Mary turned to take in the wreckage and the room tipped. She felt herself float, only seeing the image of the room sway before her, as though they were vapors of a desert mirage. As the mirage faded into black, all she could think of was the man that believed enough in her to give her a chance at a new job, King. It was her last thought and image that entered her mind. *Shit!* She was going to miss her first day of work.

Great way to get fired on your first day. King was furious Mary was a no-show. The guys all kept their distance because King Grizzly was ready to tear anyone's ass that rubbed him the wrong way.

He reloaded his mag and slapped it into place, chambering the first round. He took his aggression out on the target, riddling it with five rapid shots.

Why even come for the interview, go through the whole charade and rigmarole, only to not show up?

Mary didn't seem like the type to ghost her job, but maybe she had a change of heart and didn't know how to politely decline? No, that didn't seem to be her M.O. She had no problem letting her position be known at the interview.

King moved from the range to the mock-up of rooms he and the team used to hone their skills and keep them sharp, precise, and clean.

She wouldn't be the type to rant a tirade and then be too docile and timid to call if she changed her mind. That got King concerned. Mary wouldn't just leave him in the lurch. He saw it in her eyes and in her excitement during the interview, how much she wanted the job. Something niggled in the back of his mind. His brain couldn't shake it. Mary was too fired up not to show up.

Mary waited for the doctor to return to her bedside, all the while thinking of a way to get a hold of King. She didn't have her phone, which was the only place she had his number. It's not like she could Google, "Hellforce," and they weren't in the phonebook. She was tempted to ask the nurse if he could look up Henry Clark and see if he was in the directory, on Facebook, Snapchat, Twitter, anything that she would be able to get a message to him. He must be furious that she didn't show up this morning. She should've asked the police officer if he could stop at the nondescript building and give King a message. Yeah, that probably wouldn't go over well, with the fortress of security outside and inside the building. The Bat Cave had less security than Hellforce.

Shit! She was screwed and would have to wait until she was released to go to work. Hopefully, King would be understanding. After all, it wasn't like she purposely skipped work. None of this was her fault, and it was out of her hands.

She had nothing but time, and the thoughts of what happened at the house played out in her mind. It hurt to think, but she replayed every aspect of time she could recall. Over and over on a loop, she scrutinized anything she could recall, searching for the most minute clue. *Where was Trent? How did I not know someone was in the house? Did they enter when I was in the shower? How long had they been there?*

The thought of someone in the house while she was vulnerable, naked in the shower made her run cold with a shiver. What could have happened if they would've found her in the bathroom?

She kept the house doors locked, so either someone forced their way in, or maybe Trent left the door unlocked.

The safe was the part of this whole scenario that weighed on her the most. Whoever was in the house knew there was a safe and knew exactly where it was located. *Would Trent burglarize his own house?* It seemed absurd, but then again, his erratic behavior and change in mood had her thinking it could be a possibility.

And, the man in Trent's room. Who was he, and what was he looking for? If he was there for the safe, why wreck every room? Every room in the house was tossed. Did they get up to her room or just stay on the main level of the house? The thought of her room being vandalized sent pricks of tears to her eyes and filled her veins with venom. Her things being gone through, pilfered, or destroyed. Her gut ached and her head throbbed.

The pain medicine they gave her was beginning to take effect. Her eyelids were heavy, and the throbbing in her head was dissipating. She was tired. She peered out of one eye and checked the clock, hoping it was still morning and not too late in the day. She could still make it to work. 12:15. Over four hours late. *Crap.*

CHAPTER 8

The niggling in the back of King's head wouldn't go away. After a few hours on the range and a couple more in the armory, he couldn't shake the feeling something awful had happened to Mary. Again, he tried her cellphone. Nothing. He didn't leave a voicemail.

"Wanna ride along?" King popped his head into Arctic's office. His initial anger had turned to concern.

Arctic looked up from the report he was reading, catching King with a worrisome expression. "Where?"

King stepped through the doorway, rubbing his left forearm with the tattooed sleeve that hid his hideous scars from the IED, "Mary's house."

Arctic's expression deepened, and King answered his unasked question, "Something isn't right." Arctic stood and King continued, "Got a bad feeling. Something's wrong. Can't shake this suspicion."

All the guys on the team knew to never second-guess a gut feeling or a sixth-sense. If anyone on the team had learned that lesson—all too well—it was King and Arctic. "She doesn't seem the type that'd just not show up, no call or anything. Gonna run past her house, make sure everything's good."

Arctic made his way around the desk, following King out of his office. "She's still not picking up?"

"No."

King pulled his FOB out of his pocket and headed out the back door to the employee parking lot, jumped into his truck, and entered Mary's address into the GPS. Arctic hopped into the passenger's seat and they hightailed it out of the lot towards Mary's house. His hackles were up and the pit in his stomach was growing, telling him that what he would find at Mary's wouldn't be good. Thoughts of, "what if," ran through his mind. King wasn't a "what if," guy. He dealt in facts. He was always looking to connect the dots, if A happens, then do B. If that doesn't work, move on to C.

There was always a plan for any scenario he headed into, but today, he was flying blind. Multiple scenarios ran through his head, but not having a starting point to construct a plan from, he essentially had no plan. All he knew was the feeling of dread built within him, and he didn't like it.

The ride was mostly silent, neither needing to explore possibilities, knowing that they would have at least some answers once they arrived at her house. Either she would be there and they could find out why she didn't show up to the office, or she wouldn't be there and they could start tracking her down.

King didn't want to be too aggressive, in case she'd changed her mind and ghosted him. If she wasn't home and continued to not pick up her phone, Cy could start to track her by cell phone, her debit and credit card transactions, and then if need be, they could track her vehicle looking at cameras in the area, see which direction she was heading, but only if it came to that point. He could also make a call to Tex, a computer guru in all aspects of ops, missions, tracking, and delivering. King didn't want to get ahead of himself, but if Tex's genius was needed, King wouldn't hesitate to make that call.

Something Mary had said during the interview concerned King. When he mentioned that the company would supply her with a phone in case she was needed at some hour she wasn't scheduled, Mary had mentioned that she was never without her phone, so King would be able to contact her 24/7. If she was ghosting him that would be on her, but if she wasn't answering because she didn't have her phone, that would mean it was not by choice.

Tension built in King's muscles, especially in his arms and fingers gripping the steering wheel, as they drew closer to the GPS destination. He was never high-strung, so the anxiety he felt had him off-kilter.

Out of his peripheral vision, he saw Arctic drumming his fingers on his knee, and that alone threw up alarms. Arctic may have been one of the most closed-off and private people King knew, but he was also one of the most relaxed, laid-back men. Never jumpy.

Never startled. Never nervous. So, to see that even he was feeling antsy didn't bode well for what they would find when they got to Mary's.

Both he and Arctic had survived the worst together, the loss of their entire team. It was on that mission as well—King driving and Arctic in the passenger's seat of the Humvee—that both had the deep gut feeling that doom was around the corner. And then their Humvee lay ripped into pieces around them, neither knowing if the other survived. It wasn't until they met up at Walter Reed that they both discussed knowing something bad was going to happen on the mission. So, knowing they were both feeling dread driving to Mary's, had him experiencing Déjà vu.

King rounded the final corner of Mary's block. His blood ran cold when he saw a myriad of police cruisers parked haphazardly in front of the house. King pushed the pedal to the floor and raced to the scene. The hair on the back of his neck was standing on end, and his adrenaline was pumping. *What happened? Where's Mary? Is she okay?* The thoughts came in succession. He calmed himself. *Precision.* King the man became King the operator.

When he reached the scene, he jammed the truck into park and rolled out of the cab with ease and purpose. Arctic did the same and followed King to the first cruiser that was draped with yellow police tape, anchoring it to the next point, keeping all the looky-loos at bay. King ducked under the tape as an officer approached them. Police tape wasn't going to keep King from finding Mary.

"Please step behind the tape, sir. This is a crime scene."

Crime scene. The words made King's stomach turn. King proceeded to make his way to the house.

Placing his hand on the yellow taser on the front of his utility belt, the officer threw out another stern warning. "Sir, I won't ask you again, step back to the other side of the tape."

King again disregarded the warning and kept walking. It was as if he were in a trance. Singular vision. Singular mission. Honed in on getting to Mary.

The officer pulled his taser and aimed it directly at King. "On the ground!" The command was loud and forceful. "On the ground, now!"

Arctic made a grab for King's arm to halt him from going any farther.

The commotion grabbed the attention of the other law enforcement at the scene, and they quickly ran to assist, pulling their tasers as well.

King met eyes with one of the Rangers he knew. "Where's Mary?" Two words. That's all he said.

"Stand down! Stand down! Officers stand down," the Ranger yelled to the men standing at their ready, and they lowered their weapons. "He's good. A friendly."

"Chambers, where's Mary?" King ordered the question, not the least concerned that he had at least five officers ready to take him down just a few seconds ago.

Ranger Daxton Chambers made his way over to King and Arctic, waving a few of the other officers away. "King, you can't cross the tape. You know that," Dax said with a chuckle. "Doesn't matter you're a force to be reckoned with, you know the rules."

King stood stock still, no smile, only concern masking his face, waiting for him to answer his question. "Mary, where is she?"

Ranger Chambers drew a hand down his face and said, "Can't disclose any information."

King knew the rules. If you weren't family, no information would be given. "She's my fiancée." The lie just rolled off his lips before he could think better of it. King wasn't one to lie. Ever. He despised liars. Couldn't stand them in his company. He was honest to the core, so it surprised him when the lie slipped easily through his lips, but he wouldn't take it back. "I need to know where my fiancée is? Mary, where is she?"

Dax studied King with a wary eye, not buying the bit. He scrubbed a hand down his face again and turned his attention to Arctic and raised a brow. Arctic didn't say a word, just gave him a curt nod of his head. Dax took that as truth and turned back to King.

"Looks like there was a break-in. House is ransacked. Everything is turned on its head."

"Mary." King forced the word out with demand.

"She must have walked in or interrupted the burglary in progress. She was tossed around and sustained some injuries..."

King didn't hear anything Chambers said after that. Someone dared to lay a finger on Mary. King was in operator mode. Someone was in for a heap of trouble when he found them. King headed to the house, taking the front steps two at a time onto the porch, with Dax and Arctic on his tail. He stopped when he entered the front door which led straight into the dining room.

Everything was trashed.

The china cabinet doors were flung open, and the table chairs laid on their sides. Whatever had been sitting on the table was now swept onto the floor. King looked to his right into the living room and was met with the same. Couch cushions pulled from their place, the entertainment unit ransacked, the coffee table upended and the recliner tipped forward. Even the outdated box television laid face down and busted on the floor.

King studied it through the eyes of an operator, categorizing each area, compartmentalizing the information. He knew what he was looking at was a staged scene.

King walked farther into the house, into the kitchen, taking in the disarray. He found the kitchen the same as the other rooms. An overkill of destruction. He walked down the hallway, to the right, passed the banister rail leading upstairs, and went into the master bedroom. This room was a disaster as well. But again, too tidy of a disaster. Dresser drawers hung open, some pulled all the way out and the contents dumped on the floor. The items on the dresser were swept clean, and to King's mind, this scene was too damaged.

If a burglar were looking for something, especially something specific, they wouldn't go to the extent of clearing the dresser tops. The only reason someone would damage personal items would be for a vendetta or someone trying to stage a scene. King thought this scene could be both.

"The safe was taken." Dax pointed to the open closet. "Seems whoever this was knew the safe was in there. It was hidden in the wall behind some suitcases and covered with a wooden panel. It was dragged out of the closet. Must have been removed on a cart or carried by a few people. The size would be pretty impossible for a single person to carry it."

King crouched down, peered into the void where the safe once sat. The wall was busted around the hole, probably to make it easier to pry or pull it out. He knew better than to touch anything, which made him demand, "Fingerprints. I want this place dusted."

"Detective Meyers is on that. He's starting in the basement. That's where Mary encountered the burglar."

King's blood boiled and he fumed, his original question returning. "Where's Mary?" He strode back into the kitchen looking for the basement doorway.

"Regional Medical. She was taken by ambulance once she answered some questions. She didn't want to go, but the EMT almost demanded it. She refused, but once she lost consciousness, she had no choice."

King just about lost his mind. He turned, stepping close to Chambers, crowding him with the bulk of his torso. "Lost consciousness! What the hell happened?"

Arctic placed his hand on King's bicep, keeping him from assaulting a Texas Ranger. Friend or not, King wouldn't be kept from a jail cell.

"How bad is she hurt?"

Not being intimidated, Dax stood his ground. King stood solid but reluctantly took a step backward with a pull from Arctic, after which Dax, too, stepped back.

"Well, to start, she's got a knot on her head rivaling a tangerine."

This information didn't bring the calm King was hoping for. Actually, it did the exact opposite and had him wanting to tear someone apart.

Dax continued, "She's bruised pretty bad on her side, across her ribs, but that may be an older injury. The swelling on her face didn't look good."

King felt a burning tingle in his hands; hands that were turning white from the fists he was squeezing. The thought of how Mary may have gotten an older injury burned with fury and intensity in his chest. "How long ago was she taken?"

Dax looked at his watch, "Hour or so? She came up from the basement and called from the house." He pointed to the rotary phone hanging on the wall. A phone from a bygone era.

King knew she mustn't have had her cell phone if she called from the ancient relic hanging on the flowered, wallpapered wall.

King headed for the doorway leading to the back door and took the two steps to the landing, which also led to the basement stairs. He bounded down them, scanning the area that was in no better shape than what he'd found upstairs. He caught the attention of Detective Meyers and his team combing through the chaos.

"Clark!" Meyers walked up to King.

It took King a minute to realize that Meyers was addressing him by his last name. No one called King anything formal, unless he was meeting with the brass and alphabets that came to his office. Even then, after formalities were exchanged, people addressed him as King.

"Meyers," King answered back with a nod. "Any idea who did this?" King wasn't in the mood for chitchat, he wanted answers.

Meyers didn't answer his question. "You can't be on the premises, Mr. Clark."

King knew that Meyers was pulling rank. Animosity ran deep between the two from years past, when King and his team cracked a case Meyers had been working on when he was a seasoned junior detective in Vegas. The case was at a standstill. The family appealed to Hellforce to find their daughter, who'd gone missing on the Vegas strip during a bachelorette party gone wrong. The girl was missing for months, and Meyers was leading it directly into a cold case file.

Four days upon getting the case from Vegas PD, King and the team had found the girl held in a Columbian fortress, caught up in drug smuggling and human trafficking ring. The team was too late to keep her from finding out the atrocities of the Columbian sex trades, but at least they were able to return her to her family and get her on a road to recovery and healing. It was a slap in the face to Meyers when he was let go from the Vegas detective squad a month later, then later joined the Texas detective division, and he never let go of the vendetta.

To King, it didn't matter who rescued her, or who received the credit, all that mattered to him and his team was the fact that she was found.

Before King could tell Meyers that he wasn't leaving the premises, Ranger Chambers spoke up, "His fiancée was the victim."

Victim. The word curdled in King's stomach.

"Still, crime scene," Meyers circled his finger in the air to the surroundings, "gonna have to ask Chambers here to escort you *out.*" He punctuated the last syllable, and his smugness grated against King.

King wasn't backing down, "I need to know what you've found."

Detective Meyers stepped forward, catching the coolness coming off King, "You *don't* need to know, and you *won't* be interfering with *my* investigation."

King wanted to reach out and snap the pencil-necked detective. One squeeze and twist would give King the satisfaction he craved, but Meyers continued, "And, I don't want you and your lackeys poking around here. One whiff of you interfering and sticking your nose where it doesn't belong will have the full wrath of the department at your doors." Meyers played a bravado that his demeanor couldn't cash. He thought he was intimidating King, which was a joke.

King crouched down, took a pen from his shirt pocket, and

began sifting through the broken debris at his feet. He'd be finding out what the investigators found, and he'd be coming back to the scene once the tape was lifted on the premises.

Meyers stepped into King's personal space, expecting King to look up, which was not the case. In actuality, King straightened to full height, and by the flare in Meyers' eyes, King standing six-foot-two inches over Meyers' five-foot-eight, King knew he had the upper hand.

Meyers faltered in his next words, and if King wasn't mistaken, he thought he saw Meyers' head tremble when he pulled back, looked up, and attempted to dress King down. "You and your *boys* think you rule the roost. A bunch of retired Rambos playing vigilantes in the streets thinking you're above the law."

King stood toe-to-toe watching the detective play grade-school bully, his "Little Man Syndrome" shining like a beacon,

"Sorry to break it to you, Clark," he spit King's last name from his lips, "I'm the law here, and you and your group of Merry Men won't dare attempt to get into *my* investigation." King took his empty threat to be a direct invitation to the party. "I get the sense you're interfering, I'll have *hellfire* raining down on Hellforce." Meyers seemed to take glee in his play-on-words, but his face fell a few shades when King addressed him.

"Don't know why they would assign a washed-up detective to secure this scene," King mimicked the detective's earlier motion by circling his finger around the room, "but, if I find out you fucked up one piece of this crime scene, crossed one *T* wrong or forgot to dot a single *I*, I will have your ass on the chopping block so fast, you won't know it's missing until it falls off the table and onto the floor. You may think we're nothing, but we Rambos and Merry Men," he threw a thumb towards Arctic without losing sight of Meyers, "we hold a lot more pull in Sherwood Forest and beyond the King's realm than you can imagine."

Meyers' face blanched even more. "One fuck-up, Meyers, just one," King held up his index finger, "that's all it will take for you to be packing a banker's box with the awards you don't have and accolades you haven't earned, and you'll be moving out of that cushy office where you solve and close nothing, and you'll find yourself in the back end of the unemployment line...again. You want to measure dicks, that's fine with me because I know what you're packing, and the chief of police, the commander, your boss, will be more than happy to let you know who the winner of the contest will be. So, just keep spouting off, and we'll see who comes out on top."

King turned to leave and saw the smirk Dax was holding back. King led Arctic to the stairs and took one last look over his shoulder, "Have a productive day, Detective." He turned and made his way up the rest of the stairwell.

CHAPTER 9

If King thought the fury he felt when he heard Mary had been taken to the hospital was maddening, it was nothing compared to the rage that burned through his veins seeing her lying in a hospital bed with her left eye swollen shut and her cheek bruised. Her head was turned slightly away from him, and he could clearly see the stitched-up bulge behind her ear. After playing the fiancée card at the administrative desk, he was now standing at her bedside, uncontrollable anger seething through him.

"Tamp it down, boss." Arctic's voice came from beside him, and King had to put himself in check. The last thing he wanted to do was scare Mary when she opened her eyes. "She's safe."

Arctic's words did nothing to reassure him. Just because she was in the hospital, didn't equate to her being safe. Whoever did this to her was still out there and may be looking to bring her more harm. King studied Mary's face. Even in its punished form, she was still beautiful. He wanted to reach out and run his finger down the unbruised side but didn't want to startle or wake her.

From the doorway, he heard a throat clear and he turned, only to find a younger-ish doctor, maybe late twenties, early thirties at best, making his way over to Mary's bedside. King eyed him with suspicion, and he knew right away he didn't like him. Even being a guy, King thought the doc was way too good-looking to be a doctor. His hair was coiffed and his shirt was three sizes too small—definitely purchased from the children's department.

His skinny jeans wrapped around his skinny ankles and King

wondered how the toothpicks even held the slight man upright. To King, he seemed to be one of those TV doctors that ladies seemed to swoon over. *Why was Mary assigned such a young, handsome, debonair doctor?* It made King angry. *Was he even old enough to be a doctor?*

King wanted to demand his credentials. *Did he skate by through medical school on his looks?* Maybe he wasn't even a real doctor. Maybe he was a resident who hadn't passed the medical board and wasn't allowed to practice medicine without his mentor looking over his shoulder.

The man held out his hand to King, "I'm Dr. Whitmore."

King eyed it suspiciously and then looked at him directly, "Where's your mentor?"

Dr. Whitmore's brows knitted in confusion, "My mentor?"

"Yeah, the doctor in charge. Your boss?"

He dropped his hand. "I *am* the attending." Whitmore crossed his arms across his narrow chest.

Not to be outdone, King crossed his arms also, took in a breath, and inflated the bulk of his torso.

"I'm Cole," Arctic interjected and held out his hand to the doctor, but not before catching King's eye, his face telling Arctic that he was a traitor and would be charged as such with mutiny.

"Are you the fiancée?" Whitmore smiled and shook Arctic's hand.

"I am!" King blurted before Arctic could open his mouth, "I'm her fiancée." It sounded too forced to King's ears, but like hell he was going to let anyone else be in charge of Mary's keep.

King softened his tone, "She's mine," King corrected, "um, my girl." He held back his former reservation of the doctor. Maybe he *was* a well-trained doctor?

"Oh, I'm sorry," Whitmore apologized with his sincere embarrassment showing, "I just assumed..." he looked from King to Arctic to Mary, "um, the age difference..."

King was back to pissed. *Arrogant fuck! No way he's a doctor.* King was murdering him in his mind.

"How's Mary?" Arctic knew King was planning where to bury the body, and he wanted to move the conversation along. "Will she be all right?"

King held himself, waiting to hear what this Fisher-Price doctor had to say about Mary's condition. Then, he would hunt down the most senior of the medical staff and see what the truth was about her condition.

"She seems to be doing all right..."

King didn't know if the doctor was blind, but Mary was far from all right. She had bruises on her face and her eye was damn near swollen shut, and she had stitches in her head. And, those were just the injuries he could see.

"...she sustained a contusion behind her right ear..."

King bit his molars.

"...and after her initial examination, we think she may have suffered a minor concussion related to the abrasion to her cheek..."

King tightened his arms.

"...and bump to the head."

"Okay, that's it," King threw up his hands and roared, at a decibel way too loud for a hospital ward, let alone a patient's bedside. "Arctic, call Slate, get him over here to run a complete examination on Mary. Pronto."

Dr. Whitmore stood in shock, and Arctic just stood in amusement, chuckling.

"You can't just call in another doctor into the hospital!" Whitmore exclaimed.

King saw that Arctic wasn't heeding his warning and pulled his own cell from his pocket. He swiped to unlock the phone and began to enter his security code.

"*I'm* her doctor and *I* have thoroughly examined her."

The statement brought blood whooshing into King's ears at the thought of this *doctor* eyeing and examining his woman. *His woman?* The thought didn't have his usual reaction of repelling any woman who had stars in her eyes and the scheme to bag a military man. King was the one with starry eyes.

"Well, obviously you aren't a very good one if you think she's alright, *Doogie*."

The doctor looked dumbfounded.

This made King not only mad but also feel old, that the doctor wasn't even old enough to understand the Doogie Howser, MD reference.

King went on, "That's more than an "abrasion" to her cheek where someone clearly clocked her, and she has more than a "bump" on her head if that knot behind her ear is anything telling."

"Believe me, Mr... I'm sorry, I didn't get your name..."

King didn't offer it.

Dr. Whitmore continued, "I'm certainly a qualified doctor to evaluate Ms. Jones. And, you are not authorized to bring in another doctor for a second opinion."

"Not a doctor, he's a friend." King started to dial his cell.

"Even more preposterous," Whitmore was genuinely shocked, "you can't bring an unlicensed person in here to make a medical diagnosis. Either you leave now, or I'm going to have to call security to escort you from this room."

"Slate? King. I'm going to need you—"

The phone was torn from King's ear before he uttered another word.

"Yeah, Slate, Arctic here. Never mind, King," Arctic ignored King's glare and dodged his attempt to take his phone back, "he's just temporarily lost his mind. Yeah, I'll call you in a few."

Arctic pocketed King's phone to prevent him from making another rash phone call to any of the others and played damage control.

"King, in the hall." Arctic pointed to the doorway. King stared at him in astonishment that Arctic would heed the warning and banish him from Mary's bedside. Arctic only hardened his stare, and King reluctantly turned from his stance and stepped towards the doorway. He lasered Arctic with a stare and seared him with a death look that said, *We'll discuss this later and it won't work out well for you.*

If anyone could make this situation better, it was Arctic. And, King knew it. He was a smooth-talker and the negotiator of the team, and his Oscar-winning looks didn't hurt in the least. When things needed to be smoothed over or worked out in compromise, he was the go-to man.

When King cleared the doorway and the door shut behind him, Arctic turned to the doctor and took in a cleansing breath. "I apologize for my friend, King. He's kinda a little stressed and hot-headed right now, understandably." He pointed to Mary's bed.

The doctor raised his eyebrows and gave him a knowing look.

"Look, I know you want to throw him out on his backside, but he's normally not this big of an asshole." He heard a pound against Mary's door from the outside—obviously, King was eavesdropping. "He's just concerned about his," Arctic looked at Mary laying in the bed, "his fiancée." He hoped he was believable. "Please, Dr. Whitmore, please allow him to stay."

The doctor twitched his lip to the side, contemplating his decision.

"Please," Arctic chuckled, "otherwise I'm going to have to sit with him, and please don't put me through that." Arctic gave him a mocking plea of his eyes and flashed his never-fail smile, trying to lighten the moment with humor.

Dr. Whitmore smiled, but with seriousness said, "I'll allow him to stay, but he *cannot* bring any unlicensed medical personnel to examine *my* patient. And no more outbursts or he's out without a warning. Ms. Jones is *not* to be disturbed or agitated."

"Understood." Arctic leveled the doc with a nod. "Is she sedated? Will she be waking soon?"

"She was a bit agitated when she was brought in, so we lightly sedated her for the CT scan." He looked at the clock on the wall. "She should be up soon."

"Thanks, doc."

"You're welcome." He walked to the door. "I'll send your friend in."

Arctic nodded and took in a deep breath, thankful that all went well. A few seconds later, King came barging through the door with the pent-up fury of a bear.

"*I'm* an asshole? You fucker!" King bellowed, striding to Mary's bedside in three steps.

Arctic brought his finger to his lips and said, "No more outbursts! They'll kick you out on your ass if you disrupt this hospital one more time, and they aren't kidding, King."

King narrowed Arctic with a glare and said through gritted teeth, "We'll discuss it at the office," but his tone was still deadly.

Arctic knew King was more growl than bite with the guys and wasn't worried in the least that King would reprimand him. If anything, King should be thanking him for not getting him barred and banished from the joint. King turned to Mary, and his countenance softened.

"Think she'll be all right?" King pulled a chair as close to her bed as possible but didn't sit.

"According to, 'Dr. Howser,'" Arctic chuckled, "she'll be okay."

King's phone began to ring, and Arctic pulled it from his pocket. Mary stirred.

"Slate," Arctic said to King as he looked down at the screen, "I'll take this in the hall." He walked out of the room, giving King the privacy he knew he wanted.

Mary blinked her eyes, then kept them closed and squeezed them together tightly.

"Mmhhhrrr," Mary moaned, and her hand lifted to touch behind her ear.

King caught her wrist, "No, Sugar, you don't want to do that."

Mary's eyes popped open at the sound of the masculine voice, and she flinched before realizing it was King. "What are you doing here?" The question came out more forceful than Mary meant it to, and her own voice hurt her head.

King reeled back and let go of her wrist. "Sorry, didn't mean to startle you."

"You didn't."

King knew it was a lie but let it go. "You got a nasty knot behind your ear that needed to be stitched and a good-sized welt on your cheek. Can you tell me what happened?" King used a gentle tone and not the forceful interrogating tone he would otherwise use in a scenario to get information.

Mary's hand immediately went to her ear again, this time without King making a grab to stop her. King knew since the injury was bulging outward, that it was a good thing, and the swelling was outside of her skull, not causing any pressure or damage in her brain.

"Sssswwwsss!" Mary sucked in a wince when she felt the bulge.

"Easy, Sugar. Careful." King crooned in a tone he had never used before. The tone sounded foreign to his ears. "Tell me what happened." He pulled the chair beneath his legs and sat at an angle facing her. He gently pulled her hand from her examination of the wound and cradled it in his hand, interlacing his fingers with hers. "Anything you can remember?"

She closed her eyes, one almost swollen shut already, and tried to recall what had happened. The throbbing in her head made it hard to concentrate, but she remembered waking up on Trent's bedroom floor.

"Take your time, Sugar, no rush." King caressed her thumb with his massive bear paw.

Her next words weren't what King expected. "I'm sorry I missed the first day of work." She took in a deep breath and exhaled on a tremor. She looked over at King, "If it's not going to work out, and you need to let me go, it's perfectly understandable." The words betrayed the way Mary was feeling. She needed this job more than anything, but if King didn't want to be wrapped up in the craziness that was her life, if he had to cut ties, she would understand.

King blinked in astonishment. Was she really thinking he was going to fire her? And at her bedside, no less? "Mare, that's not going to happen." He used a more authoritarian voice than he needed and then gentled his tone. "That's not going to happen, and that's not what's important at the moment. What is important is you telling me what happened."

"I still have a job?" Her voice was just above a whisper as if she said it too loud it would spell her demise.

King chuckled not at her weariness, but at the disbelief of the situation. "Yeah, Sugar, you still have a job. Now, tell me what happened."

Mary closed her eyes but turned her head in King's direction. She sucked in a deep breath and exhaled. "I'm not sure what happened," she paused, "I was putting away the laundry I folded and went to put it in Trent's room…"

"Your brother?" King knew he was Mary's brother from the background check Cy ran earlier.

"Yeah, he's my brother. He lives with me."

"Your thirty-two-year-old brother?"

"Yeah?" Mary didn't understand where King was going with his questioning.

"And, you do his laundry?" The thought of Mary doing her thirty-two-year-old brother's laundry pissed him off. It was absurd. He was a man-child, but King kept the comment to himself.

Mary nodded slightly, ignoring the pain in her head, embarrassed at the fact that she did Trent's laundry. But, if she didn't do it, it wouldn't get done, and then things started to stink. So, in a way, doing it before it piled up just made better sense.

King knew he was getting off-track, and he didn't want to agitate Mary any further. "Sorry to interrupt you, Sugar, go on. You were putting away laundry. Then what happened, next?"

Mary settled, delving into her memory. "I walked into the room and I saw a man going through Trent's dresser drawer."

"Did you recognize him?"

"No. At first, I thought he was Trent, but Trent left earlier this morning, which was unusual in itself, but then I realized this was a stranger, and I screamed."

King made a mental note to get a description of this guy from Mary later, but didn't want to interrupt her again. "Then, what happened?" He caressed her thumb below his own.

Mary furrowed her brow, reliving the moment. Her breathing increased and she winced. "I turned to get away, but I wasn't fast enough." She quieted, "He hit me…on the cheek." She brought her free hand to the reddened welt that marred her beautiful face.

King wanted to roar with the anger that bubbled to the surface. All he allowed was a low growl deep from within his chest. His teeth clenched so hard, he thought he would crack a molar. He made a solemn vow to find the son of a bitch, and when he found them, he would unleash the hounds of hell. No holy entity would save them.

King stood, making Mary open her eyes. He grasped her free hand from her cheek and brought it to his lips. "Sugar, I'm so sorry."

"It's okay. It doesn't hurt that much," she lied.

King leveled her with his eyes, eyes that blazed fury, "Don't lie to me, Mare. Ever." His eyes relayed the truth that he wouldn't be lied to. He gentled his stare but kept it direct, poised on her gaze. "No one, and I mean *no one*, is ever allowed to hit you." It went without saying, but King couldn't stand to imagine the scumbag hitting her and couldn't stand the fact that Mary would brush it off as if it was a common day occurrence. He sat back down, not wanting to intimidate her.

"I know." Her words were small.

"Mare, look at me."

She already had his gaze, but she stared at him with intensity.

"Has anyone ever laid a hand on you in the past?"

Mary knew at this point the intensity that was King. She didn't want his wrath. Embarrassment ran through her so she looked away.

"Mare." His deep timbre and fierce tone snapped her attention back to him. "Who." It wasn't a question. It was a command.

She wanted to look away from the fury in his eyes, but the richness and depth of the sapphire sucked her in, unable to break her hold. How could such a Goliath, with such ire within him, have such transfixing eyes? They were wild with rage and turbulence, yet benevolent, tranquil, almost serene all at once. They looked into the depths of her soul and pulled the truth from within her. She had to close her eyes and look away before the answer was pulled from her lips.

The words were silent. Only her lips moved. "My brother."

～

Rage. That was it. Pure, white, blinding, hot rage filled King. He stood so fast, his chair clattered to the floor behind him, sliding a few feet before coming to a rest. *That motherfucker is going to die.*

"Ow!" Mary's shriek snapped King's attention back to her. *What's hurting her?* But then, the *what* became a *who*, when King realized *he* was squeezing her hand. His fingers, interlaced with hers, were white-knuckled. He loosened his grip and let go of her hand.

Arctic threw open the door and was at Mary's side in a flash. "What's wrong?" His eyes, too, burnt with concern.

"Nothing, I'm fine." Mary tried to placate the two hulking men.

"I squeezed her hand too hard," King told the truth.

Arctic saw the fury raging in King's eyes and sent him a question, asking if he needed ten to walk off whatever was seething within him. The guys on the team worked without verbal command on execution, so when King shook his head, Arctic knew he was okay. At least for the moment.

"Where's your brother?" The words burnt from King's lips, as he couldn't tamp down his anger.

"I... I, um, I'm not sure." There was more fear in Mary's response than worry, and she began to tremble. King hated it.

"Mare. I will not hurt you. You understand me?"

"Y-yess."

"Your words say, *Yes*, but your voice says, *No*."

Mary tried to summon her bravado, but her angst won out. "I believe you."

King hated himself. "Sugar, look at me. I. Will not. Hurt you." He motioned with his head to Arctic without losing eye contact with her. "See this man here, my brother? He would gladly remove me from the face of the earth if I *ever* dared to knowingly hurt you and bring you physical harm." Arctic nodded when Mary's eyes shifted to him. "He, and the other men that stand at my side, would never let any harm come to you by my hands. Don't ever be afraid of me. I would rather die a thousand agonizing deaths than to hear you fear me. I will never harm you. That's a promise I vow to you."

Mary seemed to still at King's words. It wasn't that she thought he would hurt her physically, it was the overall anger and venom that surrounded him that scared her to the core. He was like Jekyll and Hyde. The teddy bear that Ember had spoken of was the same teddy bear that sat across from her and laughed at her interview and subtly flirted with her through text messages. But, this King wasn't even a grizzly. He was an inferno of fire and hostility. He was malevolent.

King was scaring her, but his fury was at DEFCON 1. He needed to walk before he did irreversible damage. Taking a well-needed, calming breath, he turned to Arctic and said, "Back in ten." He gestured his open hand to Arctic, and he placed King's cell in his palm. King gave Mary a guarded grin and her arm a light squeeze. Then, he left without saying anything more.

"King?" Mary's words died as the door drew closed.

∾

Mary is afraid of me.

"Damn it!" King brought his hand to his beard and coaxed his fist around it. He repeated the motion as he walked the hallway, no destination in mind. Finding an empty waiting room, he drew his cell from his pocket and had Cypher on the other end in less than a minute.

"'Lo?" Cypher's voice came through the earpiece.

"Cy, King. I need a check on Trent Jones. Mary's brother."

King could hear Cy clicking away at the keyboard he always had in front of him.

"How far to dig?"

"Roto-Rooter."

"Gotcha."

King wanted him dug into so deep, he'd know what his placement was in his third-grade Spelling Bee.

"I need a placement on him and also a trace on anyone he's associated with."

Cy continued to do his voodoo of finding whomever King needed him to find. King didn't ask questions, because Cy always got results. He'd learned tricks of the trade from *the* Tex Keegan, Mr. Dark Web himself. Cy'd never compare himself to the infamous Tex, nobody could ever compare, and a comparison would be an insult, but just having his guidance and reliability allowed Cy to become Hellforce's Mr. Dark Web. With Cy's genius IQ, and Tex's tutelage, the webs Cy spun were incredible. CIA, NSA, DHS would all love to get their hands on him, but Cy wasn't poachable. His loyalties ran deep with his team, and he was the least trusting of all the team when it came to the alphabets, because he knew the tricks of their trades. And that was saying a lot, as King's distrust for them ran leagues deep.

Though King ran contracts with the agencies, he did it only out of the need and necessity for them to procure pro bono work for families in desperate need of his team's services. He did the country's bidding when he was an enlisted man, and he preferred to not do their bidding as a contracted operator. But now, he could at least pick his poisons.

"Rap sheet a mile long. Associates even longer." Cy relayed his findings as he worked. "Will get a trace on him within the hour. Need me to call you back with the locale?"

"I'll get it at HQ."

"Ya got it."

King thought about what he was going to ask next. It was probably a complete betrayal of Mary's trust, but King knew in his gut what he would find. A background check was within the norms of what he would do on ANY employee. It was standard and happened all the time to thousands of people a day, but King needed to know the truth. Needed to get answers to the questions he hoped didn't exist.

"Cy," he paused, I need you to do something else."

King disconnected and forced down his anger. He could put it aside until it was needed. Needed when the trace came through, and Trent Jones would be on the receiving end of his fist, just as his sister had been. And, if his intuition was correct, and Cy came back with what King knew was almost a certain truth, no mercy would be granted.

CHAPTER 10

King reentered Mary's room exactly ten minutes after he left. Arctic side-stepped when King approached her bedside. Gone was King with the rage, and the cool, calm-demeanor King stood next to her and reached for her hand.

"You're back," Mary said it with a sense of relief as if she doubted he would return.

"I am." King soothed her fingers with his.

Mary looked down at their joined hands then back up at his face. She didn't see any anger in his sapphire eyes. The winds had taken away whatever had riled him and ushered in a tranquil regard. Mary loved the depth of his gaze.

"Better?"

"Better."

King ran his free hand over the top of her head and gently grazed the swell of her cheek, careful to not cause her any pain When she didn't wince or pull back from his touch, he gave her his trademark, crooked-half-grin.

"I'm glad you're back." Then her eyes shifted to Arctic, and she added a caveat, "Not that I didn't enjoy your company."

"Understood," was Arctic's reply, while his curt smile pulled at his mouth.

"Will you finish your story? Explain to me what happened after," he swallowed, "after you were attacked?"

Even beneath his beard, Mary saw his Adam's apple swallow

hard. She knew he didn't want to hear about her being hurt any more than she wanted to be on the receiving end of it.

"You're a brave one, Mare." King caressed her hair once more.

Mary began, "After, ya know, the hit," her eyes were downcast and her words were tentative, "um, I must've fallen and hit my head. I don't know how long I was down, but when I woke up, um, the room was torn apart, and I didn't know what happened or where I was."

Mary recounted the story to King and Arctic, while they both held themselves in check. Both were murderous and wanted nothing else than to get their hands on whoever was in her house.

When she finished telling him what took place, she was drained. Between the trauma to her body and the retelling of her story, she was exhausted.

"I can't believe this happened. You know, you always hear about things like this happening to other people, but you never think it'll happen to you. I mean what are the odds?"

King wanted to tell her the odds were great that something would happen to the average person walking down the street. The stats and statistics he could recite to her would have her trembling and locking herself away, if she knew what scum of the earth walked among the general population each day.

"We'll find whoever did this. I promise you that, Mary."

"Do you think I'll be able to find my mother's rings? I mean, I know they are just material possessions, but they were my grandmother's and I can't stand to think they're lost." She shook her head, wincing a bit, and added, "I know they won't be found, but I guess I hoped…" She swiped at a tear that pooled at the corner of her eye, turning as if not to let them know it was there.

"We'll find it, Mare." King pulled her chin up with the knuckle of his finger. "I'll find them for you."

Arctic wanted to chime in, warning King that a promise like that was unlikely, at best, and most likely her grandmother's rings were already pawned, resold, or melted down by now. But he bit his tongue, not wanting to bring any more sadness to Mary.

Mary's eyes were drooping, and King knew she needed to sleep. "Gonna let you catch some Zs, Sugar."

"You're leaving?" Mary almost jackknifed up and cradled her side with a stifled cry.

"Mary!"

"Sugar!"

Both men were at her side in an instant.

"I'm fine, I'm fine," she took a few gasps of air through her nose and held them before releasing them. She tucked her chin to her chest, reeling through the pain.

King had an arm around her back and the other pressed against her side. "I gotcha, Mare." He threw Arctic a side glance, and he dutifully pressed the *call* button on the bedside panel.

"Really, I'm fine," Mary was catching her breath and was leaning back. King removed his arm and slowly lowered her to her pillow. Her bed was reclined and she adjusted herself, King raising her pillow behind her head.

The crackling voice from the nurse's station came through the speaker on the bed rail. King spoke before Mary could and told them she needed assistance for pain. The muffled voice said someone would be right in. Mary complained that she'd be fine. King was doubtful.

A few moments later, Doogie entered the room, and Arctic nudged King when he didn't move from Mary's side. King gave Arctic a low grunt and side-stepped but didn't give the doctor a wide berth. He would be at the ready in case Mary needed him. The doctor looked over his shoulder at King as he crowded him, but said nothing. *Smart man* was all King thought.

Dr. Whitmore asked Mary about the pain she was having, and she said it was from a previous fall. King was on alert when he heard those words. *Previous fall.* He'd seen a lot of women who'd succumbed to "previous falls," and it was never anything he wanted to see.

The doctor lowered the bedrail and told Mary to roll to her left side. She was facing away from King. "Would you like some privacy, Ms. Jones?" Whitmore asked, which was a polite way of asking if she wanted King and Arctic to leave.

"No!" Mary's answer was instant and a bit too eager for either of the guys liking. Arctic and King stayed close. "I mean, um, I don't want them to leave." She hesitated, "Um, can you come where I can see you?"

Neither of the guys knew who she was speaking to, so they both walked around to the other side of the bed. Mary reached her hand through the railing and King grasped it. He laid his other hand over hers and gently rubbed it in reassurance. Arctic stood a few feet beside King further down the bedside but still in her view. Mary gave him a small, but grim, smile. Arctic gave a smile back. Mary blew out a breath.

King had seen some gruesome shit in his time. Things no sane person would ever want to witness. The horrors of traffic houses and cages of women and children being readied to be shipped to their new "owners." He'd seen the effects of abuse and maiming of forced workers in the sex trade, to the monstrous, grotesque disembowelment of human drug mules. The atrocities never ceased. King knew to never think it couldn't get worse because in his line of work, it always did. The savagery of the human race was barbaric. If only the average person knew. King saw the ghastly images replay in the night terrors of his dreams. He would gladly settle for nightmares because in those, he only viewed the grisly scenes. He didn't have to relive each sickening horror, feel the nausea build in his gut and the bile in his throat, or feel the devil rage in his blood and smell the stench of sin and fear. No, nightmares would be a joyful burden. But, King's night terrors kept him reliving the most atrocious of days. If only King could be so lucky to be blessed with nightmares.

So, he braced himself for what may be the source of Mary's pain. He expected to see a bump on her side, maybe a small bruise or two. He knew he was lying to himself because he was not prepared for the sight of Mary when the doctor pushed her gown forward and over her torso. He heard the intake of breath from Arctic beside him, and he steeled himself, mentally reminding himself not to crush Mary's hand in his grasp.

Mary's ribs were covered with a long and widening bruise that ran the short side of her back alongside her torso. It ranged from a yellowish-brown along the edges to a deepened blackish-purple at the center of her rib cage, obviously the site of an impact. It wasn't a fresh bruise, probably a week old by the coloring of it.

The center impact, where the blackened skin met the dissipating purple stain, was most concerning to King. He'd seen that bruise on himself, and some of his team, at the site of cracked ribs. He could empathetically feel the pain Mary was going through. As if the bruising on her torso wasn't enough, he saw what appeared to be fingerprints bruised into the upper part of her bicep just below her armpit which earlier was covered by the sleeve of the gown. And, now that her caramel-colored hair was swept away from her neck and her gown exposed her shoulder, King's blood ran cold. Not just cold, it ran pure ice.

Along her clavicle were faint traces of yellowish bruises that were consistent with an open grasp of a hand. Someone had choked her or pinned her down by her neck. King was livid and he barely contained his rage.

"We'll get you something for this bruising, but as I said, there's not much we can do for cracked ribs."

There it was. Cracked ribs. *Previous fall.* Unless the fall was also on her armpit and collarbone, someone had put their fucking hands on her. He felt himself tremble, and then a hand reached across his shoulder and squeezed. Hard. So hard, that King felt the bite and burn in his traps. Arctic was telling him he saw the horrific state Mary was in and he too was enraged.

King looked down at Mary's face, but her eyes were closed. King wasn't sure if it was a good thing she couldn't look him in the eye because there was no way he was hiding any of the anger that was consuming him.

Dr. Whitmore lowered Mary's gown. "I'll be back with some heat for these ribs. Since it is an older injury, ice won't help, but heat will increase blood circulation and get the bruising to heal. I'll also order some pain meds for your IV. Rest and heal, Mary," he readjusted her blankets. "Doctor's orders." Then he laughed at his own lame joke and left the room.

King didn't laugh at his douche humor. Nothing was humorous at this moment. He wanted to murder somebody, and he was positive that somebody was Trent Jones.

"It's not as bad as it looks." She spoke without opening her eyes.

King didn't respond to her absurd statement. He felt Mary squeeze his hand. That cued him to continue to rub it. He concentrated on the small circles he kneaded into her skin, incessantly massaging concentric circles into her thumb.

His phone sounded with an incoming message and King hoped it was what he was waiting for. He didn't want to let go of Mary's hand but he needed to see what Cy had sent.

He threw Arctic a glance, catching his gaze. Without speaking, Arctic stepped closer behind King, ready to take his place. "I need to check a message." He rubbed her hand and she held onto it with a death grip, not wanting him to leave. Reading her thoughts, he said, "I'm not leaving, Sugar, just need to step aside and read it quick."

Keeping his composure was an act of God because the fuel that was burning in him after seeing the result of the brutal attack on her ivory skin was too much for any human man to restrain on his own. He'd seen atrocities like this overseas on missions. There, he could dispatch the sons of bitches with a one-and-done or a double-tap. Here, he felt helpless. He needed to find her brother. Hell hath no fury when King would meet him eye to eye.

"Promise you won't leave." Her strangled words broke his soul. A plea spoken with fear and uncertainty.

"Promise you, Mare. I won't leave this room."

King leaned forward and brushed a kiss against her forehead, lingering a bit longer than needed telling her she'd be all right. She gave his hand one more squeeze, giving him permission to go, but in doing so, also gave herself the strength to let him leave.

He stepped aside and Arctic immediately took his place. He laced his fingers with Mary's and for a fleeting moment, it piqued his jealousy. But he settled, knowing Arctic was comforting her and it was no more than that.

King stepped to the other side of the room, to the side Mary was facing away from, and pulled his phone from his pocket and entered his security code. Cy had come through. He clicked on the message, opening it and knowing almost instantly he wasn't going to like what he found.

CY: *Figured you'd want this info right away before coming back to HQ. Keep a cool head. Don't do anything rash. Remember, Mary needs a rock, not a hothead who is enraged. Read this alone, far from her, so you can collect yourself before going all out "King" and scaring the shit out of her. Still working on the trace. Cy.*

His finger hovered over the attachment. He debated on opening it. He'd promised Mary he wouldn't leave, but Cy wouldn't heed the warning of opening it in private if it wasn't something he knew would set King on the heels of the Hounds of Hell. He looked over at Mary, her backside to him, and he knew what lay under that gown. Knowing that, and almost positively knowing what was in the report Cy sent was going to set him off, he took the path of the unwise and foolishly opened it.

～

It was a lie. A bold-faced, absurd lie. Simple truth. He lied when he inwardly told himself he could handle whatever he'd find in the report. Complete and utter bullshit.

Anger wasn't even the strongest description of what he was feeling. Wrath? Infuriated? Outrage? Ballistic? None expressed and depicted what he was experiencing. Revenge. Retribution. Murder. Vehement vengeance for the atonement of sins. A better portrayal of his malice. Cy was right. He should have been alone, segregated himself from the sane, so at least he could rant, rave, and rage, and put a few well-deserved holes through a few walls. His fist balled with force.

The attachment of Mary's medical records was novel-thick. Cracked ribs. Fractured arm. Dislocated elbow. Stitches along her hairline and back of her head. Multiple emergency room visits. The list went on. Hematomas. Concussion. Contusions. Shin fractures. Inner ear rupture.

King read that with each visit her brother was present, listed as her accompanying visitor. *What. The fuck?* Why wasn't this a huge fucking red flag? Why wasn't this turned over to police as possible abuse? How had she fallen through the cracks? The answer came when he realized she was seen at multiple ERs and Urgent Care walk-ins. Never recurring visits to the same medical facilities within a short timeframe. No wonder red flags weren't raised.

Still, the fact burnt him. All these injuries were listed within the last eighteen months. The same amount of time Mary's mother wasn't in her home. What the fuck had she received at her brother's hands? King gripped his phone so hard his knuckles whitened. It was possible he'd shatter it at any moment. He must have let out an audible groan, because Arctic cleared his throat, catching his attention.

Scaling it back a bit, he set his concentration on Mary. She didn't deserve his wrath. She needed him to be her rock, her strength. Everything had its time. Trent Jones would certainly have his, King vowed to that. He wrangled his anger. Tamped it down. Capsulized it. He'd crack that lid when its time came. But, for now, Mary needed him.

Back at her bedside, Arctic moved to the side when King took his place. King handed him the phone, gesturing for him to step away and read the report. He walked to the same place King had been and studied the phone.

"King?" It was a whisper.

"Yeah, Sugar?" He used everything within himself to keep his voice at a soothing level.

"Say something."

King closed his eyes and counted the seconds of his inhale then focused just as hard to exhale. He couldn't speak because his jaw was clamped shut, keeping all the things he wanted to wail at bay.

Mary grabbed and squeezed his fist and didn't let up. The pressure was strong. Opening his eyes, he saw their hands clasped together. Instinctively, his eyes roamed up to hers. Tears were gathering on her pillow, cascading from the wells in her eyes. Even her swollen eye was slowly leaking, brimming with unshed tears. King felt his heart shatter. It fell to the ground and splintered into a million fragments.

He hovered over her, cradling her the best he could in their awkward position. Because he was leaning into her, he got an up-close and personal look at the hideous bruises at the base of her throat.

"I'm sorry."

At first, King wasn't sure who whispered the words, he or Mary. The words were on the tip of his tongue, but it was Mary who uttered them first. King pulled back, taking in her tear-stained face.

"What the fuck are you sorry for!" King bit back the words, but it was too late. He vigorously shook his head when Mary pulled back "Sugar, I'm sorry, I didn't mean that to be so harsh," he pulled her close to his chest and spoke into the shallow of her neck. "I may be former Army, but I have a sailor's tongue. What I meant was, 'what are you sorry for?' You have absolutely nothing to apologize for."

"I don't know. I'm just sorry and embarrassed you have to witness the fuck that is my life." Neither said anything until the silence was broken by Arctic.

"I need a name." Four words, spoken with venom and spite.

King turned to his friend.

Arctic stood next to King, in Mary's view, with rage. "Mary. The name. I need a name."

King wanted to tell his friend to take it down a notch, but in this case, the pisstivity level was high.

"Who did this?" King laid his hand lightly on her bruised ribs. "Tell me."

Mary shook her head. "Please, don't."

Her plea hurt his ears, and his heart wanted to surrender, but vengeance didn't reside in one's heart. No, it ate at a man's soul until it's purged with the satisfying hunger of retribution.

King stood to his full height, softly stroking Mary's hand. He wouldn't play games, and he didn't want to scare her, but there was no way he could allow this horrendous deed to go unpunished. This is what he did. This was who he was. It was now his crusade to chasten the unrepentant.

King's single word was tainted. "Trent."

It wasn't a question.

He waited.

So did she.

He heard the second hand of the clock echo in the silence of the room.

He nor Arctic moved a single muscle. They waited.

A lone tear streaked down Mary's bruised cheek. King caught it with his knuckle before it hit the pillow. He lifted the finger and kissed the dab of moisture to his own lips and held Mary's eyes.

She didn't speak, but slowly nodded her head, as rivulets of tears streamed onto her pillow.

King nodded back.

She broke into sobs. Sobs so deep they wracked her body. The heaving must have hurt like hell, excruciating.

If a moment could break a man, this was it. He was caught between comforting his woman and waging retribution for the atonement of sins.

King leaned down and spoke into her ear. "Mare, I know, you know, we aren't simply men."

She nodded.

"We're men who've attained special skills."

She nodded.

"You know what's coming?"

Her nod was slight, but still, King felt her acknowledgment.

"You know this is still in your hands?"

She nodded again.

"I'm of flesh, and I can't let this go."

It wasn't a question, but still, she nodded.

"I'm not asking for your blessing. This isn't on you, but I need to know, you know where I'm going."

Her nod came against his cheek, and he prayed she knew why he had to go.

"If you say stay, I'll stay."

A moment passed between them and Mary whimpered.

"Tell me not to go." His plea was ripped from his soul.

King nuzzled his beard against her neck, caught between the torment of staying or leaving.

When she whimpered again, King kissed her jaw. "Talk to me, Mare."

Her words were soft but loud enough for Arctic to hear, "Before you go, grant me one prayer."

King didn't know if it was possible, but at that moment, holding a broken Mary in his arms, he would grant her anything.

"What's that, Sugar?"

Mary swallowed twice then pursed her lips, holding in a sob. "Don't take his heartbeat."

King knew what she was saying, or asking, and he had to reassure her of one thing. "Mare…"

She nodded with the slightest motion.

"I'm a killer."

Mary stifled a sob.

"I've killed for my country. I've killed for my brothers."

Her tears mingled with his beard.

"I've wiped men from this realm and sent them to their judgment," he paused, "the same judgment I will someday stand before when my name is called."

Mary pushed her head into his face.

"But, I have never killed in cold blood. I've never killed for vengeance. My soul bears many marks, but each one I am accountable for and will stand before my Maker with a clear conscience." King stopped and measured his words, hoping he could make good on his promise and not blacken his soul with an indelible mark he couldn't justify when his day of reckoning drew near. "I swear to you Mare, your brother's time will not be called by my hands or those of my brothers. I swear on all that is Holy, he won't succumb to us." King's heart was beating against his chest and he swore it could be heard in the stillness of the room. He was whispering a lie, and it burnt his soul to know he'd dole out retribution at any cost.

The door opened and a nurse swayed cheerfully over to Mary's bedside. "Gonna get you feeling better in a jiffy." Her all-too-cheerful voice rang in stark contrast to the gravity happening between the three. She seemed oblivious to their somber moment.

"One more request."

"Which would be?"

"Have mercy." She whispered the words into his face, and the words mingled beneath his beard, then dissipated into the air. Solemn words vanished into the universe, hardly heard and barely spoken.

Mercy. The one thing he couldn't promise.

"King."

"I gotta go, Sugar."

At first, King thought she was going to beg him to stay, but as he started to pull away, he felt her nod and whisper, "Okay."

King straightened and scrubbed his hand down his face so no one would see the unmistakable tears streaming from his eyes.

King headed to the door with Arctic right behind him. They made a fast clip out her door and down the long corridor to the elevators. Neither spoke, nor made eye contact with each other the entire way out of the hospital. At his truck, King flashed the locks and they both piled inside, each shutting their door with more force than necessary. King didn't miss Arctic scrub his face, and he also ignored the quick inhale of Arctic's nose. King was never one to say, "Men don't cry," he knew firsthand that men wallowed in their sorrows, trying to purge the demons, hoping their tears would also cleanse the stains on their souls. But, King and Arctic tended to their wounds with unspoken assumptions.

King put the truck in gear and headed to headquarters. The same words resonated through his mind as he drove and still echoed when he pulled into Hellforce. They got out of the truck and King flashed the locks. They headed to the back door, King trailing a few steps behind his friend. Arctic punched in his fifteen-digit security code, and the triple locks disengaged. He entered the first security premises before the finger and palm reader, and the retinal scanner at the next checkpoint. He held the door for King. With the door ajar, King removed his sunglasses and peered into the unblemished blue sky, looking for an answer or blessing of some sort. He kept his gaze skyward, hoping for a last-minute reprieve. It didn't come. He lowered his head and made his way into the darkened hallway of Hellforce. The same darkness that would soon mark his soul. An indelible mark that couldn't be erased.

Mercy. How could she ask him for the one thing he wouldn't give?

CHAPTER 11

It'd been four days since Mary was released from the hospital. Six days since King was on a warpath trying to locate her brother. Trent was gone in the wind and each day that passed made King angrier and more unbearable than the last.

"How in the fuck can we not find him!" King's bellow reverberated off the walls and every man, and woman, in the room felt his wrath. He threw the file folder down on the table and leaned against his fisted knuckles. The rolled, three-quarter length sleeves of his starched shirt showed the strain of his muscles on his tatted forearms as he leaned forward into the table. "We've had better luck finding a third-world, goat herding ISIS fighter holed up in a fucking Afghani mountainside living in a motherfuckin' rock cave with no electronic or digital footprint than we have finding a piece of shit, fuckwad who is skating right under our nose."

The guys didn't reply because what was the use? King was on a tirade and nothing they said would make a lick of difference.

"I want fucking answers!"

King loosened the tie around his neck, pulling the silk fabric through the knot and out of his collar and off his rounded shoulders. His neck was the size of a tree stump, so there was a lot of tie to be shed. He was high-strung because the only days King was found in a starched white shirt, cufflinks, and tie were on the days he met with high-profile clients or men with more brass on their shoulders than could be found in Hellforce's armory. Today was one of those special days everyone in the office was treated to King's irritability. And now, with the matter of Mary's brother gone in the wind, King's rants seemed more like tantrums, though no one dared to call him out. Better to listen to him piss and moan than to let the bear out of the cage and send the wrath of God upon everyone in his path.

"King, the guy's dead on the digital front. I've scanned for every digital footprint, every electronic device he has, as well as the shit-bags he hangs out with, and there is nothing. Not a blip on the radar." Cy stretched his arms over his head, pushing his interlaced hands behind him, and waited for the satisfying crack of each verte-bra. He'd been hovering over his computer for the last few hours, essentially searching for a ghost. Trent Jones was off-grid.

"Unless he's dead in a ravine or joined some outcast cult, I want him found!" King rubbed his left forearm and then ran the length of his face with both hands. His appearance was haggard. He looked like he just returned from a month's long mission surviving on MREs and little-to-no sleep. The only reason he showered today was the high official meeting he had at 0700. Out of all the team, King could wait out the enemy as long as it would take. The man had the patience of a praying mantis and the ferociousness of its appetite, as well. So, he'd wait out Trent Jones as long as it took.

Slate was the next to speak, and King wasn't taking kindly to any information that wasn't related to Mary's brother. "Got feelers out at all the known drug traffics and also got probes into all the local pawn shops in the tri-state area. Anything resembling the jewelry that was in the safe, we'll be first to know before it's transferred through the shop." Slate rubbed the back of his neck, "King, man...you may have to accept the fact that this guy is going to wait us out. Whether he knows you're waiting for him or not, the world is still circling here at Hellforce."

"You think I don't know that?" King bit the words out. "I know my own fucking business, thank you. Who the fuck do you think I was meeting with at the ass-crack of dawn? Wasn't your fucking mother!"

Slate stood to his height of six-foot, only a few inches shorter than King's six-two. "Bring it down, King." Slate's tone was ice.

King turned to Slate, the six-foot conference table separating them, and narrowed on him. "Excuse me?"

Slate wasn't backing down, "You heard me. You need to bring it down to a sane level, so we aren't all caught in the path of the tantrum you're throwing."

The room went silent. Shit was about to become real.

King was on the move. The scary thing about him was the fact that everything was methodical. The way he moved. The way he carried himself. His disposition. Thought out. Calculated. Nothing erratic or unsettled. So, when he rounded the table, calm, cool and collected, long, smooth strides, it heightened the danger level to a magnitude of the highest scale, and everyone braced for the impact of what was about to become a shitstorm of the century.

King stood a chest's width apart from Slate when he came to a stop and stood toe-to-toe with him. Slate was well-built, but mostly toned muscle and nowhere near King's bulk of a well-built brick shit house. King was impressive in mass and it made a statement of its own.

King's stare was a close match to Slate's steel-blue that gave him his moniker. Though King's were piercing, and Slate's burrowed in-depth, both men locked in on each other. Like two rams ready for battle, both not backing down, waiting for the other to blink.

The tension built. King was not a man to be fucked with, and Slate wasn't a man to mince words. So, the room was volatile between the two.

Surprisingly, and uncharacteristically, King spoke first. "You got issues, Slate?"

"Not the one with the issues, King."

The tone was cold between the two, neither breaking their stare.

"I know you're hooked on finding this piece of shit, but it's become an obsession. For a week now, you've done nothing but probe and press us all for information that simply isn't there." Slate broke the stare and picked up the file folder from the conference table. "We've got other matters at hand and you're throwing them to the wayside. You've become a team of one, and you're using resources and time that needs to be spread in other areas."

King looked like he was about to stroke out. The vein that ran alongside his temple was throbbing and his blood pressure had to be off the charts. The tips of his ears were reddened and that was a sign they'd seen on missions that said King was going to blow. Cy slowly pushed his chair back from the table and closed his laptop. He rose quietly, not wanting to draw the attention of the two pressure cookers to the left of him. The guys had never come to blows, but then again, rarely did anyone ever step to King. Luckily, Cy moved to stand next to T-BAR and Trip.

"Look at this family, King," Slate held up the folder and then opened it, revealing a picture of a pretty fourteen-year-old girl with big, brown doe eyes and a beautiful smile, and then another of her standing with her parents holding an award of some sort. "She's gone. Taken from the streets of her own home close to the Texas border. We all know how those cases end." He picked up another file that was already open. "See this boy." Slate held up the opened folder. "Gone." He pointed to three more files. "Each family has come to you in desperation, in the hopes that you'll return their loved one, or at least give them the closure they so desperately seek, and answers as to what hell the missing may be experiencing. College student, foreign aid worker, mother of four," Slate shoved the files across the table, scattering their contents, a few of the papers floating to the floor. "You don't give a shit, King. Each file *you* hand-picked and made a promise to each one of those families that you would give a fuck. But, I don't know, King," he rubbed the back of his neck, "I know Mary's the number one priority, but when the trail's dead, it's dead. You know the key to sit and wait better than any of us. Time away is time gained, not wasted. You taught us that." He bounced his index finger off King's steel chest. "I know Mary is important, God, we'd each gladly put our lives on the line for her, you know that, but King, look at all those other faces," he pointed to the files now scattered across the table, "and tell me those families aren't begging for answers of their loved ones, just as bad, if not more, than you're asking for answers for Mary."

King's eyes never lost Slate's throughout the lashing, but he turned his head and took in the files scattered across the table. His eyes rose to the men standing across from him—T-BAR, Trip, Arctic, and Cy—and saw their agreement, though no one spoke or moved from their places.

King looked back to the folders, at the picture of the fourteen-year-old girl that had come loose from her file. Slowly and methodically, he reached across the table and gathered the open files. Trip and T-BAR gathered the papers at their feet and set them on the edge of the table. King finished stacking the folders and collected the single sheets.

"King," Slate called out to his team leader, but King didn't turn or acknowledge the call.

He walked past the others. All eyes were on him as he left through the door, then all eyes volleyed to Slate. He didn't say anything the others weren't thinking, but he felt like an ass for dressing down his friend. He didn't regret what he said; all of it was true, but now, he second-guessed the delivery of the message. It would have been more professional and in keeping with practices for Slate to talk to him privately in his office. But, just like the rest of the team, Slate was fed up with King's obsession and daily grindings, tirades, and outbursts, and yes, tantrums, pushing the guys for things none of them could produce.

King's obsession had gone beyond the normal measure. Each one of the guys had obsessed over cases before. But they all knew that with obsession, in most cases they found irrelevant things that became the focal point, but in reality, they threw the team off-guard, pulled their attention away from the important aspects, and had them wasting time, all in desperation to break the case. Time that could be allocated to actual aspects of other cases. That's what King was doing. Everyone knew it, and by brow-beating the team, it was breaking them. Cy would find Trent's trail the minute he had any electronic presence. Eventually, everyone either slipped up or thought they were off the radar and made some type of electronic footprint. It was inevitable in today's age. Cy was ready the minute something surfaced. King had lost the one thing that had forged his presence among the teams. The thing that made his success rate stellar among the Special Forces community. His ability to wait and let his prey come to him.

King rounded the table and gathered the last of the files then left in silence, heading to his office. All eyes went from King and fell on Slate. It was short-lived, because they all volleyed to the doorway, onto Mary who entered, taking only a few steps into the conference room. How long had she been standing outside the door? How much of the conversation did she hear? Ember stood behind her, and Mary asked the question no one wanted to answer.

"Is he really blowing everything off to find my brother?"

"Fuck." Slate ran his hand over his neatly trimmed beard.

T answered her open question. "He's just a bit overzealous."

Mary turned to T-BAR who was now in the hot seat. "Overzealous? Is that a new way of saying obsessed?"

She had definitely heard the conversation.

"Sometimes it gets that way." T adjusted his stance and shifted his weight. "We've all been there." He gestured to the rest of the room and a throng of heads nodded in agreement.

"I need to talk to him." Mary started to leave when Arctic reached out and held her bicep. Mary flinched and Arctic dropped his hand. It was a stark reminder of what she'd been through, and it gave reality to the fact that her brother was a piece of shit and needed to be found.

"Not a good idea, Mary." Arctic shook his head.

"But, I gotta tell him to stop. He's putting things aside that need to be his priority. If he doesn't—"

"He needs time. King's the type that needs to process and doesn't need to be placated. He'll emerge from his hibernation when he's ready to join the living." Arctic let out a huff in the realm of a chuckle. "I think he should be left alone."

Mary didn't agree with Arctic's suggestion, but his team knew him better than she did.

Today was Mary's "official" second start date. She wanted to come to work at the beginning of the week, but King insisted she take time off and rest. She hadn't returned home. One, her house was trashed and two, she didn't want to stay there in case her brother or his friends returned. After leaving the hospital, King called Ember to stand guard at her bedside. Mary and Ember bonded over the two-day stay at the hospital, and now Mary was staying at Ember's house since a new friendship had blossomed between the two. With Ember being a former Army Ranger with sniper abilities, and owning a gun range, her armory at home rivaled Hellforce's, so King was appeased at the thought of Mary being safely protected, though he was pissed he wasn't the one by her side.

He wanted to be the one protecting her, but Mary put the kibosh on that immediately. There was something that ran deeper than a natural attraction between the two, but Mary wasn't as forward as King when it came to them being together. King had laid claim to her. Whether Mary was aware of the fact didn't change things, but King made sure everyone around him knew where he stood. Mary was *his*.

"Have you seen the range yet?" Ember's question came out of the blue.

Mary seemed uncomfortable and fidgeted a bit, biting the corner of her bottom lip and letting it roll beneath her teeth. "Um, no... I haven't seen it." The conference room was too crowded for her.

"It's badass!" Trip joined the conversation, "State of the art... all the newest bells and whistles King could cram into it. You can use it anytime. Sharpen your skills around the clock."

Mary didn't reply.

"Come on, I'll take you down there." Ember motioned to the hallway outside the door.

"I don't shoot."

It was a statement that seemed odd in the confines of a security company. Especially when handling arms was second nature to all those in the room.

"Ever?" Cy's words broke the awkwardness.

Mary looked embarrassed and suddenly found the floor very interesting. "My dad, he hunted, and I went a few times. He showed me how to work a hunting rifle, but I've never shot. I mean, I think I'd know how to, but, um...I just never—"

Her sentence trailed off as if she didn't know what else to say. It felt like an apology for not knowing the skills the others honed as an extension of themselves.

"Working here, you'll be sharpshooting in no time." Trip lightened the mood with his charisma that never ceased. "Any one of us would be happy to teach you and spend time with you on the range," he gestured to the team. "Hell, any excuse to spend a few hundred rounds is time well-spent." A quiet barrage of agreements and volunteering to help her came from the guys.

"The outdoor range is killer, too, if you want to hone rifle skills instead of pistols," Ember chimed in. "And, you're always welcome at my range if you don't want to hang with these yahoos." She gave a snide grin to the guys.

"Girls and guns..." Mary relaxed and chortled, "it'll be like a fun girl-date."

"Done!" Ember closed the conversation. "Come on, I'll show you around."

The two left and it put the team into action. Cy went back to his seat in front of the computer and the others went to their respective offices.

Cy shut the conference door and picked up the phone on the desk, dialing a number from memory. He waited for the line to pick up. It did in less than two rings.

"Cy."

"Tex."

"What can I do for you?" His Texas drawl was all his own.

"Need a trace. Name's Trent Evan Jones. Age thirty-two, DOB..." Cy rattled off Trent's information and he could hear Tex hammering away on his keyboard.

"He's underground and hasn't surfaced." Cypher laid out the details of Mary's brother, and he could sense a change in Tex's voice.

The usually laid-back Tex hardened his tone. "I'll find him. No hole deep enough to hide him."

"Appreciate it, Tex. I'll let King know you're on it."

"Done."

Tex disconnected before Cy could thank him, though a thank you was always sworn off by the cyber genius that a lot of the ops community relied on.

Cy would head to King's office later in hopes he'd simmer down by then.

The day was just beginning, and most of the team was already spent. It was going to be a long day.

CHAPTER 12

Mary spent an hour with Ember and felt like a badass with all the different pistols she allowed her to fire, although a skirt, blouse, and four-inch heels weren't the ideal gun range attire. It came as a surprise when she found shooting to actually be fun, and she wasn't as scared as she thought she'd be. Ember was a great teacher and answered the million and one questions Mary threw at her. Ember showed her how to handle things safely, and Mary caught on quickly. He'd been gone seven years now, but her father had a pistol he'd kept in the safe. Although, now whoever had the safe also had the gun. To tell the truth, Mary wasn't sure what all was in the safe. She'd only been in it twice, once to put her father's ring in it after he passed, and then again to put her mother's wedding ring in it before she moved into the senior living home.

Ember had left to go to her own range, and Mary was on the fence about going to King's office. It was her first day on the job, and she didn't know what to do. She thought about stopping in Arctic's office. Besides her brief encounter with the guys, he was the only other person she knew, so he'd be her best bet. She headed towards his office but then thought better of it.

She faced King's closed door. *Just knock. He knows it's your first day. He knows you're here. He's expecting you.* Mary was giving herself a much-needed pep talk. Why was she so nervous? *It's just King.* That statement alone told her why. It was King. Her stomach fluttered and tingles radiated in her core. She felt like a schoolgirl with a playground crush. *King.* She shrugged her shoulders, and held them there, as the smile crossed her face. *King.*

She pressed her thighs together, suppressing the ache she definitely needed to relieve. He'd spent the last few evenings with her at Ember's, and she couldn't get him off her mind. The nights after he left were torture. She wasn't sure how she was going to relieve the ache. It'd been building for days, and she didn't know how long she could hold it. She wasn't able to deal with it as she normally would, seeing she was staying with Ember, but maybe she could find relief during a nighttime shower? Somehow, relief was on the horizon.

She ran her hands along the length of her pencil skirt, a dual purpose to flatten out any wrinkles and also to wipe the moisture from her palms. She straightened her blouse, making sure the buttons were fastened and nothing indecent was popping out, and tucked a loose strand from her messy bun behind her ear. She tapped her pencil's eraser on her notepad. *Just knock.* She shoved the pencil into her bun. *Safekeeping.*

She was always losing her pens and pencils while at the diner, so it'd become a habit to keep them in her trussed-up locks. She clutched the notepad to her chest. *All right, you're pulled together.* Tentatively, she knocked on the solid door, pushed her black-rimmed glasses up, and waited.

King's muffled baritone voice called from behind the door, "Come in."

King was growling to himself as he looked over the files from the conference table. It was useless because none of them had his full attention. He couldn't concentrate. He shut the top folder and pushed back from his desk. *Am I really this disconnected?* Some of the information was new to him, and it pained him that he wasn't on top of the newest intel, like the rest of his team. He knew he was giving Mary's case a *little* more attention but didn't realize he was pushing so many things aside. He pulled his elbows behind his back, stretching his ribs and torso, feeling every prior injury and feeling older than his age. He wasn't old in the least, but at thirty-eight, he had punished and damaged his body more than the average person. The grunt that emerged as he lifted himself from his chair had him feeling double his age. *Grandpa noises.* That's what his team called them. He was their senior, except for T-BAR who was closest to his age, who also made the same "Grandpa noises" as him.

He walked to the wall of windows and looked across the small courtyard between the building and the security perimeter. He had to pull his shit together. But, the ire that churned in his gut at the thought of Trent Jones out there somewhere made him grit his teeth.

He didn't appreciate being dressed-down by Slate, but Slate was right in the aspect of needing to wait. King knew the best thing to do when a trail ran cold was to wait out your opponent. Eventually, and inevitably, either the enemy became too arrogant, too bold, or too stupid *not* to be found. He had to get it together. Trent Jones' time would come, and when it did, King would be ready. It was a waiting game, and though he hated to wait, he would come out the victor.

Back at his desk, he flipped open the top file. It was the missing fourteen-year-old girl from a small town that bordered the outskirts of Laredo. Unlike Slate had thought, King knew the desperation a family felt when one of their own went missing. It was the drive that drove him to open Hellforce. He wondered for the millionth time if he would be an uncle, or how many nieces or nephews he would have had. The thought, as usual, brought the familiar ache to his heart, and he felt the pinpricks behind his eyes.

Most people thought of women and young girls when they heard of sex trafficking. All too often the boys taken and forced into the trade were forgotten or completely unthought of. King rubbed the ridge of his brow, pinching the bridge of his nose waiting for the ache to pass. It never did, but he welcomed the day it would lessen. Thirty-one years later, and still it was there, strong as day one. He still missed his brother.

A knock came at the door and he wanted to send away whoever it was. He wasn't up for another round with Slate, and he didn't need any of the others coming to discuss his shortcomings.

"Fucking hell." He muttered the words under his breath. Grousing, he called, "Come in."

He was gearing up for a fight. He expected another round. But, what he didn't expect was to see Mary come through the door. God Almighty in heaven, she was a sight!

He stood when she entered.

"Mary!" It was a stupid way to greet her, but he was at a loss for words. All the blood from one head rushed to the other. He stopped himself from adjusting his slacks. Good thing they were black and hid the outline of his hardening erection. "I thought maybe you left."

"Not on my first day." She corrected herself with a laugh. "Well, actually, my second-first day, if we're getting technical."

King didn't return the sentiment, bringing to mind why she didn't make it into the office on her original first day.

She composed herself and followed up, "I hope I'm not interrupting?"

"No, no, have a seat."

King rounded his desk and gestured to the leather chair, pulling it back slightly so she could sit.

Mary looked around at his disheveled office. If possible, it was worse than when she was there a little more than a week ago for her interview. More papers and files were stacked on the over-stacked piles. She really needed to get him organized.

"Sorry about the mess. I need to get things in order." It went without saying as he looked around his office. It had never bothered him before, but suddenly he felt embarrassed. Rarely did King get embarrassed, so the feeling was off-putting.

"Guess that's why you hired me." Mary sat and crossed one silky-smooth leg over the other. King swallowed hard. She wasn't wearing nylons, but her legs were silky and shiny. *Fuck.* Luckily, he was standing behind her. He had to get seated behind his desk before she got a look at his crotch, which was now eye-level since she was sitting.

"Okay, where to start?" She leaned back and set her notepad on her lap then pulled the pencil from her hair, and King had the dirtiest thoughts run through his mind. *Get a hold of yourself.* She had the whole secretary/dirty librarian vibe going and he doubted she knew it. King wanted to swipe his desk clean in one fell swoop, and either toss her on top of it or bend her over it. It was every man's fantasy to—

"…and, then I was thinking we could get a few more cabinets to match the decor, and I could get them filled, so you'd be able to use that space over there." She motioned with the pencil at the small sitting area on the far side of the office behind her. The area, of course, was also littered with files and overflowing paper.

King was lost to the conversation. *She's here to help, not to fuck.* He chastised his conscience and tried to carry on with the discussion, but when she put the tip of the eraser to her lips and sank her teeth into the pink, fleshy tip, he was a goner!

His thoughts turned to last night. Even though Mary wasn't
staying with him, it didn't stop him from spending the evenings
with her at Ember's. Although, with Ember fluttering around the
house, he felt like a teenager trying to get to first base while on his
mother's sofa. Trying to woo Mary wasn't easy. He hadn't gotten
anywhere near first base. And, the chaste goodbye kiss left much to
his desire.

When he got home, he spent thirty minutes in the coldest
shower trying to tamp down the lustful and sinful thoughts of all the
things he'd like to do to her. Even after thirty minutes of the cold
beating down on him, and a hard-on to rival all hard-ons, a quick
handjob did the trick. That was until he climbed into bed and his
mind filled with more indecent and tantalizing thoughts of her. He
may be reaching forty, but his dick hardened within minutes, and
his hand went back to work. He fell asleep sated, and his normal
fitful sleep and night terror dreams subsided, turning to Mary
instead. He wasn't surprised when he woke to a prepubescent wet-
dream.

"King?" Mary was waiting patiently with her pencil in hand,
resting on her notepad.

King cleared his throat and turned back into Mary's question.
"Yeah." It was a dumb way to enter back into reality, but it was the
best he could do when he had no idea what she'd said.

"I was wondering about my own security code to enter into the
building? Today, I had Ember with me, but tomorrow, I'm on my
own."

There was no way she was going to be on her own tomorrow.
No way in hell was she driving herself. "I'll be picking you up
tomorrow morning and driving you back to Ember's this evening
until further notice."

Whoa! This was news to her.

King picked up his phone before Mary could interject, and had
Cy on the line. He explained Mary would need building clearance
along with security clearance. He hung up in less than a minute.

"Cypher will get you set up. He'll also get you familiarized with
the computer setup and the network. He's the brains of the business.
I just work here." He set off the statement with a grin.

Mary knew he was downplaying and shortchanging himself. No
way could he have built this company and not had the brains to get
it running and keep it going. But, that wasn't her concern at the
moment.

"Wait, wait, wait. What do you mean you'll be picking me up and driving me home?"

King looked at her like it was a no-brainer and tilted his head in a questioning manner. When she didn't respond, he laid it out. "You need to have twenty-four-seven protection. Whether that's me, one of the guys, or Ember, you won't be driving by yourself or going out in public on your own."

It unnerved her that he was telling her instead of asking her. "King, I'm perfectly safe making the twenty-minute drive across town and the country roads to get here."

King raised an eyebrow and she felt herself dampen. She crossed her legs a little tighter, squeezing her thighs, hoping it wasn't obvious and her arousal wasn't noticeable. God, he was sexy. Just that one twitch of a brow muscle had her randy.

He softened his tone, "Sugar, anytime you're without one of us you're vulnerable."

She thought about her twenty-year-old VW Beetle, the G-ride she lovingly named Sophie, and she knew how unreliable it was. What if she broke down? She'd been taking a ride-share to save money because Sophie was on her deathbed. And, she didn't even want to bring that up. If he knew, there was no way King would allow her to take a ride from an unknown person, someone he'd conjure up to be a lone assailant or an ax murderer.

She acquiesced. There was no sense fighting it. She needed a ride, and he was willing to provide her with one. Case closed.

King clasped his hands. "Okay, that's settled. Now, why don't we—"

There was a knock on the open door and Cypher walked in holding a few gadgets.

"Hey, boss. I'm ready to scan her."

Mary didn't know what he meant but King clued her in

"You'll need a fingerprint and retinal scan to enter the building along with a security code."

Mary saw Ember enter that morning so she had an idea what it involved.

Cy set down the small electronics on King's desk, then held out what she thought was a cell phone. The screen was blue and she looked from it to Cypher.

"We'll need to get your fingerprints. It's a digital scanner. If I could have your hand?"

Cy squatted beside her chair, then tore open a packet that held an alcohol wipe. He turned her hand and thoroughly wiped each finger. When he blew across her fingertips, she thought she heard a low growl come from King. She looked over at him and he was eyeing the process but said nothing.

Next, Cy pressed each of her fingers to the pad and keyed in information. Mary had never been fingerprinted before, and even knowing it was for the job, it was still unsettling.

"You'll need these for DOD security clearance as well." When Cy was done with one hand, he did the same with the other. This time he neglected to blow on her fingertips to dry the alcohol. Cy picked up a small tablet and pressed her hand for a palm scan.

She started to realize that Hellforce didn't take security lightly, which was blatantly obvious with their line of work. She inwardly chuckled thinking Fort Knox probably wasn't guarded as tight as Hellforce.

When she thought she was done, Cy picked up the rectangular box and had her hold it to her eyes. He answered her question before she asked. "It's a retinal scanner. Stare straight ahead and focus on the dot. Try not to move your eyes or look around."

It was easy to keep her eyes looking straight ahead until she was told not to move them. She had to fight the urge. Essentially, it was like looking into a set of binoculars.

When that was done, Cy produced an empty vial from his pocket, donned a pair of medical gloves, broke the seal on the top, and handed her the two cotton swabs on wooden sticks. She looked from the stick to him, not knowing what he was requesting.

"DNA. Hold the swabs in your cheeks and rub them against the walls. It'll only take a few seconds."

Mary did as he said. She felt stupid, but if this is what they needed for employment, she'd do it. Cy studied his watch as she rubbed her inner cheeks. A few seconds turned out to be ten, which in actuality, was a long time to collect whatever they were collecting. She pulled the slobbered sticks from her mouth and slipped them into the vial he held out to her.

"That was fun." Mary let the sarcastic comment slip. Cy and King both laughed.

Cy quipped, "When we say this job is blood, sweat, and tears, it's not far from the truth."

After sealing the vial and removing his gloves, he voiced her a sequence of numbers. When she started to write them on her notepad, Cy stopped her.

"This is your security code. You have to memorize it. It can't be written anywhere."

Mary looked at him and laughed until she realized he wasn't joking.

"That's fifteen digits," she stared at him wide-eyed. "That's a long code. How am I going to remember it?" Mary drew a blank. She had a hard enough time remembering her social security number, let alone fifteen digits.

"Not everyone has an eidetic memory like you, Cy." King had that eyebrow cocked again, and it was doing naughty things to her insides. *Focus!*

"Don't think of it as individual numbers. Break it down into a sequence of smaller numbers. Group it into thousands."

With his trick, it was easier to memorize the batches of numbers, but it was still a pain in the ass. She repeated the code over and over until Cy was comfortable that she had it down.

"So, if I enter the code wrong, is a laser going to blast me into vapor, or a pit of lava mysteriously pool at my feet and disintegrate me?" She laughed at the thought, "Or, maybe a large pit of man-eating piranhas will open where I stand, and I'll plunge to an agonizing death?"

King laughed. "Ooh, a pit of piranhas? I like that. Cy, look into the logistics and put it on my to-do list."

Cy turned as he was leaving. "Not your secretary anymore, King." He pointed at Mary, "Glad you have her. She can put it on your to-do and keep you in line."

Mary smiled. She didn't think anyone kept King in line.

King gave Cy the finger, and he returned the gesture.

"Laters!" Mary waved to him, and he held up a hand as he walked out.

"Okay, now to get you organized." Mary bit into the tip of the eraser.

For King, it was going to be a hard day to focus.

CHAPTER 13

King spent the day with Mary, showing her around the building and grounds. The offices, break room, gourmet kitchen, and lounge. Mary was surprised to see the lounge where the guys could kick back and relax. Besides the over-the-top, too large television that took up one whole wall, there were comfy recliners and multiple gaming consoles, but the part she loved the best was the wall lined with the retro arcade games, a dartboard, and a few pinball machines. They were a stellar touch. She liked the tables next to the windows with half-finished puzzles laid out, and she also liked the cabinet filled with board games and books. It was a relaxation paradise.

After beating King in back-to-back games of Pac-Man, which she was almost certain he'd let her win, she was ready to see the rest of the building. They toured the upper supply floor, the ready rooms, weight and locker room, the armory. At the end of the day, they ended up at the range. King was surprised she had never shot until today and gave her a personal lesson of her own.

When he leaned into her, showing her the right way to sight a target, or when he wrapped himself around her, engulfing her into his torso to help her grasp the firearm, she could smell the day's worn scent of his cologne, and it drove her crazy. Maybe it wasn't even cologne? Maybe the scent was all King? When the strands of his whiskers tickled her neck, and the low timbre of his voice wafted over her ear, it took all her strength to concentrate on the technique he was teaching. She didn't know if he was purposely torturing her, or if it was just his way of teaching, but good Lord, she would take his lessons in multitudes.

At the day's end, the drive home was quiet. The silence was comforting just having King at her side. She thought he was going to drive her to Ember's, but when he made a detour to a small hole-in-the-wall mom and pop diner, she was thrilled. The day wasn't over yet.

They ate and made small talk over bread and pasta, two things she thought would never cross his lips considering there wasn't an ounce of fat on him.

"Tell me a little bit about yourself." King leaned into his folded hands and rested his chin on his knuckles.

Mary didn't like to talk about herself. Her life was anything but normal. She'd rather King told her about himself, but he was closed off, and she assumed he liked his privacy.

"Not much to talk about, really. You know mostly everything about me from my interview."

King knew more than she thought he knew.

As if reading his thoughts, she added, "And, I'm sure you ran a thorough background check on me, and know how many speeding tickets I've had, and who my middle-school homeroom teacher was." She sipped the sweet tea from her straw and peered at him from beneath her lashes.

King controlled the twitch in his pants when she pursed her lips around her straw and did all he could not to grab her and seal his lips to hers.

"I didn't run a background check." He leveled her with a half-grin.

Mary was about to call him a liar when she figured he was tactfully evading the truth, and structuring the answer as not to perjure himself.

"Cy?"

King lifted his brows and pulled a frown that brought his chin to his pursed lips. "Never tell."

Mary liked the cute banter between them. She didn't understand how she could be falling for him so fast and hard, when less than two weeks ago, she didn't even know him. But, it was unmistakable how bad she had it. She just wasn't sure if he felt the same. Maybe she was reading the situation wrong. He was her boss. Fraternizing was grounds for termination. She knew this because she scoured the employee handbook she received after her interview. Relations within the company would get her fired, so wanting to sleep with the boss was, most likely, frowned upon.

"Your mother's in assisted living?" The statement came out of the blue, and it set Mary back in her seat.

King corrected himself before she could say anything, "Sorry. I'm so sorry, Sugar. I didn't mean to be so brazen. I just, I saw it on the background check I didn't run and was curious how she was doing?"

Mary sat a little straighter. She didn't want to talk about her mother. But, on the flip-side, she had no one to confide in. Did she want to burden him with the fuck that was her life? It'd been ages since she was able to unload her thoughts and feelings. She had no close friends, and her mother was her lone sounding board. She took another sip of her tea and mustered all the courage she could.

"She's been in the senior home for eighteen months now. I miss her dearly." She was talking to the tabletop and ran her fingernail over the red-and-white-checkered tablecloth. "She'd always been my biggest cheerleader and my best friend." She smiled at the memory, "We never went through the whole *teenager versus parent* fiasco. I figured my parents had their hands full with Trent, and I just never had the urge to be defiant."

King figured Mary as a rule follower. He couldn't picture her as a hellion or troublemaker.

"Shortly after my father passed, when she first started showing signs of dementia, it was small things, like forgetting her keys or phone or misplacing her purse, which is common even for cognitive people, but over time, I could see she declined quickly." Mary sucked in a breath and continued. "Things got progressively worse, and she started to become a danger to herself. Leaving the bathwater running and flooding the bathroom. Forgetting she had supper on the stove, or in the oven, not realizing until the smoke detectors blared throughout the house. It was at that point I knew she couldn't live on her own, so I moved in with her."

"Didn't your brother still live at home?"

Mary cocked her head, "Non-background check info?"

King stared back at her with a mischievous grin but said nothing.

Mary let out a huff. "Yes, he did, but...it's Trent, so..."

"Say no more."

"Exactly." Mary felt her face redden. She had no reason to feel embarrassed about her brother. She wasn't his keeper in the sense of the word, though she did support him with room and board, not to mention the money she knew he was stealing from her purse, his deadbeat ass wasn't a reflection on her.

She continued, "Things worsened for Mom. She forgot appointments, birthdays and holidays, and even simple tasks like feeding the cat. I tried to brush it off as just absent-mindedness." Her tone sobered, "I walked in on her staring absently at the washer, trying to figure out if she put the clothes in, or if she was supposed to take them out. My concern heightened, wondering if the progression of forgetfulness was caused by stress or anxiety, or some outside force that could be rectified, but the neurological tests confirmed my worst nightmare." Her voice broke, "Mom was declining and had the beginning stages of dementia. That was a little over eighteen months ago and watching her decline is heartbreaking. I mean, she's my best friend and confidant, and she's slipping away."

Mary hated the thought that her mother's memory was almost non-existent. Like a breeze carrying dandelion's seeds, her mother was wisping away in the breeze, carrying all her memories and scattering them.

"The day I knew I had to make the agonizing decision to put her in the home was the day I walked into the house and my mother shrieked in horror, screaming at me to leave her house, to get out, screaming in terror wanting to know who I was, and why I was in her home." She quickly swiped at the wells of her eyes. "My mother didn't recognize her own daughter, and it tore my heart from my chest." The last words were a whisper.

King moved to her side of the booth and cradled her in his arms. She went willingly and burrowed herself into the depths of his chest. They sat in silence. No one needing to say a thing. There was nothing to say. He would be her rock. He caressed her hair and gave her the respite she needed. He wasn't sure how long they sat, but he would've stayed all night if she needed him to. It wasn't the intimacy he was craving, but he felt closer to her than any of the previous evenings they'd spent together on Ember's couch.

She sat up, swiping at her tears, and began to apologize. "I'm sorry, I'm a wreck." King handed her his cloth napkin. "Just the way you wanted to end your evening, right?" She wiped her eyes then pulled a compact from her purse. She opened it to check that she didn't look like Alice Cooper, with her mascara running from her eyes when King reached over and clasped it shut.

"Hey, I need to check my face." Mary scolded him in a half-joking manner.

"You're beautiful and don't need to check anything."

Mary scoffed, imagining her Uncle Fester eyes caked in dark circles. She tried to get him to scoot out of the booth, but he wouldn't budge. "King, I need to freshen up. Will you move?"

He sat solid, not moving a fraction.

"King!"

"Do you need to hit the head?"

Mary scrunched her face, "Excuse me?"

"Do you have to do a..." he held up first one finger and then a second.

Mary got the gist. "Ewww, no," she felt herself flush, "I need to check my face." She knew she was reddening by the heat rising up her neck.

"I already told you, you're absolutely beautiful. There's nothing but perfection."

Mary glowered at him.

King laughed. "Take the compliment, Sugar."

Hearing his endearment set the butterflies fluttering in her stomach. Forgotten was the fact that her makeup was most likely melting off her face. All her brain was focused on was the way the man beside her could make her heart flip with a single word.

King pulled his phone from his pocket, tapped the screen a few times, then held it out at arm's length, while pulling Mary close with the other.

"What are you doing?" Mary's shriek was muffled when she dipped her head into King's chest.

King loved the feel of her burrowing into him. "Taking a selfie."

"No way!" She burrowed deeper, "I look a fright, and you want to take our first picture? That's a hard no!"

King chuckled at her antics, then said, "Either way, you're in the picture. Whether your face is in my armpit or looking at the camera, it's going to be my lock screen pic."

"King!"

"Say cheese on three. One, Two..."

Mary looked up at the phone outstretched in King's massive grip. Mary quickly snuggled close to his side, and King tightened the grip around her shoulders to keep her nestled.

"...Three."

He took the picture and caught the two of them in the frame, then brought the phone in, never loosening his grip on Mary. He studied the image but said nothing. She turned her face up to him. He was handsome. No, scratch that, King was *hot*!

"Let me see!" Mary protested when King shut off the screen and pocketed the phone.

"King!" Mary wiggled out of his hold. "I want to see the picture." She gave him a yearning plea, "I want to see if I look all right."

"You do."

"I want to see it." She held out her hand.

King ignored her.

Catching her off-guard, he leaned into her and pressed his lips to her temple. The kiss was chaste, but it sent tingles throughout her body and straight to her lady bits.

"Let's call it a night, Sug.'"

Before Mary could protest, he stood from the booth, held out his hand to help her stand, then ushered her forward with a gentle and light hand to her lower back, all while saying nothing as they made their way to the counter.

She didn't want the night to end. She didn't want to go to Ember's and spend the night alone. Could she be forward enough and put herself out there...ask him to spend the night with her? After a second thought, she was a guest at Ember's, and inviting King to stay the night would be absurd and out of the question. And, she wasn't about to ask him to take her to his place. She'd die of mortification if he turned her down. She knew a late-night shower would beg to her, offering her sanctuary to relieve her throbbing innards.

After he insisted on paying the check—and being insulted when she tried to pay her half—he walked her to his truck and opened her door, which she thought was just the way King did things. He wasn't trying to be chivalrous, it was just him being him. It was one more thing that made her fall deeper for the man.

When they arrived at Ember's, King turned the truck off and they sat in silence. The moon overhead was full and illuminated the inside of the cab. An awkwardness ensued when neither of them spoke and the quiet lingered a little too long.

"I had a great time—"

"Thank you for supper—"

They both spoke at the same time and then stumbled over themselves, insisting the other speak first. Mary won out when King remained silent.

"Thanks for tonight. I had a wonderful time," then she added, "up until I blubbered on your chest." She reached over and smoothed his shirt over his pec. The gesture was innocent but felt intimate. She let her hand linger a bit and then let it trace over the muscles of his rib cage. Her eyes went from her roaming hand to his eyes that caught the moonlight and mesmerized her.

When he spoke he didn't turn to her but spoke straight into the night. His low voice was soft, yet filled the air around her. "You know what I am, Mare."

It wasn't a question, so she didn't answer.

"You may not be privy to the inner workings of the company, but I need to know you understand the things I do," then, he added, "the things I've done, and the things I'll continue to do."

Mary didn't answer right away. She took in his words and contemplated their meaning.

King waited, giving her time to absorb what he was saying.

"I understand." Her voice was timid.

"Do you?"

"Mmhuh." She was looking at her hands, picking at her cuticles.

"Mare, look at me."

Her chin came up and she met his darkened stare. The moonlight still caught his eyes, but something was clouding them. Something dark, and she didn't like it. When she tried to look away, he caught her chin with his knuckle and turned her to him. His touch was forceful, but gentle at the same time, and she didn't know how he was capable of both.

"Like I told you before, I have marks, Mare. All I feel are justified, but ultimately, I won't be my own judge and jury."

The sentiment made her swallow, and it was loud in the still of the night.

"Most of the time we have scheduled missions, and you'll know when I'll be leaving, but there'll be times I'll be called away at a moment's notice."

She nodded, and in the moonlight, he could see her acknowledgment.

"Because you're an employee, you'll most likely know where I'm going, but not when I'll be returning. Most of the time we don't even know how long we'll be OCONUS. But, knowing when I'll be leaving won't always be the case, especially when we are sanctioned by the government. I can leave without notice, and you won't know where I am, or when I'll be back. It's a life I love to live, doing what we do, and it's a life I'll continue to live until my body gives up or my number is called."

The thought of him leaving made her sad, but the possibility of never seeing him again made her stomach churn, and she tasted bile in the back of her throat. She never thought of him not returning home. Though he didn't tell her in so many words, she knew what he and his team did. He told her a bit in the hospital.

"OCONUS?" Mary knitted her brows.

"Outside the Continental US."

"Oh." It wasn't a great reply, but she wasn't familiar with military jargon or the acronyms she knew she'd hear around the office. But, then it really hit her. He'd be gone. Not just gone somewhere on US soil, he'd be gone somewhere in parts of the world most people didn't even know existed or could point out on a map. He would be willingly placing himself in danger. *Could I be with him knowing I'd possibly be setting myself up for heartache?* The thought caused her to tear up.

King saw her turmoil. She wore her emotions on her sleeve and wasn't doing a good job of hiding them. He hated to put her through this, but it was something that needed to be decided before he acted on his emotions. This was a first for him. He'd never laid out an ultimatum before. He never had the need to.

Barrack bunnies were a dime a dozen and were looking for no more than a romp in the sheets, and were just as eager to leave his bed as he was, so it was never an issue. Clingy bar hogs were never a prospect, and he cut them loose before any underlying emotions could surface, so again, a talk like this was never warranted.

Mary was the first woman he'd ever even considered or felt deep emotions for, that he could see a long path forward. He was falling fast and falling deep. She was more than someone he wanted to fuck and leave. The reality was what it was; he had no more attachment to a one-night-stand than the next one that rotated beneath him. He wasn't a man-whore, but he'd had his share of honey wells. He'd never regretted it because he was nothing more than an easy orgasm for the woman who used him for what they needed.

Tit for tat.

No regrets.

Until now.

The thought of the bedposts he notched sickened him. The thought of someone using Mary as a hump-and-dump, like he'd used women, riled his gut.

He turned from his thoughts and saw she was still caught up in hers. "Mare?"

Her name made her meet his eyes. Gone were the welled-up tears, and determination was set on her face.

She could do this. It would suck, but she knew in her heart that she could do it. There were no guarantees in life. He could as easily get killed crossing the street as he could on some foreign soil. Her stomach flipped again, but it didn't change the fact she'd never felt for someone the way she did for him. Call her crazy, but it was the honest-to-God truth.

She'd read romance books, and seen the movies where the hero and heroine fall in love at first sight, or fall in love in a whirlwind romance over the span of a couple of days, and the concept always seemed unrealistic and unbelievably far-fetched. But, she was living proof that it happened. She was falling for King.

Scratch that—she'd already fallen. Was it possible? He hadn't given her more than a chaste kiss. They hadn't spent much time together, especially alone, and they definitely hadn't slept together. So, how could she feel this strongly?

Am I crazy? Setting myself up for a fall? No. She knew it in the marrow of her bones that what she was feeling was genuine and not a fly-by-night crush or fling.

"Mare?" King calling her name again broke her from her thoughts, and she knew she could give him an honest answer.

"I need you, King. Not want, but *need* you."

He tried to interrupt, but she spoke over him.

"I know it won't be easy. And, I know I'm most likely setting myself up for heartache, but I'll chance the good over the bad. I have three scenarios. Two I lose, one I win.

"Which is?"

"If I don't allow my soul to be yours, I suffer now. Or, I give you my soul and you crush it, and I suffer later..." She trailed off.

"Or?"

"Or, I give you my soul and get everything I never knew I needed."

She swallowed hard when he pressed the button to unlatch his seatbelt, not losing her eyes for a moment. When he lifted the center console and reached over and unlatched her belt as well, she felt the familiar pang as her muscles beneath her skirt clenched in want and need.

The throbbing of her inner walls was tight and steady. She didn't know who would have a harder time scooting over, King with his massive bulk or her in her restrictive pencil skirt. Of all days not to wear a flowing dress. *Damn it!*

But, it was King pushing himself away from the steering wheel and pulling himself over to the middle of the bench seat that had her stomach flip-flopping and her heart galloping out of her chest. *Holy shit!*

He said nothing, but brushed his lips against hers, giving her time to rebuke him or pull away. She did neither but leaned in and pressed her lips to his. It was a chaste kiss, but when he ran his tongue across the seam of her mouth, she opened, and he took what was his.

It wasn't ravenous, passionate, and hunger-laden, but a slow, sensual, burning kiss. One of desire and fueled by longing.

He knitted his hands in her hair and she grasped the shirtsleeves over his biceps. They were huge and solid as granite. The man was a fortress. How someone that big could be this gentle was beyond her.

The kiss deepened but wasn't rushed. She was grateful. She didn't want it to end. Soon, they would need to break, come up for air, but until then, it didn't matter. She was drowning in everything that was King, and she welcomed a slow death if it meant he'd never take his lips from hers. A small whimper came from within her and was met with a rumbling moan from him.

They parted and he took her in, but only for a second; then he was back with a vengeance. The passion ramped up, and she was throbbing and every inch of her was aching for him. One hand left her hair and wrapped around her back. It was short-lived when she felt his thumb trace the underwire of her bra and cup around the side-swell of her breast.

Another whimper found its way out of her, and she felt his moan deep in her chest. She was swallowing his every emotion. He massaged his palm over her breast, and she felt her nipple stand erect and jut from beneath her lace bra. Her blouse was thin, so she knew he could feel the protrusion. She fisted his shirt and brought her hand to the side of his face, caressing his beard with her thumb. Again, she mentally cursed herself for wearing such a tight skirt, vowing to throw away every one she owned when she returned home.

King nibbled at her lobe and she tilted her head to allow him room to entice her more. He obliged, then trailed a length of kisses down her jaw. She felt her own wetness and drenched herself when his head dipped into the V of her blouse and disappeared into the flesh of her cleavage.

Her breathing was heavy, and her chest rose and fell with every erotic intake, so she gave him plenty of room to explore. His lips roamed the swells of her breasts, and she felt the bite of his mouth when he sucked in her sensitive flesh above the lace of her bra. The thought of him marking her aroused her even further, and she needed to feel him.

She'd never been in this situation. Never felt a man above or below his slacks. She felt empowered and emboldened. The mixture of erotica and nerves was a volatile mix. The way King was ravaging her gave her a sense of mischievousness she'd never experienced before.

She reached out and ran her hand up his thigh. Her hand ran smoothly against his leg and then, there he was. His erection was hardened beneath his slacks, and the sheer size of him astounded her. There was no way that was humanly possible. She had to be feeling something other than his cock, because only people in porn packed that mammoth size.

He must have read her thoughts because his head came up from between her breasts. "It's all me, Sugar."

When she gasped, he took full advantage of the moment and plunged his tongue deep in her mouth. He turned her to the angle of the seat. She was leaning against the corner of the seat and the door.

Once again, she hated herself for wearing such a tight skirt. It was no feat to King, who shoved it up, bunching it over her hips, exposing the white lace underwear she bought to match the bra. She brought one leg against the back of the bench seat. The seatbelt latches dug into her thigh, but at the moment, she didn't care. Her other leg rested on the floorboard, putting her spread-eagled before him.

He broke the kiss and noticed her rearrangement. The lowest growl she'd ever heard came from the man before her. He literally growled. She was so wet, and without the barrier of her skirt, she hoped she wasn't leaving a wet spot beneath herself on the leather upholstered seat.

King's eyes narrowed in on the scrap of fabric that was now drenched with her juices and covering her bare pussy. She swore her inner thighs trembled with the need to be touched. Mary was untouched, so the throbbing of her inner muscles was screaming to experience the touch of a man for the first time. She was lost in the thought of what his hands would feel like, and if it would hurt if he shoved his fingers into her virgin sheath when King ran his finger just below the fray of the lace, starting at her mound and running it slowly down to the gusset of the apex of her core.

She shuddered and unconsciously brought her hips forward, hoping to feel the impalement of his fingers. Her eyes were glued to his fingers millimeters from her wet folds when he eased the gusset forward and hooked his fingers beneath it.

"Soaked."

All Mary could do was whimper an incoherent, "Um-huh!"

"For me?"

Her gaze met his when his eyes broke from her core to her emerald eyes. Again, she was aroused out of words and just nodded her head. She knew he could see her in the moonlight because she could see him, and herself spread on display.

He inhaled her arousal and she cringed with embarrassment.

"Heavenly scent." His fingers ran the length of the lace and she thought she would die of torment. She wanted the thickness of his fingers inside her.

"Tell me you want this."

She must've heard him wrong because she thought he was asking if she wanted this. Couldn't he tell how much she wanted this? She knew she was coating his finger just by the soaked lace of her underwear. He was taking his time and was slowly torturing her. She wanted to yell at him to hurry up and take what she was clearly offering.

His sapphire eyes never left her watch. He was waiting for her response.

She nodded her head and her breasts heaved in anticipation when she muttered a sound of approval.

"Words, Mare. Tell me you want this, and I can take what's mine."

What's mine.

The words sent shivers up her spine.

"Yes." She jetted her hips, lifting them to him.

Just when agony was about to set in, King's phone pealed a tone into the night, breaking their hold with a start. That growl came again from King, though this time it was a mournful cry. He sat back at the center of the bench seat, clearly in as much agony as she was in. She missed his touch, though she never had it. She never knew her arousal could hurt so much.

"I gotta get that, hold that thought." He unabashedly adjusted

himself in his slacks and pulled the phone from his pocket. "King."
The word was clipped and fast. She knew he would make the call
quick and hoped they'd pick up where they left things.

"Fuck!"

She could only hear his side of the call, but by that one word, and
his tone, she knew they wouldn't be starting where they left off.

With the euphoria leaving her, she looked down at herself, her
blouse askew, buttons popped open, her oversized breasts hanging
out of the cups, barely contained in their holdings, and her skirt
bunched up around her waist. She was exposed and embarrassed.

Her lady bits were on full display, out in the open, in view, like
an anatomy exhibit.

She lifted her leg from the floor to the seat and brought her
thighs together to hide herself, hoping to lessen her vulnerability.
King stopped her closure with a hand to her uplifted knee, keeping
her open to him, though he was staring out through the fogged
windshield. She felt the coolness of the night air cross her open
core, and she realized just how wet she was.

Embarrassment turned to mortification. *Am I really making out
like a high school teenager in front of Ember's house? Has Ember seen or
heard us pull up, and is she peering out the front window?* How could she
face her new friend when she would clearly know what she and
King were doing for the last fifteen minutes? What if things had
gone further? Would she really have wanted to lose her virginity in
the front seat of his truck?

You're a hussy! She internally laughed at her inner musings. She
wanted to be a hussy!

King's voice broke the moment. "Okay, give me ten." He ended
the call without another word. His demeanor changed, and he went
cold.

"Raincheck?" Mary tried to keep the mood light.

King took in a breath and let out a controlled exhale. "You meant
what you said? Can you handle being apart?"

He was dead serious.

Mary swallowed. "You have to leave?"

He nodded.

"Is this somewhere I can know where you're headed?"

He shook his head, and she felt a pit form in her stomach.

She couldn't crumble or go back on her word the first time she
was tested, so she dug deep and found the strength from within.
"Okay."

"You sure, Sugar?"

She nodded, "I'm sure." She hoped she wasn't lying to herself. What choice did she have? She would deal when she needed to deal, but she wouldn't break in front of him.

Again, she realized she was exposed to him and didn't miss when his eyes fell to her still-throbbing core. He slowly grazed the outside fabric covering her clit, rubbing twice over the hardened nub, and then let go of her knee, and she closed her legs.

"Definitely a raincheck." His voice lingered with disappointment.

If he'd only rubbed a time or two more, she would have gone off.

He rubbed the length of himself through his slacks, and his hand rose to his waistband where he squeezed and let out a groan. Mary knew his cockhead couldn't possibly reach that far, but she couldn't fathom what else he would be squeezing. His painful groan told her two things: one, it was most definitely his cockhead, and two, his cock was aching as much as her core.

"I need to leave, but I'll walk you to the door." He reached for the bunches of her skirt and pulled the material down when she lifted her hips. "Wait for me to come around." He scooted back behind the wheel and opened his door. His stiffened walk told her he was still hard.

She dutifully waited, adjusting the rest of her clothing and wondering if it was possible to walk to the front door without orgasming with each brush of her thighs.

He opened the door and helped her out of the truck, and as promised, he walked her up the front walkway to the door. The porch light was lit and she could see the television through the window, so she knew Ember was home.

"I'm so sorry to have to split on our first date, Sugar." He wrapped his arms around her waist and she felt like a tiny fairy in his embrace. She was hoping there wasn't a wet spot on the back of her skirt, matching the spot she was almost certain she left on the leather interior of his seat.

"So, this was a date?" She tried to bring her arms around his neck, but it was damn near impossible, so she settled for placing her hands on his shoulders.

King chuckled at her attempt and answered her question, "Yes. I hope so." Then, he sobered, "I never do that," he motioned his head to the truck, "on a first date."

Mary scoffed, "You've never had a one-night-stand?"

King seemed miffed and replied, "Yes, but I've never dated, so I've never had a first date until tonight."

The thought of King never dating was preposterous. Women had to be throwing themselves at him. Why would he lie and say he never dated? It wasn't believable.

"Mare, I see that brain working, and I'm telling you the truth. I've never dated. Yes, I've hooked up. I've had one-nighters. I've taken girls out for dinner, with both parties knowing where the night would end, but I promise you, swear on my team's lives, I've never had a first date."

She didn't like the first part of his confession, the thought of him with other women. But the truth that she was his first date, someone he wanted more than just a 'one-nighter,' as he called it, brought the euphoria from earlier flooding back to her veins.

With them wrapped in each other's embrace, Mary didn't want the night to end. She screamed internally to ask him inside, or to take her back to his place, but she knew that wasn't an option. He had to leave, and suddenly the euphoria turned to sorrow. She didn't show it. Instead, she turned on her charm and met his deep sapphire eyes glistening in the moonlight.

"Well, Mr. Clark, I think it's customary to give your date a good-night kiss."

"Well, Ms. Jones, wouldn't want to break customs."

He leaned down and took her lips just as tenderly as he did the first time. It rose into a slow burn, but all too soon he pulled back.

"Gotta run, Sugar."

She wanted to ask him to promise her he'd come back, but it felt needy, and she didn't want to be "that" girl or want to put that kind of pressure on him.

Again, he read her thoughts. "I'll come back to you."

Her heart did a somersault. "I'll be waiting."

He went in for one more kiss. She savored his taste, his scent, all of him, knowing it would need to last her until he returned home.

He pulled back but his lips still brushed hers, "I really gotta go."

"I know," was her breathy reply.

"You know you're mine, Mare." It wasn't a question. It was a claim. "You've taken over my soul, and I don't know how it's possible, but it is. It's not understandable, and I'm not going to spend the time to try and make sense of it. You. Are. Mine." It was final.

Mary let his words drown her. Let them seep into every pore of her being. She loved him. How, by the speed of light, she didn't know. But, she knew she loved him.

"I want to say the words, but the timing isn't right. I want to lay you down and explore every inch of your body, and when I come up for air, you're going to be my saving breath. I want to ravish you with the words I feel in my soul that I'm sure you're dying to hear."

Mary. Was. Gone.

Hearing him wanting to tell her the same words she was dying to tell him had her soul bursting. He loved her. And, he would tell her in ways she couldn't wait to be told. She nodded to him with a guilty smile plastered from ear to ear.

He stole one more peck. "I need to make sure you get inside safely."

"The door's right here."

"Yes, but until I see you go through it and hear the locks engage, I can't move from this porch."

"Maybe I won't go inside then."

His rumbled growl turned her on, but she knew he needed to go. He was already past his original ten-minute mark, and just on cue, his phone rang from inside his pocket.

"I gotta go, Sugar. Get your ass inside so I can get mine gone."

"Bossy," Mary sassed.

She pulled her key from her purse, unlocked the knob, and unbolted the deadbolt. "I'm in, you can go."

His phone was still ringing. "Not 'til I hear you lock up."

With a small wave, she shut the door and he heard both locks engage. He pulled his phone from his pocket and answered with a curt, "King."

"I've got movement." Tex's southern drawl came over the phone.

"On my way to HQ."

Tex ended the call before King.

He felt a satisfying calm come over himself. The same calm he felt every time he geared up for a mission.

He strode to his truck, started the engine, and sent up a prayer. A prayer to help him with the indelible stain that would soon mark his soul, because this time, the mark *he* could justify, would be one he knew his Maker wouldn't.

Because this time...it was for vengeance. Trent Jones would be cast for judgment.

CHAPTER 14

King had to restrain himself from peeling out from the curbside in front of Ember's house and laying rubber down to get to Hellforce. He eased his way away from the curb, knowing Mary was watching him from the window. He eased the gas pedal with moderate pressure until he turned the corner, then smashed it down, racing balls out to Hellforce HQ.

Trent Jones was on the move, which meant King and the boys were on the hunt.

Images flashed in his mind of Mary lying in her hospital bed with her gown drawn, and the hideous black, purple, and yellowing bruises littering her silken flesh. He knew the pain of impact injuries —he and the team had suffered them many times—and he knew recovery was a bitch. Whether it was taking a round to a chest plate, a hand-to-hand fight, or a nasty fall on jagged rocks or boulders in rough terrain, broken ribs were a healing nightmare. His blood flooded with venom at the images settling in his mind, and he knew it was a matter of time before he would feel sweet relief.

∼

"He's in Carrizo Springs, about twenty miles east, so you can be on-site in less than an hour." Tex's voice came over the speaker in the middle of the table.

Cy pointed to a map on his tablet that projected onto the monitor on the wall, as the rest of the guys gathered around in the tactical ops room. This was the room where all missions were discussed, briefed, planned, and rehashed in debrief after execution.

"He logged into an auction site online when his location was pinged."

"Do we know if he's alone?" Trip was sitting at the table, twirling a pen through his fingers.

"Seems he's with someone. I couldn't get a detailed visual, but I "borrowed" the CCV traffic cam and saw them parked behind a warehouse parking lot. Two individuals are in the vehicle, one we know being Mary's brother because that's where his cell location pinged." Tex was always "borrowing" things.

Cy tapped a few times on the tablet and brought up the CCV vid. "I have the feed running facial recognition, so we should know the identity of the other person if it hits."

"This is a live feed?" King barked out the question, but no one addressed his tone. They all knew he was high-strung at the moment, definitely in leader mode, and no one could blame him for wanting every detail.

Tex ignored King's outburst "Yup. If they move, I'll be on them. Call you if they move."

He disconnected and the line went silent.

Cy put the tablet down and turned to King. "What's the plan, boss?"

King wanted to move now!

"Gear up. Kit out."

"Whoa! King, this is a civilian town, not the outskirts of some third-world, destitute mountain village. This is sovereign soil. We're not operators here. We can't storm in there on a rampage and capture him. If we can see him on CCV, then someone can see us. Gotta think this through." T crossed his arms over his chest, not in an intimidating manner, but just adjusting his stance, waiting for a plan to be hatched. Of all the guys, it would be T that wouldn't be the sensible one. His MO was balls-to-the-wall on a whim, which earned him his moniker. So, to have him as the voice of reason and the sensible one of the group was bizarre.

"We're not sitting on this." King paced over to the table and stared at it blankly. The thoughts of Mary alone, carrying the burden of her mother's care, striving to stay afloat while her dead-beat brother did nothing, infuriated him. Trent's days of taking advantage and freeloading were over.

Mary's battered body came to mind. Every tear she cried into his chest now burned against his flesh. He relived the sobs that wracked her body as she lay in the hospital, afraid and broken. As rage built, the time for retribution and atonement was at his hands, and he wouldn't be denied his justice.

"I can track him in live time, so we could stake out his location and wait for him to move to a less visible and more *desirable* location." Cy, as usual, was the sensible one, so all eyes were on him. "He's gotta move sooner or later, so if we're at least in his vicinity, we can keep on his tail until we can 'confront' him."

"Confront him?" King whirled around and it was to him that everyone's attention was drawn. "That piece of shit is being more than confronted." King's voice reverberated with lustful revenge." He's going to feel every bruise he put on his sister. This isn't going to be a touch-and-go mission, we need a locale to beat his ass down. He won't walk out."

"King—"

"Fuck off, Arctic! You saw her. You know as well as I do the state she was in and how every mark and bruise got there." King walked to the other side of the room with long strides. "You remember the handprints on her arms?"

Arctic kept his eyes on his boss and felt each lash of his words.

"You remember each fingerprint that was carved into the base of her neck when her brother choked her?" His words struck each guy. "Those weren't fresh, so they weren't a result of the motherfucker who attacked her during the break-in."

Though he was confronting Arctic, he spoke to the room.

King walked over to a folder and threw its contents onto the table in front of the team. They all looked at what was scattered and saw photos of Mary's body. Pictures the investigators took after she arrived in the ambulance. The team hadn't seen them before, but now King made his point. Some of the guys stared at the gruesome pictures, but a few looked away with fury in their veins.

The guys knew if King had his way, Trent Jones wouldn't see the light of another day.

They'd all had their moments when they went past the tipping point, and anger and retribution were doled out. That's when they relied on their brothers to pull them back from the edge and remember they weren't judge and jury.

When enlisted, military Rules of Engagement were in place to avoid such conflicts, but in actuality, it tied their hands more than necessary. Hellforce had a set of ROEs, but they were lax since they weren't sanctioned to the confines of enlisted men, though the Geneva Code was still in place.

"Let's set a plan and get on site." T-BAR rounded the table and grabbed a seat, looking once more at the pictures in front of him. The rest of the guys sat, and the brainstorming began. Each countered and balanced the discussion with different tactics and set a plan, and backup plans, in motion.

They geared up but not in the usual sense of a mission, where they'd load gear to the hilt. This time, each carried a sidearm and plated beneath their black shirts and black cargo pants. They weren't taking any chances considering Mary said her father's gun was in the stolen safe.

Their clothing was in line with street clothes, all black, no logos or tags, and each had a black hood in their pocket. Normally, the team would be fitted with sidearms and rifles, their KABAR knife, plate carrier, helmet, NVGs, extra mags, and all the gear needed to make an HVT stealth op possible. But, seeing as they were in a populated area, with surveillance cams, be it public or private, they wanted to be as unnoticeable as possible.

They'd completed jobs on US soil before, but nothing with the emotional connections this plan had attached to it.

Trent wasn't listed as a government interest and wasn't on anyone's radar as a person of interest, so Hellforce was breaking a shit ton of civil laws, apprehending him and holding him for "light interrogation." If they were caught, the hammer of the law would come down on them, and no one wanted that to be a possibility. King had his connections, but there was no way any law enforcement could, or would, look the other way.

"Let's roll, boys." King headed out the door.

Mary watched as King pulled away from the curbside and disappeared into the night. Her heart was beating out of her chest, knowing that he and his team were leading themselves into danger, probably halfway around the world to a country or village no one had heard of. *What if he didn't come back? What if he was wounded? Would anybody tell me?* She supposed someone would contact Hellforce if the team didn't come back. *What if only the rest of the guys came back without King, would they be able to tell me what happened?* Her mind was going crazy with different scenarios and coming up with questions she couldn't answer.

"King leave?"

Mary about jumped out of her skin when she heard Ember's voice from behind her.

"Holy shit!" Mary screeched with a start.

"Oh my God. I'm sorry, I didn't mean to scare you. I thought you heard me coming out of the bathroom."

In any other circumstances, Mary probably would have heard her, but with her mind playing twenty-million questions, she wasn't engaged. She clutched her chest and steadied herself, "No, I didn't hear you. I was watching King—"

Ember gave her a grinning smirk. "So, did he round any bases?"

Mary unconsciously straightened her clothes, knowing they were still in disarray, and her hair must not have fared well either by the way Ember was giving her a once-over from head to toe. Mary felt the flush creep up her neck and knew Ember saw it as well. "A woman never tells."

"Enough said." Ember took her seat back in the overstuffed armchair and grabbed the remote and the bowl of popcorn from the coffee table.

Mary knew standing by the window wasn't going to bring King back to her any sooner, and she hoped her wrinkled skirt wasn't showing any signs of the last fifteen minutes. She headed to the guest room to change. When she returned in her elastic fat pants and oversized tee, she curled up in the corner of the couch, closest to Ember's chair. She threw the throw blanket over her legs and settled in to watch whatever was on television.

Ember stuffed a handful of popcorn into her mouth and held out the bowl to Mary, "Wan 'schhum?" she said around the mouthful.

Mary grabbed a handful of the snack.

"So, you have a good time tonight?" Ember swallowed the popcorn with a swig of water, then popped a few single kernels into her mouth, waiting for Mary to answer.

"Yeah, I really did."

"Where'd you go?"

Mary relived the night in her mind, as images flashed of supper at the quaint diner, her breakdown, her recovery, the sweet scent and taste of King's kiss, the way he teased her tongue with his, and how he cradled her face with his gentle touch, but also took her with passion and need.

She heated at the thought of herself spread open to him, offering herself, and the way he looked at her with hunger in his eyes. She felt the want of his touch, the want to be touched by him for the first time, and she shivered.

"That good, huh?"

Mary blushed when Ember's grin just about split her face. She wasn't sure if Ember knew they'd been sitting out front getting heavy and heated, or if her grin was because of the visceral reaction Mary had to her own thoughts, and Ember was just happy for her new friend.

Mary shrugged her shoulders with glee and wrung her hands.

"You and King! Way'da go, guurl!" Ember's enthusiasm was contagious. "So, are you official?"

Mary wasn't sure how to label themselves. Were they seeing each other? Were they dating? Were they exclusive? She'd have to say, 'Yes,' to all of the above by the way King made his declaration.

Ember went into the kitchen and came back with two glasses and a bottle of wine. "Dish, baby. I want deets. Don't leave anything out!"

There were definitely parts Mary was going to leave out. Everything at the curbside. She'd never had a friend close enough to be considered a "girlfriend" to share secrets with or have a girl's night, hanging out, doing girly things, swapping guy stories. She hoped that she and Ember would have a sisterhood like other people had.

Ember poured the glasses and handed one to Mary and plunked herself back in the armchair, eager for Mary to start the "tell-all."

Mary took a sip of wine. It was only a little after nine p.m. so she'd be up for a few more hours.

"Well, come on...what'd ya do?" Ember's impatient mocking voice sent Mary into laughter.

"Well, after you left, I went to his office—"

"Whoa...bold move! No one ever confronts King until he's cooled."

Mary didn't know the quirks and rules of the guys, but she was sure she'd learn them over time. Either through the advice from the others or by trial and error.

Her phone chimed with an incoming message and she looked at the screen lying next to her legs curled beneath her. It was a message from King. She wanted to pick it up and immediately read what he wrote, but she didn't want to be rude to Ember.

"Is that lover boy?" Ember teased in a singsong voice.

Mary felt giddy at her teasing; like a teenage girl at a slumber party talking about boys.

"Yes," was all Mary replied with a chortle.

"Look at you...Smitten Kitten!"

Mary blushed at the good-natured razzing.

"Go ahead. Answer it. He's waiting," Ember bounced up and down in her chair, exaggerating her excitement, "see what he's gotta say!"

She picked up her phone and clicked on the message.

KING: *"If all the world's wishes were bottled up and thrown into the ocean, yours would be the only one I'd ever want to find."*

Mary read the message privately, and she wanted to bawl. One, because his sentiment was breathtaking, and two, it made her heart ache for him and miss him even more than when she left him at the door. How would she stand to be without him until he returned? She held the phone to her heart as if holding his words close would soothe the ache.

"Well?" Ember stared with an expectant look on her face.

She reread his message once again to herself and contemplated whether King would want her to share such a private, intimate message between them.

Another chime and she opened the message right away.

KING: *"FYI. If you're near Ember when these come through, letting you know, she'll badger you, relentlessly, until you share. The choice is yours. I would yell from the rooftops if I could, for all to know how much you mean to me."*

Mary's heart swelled, and she breathed relief, knowing she wouldn't be violating any trust between her and King by sharing his messages. She typed a message back to him.

MARY: *"You'd be the only one I'd want to reply to my ocean bottle."*

. . .

Then, she replied, again, *"Stay safe. Watch out for each other, and I'll be waiting for you the second you get back."*

She didn't want to make the message sappy or want to give him any cause to know she was worried for him and the guys.

KING: *"We'll pick up where we left off. That's a promise. I know where you live, and I know where you work. Either way, you're coming back to my place."*

Mary tingled with excitement and anticipation. He couldn't get back soon enough, and she'd be ready and willing. She wanted to keep things light, so she typed back with levity.

MARY: *"I don't know. I just got a new job and my boss...he's a ballbuster, so I don't know if I'll be able to get time off."*

She giggled when she hit the send button and watched as the bouncing dots appeared, letting her know that he was replying.

KING: *"I have it on good authority that your boss will give you all the time you need and won't object to you being carried straight out of the office and spending a three-day "staycation" at my place."*

Mary replied with a bunch of thumbs-up emojis and ended it with a heart.

"Hello?" Ember got her attention. "Kinda waiting here." She sipped her wine with utter arrogance, then laughed when she couldn't keep the ruse up any longer.

"Oh my God, don't shoot wine out of your nose!" Mary was laughing at the dribble of wine leaking down Ember's chin and the few droplets that landed on her jamma top.

Ember wiped her chin with her sleeve. "If you're worried about sharing, you can totally keep it private, but I'll tell you what—the guys will know all about you by noon tomorrow, tops! That group of hard-ass, over-muscled, alpha boys is the biggest bunch of gossips this side of Texas!"

Mary's eyes widened. *Would King actually tell the guys about our time in the truck?*

"And before you get worried wondering if King would spill any of the deets about you that would embarrass you, he'd never disrespect you like that. Trust me. King keeps people's secrets. He's a gentle giant."

Mary thought of the gentle words he messaged and how he comforted her in the diner, a gentle teddy bear.

"How do you know about his gentle side?" It was an innocent question, but she could see Ember pull into self-reflection, and suddenly she regretted asking. Before she could correct herself, Ember spoke.

"When I came back from my last deployment," she paused, "He, um, helped me out a bit. Helped me navigate through some heavy things."

Mary didn't know what she'd been through, but she knew that if someone needed help, King would do whatever he could to help them.

"But, things are good now, got the range up and running, got my family, old friends, a new friend," she raised her glass to Mary, "and, wine. Life's good."

Both took a drink, and Mary set her glass on a coaster.

Her phone chimed the same time Ember's did. Both checked their messages.

KING: *"Going dark. I'll message you when I can. Stay safe. Don't leave Ember's sight. This should be quick, and we'll be out on date number two before you know it. Take care, Sugar. See you in your dreams."*

MARY: *"My dreams belong only to you. Be safe. Laters!"*

Mary lingered a bit seeing if he would reply. When nothing came, she looked over to her friend.

Ember looked longingly at her phone. "Guys are out." She placed it on the armchair and curled into the chair, bringing her feet under herself. "Must be spur-of-the-moment."

"Did King text you, too?" Mary was curious.

"No. Slate."

Mary wondered if they were a thing. "Are you two dating?"

Ember laughed, knitting her brows and shaking her head. "No. We're not like that. We're just friends."

Mary thought they seemed to be more than friends, but she was new to the group, so what did she know?

"We grew up together. He's sorta like my brother."

Mary still wondered but let the moment pass.

"I hope they'll be all right." Mary was worried again.

"They'll be good. They always are."

"They've always come home." Mary assumed they were always a team, so her assumption was based on the six of them.

Ember smiled stiffly, and Mary sensed there was more to the story, and the guy's history, but she didn't want to dwell on that. Any stories about things gone wrong, or the guys getting injured would only make her worry, and she had enough of that flowing through her at the moment.

Ember grabbed her glass from the table, "So, are you going to tell me what happened after I left and why you came home thirteen hours later, or do I have to guess and let my imagination run wild."

Mary picked up her glass and took a swallow. She was going to enjoy the evening with her new friend and put the worry in the back of her mind.

"And, don't leave anything out!"

It was definitely going to be a "more than one glass of wine," night.

CHAPTER 15

Six guys sat in an unmarked van outside the rundown industrial park, Trip at the wheel. Cy was in the passenger's seat, King and Arctic sat directly behind the front seat on the van's floor, and Slate and T-BAR kept watch through the back windows making sure they weren't followed. Cy was tracking the real-time location map, watching as Trent and his companion headed down McAllan Way.

"It's clear." T-BAR said as he hung up the burner phone and pocketed it. "Everything's set, and there won't be anyone near this warehouse for the next twenty-four hours. Transfers made, and Tex says we're good to go."

King looked over Cy's shoulder, through the windshield at the abandoned building, and Trip eased the van away from the alley between the two warehouses. The drive to the neighboring town didn't settle King's rage any less than it did before he left HQ. The only reprieve from his wrath was the texts he exchanged with Mary before they loaded into the van. Once the van door was closed, he seethed for retribution.

"Looks like they're heading west. There are three pawn stores in the next seven miles." Cy followed the tracker, as Trip tailed the four-door, '92 Ford Taurus. It wasn't hard to tail, with its two-tone rusted and flaking paint job, missing hubcap, and broken rear taillight.

"Wanna make some calls?" Arctic looked to King, even though the windowless van was dark, and they could barely see each other.

"Negative. Wait to see where they slow." King had close ties and knew people who knew people. If he needed a fix at a location, one call would get him the information he sought or a marker cashed.

He wanted to PIT maneuver the shit box car Trent and his friend were in, but they'd make more of a scene than what was warranted, and although the traffic was minimal, everyone was a cameraman these days with cellphones and the internet—they'd be guaranteed to end up on YouTube by the night's end. So, overall, patience would win out.

"ID just came back on the driver. Chet Richardson." Cy read the status Tex sent, and the mile-long rap sheet that followed. Trent Jones was in rough company. King doubted Trent had any clue how deep he was in. Compared to Chet's prior convictions, pleas, jail, and prison time, Trent's run-ins with law enforcement looked like child's play.

"Looks like they're stopping at Paul's Pawn Mine, Twelfth and McAllen. Trip pulled into a parking lot adjacent to the pawnshop and parked alongside a twenty-four-hour laundromat.

King put feelers out to all the pawn shops in the tri-state area about the missing jewelry and pistol and sent Trent Jones' picture to them as well. Most shops usually wouldn't take a second look at the info, but since it had King's name attached to it, he knew scouts would be on the lookout.

King took the burner phone from his pocket and dialed the twenty-four-hour pawn shop.

"Paul's Pawn Mine," the man's uninterested voice answered.

"This is King."

The voice perked up on the other end, "King, buddy...it's been a while. What can I do for you?"

"I've got a mission execution of the tangos you were notified of earlier this week."

Paul, the owner of the shop, listened intently. He was a former Ranger, and he and King had ties that ran deep. A longtime acquaintance. He was a good guy, and King trusted him. Of all the places Trent could've unloaded the goods, King threw a prayer up that it was Paul's shop. He knew this would be a swift takedown.

"Two men, names of Trent Jones and Chet Richardson, are sitting outside your establishment. He'll most likely be coming in to pawn jewelry and a gun." King rattled off a detailed description of each guy.

"Got your six, King."

King knew he would, but hearing confirmation from Paul was a great reassurance.

"Do you have a make, model, or the serial number of the gun?"

"CZ75, 9mm pistol.... serial number's unknown."

"And the jewelry?"

"A man's plain silver wedding band and a women's antique wedding set."

"Description of the antique?"

The ring was Mary's grandmother's, her mother's, and would one day be hers.

"One-carat, princess cut diamond, center round, white gold, with smaller diamonds surrounding the face and band of the ring."

A low whistle came from the other end of the line. "That's impressive. And, unmistakable."

"I need a head's up if either comes in." King would capture Trent whether he was pawning the items or not. "We'll be storming the castle."

"You in the area."

"Roger. Right outside your keep." King went on and laid out a detailed plan with Paul, and he was happy to help in any way he could. King pocketed the phone.

"Plans in motion."

Nobody liked the waiting game, but it was crucial to the success of so many of their missions. They were masters of the game, so no one complained. Waiting and watching let them reap rewards.

A few minutes passed.

"Got movement." Everyone's head lifted at Trip's voice. "They're entering the shop."

"Verify."

"Verified." Cy seconded King's request, as Trip slipped the van into gear.

"Showtime, boys!" King's voice was rich and laden.

Arctic put his hand on King's shoulder. "Easy...Mission mode." Arctic reminded him.

King nodded in the darkness and drew in a breath. He put all thoughts of Mary out of his mind, which was harder than usual to compartmentalize. She was monopolizing his every thought, so to set her aside felt like a betrayal. It was unsettling.

King never had to harbor his thoughts of a woman to do his job, but he needed to have his wits and bearings about him. He set his thoughts to the mission. *Operator.* The single word calmed him.

There would be time later to unleash his frustration, anger, and ruthlessness. But, now, he had a job to do, and he would execute it with precision.

Trip pulled the van around the back of the pawnshop and kept the engine idling. King's phone lit with an incoming message.

PAUL: *Targets and items in store. Description confirmed. Jewelry; no gun.*

It was short, sweet, and exactly what King wanted to hear. They had to give time for the stage to be set, and the fifteen-minute wait was agonizing.

He checked his watch. "Let's move, boys." King grabbed his black face-covering and placed it over his head, as did the other five men in the van. Each checked their sidearms, having a round in the chamber. If all worked out as planned, no one would lay down a single round, but when targets panicked all hell could break loose, and the guys were ready for any scenario.

King knocked his vest beneath his shirt. *Plate in place.* He was ready.

"Check One," King called out.

"Check Two," Arctic sounded.

"Check Three..." The guys called off in sequence, keeping their comms open.

When everyone was sounded off, Cy and Trip exited the front doors. Cy methodically opened the side doors behind the passenger's seat, where King and Arctic barreled out. Trip rounded the rear, opening the doors for Slate and T-BAR. The side doors stayed open and the van sat idling.

"Like we planned; clean, quick and easy." King spoke the same words he did every time they got underway. Though his voice was low, all the guys nodded and knocked fists on top of one another. If asked, they'd say they weren't a superstitious bunch, but they never broke routine.

Arctic and Trip circled around to the front of the shop, covering the doors in case Trent and his pal decided to make a quick exit, while King, Slate, and Cy made their way to the back of the shop.

T-BAR stood sentry between the van and the shop's back door to provide cover in the event one of the assholes were able to evade the ambush and rush out the back exit. The chances were nil, but every aspect had to be accounted for. No one wanted to be the catch-all, everyone wanted to be part of the action, especially when the wait had been a long time coming, but in reality, the sentry was the ultimate guardian, the saving grace, if all went to hell and became a cluster fuck. T would be the gatekeeper.

The back door to the shop was always locked and bolted shut, but King slowly eased the handle and the door opened without a hitch. *Just as planned.* King's thoughts were echoed by the others with their curt nods. Each man unholstered. King took one last look at his brothers, then threw the door open and it began.

The hunt was on.

~

Trent fidgeted as the clerk looked at the items on the counter. A plain men's silver wedding band. Plain. No gems or stones. No lasered design. Just an inscription that said, *'My dearly beloved.'* It looked sad compared to the ring next to it. An eloquent engagement ring with an intricate inlay of accent diamonds around the master princess cut stone.

It was a sight.

The bridge of diamonds, lying just below and encircling the main diamond, glistened under the store lighting. At a jeweler's, the ring would easily appraise in the upper five to lower six figures. Paul knew this was what King was looking for.

Trent tried to play it cool, but Paul noticed the beads of sweat on his upper lip and a sheen across his forehead. He nervously bounced his leg and it seemed he didn't know where to put his hands, crossing and uncrossing them.

His buddy, Chet, stood calm and collected like this was old hats to him. This was the first time he'd been to Paul's store, but Chet probably knew he couldn't unload the jewelry in the Heights where he lifted it from Trent's house. Harker Heights had no pawn shops, but Killeen and the surrounding metropolis had plenty. The gun from the safe was tucked beneath his front waistband in case the owner needed *persuading*, and Chet needed to *help* the transaction.

Paul picked up the lady's ring and examined it. "Pretty exquisite piece. Someone sure is an unlucky lady." He grabbed the loupe from the island behind the showcase counter and took a closer look at the diamonds. "Wow, this is impressive. Where'd you come across a gem like this?"

"How much you offering?" Chet wasn't in the mood for small talk. He wanted to unload the shit and get the cash. It would be a great payday. Trent thought it would be a fifty-fifty split, but Chet had no intention of splitting the payout.

Paul took his time, pretending to examine it, taking only one eye from the two POS in front of him. He kept them in his peripheral vision at all times. Besides the fact that he knew King and his team were surrounding his store, he knew his night security, Nick and John, would take care of any foul move either one of them made while he was "distracted."

Being a twenty-four-hour pawnshop meant a lot of street thugs, thieves, and looters were a common occurrence. If riff-raff came calling, Paul's friends and former teammates would haul their asses out of the store, rough them up, and go as far as a full beat-down if necessary. The pair were not a force to be reckoned with.

Paul ran a legit business, so when trash like Trent and Chet came in with things that looked *too* good, Paul knew where the goods came from, and he didn't buy or sell anything he thought would be a find for the authorities. It was just bad business practice. If the hock was hot and police confiscated it, it was money out of his pocket. Although he worked with law enforcement, always on the lookout for reported items, he wasn't in the habit to buy hot goods.

So, when he got the report that King was on the hunt for jewelry and a weapon, Paul kept his eyes peeled. He thought it would be a longshot, but when King called and said the trash was outside his store, *hot damn*, the adrenaline flowed. He and his staff were ready.

Paul put down the antique 1920s era ring on the jeweler's mat. "This silver band, they're a dime a dozen." He pointed to the mat in the display case, where rows of plain gold and silver bands nestled between ropes of velvet. "Don't know what I can give you for it. Don't really have a demand for them, especially silver."

Chet got antsy, "Put a price on it."

Paul was stalling for time. He knew King would be coming through the back any minute. He'd unbolted the door after King called, something he'd never do under normal circumstances for anyone other than King.

John was at the entrance to the hallway that led from the store floor, directly to the alley behind the building. He was tucked into the shadows and Nick was in the surveillance room watching the monitors like a hawk. Nick was always itching to crawl into a brawl, so when Paul told him King was on the prowl, he looked like a kid on Christmas morning.

Paul fingered the silver band and he felt a pang of sorrow. He didn't know who this belonged to—if it was stolen, robbed, or even mugged from its owner. He knew these two were nothing but street ruffians, and he would normally never allow them in his store. The fact that King and his team of Hellforce were going to rain down on them, gave him a gleam of satisfaction.

"Fifteen bucks. Take it or leave it."

Chet stepped forward, and Paul scrutinized his every move.

"Fifteen! That's a joke. Chump change!" Chet settled his hands on his hips, his right moving a little too close to the gun Paul knew he had in his waistband.

Paul stood from leaning against the counter to his full height of six-foot-four, just as John stepped from the hall, hand on his holster, sending a message. His fingers twitching like an old western cowboy at the OK Corral. Nick stayed in the surveillance room, but if shit got hot, he'd be out in a flash.

"Might want to step off, son." Paul's smooth baritone sounded.

Chet was smart and crossed his arms over his scrawny chest. John watched from a distance.

"Don't like the price, you can turn around and walk your ass right out the door. I ain't a crown jeweler, I don't yank chains. I offer you what I offer you, and you decide if you want it, then you take it. Otherwise, you walk. Now," he turned back to the counter and picked up the woman's ring. "This is a different story."

Trent stepped closer to the counter. Paul looked up at him and gave him a silent direction to step back. Trent read it and gave him space, but not a wide berth.

"That's antique. Real old." It was the first time Trent spoke.

Immediately, Paul didn't like him. He was a weasel. "How do you know it's old?"

Trent fidgeted some more. "Just do, man. Looks old as shit. Gotta be worth a few hun'ered."

Chet came up and elbowed Trent in the gut, causing him to clutch his side and stumble back.

"Shut the fuck up!" Chet bellowed. "Don't you ever interrupt business!" He stepped two paces into Trent causing him to stumble back further.

John stepped onto the showroom floor and casually leaned next to the door to the surveillance room, but not before Nick was out in full force. Nick had two modes: eager, and eagerly eager. He wouldn't be left out.

"But, they're my things." Trent muffled the words but they were loud enough to catch Paul's attention.

"Not anymore." Chet seethed out the words between his teeth.

Paul played coy and showed astute interest in the ring.

"Gotta be a few G's, at least." Chet was crowding the showcase. Paul kept quiet and brought the loupe to his eye, again, and examined the accented diamonds cresting the side of the band.

Chet got antsy, and Trent got twitchy, and then, all hell broke loose.

~

"Execute." King threw open the door and barreled in, with Slate and Cy hustling behind him. Each had his weapon drawn. Arctic and Trip came through the front on King's command and blocked the entrance.

"Get down! Get down!"

"On the ground! On the ground!"

"Now! Now! Drop down!"

All the fury of Hellforce came down in about one-and-a-half seconds. Each man was precise in his duty, engaging his role, barking out commands of compliance. Paul stood three feet behind the counter, gun drawn. Nick and John stood on the other side of the room, guns drawn as well.

Trent panicked and scurried away from the force pushing their way through the back door, rushing the hallway, and into the main room. He turned to bolt out the front door but was met by the wall that was Trip and Arctic. Backing up, he stumbled over his own feet but didn't take his eyes from the two men crowding him, yelling for him to get down.

Chaos ensued, and Trent wasn't sure what to do.

That decision was made for him when an arm from behind came around his neck, crushing his windpipe and pulling him into a body of stone. His hands instinctively went to his throat, trying to pry the massive arm and prevent it from choking him, but it was unmovable. A futile attempt. The hold tightened and squeezed harder. Blood rushed to his face and black spots danced before him. Panic. Pure, cold panic doused him.

He clawed at the hold in a frenzied attempt. Just when he

thought he was going to pass out, he was hurled to the ground, his head bouncing off the concrete floor. More stars danced in his vision. Then a blinding flash of white light hit him when a crushing blow struck his temple and impacted his right eye. A burst of pain shot through his head as he winced and tried bringing his hands up to cover his face. It was in vain.

Before he knew what was happening, a mammoth man hooded in black was on top of him. A single hand bridged his neck, choking him and pinning Trent to the ground. His eyes bulged and he wrapped his hands around the man's corded arm, trying to pull it away, but it was like moving a steel girder. It wasn't going anywhere.

～

King was on a singular mission and that was to get to Trent Jones. He barged through the door to the shop and his eyes landed on his target.

Bingo!

King holstered his Sig with lightning speed as Trent backed away from Trip and Arctic. He had his back to King and that made the grab all the sweeter. King wrenched his hold around Trent's scrawny neck, choking the cocksucker as he flailed, while he tried to pry the girded hold from his neck, but it only made King's squeeze tighten. It was a futile attempt.

Unlike this shitbag, King was a trained operator, a deadly force when needed, and hand-to-hand combat was his forte. He had Trent in the hold in a matter of seconds.

King threw him to the ground with more force than necessary and was on top of him in a heartbeat. The width of his outreached hand spanned the flesh of Trent's slender neck, pinning him in place, and King glared down, meeting him eye to eye. The fear flooding Trent's bulging eyes was satisfying, fueling a need inside King's being.

King leaned into him and his words calmly fell from his lips. "You bitch-ass motherfucker, you like this? You feel this?" He tightened his grip. The words weren't forced. They were spoken in a calm demeanor, which made them all the more terrifying.

Trent could barely hear them over the whooshing of his own heartbeat in his ears.

"You think I'm playing?"

Trent tried to shake his head, 'no,' but the fingers wrapped around his throat, pinning him to the floor, made it impossible.

Mercy. The words hit him like a bath of ice water. Mary's words swept over him and echoed in his mind.

No. Not now. King tried to shake the words from clouding his objective, but they resounded in his head.

Have mercy.

King flipped Trent to his stomach and jammed a knee between his frail shoulder blades, purposely settling too much of his weight onto his spine. When Trent let out a scream, King didn't relent. He grabbed Trent's free arm frantically waving about and pulled it high behind his back.

Trent's other arm was trapped beneath him, so King left it where it was, knowing its position would be crushing against his chest and causing even more pain. Trent tried to buck his body and flail his legs but stopped when King wrenched his arm higher. He let out another scream and his eyes flooded with tears.

It was a perverted pleasure King found in this takedown.

Normally, a target was taken down with the least amount of force, with minimal damage. They were operators, not tyrants. Their only objective was to secure their target and then let the people above their pay grade deal with the aftermath. But, this was personal. The piece of shit beneath him had laid his fucking hands on Mary, and King was just getting started.

He fisted Trent's hair and pulled his head back beyond its normal range, knowing the pain he was inflicting was excruciating. Cy approached and tore a wide piece of tape from a roll and slapped it over Trent's mouth, muffling his scream.

King leaned down, and in the lowest of low tones so his teammates didn't hear, spoke into Trent Jones' ear, "You are going to know the fury of hell, and I will be your executioner."

He grabbed the hood Trip held out to him and bagged him, dropping his head with a shove. Trip and Arctic took over cuffing him and King got up, feeling the blood of the devil fill his veins.

The takedown was satisfying. He had only one regret. He couldn't give Mary the one thing she'd asked for, the one thing he didn't promise.

Mercy.

~

"Get down! Get down!"

"On the ground! On the ground"

"Now! Now! Drop down!"

Chet saw the wall of men storming down the hall, and he knew it wasn't going to end well. He didn't know who it was, local police, SWAT, or any other lawful entity, but he wasn't surrendering. He wasn't going back to prison.

He turned to charge the front door but two men stood like mountains, blocking his getaway.

The first man barreling down the hallway took Trent down in a flash. He wasn't going down like that. He lifted his shirt and pulled the stolen gun from his waistband and brought it up, aiming it at the hulk of a man rushing towards him, and pulled the trigger.

Nothing.

To his detriment, he didn't have a bullet chambered and didn't have time to rack the slide before the man was on top of him, coming down with a fist of fury.

One of the men swung his arm into the one holding the gun, knocking it out of the way and making Chet loosen his grip.

Keeping momentum, Slate stepped into him and grabbed his forearm, twisting it into his own body and grabbing the wrist holding the gun. He brought it down across his own knee and felt a sickening, but satisfying snap, the giving of bone, and Slate smiled. Chet's wrist hung limp.

Chet let out a howling scream, curdling to everyone's ears. He buckled at the knees and Slate took advantage of his lowered stance and drove an elbow back into his face, leaving Chet grasping for his nose with his free hand as he fell back.

Slate "nudged" him with his booted foot, turning him onto his stomach. It wasn't hard enough to break any ribs, but enough to knock the wind out of him. Trip handed Slate a pair of flex-cuffs.

Because of his now-broken wrist, he couldn't be cuffed in the usual manner, so Slate cuffed his arms behind his back, elbow-to-elbow. Slate pulled the black hood from his cargos and bagged it over Chet's head, cloaking him in darkness. The takedown operation was over in less than a minute. Both men were bagged, and it was time for phase two.

Cy and Slate picked up Chet, got him to his feet, and marched him down the hallway. They nodded at Nick and John, as well as Paul, on the way out. Paul would definitely have a marker with King if he ever needed it.

Arctic and Trip had a little tougher time getting Trent out of the shop. He was dragging his feet and resisting the two leading him down the hallway. An elbow to his ribs from Arctic, and a blow to his solar plexus from Trip, gave the guys the control they needed to get him out with ease. Because he had his mouth taped, the gasp for air had him fighting consciousness, which helped to subdue him.

All four men dragged their captives out the back door, and with the van doors open, they threw them into the awaiting vehicle. T-BAR stood guard as the *cargo* was loaded.

"I missed all the fun," T-BAR laughed.

"Party's not over yet," Trip quipped.

King remained inside. He walked to where the gun lay on the ground and picked it up with his gloved hand. He dropped the magazine and pulled the slide back, clearing the chamber. Since Chet never put a round in, it was clear the entire time. King shook his head and put the gun and full magazine into his side cargo pocket.

Still masked, he walked up to Paul and nodded. Nick and John stood beside the counter, wishing they would have gotten to participate in the takedown, but were damn happy to see the thugs get their asses handed to them.

"Would 'preciate if your security feed was on the fritz, maybe for half a day or so?"

"Already taken care of," Nick chimed in from beside him, "you were never here."

King looked over at him and nodded then did the same to John. "You all have a marker." He looked at the three, "Use it wisely."

Paul handed King a small black velvet pouch, cinched by a drawstring. "Believe these are what you were looking for?"

King took the bag and clutched it in his hand. His emotions ran deep. As much as he relished the fact he had the two men who were responsible for destroying Mary, he was more grateful to have her rings back in his possession. King swallowed hard, gave a single chin lift, and exited down the hallway then out the back door.

The guys were loaded up in the van. Cy was waiting at the open side doors for King to hop in. King shook his head, then pointed for Cy to get in the back. He went without question, and King closed the two doors. He hitched himself up into the passenger's seat, shutting the door as he settled.

As soon as the door shut, Trip pulled the van out of the alleyway and then onto the main drag, towards the warehouse from earlier. King knew it would be vacant. Knew there were no CCV cams along their route and no cams on the warehouse or surrounding buildings. He'd cashed a marker, and he was going to use it to its full advantage. The warehouse was his.

He removed his gloves and palmed the velvet bag. He caressed it beneath his fingers, thinking of how happy Mary would be when he returned them to her. The items she thought were lost forever would find their way home again.

Home.

That single word set bile in his throat at the thought of the reason the rings were taken. Her home was violated. Mary was violated. He squeezed the bag and a roaring, heated rage began to burn in his gut.

The blood pumping through his veins boiled with the thoughts of sweet Mary, and the pain that was inflicted by the two sons-of-bitches on the van floor behind him. He wished now that he would have taken Cy's place in the back with the worthless cargo.

Images of Mary flashed in his mind, and not the good ones from their first date, or the moments from earlier tonight in his truck.

No, the pictures flooding his memory were from the police, of her battered and bruised body. One after the other, after the other, an endless loop played. He squeezed his eyes shut to try and ward away the images, but they still littered his mind, over and over, image after image.

Trent Jones had the wrath of the devil at his doorstep.

Mary had asked for mercy, but King couldn't grant her wish.

King knew tonight his indelible mark would come.

CHAPTER 16

King felt the pain radiate in his knuckles and down his forearm as he made contact with the bony structure of the rib cage.

The man handcuffed to the cast iron pipe above his head screamed in pain. Lucky for King, not so lucky for Trent—with his hands extended over his head, it made his ribs conveniently accessible.

When the team arrived at the warehouse in the dark of night, the guys removed the trash from the van, Trip and Cy handling Chet, and King and T hauling Trent. The guys hustled from the van into the warehouse, though King's contact said the area would be cleared for twenty-four hours—they weren't taking any chances. Slate rolled the heavy metal door open on the loading bay, giving a wide berth to his team that marched the hooded men inside. The light was non-existent, and the musty smell of emptiness permeated the air.

Arctic cracked the neon phosphorus glow sticks and clipped one to each of the team's shirts, giving them a bit of illumination to navigate in the dark.

"That one stays up front," King pointed to Chet who was to be secured in the front of the warehouse. "I got something special in store for this one." King spoke to the crest of Trent's ear beneath the hood. Trent moaned a muffled sound and shook his head, flailing to pull away from King's grip. King tightened his hold, squeezing the muscle and flesh to the point of pain if Trent's wincing and smothered cry were any sign of his discomfort.

King pushed down on the back of Trent's neck, bowing him forward and leading him through the open space, back through a few divided corridors, coming to a halt in the back of the warehouse to an open but confined room, far from the others.

Arctic and T-BAR followed at a close pace making sure that King had cover and backup if needed. Arctic set down the large duffle when they entered the room. He got to work unpacking the low illumination LED lantern, setting it to a dim glow, and an umbra of shadows danced against the walls, matching the eerie sense of gloom, setting the stage for what was to come.

The room was sparse, void of furniture or crates, but had a few old pipes and lengths of wood strewn about here and there, and a large metal fifty-five-gallon drum sat in the far corner.

"Hand me the rope." King barked the words to Arctic, who dug in the duffle and pulled a length of braided, polypropylene rope from its keep. Trent flailed, but King had a death grip on him, probably bruising his flesh beneath his grip. Soon, a bruise would be the least of his worries.

"Settle down!" King shook Trent with jarring force.

T came alongside him, grabbing Trent's other arm and manhandling him into submission. "Hang him, boss?" T knew his words would frighten the ever-living shit out of Trent, but he was pointing to a large water main running along the low part of a header across the length of one section of the room.

Trent fought with all his might even though he was cuffed and hooded, and he was scared to his core.

Beneath his mask, T gave King a sinister grin as they dragged the fighting captive over to the main. T-BAR, standing at six-foot-four, easily looped the rope around the main a few times, securing it with a bow-line knot that could withstand thousands of pounds of pressure. With that knot, they were sure it would stay secure. King forced a struggling Trent over to T who grasped his cuffed hands. Trent let his legs go limp, collapsing backward against King.

T dropped the rope and grabbed Trent to his front, hoisting him in the air as King fastened his bound hands to the remaining rope.

"What the fuck! Did you just fuckin' piss on me!" T's roar was deafening. He stepped back from a now secure Trent, his hands above his head and his feet still able to touch the ground. Trent now had a darkened stain running down the front of his jeans.

T stared down at his own cargos; though black, they glinted with wetness in the low light of the room. He didn't say anything but jacked Trent in the side with a quick blow. "You fuckin' pissed on me, you piece of shit!" T fumed.

Trent let out a strangled grunt, trying to cradle himself as best he could without the use of his hands. Arctic handed T a towel. He took it without words and proceeded to clean the piss from his pants.

"Need you to leave." King's stone-cold voice struck a chord with the other two. It was a tone that rumbled from deep in his chest, his usual baritone timbre an octave lower, and his eyes spelling death.

"King—"

"Shut it. Out."

Arctic tried to intervene again, "We're not leaving you to—"

"I. Said. Out." King grabbed Arctic by the arm and shoved him towards the open door.

Arctic didn't take kindly to being handled by King. Boss or not, the guys had a code, and that code bound them as a team, as brothers. They'd exchanged words, but never came to blows, but Arctic was teetering on the edge waiting for King to come at him again.

T-BAR raised his concerns next, "King, we can't—"

"Plausible deniability. Out!" King met his friend's eyes as anger radiated out of every syllable.

"You know we don't separate—"

King cut him off, crowding his space. "Are you going to defy a direct order?"

"Yes." T and Arctic answered at the same time.

King was two inches shorter than T's six-foot-four inches and two-inches above Arctic's six-feet, so the guys were evenly matched in height, but King had mass on his side. He and T were almost the same age, so Arctic had the advantage of being a bit sprier, but all scales tipped in King's favor if it came to a brawl.

"I'm saying it for the last time because words won't follow. Leave. Now." The words were so cold they slid off the ice of his tongue.

Both men stood their ground, unmoving.

Just as King was going to force them from where they stood, both guys reluctantly turned for the door.

Before leaving, Arctic turned. "You know if you go beyond the line, it's not just career suicide for you, but prison time, and where will that put Mary?" He didn't wait for a response from his boss and best friend. He walked down the dark hallway, his green glow diminishing as he disappeared.

T stayed behind and leveled King with a stare. "You know he's not wrong."

King didn't reply, just stared at the wall over T's left shoulder.

"I'll leave if you say leave, but I do it as your employee, not as your friend."

King's eyes met his and King gave a chin lift, then turned, setting his eyes on his target hanging bound and shaking. He heard the door close behind him.

He expanded his lungs until they burned, then exhaled on a whoosh. He crossed the room to the drum in the corner. He rocked it, gauging its contents, and discovered it was half full.

Full and heavy.

He couldn't budge it from the floor, and it was too heavy to drag. Thinking for a moment, he heaved his weight behind it, tipping it on its rim. Slowly, he rolled it on its edge, across the room, and over to the door, letting it down with a heavy thud.

Nobody would be coming through that door. Or, if they tried, it would take a hell of a battering ram and time before it would breach.

Satisfied with the placement, King turned to the man he lusted to get vengeance on.

Trent Jones was in for a rough ride.

Arctic and T made their way to the front of the warehouse, meeting all questioning eyes on them.

T raised a fist and made a sign for danger that all of them read even in the dim light. Another lantern was glowing in the middle of the room. Chet sat zip-tied, wrists and ankles, to a wooden chair, something straight out of a 1950s office, heavy and sturdy. His mask was partially raised and he had wadded cloth stuffed in his mouth.

Following the two men's gaze, Trip answered, "Needed to keep him from spewing shit." Slate and Cy nodded in agreement. "Doesn't know when to keep his mouth shut."

Besides the wadding, Chet had a busted lip, gashed open, dripping a trail of blood onto the collar of his t-shirt.

Before T or Arctic could ask, Cy added, "Had a little run-in with my fist."

T had his eyes on Chet. "Gonna make him talk?"

"What the fuck smells like piss?" Trip screwed up his face and inhaled, looking around the area, trying to pinpoint the source of the odor. "Dude, is that you? You piss yourself?" He took a few steps to the side of T-BAR. "Fuck, I can smell you through this mask." Trip exaggerated a gag. By the way T was staring at him, he was not amused.

"Really? You think I'd piss myself?" T gave him an incredulous look and pointed to the wet stain soaked into the front of his cargos. "Fuckwad in the back can't control his bladder. Pissed himself when he collapsed against me."

Trip still had his face crinkled. "Damn, of all the people to piss on." It went without saying that besides King, T was the most volatile of the team when it came to tempers. "Does he still have his dick? Did you strangle him with it after you tore it off?"

Trip lightened the mood, and T belted out a laugh, just as Trip intended.

"His tiny pecker couldn't strangle a mouse." There was laughter from the guys. "Though, the kidney shot probably didn't help his incontinence."

"Alpha One is back there giving him a good workover." T motioned with his head to Chet, who sat stock still in the chair. He perked up at T-BAR's words of a beatdown being doled out to his friend.

The guys never used their monikers around targets. They kept their identity close to the vest and closed-lipped, not wanting to give any information to a target who may want to retaliate later.

T continued, "He's singing like a fuckin' canary."

It was a complete lie, but the psychological mind-fuck they could instill into Chet would make their workover of him a lot easier. He'd talk, one way or another. How easily was up to him.

Slate walked over to Chet, making his boots thump and clop with every step, stopping in front of his chair but saying nothing. The guys could walk as silently as the night wind, but letting their footfalls be heard was another way to keep Chet guessing as to what was coming next.

Another mind-fuck tactic.

Seeing Chet stiffen let them know it was working beautifully. Slate leaned forward into Chet's personal space, bracing his hands on the zip ties, and he slowly applied pressure against Chet's broken wrist, letting his weight settle. The excruciating scream, even muffled by the cloth gag, was loud in the silent room. He threw his hooded head back, and his body jerked.

Slate wasn't normally a vengeful guy. But he, as well as the others, had read Mary's medical records, and even though it wasn't Chet who had inflicted those wounds on her, he was in the company of the one who did. So, all-in-all, it was retribution by association.

Slate let up on the pressure and Chet vibrated in his chair, gasping around the wadding. The guys would bet that rivulets of tears were washing down his face.

"Okay, you slimy fuck...you got two choices. You're either going to talk to us, or we're gonna make you talk to us. One way is simple and easy, the other is painful and gruesome. The choice is yours. I'll save you the trouble and tell you option one is your best bet." Slate backed a few steps away from the chair, then veered a bit to the right, making his boots sound and reverberate in the emptiness of the warehouse with every step.

Chet tracked his every move, turning his head, listening to the direction of the sound.

Slate walked with feather-light steps, absolutely silent, rounding his footfalls and letting his knees take each impact from the ground and cushioning the soles of his feet.

He came up behind Chet and spoke into his left ear, startling the shit out of him. "Option two—fun for us, painful for you."

Arctic also had silently come around the chair and spoke into his right ear, again startling Chet so bad, Arctic had to pull back, not wanting to get headbutted in the face when Chet whipped his head to the right. "One way or the other, you're going to talk, so save yourself the trouble and the beatdown, and tell us what we need to know."

"Fouck ahou!" Even around the muffling of the gag, the guys heard his reply. He was scared shitless, but the man had balls. His bravado was tough, but just like all targets the smart-talk was always big at the beginning, but in the end, they always broke.

For once, the guys would love to have someone just take option one and be done with all the hoopla. It would save their fists and the target's face. But, sadly, there was never a person smart enough to take option one.

"Your friend's narcing you out right now...says the whole thing was your idea." Cy was talking out of his ass. He hadn't the slightest clue if Trent was blathering, or if he, too, was taking option two. "Tell us about the staged robbery."

Chet sat still in the chair, quiet as a church mouse.

"Come on, don't make us extract the info." T turned and walked to the duffle sitting off to the side, bent down and rummaged through it, and came up with what he was looking for. "Bare knuckles will tear everyone's flesh, but for our benefit, taped knuckles will only tear yours." The sound of the adhesive of the athletic tape pulling from its roll ripped through the quietness of the room.

Nobody missed the flinch as Chet bounced in his seat.

T bit the length of tape causing a seam to tear which became more unsettling in the confines of the situation. He tossed the roll to Trip who immediately tore another length. Then he tossed it to Slate then Cy. Each guy wrapped a band of tape covering the width of their knuckles, squeezing their fists to make sure the expanse stretched and dressed the bony protrusions, to cushion each of their blows.

T approached Chet, reached out, and removed the hood from his head, jerking it with the least amount of finesse he could muster. Even with the room dimly lit, Chet still winced and squeezed his eyes shut. His eyelids fluttered and slowly opened, and the guys knew exactly what he was seeing.

Five intimidating forces to be reckoned with.

The team was intimidating under normal circumstances, but with each one dressed head-to-toe in black, donning black, fitted face masks with only eyes and mouth visible, it would make the devil do a double-take.

They all knew the instant Chet realized the five guys in front of him weren't fucking around. His eyes widened and he pulled back into the chair, pulling frantically against his restraints. The broken wrist was a bonus for the guys, as Chet howled in agony behind the mouth gag, and the show hadn't even begun.

T bent to eye level. "Gonna remove the wadding. You're going to talk. You're going to tell us what we want to know. Capisce?"

Chet's eyes spewed venom.

T-BAR grasped the piece of cloth hanging from between Chet's broken and blood-stained lips when Chet made the moronic decision, jetting his head forward and gnashing his teeth together, catching T's index finger.

Before T could yelp, his right fist sailed across Chet's face, planting between his temple and jaw.

T-1, Chet-0.

Though T would have to wait to tell Chet the score when he regained consciousness.

Lights out until round two.

~

Hooded, Trent Jones swayed from his confines, still lashed to the water main.

"What did you do?" King's words were lethal. "Tell me what you did and who you hurt?" King yanked the strip of tape covering Trent's mouth, pulling it with such momentum, he swore every cell of flesh was ripped from his lips, instantly reddening and swelling the skin around it.

Trent let out a shriek. "Don't know what you're talking about, man. You got the wrong person!" Trent folded like a jackknife when King's fist collided with his gut, pulling the air from his lungs, momentarily paralyzing his diaphragm.

"Do not. Fuck. With me." The words came out in five short syllables. "Tell me. Who did you hurt? Who did you lay your motherfucking hands on?"

Trent begged with mournful pleas, "I don't know what you want. I didn't do anything."

"Think."

"I don't know!"

The whining reply curdled King's stomach. The son of a bitch would yield. King knew his will was weak and it was just a matter of time before he caved. It was a waiting game and King knew he'd come out the victor.

"I don't know, I don't know," he sniffled some more, "I don't remember."

"Maybe this will jog your memory." King jacked him in the jaw with such force he swung him from his wrists, separating his feet from the ground. He spun with the momentum transferring from King's fist. The sound of flesh hitting flesh was sickening, but it didn't faze King in the slightest.

Trent cried out. Blood, drool, and spit dangled from his mouth and hung from his draped hood.

King caught and stilled his pirouetting body, facing him front and center. "Talk."

"What the fuck, man? I don't know what you want. Who are you? Just tell me what you want."

"I want. The everfucking. Truth!" King paced to the far end of the room, then stalked back, returning to his starting point. "You don't think I know what you did? Who you had?" King stood so close to the piece of shit, he could smell the fear emanating off him.

"You got the wrong guy!"

His tearful plea didn't move an ounce of pity within King. "Oh, fuck no...I *know* I have the right guy. You don't think I found you? Knew where you were, what you were doing? You don't think I know who you are, who you're with? You think I found you and Chet Richardson by accident?"

King read the body language, restrained or not, the upward jerk of his head when King mentioned Chet by name had Trent worried. "This is your chance to save yourself."

No one could ever accuse King of being unfair. But on the job, he never gave an option or a chance for redemption. When taking out a tango at one-hundred meters, with a headshot or a double-tap, second chances weren't warranted. But, given the dire circumstances of those occasions, those receiving double-taps weren't in the running for negotiation. Those options would either come at the Pearly Gates or the bowels of Hell. King was neither judge nor jury. He was just the delivery man.

King set the option for Trent to redeem himself and tell him exactly what he wanted to know before taking things to the next level.

"This is your chance to save yourself. Do you want to go to jail, do your time, maybe six months, get three-squares-a-day? Or, do you want to go to the hospital, spend your time healing, and drinking your three-squares through a straw for six months? Your choice."

Trent hung motionless. Only his whimpers broke the silent air. Suddenly, Trent grew a pair of brass balls. "You're not such a tough guy." His quivering vocals gave him away. "I could kick your ass if I wasn't hung here like a slab of meat. If I was able to see. Take this hood off and untie me, and it'll be you on the receiving end of my fists."

King had to give the guy credit. Not for his asinine statement, which was complete bullshit and he knew Trent knew it, but he'd give him kudos on having the balls to step to a guy who was twice the size in weight and mass. Trent's head may have been hooded now, but he'd gotten a damn good look at the team when they stormed the pawnshop. Trent shit his pants there, pissed them here, and still he was mouthing off.

King didn't know if he was truly mentally defective, lacking in intelligence and judgment, or if he was just a complete fucking idiot. King was guessing the latter.

King decided to grant his request. "You're correct." His words were measured, calm, laden with his rich, deep, baritone timbre. "I don't fight defenseless men."

He got within a hair's breadth of Trent, not touching him but making his presence known, keeping himself calm and controlled, his railed demeanor from earlier, gone. This demeanor took on a much more sinister vibe because of its calm coolness. "I know you, Trent." It was the first time King used his name. Trent went stock still. "See, you don't know me, but, I know you. You think I'm bluffing." King paused. "You play a hero. You play soldier with your friends. Get all tough-guy, become a badass in a virtual world. You fight ghosts, hunt demons, become the warrior of virtual war because you're too spineless to man-up and do the real thing. Then, you trick your mind. The lines are blurred in your reality. You fight," he corrected himself, "no, beat on defenseless women."

Trent started to shake his head.

King pushed on. "You don't think I know where you got your shit at the pawn store? Your father's ring. Your mother's ring. The gun from the bedroom safe. You don't think I know you set up the staged robbery at 357 North Crescent Street?"

King grabbed him by the throat and squeezing with an upward lift, sent Trent tiptoeing to steady himself and remain in contact with the ground. "This feel familiar?" His calm words seethed. "You lay your hands on someone like this? Think hard. All that blood rushing to your brain should give you good reason to think."

Trent gurgled beneath his hood.

"Feel your lungs burn? Feel your heart race, beating out of your chest? Feel the panic that's rising in your veins? The desperation swelling in your soul? How's it feel? You do this to someone? Think hard."

Trent tried to flail but couldn't.

"You think you're fuckin' with an amateur?" King let go of his throat. Trent's head fell, gasping. "See, unlike you, I don't *play* soldier. I don't have to pretend to rid the world of wretched souls. The Devil and the Maker know me. They know who I send them. I don't give pieces of shit like you a slap on the wrist like the cops you deal with. I don't give second chances to allow you to fuck up again. Right now, I'm your judge and jury." King was in operator mode. "I need you to tell me, who pulled the staged robbery? Who stole the safe? I need a name."

Trent gasped in gulps of air while wheezing. "Fuck you, man! I'm still tied."

"Like I said, I don't fight defenseless men. You need to make the choice…and, the choice is yours, and yours alone. You give me a name, I cut you free. You clam up, I pry it out of you. And, you take the chance of walking out, wheeling out, or bagged and rolled out."

"Fuck you! You ain't gonna kill me. There's laws."

King couldn't believe the stupidity of Mary's brother. "What? The same laws you disregard? The ones that don't pertain to you? You don't think I'd offer you up on a platter to the nearest police station? News flash, they'll gladly interrogate you. They have ways of making people sing. Just 'cuz I drop you at the station, doesn't mean they book you upon arrival. No, see, I know people," he leaned into him, "and they know me. I also know the streets. I'll gladly drop you in a neighborhood, say, 12th and Lexington?"

Trent straightened. The slight shake of his head wasn't missed.

"I know people want you. I know people that are looking for you. So, last. Chance. What'll it be? Me? The police? Or, a gurney? Either way, it doesn't bode well for you. You either give *me* a name, or you go to the police and give them a name, then when they find your friends, all your little wannabe-hero friends, they'll know they have a snitch amongst them."

Trent started to shiver.

"There's no honor among thieves." It gave King satisfaction to know he was mind-fucking him. "Tsk, tsk, tsk. That's not good," he paused for effect, "is it?"

Still, Trent ran his mouth, not smart enough to know King wasn't fucking around. "I ain't scared of you. If I wasn't tied, I'd whip your ass, old man. You're a chump! Gotta hit me when I can't defend myself. You' pathetic. You' a joke."

King stepped forward and pulled the hood from Trent's head. The light caused him to squint, but within a minute, he fully opened his eyes. He stared at King who was still masked in the black fitted head covering. King pulled out his KABAR.

Suddenly those brass balls of Trent's crawled back up his asshole because he started to stutter and stammer. "Whad'ya doin' man? What'cha going to do with that?"

"I'm freeing a defenseless man. You talk a big game of shit. Time to put your money where your mouth is. You and me. Man to man.

Mano a mano. Winner takes all. You whip me, you walk. I whip you, you talk."

King reached up to cut the ties, "I'm freeing you, but you run, you got five more of me waiting outside that door. Pick your poison.

King cut the rope securing Trent's zip-tied hands to the water main and watched as he fell to the ground. King knew from experience his arms had gone numb a long time ago and his shoulders would burn like they were torn from their sockets.

Trent wallowed in agony as the blood rushed back into his extremities. While he was still no threat, too distracted by the pain and anguish, King cut the zip ties binding his hands. He was no longer bound.

King sheathed his KABAR and took a hold of Trent by the hair, wrenching his neck, forcing him to look up at him.

"Your sister...is mine." Trent's shock mixed with confusion. "You laid your filthy, disgusting, vile hands on her. You assaulted her, and you violated her." King felt a flame ignite within him...a raging, blazing inferno that couldn't be extinguished. Though it was impossible, King knew his deep blue eyes were blackening with death. "You punched her. You kicked her. You bludgeoned her. You bruised her, and you hospitalized her." His words were flooded with hatred. "You used her. You stole from her. You damaged her. You destroyed her." He shook with uncontrolled rage, unlike any he'd ever felt. "You took what wasn't yours. And, finally, you broke her."

Slowly, King pulled the covering from his own head, revealing his identity, something he'd never done before on an op. He wanted to let Trent see who was going to take his pound of flesh. Know who was going to break his soul. Who was going to *take* his soul. "I don't play. I banish. I slay. I kill. Without reservation. Without regret."

With that, King stood, unstrapped the Velcro from his Kevlar vest, removed his plate carrier, turning and placing it on the fifty-five-gallon drum barricading the door. Then, he unholstered his Sig, placing it beneath his vest, along with the stolen pistol from his side pocket and his unsheathed KABAR. What King didn't see was Trent still laying on the ground glaring daggers at his back.

King wasn't leaving without a name and the identities of anyone else involved in the robbery. Trent wasn't going to the police or jail...not back to the streets. King wanted vengeance, readied himself for his indelible mark.

Seven men would leave and walk out when dawn broke, but only one of them would leave on a gurney.

~

Chet woke with a bitch of a headache.

"Welcome back, Sleeping Beauty." Trip quipped as the guys laughed.

Chet groaned and worked his jaw. "Fuck you, assholes!"

"Not a good way to start your wake-up call." T squeezed the pressure point between Chet's trapezius muscle and his collarbone. He dug his thumb deep into the hollow of his clavicle and the meat of his neck, sending excruciating pain down the side of Chet's body. He winced and yelled out.

"We need a name." More pressure. "Who busted the house with you? Who staged the break-in and stole the safe?"

Chet continued to howl.

"This could end quickly," Cy said nonchalantly. "Otherwise, we have all night," then added, "and... all day, so really, it's your call."

"Your friend back there," Slate motioned with his head to the back of the warehouse, "he's narcing you out right now. Says the whole thing was your idea, and he has an airtight alibi."

"Fuck you! Fuck him!" Chet screamed as T tightened his hold on the pressure points. "I gave him that fuckin' alibi!"

Bingo. They'd struck a nerve.

He screamed like a little bitch, tears welling in his eyes. T let up, and Chet slumped forward hanging his head in relief. It would be short-lived.

Chet continued, "His alibi is bullshit! I set up an interview that morning for him with my uncle to give him an airtight alibi." His breathing was choppy. "Made sure he was out of the house...before we busted the place."

"Well, not according to him." T knew all he had to do is keep the ruse up, and this pissant would spill his guts. "He's rolling on you all over the place. Says you were the mastermind. Our friend's taping his confession. When they're done, we're rollin' him to the station so he can give his statement in writing, and he'll walk tonight."

Chet fumed.

Arctic chimed in, "You don't know who you messed with. The woman that you hit, gonna be your downfall."

"I didn't hit no woman!" Chet was folding like a deck of cards.

T stepped forward, causing Chet to push back in the chair, "Your word against his. His is on tape. He'll be rolling in first. You can either help us out or when we roll you downtown, it's going to be a whole different showdown with the boys in blue."

"No way is that cocksucker rolling first."

"Meaning?" Trip questioned from behind him.

"You guys some type of spooks? Ghosts?"

The five men were like lumberjacks. Lumberjacks on steroids. With a glandular defect. How they floated when they walked...Chet had no clue.

"T-BAR bent eye level, snapping his fingers in front of Chet. "Hey, fuckwad, focus."

Chet glared at T, which wasn't his wisest move.

"Well?" T got in his personal space, placing his hand on his tortured shoulder.

"Please...No! I'll talk."

"Gotta name names." Slate added.

Chet nodded vigorously, and T removed his hand. "I want proof."

None of the guys broke their stoic facade.

"Proof?" Arctic questioned.

"Yeah, proof for the police, so you assholes can't go back on your word and roll him first. I want shit recorded." He threw his head sideways towards the back room, then winced as the residual pain from the skull punch and Vulcan grip T-BAR gifted him earlier.

Chet was dumber than a bag of hammers, requesting his own confession be taped. For a gangbanger living on the streets, he had no street smarts. He was a weasel. Willing to roll on anyone just to save his sorry ass and not have to do more time than if he was fingered as the mastermind of grand larceny and first-degree burglary, and that would turn into a violent felony, since Mary was in the home at the time it was tossed. A felony, add that to grave assault, along with his priors, would put him in prison for twenty-five or more. Chet probably figured he could get a plea deal if he rolled on Trent.

"Done." Slate motioned to Cy, who went to the duffle and got a small video recorder.

Cy pushed a few buttons and announced to the room, "Rolling."

And, with that, Chet Richardson laid out the plan, plot, mission, and execution on a fucking silver platter.

∽

While the guys up front were finding out how Trent staged the robbery to get money for drugs, and to pay off a scheme he'd been skimming from the top, King was in the back fighting to hold onto life.

After Trent lifted himself from the floor, shaking his arms out, trying to get circulation back into them, King squared off, readying himself for the shit stain to make a move.

It was actually quite comical, King's six-foot-two, the two-hundred-forty-pound muscled mass frame was mammoth compared to Trent's slender five-ten, one-hundred-seventy-five-pound smooth-muscled body. It was a joke he would even attempt to fight his way out of going to the police. If this thirty-two-year-old punk could get any licks in and take King down, it would have to be by murder. No way in hell was this thug going to take down a skilled, trained, former Delta operator. King may be thirty-eight, but he was a damn good hand-to-hand fighter. Actually, it was his forte.

Trent may play soldier boy on his Xbox gaming console, talking shit with his fellow gamers and wannabe warriors over headsets they thought were real comms, but he had none of the attributes of an actual soldier. King didn't even think he could PT him without killing him halfway through the morning five-mile run.

King knew he'd have him talking by the end of this ridiculous circus act, in which they were center ring and would soon have the names of the others involved. By daybreak, these fuckwads would be behind bars, and he would be in bed with Mary.

The image had him off-guard, and he wasn't quite ready when Trent threw the first punch, trying to land a jab with his left hand, followed with a dominant right hook, and landing it with all his might and force behind it.

It was child's play for King, who sheltered up, raising his left hand to protect his face, then pulled back for the jab, and shelled up for the body shot that followed. It was a glancing blow across his abdomen, and Trent's fists were like a toddler's with barely any weight behind them. It felt more like a weak pummeling than a fierce fighting blow.

King played defense, being more amused than going into survival mode, which was standard MO when engaged in hand-to-hand combat in the field.

Next came the pathetic attempt of an untrained fighter, or "movie fighters" as the team called them. Big, dramatic, drawn-out moves an opponent could see coming from a mile away. Like when a Western cowboy gets shot in the stomach and flies twenty feet back through the plate-glass window of the Ol' Town Saloon. Yup, this was what King was up against. If real-life slow-mo was possible, this would be Trent's Oscar-winning moment.

King braced as Trent bull-rushed him, head down, charging at him, as if King were a matador waving a red cape. Barreling into King's center and grabbing him around the waist in an attempt to knock him off his feet and onto the floor was an ill-fated attempt with lackluster flare. King easily countered the attack by stripping him away, pushing down on his shoulder, and shoving his arms away. King redirected his own body using momentum to hip throw Trent into the concrete wall behind them. It was a hard fall, but adrenaline is a funny thing when rage ensues. And Trent was enraged. King, on the other hand, was ready and waiting.

Trent came at him, again, and King had to give him gusto. He wasn't a quitter. A loser, yes; but a quitter, no. King would give him props. And like an untrained fighter, he came at King with the same move, head down, roaring like a bull, and King gladly waved his cape and charted the unknown territory of Trent's fighting style. He would be a conquistador and conquering hero of this fight.

Again, King pushed him down to one knee, and Trent braced himself with his hand trying to catch the air into his lungs he'd exerted in his folly. He had moxie and got back up a third time. King was going to get into the fight and put an end to Trent's misery, which was just sad at this point.

Since the bull-rush didn't work, Trent came at him with a straight punch, aimed for King's left jaw, but King anticipated the horrific attempt and deflected, delivering a crushing stomach blow, knocking Trent back and clutching his stomach. King thought the fight was done, but Trent lunged forward and tried to grapple King into a headlock. King had four inches of height on him, so it was a miserable, failed attempt. King blasted him with an uppercut to the jaw, hard enough that King felt Trent's clenched jaw resonate throughout his balled fist.

Fuck that hurt.

King shook his hand to diminish the sting.

To King's astonishment, Trent got up, spitting blood from his mouth along with a partial tooth. If he wanted more of an ass beating, King would gladly oblige.

Trent was losing steam, tiring out, but he came at King with half-assed momentum, plowing into him. King pivoted his hip into

Trent's, and with an easy dip, sent him onto the concrete floor behind him. Trent landed with a sickening thud, and it viciously spurred King on. If Trent wanted a fight, King had it in him. No more pussy-footing around. Anger grew within him, thinking of all Mary was put through at the hands of this piece of shit, cocksucker! There was the inferno that stoked itself with the visions of Mary, bruised and battered, helpless to defend herself, taking the brunt of her brother's fists, kicks, punches, and whatever else this cowardly ass-fuck dealt out.

"Fuuuccckk!" King's bellow exploded from his chest.

Trent laid on the ground like a candy-ass.

"Get up!" King's words weren't conscious. They rose from the depths of the unknown, a place of delirium and violent hostility, holdings from within him he didn't know existed. His temper piqued and consumed him. Hot-tempered rage seared his soul.

"Get the fuck up!" King landed a boot to Trent's head and the heavy, dull, sickening, thud of his boot making contact scourged a fever in him that couldn't be quenched.

Trent covered his skull and King raged, bent over, and picked him up by his hair.

Mary.

King ignored the vision.

"I said. *Get. The fuck. Up. You motherfuckin' piece of shit!*" King roared at the top of his lungs.

Mercy.

Don't take his heartbeat.

Not now. Why now? King shook the words from his thoughts and only had one mindset. Only one person was walking out of this room. King would bet his life on it.

Mary may have asked for mercy, but King would willingly, and ungrudgingly, mark his soul. Eternity be damned. Nothing would pull him back from the brink. Not even Mary's mournful pleas.

King wanted to mark every inch of Trent Jones' body with the exact bruises, and welts, and fractures, and contusions, and cuts that Mary wore in terror and agony. He wanted to inflict every tear Mary cried into the son-of-a-bitch's skull.

One faceplant to the concrete and his skull would crack and fracture, sending shards of bone and fragments of skull into his brain. King knew many ways to kill a man, but nothing would be more satisfying than feeling Trent's life end, literally, in his hands. *By* his hands.

Trent crashed, landing blows against King's steel body, but he felt none of them. He was numb with the wrath and fury overtaking him.

King reared Trent's head back, making sure he had eye contact, catching the depths of his soul before his rapture claimed him. He wanted to see the fear of death in him, claiming the last few seconds of his life here on earth. King wanted Trent to know who was sending his soul to the underworld.

Trent's eyes flared, filled with terror, and it put a euphoric high in King's heart.

Adrenaline surging, Trent took one more swing, a Hail Mary if one was ever needed, and his fist collided with King. And it held. Fisting the flesh in his clutch.

King froze as the blow stifled his breath. He fell to his knees, loosening the hold of Trent's hair, dropping his grip, and cradling his balls.

King felt the impact, which was odd, considering he was removed from all sense of his body. Then, came the implosion of his testicle.

Mutilated.

Mangled.

Maimed.

Obliterated.

Crippled to the world around him.

Reality ceasing to exist.

For a moment, it was surreal. Then, the explosion of pain erupted, radiating throughout every fiber of his being.

Pain. Blinding.

He gasped.

He was denied breath.

The hollowing pit in his pelvis fell and the pain of the fires of hell was the only thing that filled him.

Hellaciously excruciating pain.

Then, terror set in.

He lost sight of his target as black spots formed in front of him. He held himself with his free hand, inches from the ground.

Darkness encroached.

Stay. Aware.

Be. Alert.

Self-preservation.

Angels danced in his vision, skirting the edges as things blurred and began to tunnel.

White, blinding pain.

Hollow ringing in his ears.

Mind-shattering pain convulsing his body.

Spasm. Spasms. Uncontrollable.

Heart racing. Erratic.

Frantic throbbing as his muscles contracted. His jaw tightened, seizing him.

Bang.

Bang.

Bang.

Whiteness.

Blackness.

Lost.

Timeless.

Loss.

Mary.

Mary.

Sweet, Mary.

Darkness.

Lifeless.

Death.

~

Trent squeezed with all his might. *Pop.* The burst in his clenched fist was gruesome. He knew what it was. It was his saving grace.

King's grip on his hair loosened, freeing him from what he knew was certain death. He saw it in King's eyes. The cold, lifeless, depths of no mercy. No forgiveness. No atonement. Death on arrival.

King crouched.

Trent scrambled, scurrying like a crab beneath him to get away. He didn't stop. He kept moving backward, waiting for the salvation of the wall to meet his back, and he'd know he was far enough away from King. Out of the snares of hell. His hand slipped and rolled off a pipe laying in his pathway.

A pipe. A saving grace.

Trent grasped the two-inch pipe in his trembling hands, fumbling so that he wasn't sure if he could wield it. His hands didn't fully encircle it, the width of a baseball bat, but he gripped it with all his might.

King clutched himself, oblivious to his surroundings, not even noticing when Trent came around, King's back exposed to him.

Trent had the pipe in the air before he knew it, and he felt the crushing blow as it came down over King's back. His head fell, and his body crumpled.

Frenzied banging came from the other side of the door.

Fuck! Trent panicked and terror rushed through him.

The barrel. The barrel blocked the door. One way in. Only one way out. He was fucked if the door was breached.

He dropped the pipe and, mindlessly, Trent tried to push the unmovable barrel against the door, hoping his futile efforts would keep the group of men from entering. It didn't budge.

They have guns. I'm dead. It's over.

He spotted the Kevlar vest King wore earlier. *It could save him.* The moment the door would give way, he'd be dead. But, he had a chance. A saving grace.

He scrambled, reaching for the vest, not having the first clue how to wear it, secure it, or strap it in place. It was heavy. It had to weigh ten pounds if not a little more. He lifted it from the barrel's lid and then a clattering.

Did one of the protective plates fall out? Would it still save him?

A glint of steel peeked from under the vest. Cold, metal, cobalt blue. A gun. King's gun. Another saving grace.

With shaking hands he lifted the vest over his head, slipping it over his torso. It was too big. It could fit a tree trunk. Still, Trent grabbed the Velcro flaps beneath his arm and fastened them, pulling them as tight as he could. It was still too big, but it would have to do.

The banging was incessant. Frantic. The door would breach in a matter of seconds.

King groaned from his place on the floor but didn't move. Blood trickled from his mouth and ears. His beard absorbed the blood pooling on the cold concrete.

Trent raced. *The gun.* He had to get the gun.

He palmed the grip. It was too large for his hand, so he grasped it with both, aiming at the door. Whoever entered first would eat lead. No mercy.

He checked the chamber, seeing there was one hot—live and ready to rip. He backed around King and trained his sights on the door.

Barrages of thumps hit the door. The casing of the frame splintered. The immovable barrel rocked. They were coming. He was waiting.

The door broke. The barrel fell. The room exploded.

A hail of gunfire erupted, the sound deafening in the emptiness. One minute the door was standing, the next it wasn't there. It didn't fall down. It was obliterated.

Trent knew he had to save himself. He had one last saving grace. King. He positioned the gun on King. Helpless, lifeless, bleeding in front of him.

Bang.

Bang.

Bang.

Three shots.

His finger pulled against the wall of the trigger.

Bang.

Bang.

Bang.

Then, more rang in the air.

Bang. Bang.

Bang. Bang. Bang.

Blood pooled in his throat and he couldn't swallow it back. He was gurgling.

Tang.

Copper.

Metal.

Bang. Bang. Bang. Bang.

Endless shots followed.

Silence.

Darkness.

Death.

For both.

The sinful had fallen.

And so had the King.

CHAPTER 17

Mary jackknifed in bed, pools of sweat covering her body. Her heart was racing, beating out of her chest. Something was wrong. She checked the clock on the nightstand. Three a.m., Devil's Hour. When Mary was little, Trent tortured her with stories, scaring her half to death, about the three-a.m. hour, the hour when the devil was at his strongest. She turned on the bedside lamp, hiding the shadows in the room. She couldn't catch her breath. Something was gravely wrong.

King. Was it a dream or a premonition? Something was wrong with King.

Reaching for her phone, she checked for any incoming messages. There was one. Her heart gave a jolt. *Was it good? Was it something bad?* Her heart contracted, still racing. Her finger hovered over the message. It was King's contact, and an instant smile widened her face. It was the same smile in the picture she was looking at. Mary and King at supper. She was nestled perfectly into the crook of his arm, held tightly to his side. King's eyes danced as the light hit them just so. He was right, she did look okay. She thought her eyes would be swollen with mascara blackening her reddened, blotchy face. But it wasn't the case in the least. She stared at the two of them. They looked good together. Better than good. They fit together.

There was a message along with the picture.

KING: *If ever two souls were meant to collide, this would be the Big Bang.*

. . .

Mary drew the phone to her chest, and her heart rate spiked and was overridden with happiness. She pulled back to look at the rest of the message.

KING: *Never took a selfie before, so my virgin attempt turned out to be stellar! Hope this warms your soul to the depths that it warms mine. Keep well, Sugar. Be back in a bit.*

He ended it with a heart and smiley emoji. She smiled at the fact that big, hulking King used emojis. She checked the timestamp. It was sent after their last text, the one telling her he was going dark. She wished she would've heard the incoming text, so she could've sent him a reply back.

She wanted to message back now, tell him she was thinking of him, and he needed to be safe, but that would be needy. With the cursor lingering, waiting for her to begin typing, she waited. The temptation to type coursed through her. *No. You can't bother him.*

Mary's conscience was right, but she didn't agree. Her fingers hovered. *He won't respond.* Her thoughts were right. He wouldn't respond. Couldn't respond.

What if everything's all right, and then her message would let him know she was worried about him? She couldn't divide his attention. He needed to be focused on whatever mission he was on. Any distraction could spell certain death if he weren't one-hundred percent on task.

A flood of dread came over her. Something was wrong. She knew it to the marrow of her bones.

She tapped the picture, setting it to her home screen. Seeing it appear as her background sent shivers of want down her spine. At first, she thought it was a shiver of joy, but as she grew cold, she realized it was a shiver of concern. Of fright. The same fright she used to experience when Trent tortured her with stories of Devil's Hour.

She set her phone next to her pillow and reached for the lamp. She scanned the room looking for demons that weren't there. As soon as the lights were off, the shadows would haunt her. Quickly, she turned the switch and the room filled into darkness and grey shadows. She drew the covers tight around her neck sealing her in protection.

She was letting her mind get the best of her. Everything would be okay once the morning light came.

~

A shriek of terror echoed from the corridor where King had taken Trent. All the guys froze at the bloodcurdling scream, and in a flash, each man ran for the hallway, guns drawn, ready to intervene. Whether it was King or Trent who needed their help, they couldn't sit idly by while the screams of death came from within the building.

T-BAR and Trip made it to the door first, followed by Slate, Arctic, and Cy. T grabbed the doorknob and pushed. The door didn't budge. He tried again, putting his shoulder into it, but again, it was futile.

With his wrapped fist, he beat on the door, "King, open the fuck up!" T continued to bang as Trip put his shoulder into the door ending with the same result as his teammate.

"What the fuck!" Slate yelled while waiting for the door to cave.

"King! Open the fuckin' door!" T bellowed while continuing to bang.

Trip stepped back and Cy picked up where he left off, repeatedly ramming his shoulder into the door. The door itself was jarring open with every drive, but something was impeding their attempts. Something behind the door blocked their entry.

Arctic gave out a whistle, one they used in times of distress. It was a lifesaver in the field, so it would serve the same purpose now. When the whistle wasn't returned, they knew things were bad for King.

"King, yell if you hear us!" T bellowed through the door frame.

When no response came, they all knew whatever was happening on the other side of the door wasn't going to be pretty.

"*Kiiiing!*" T yelled once more.

"We gotta breach this motherfucker! Step aside," Arctic said from behind the guys. Everyone stepped to the side as much as the hallway would allow.

Arctic raised his Sig and let the rounds fly, emptying six shots into the latch and door frame.

T raised his fist and Arctic lowered his pistol but didn't reholster it. Still, the door wouldn't open when T slammed against it. Together, T and Trip threw their combined weight into the door, driving the barrel behind it over onto its side, and the door exploded into splinters.

Each man entered with hellfire, pistols drawn, prepared for anything.

But, the *anything* they weren't prepared for was seeing Trent standing over an unmoving King with a pistol pointed at his back. A battery of gunfire rang out, as each of Hellforce's men emptied their magazines. But, it wasn't quite quick enough to stop Trent from squeezing off three rounds, before he fell to the ground.

∿

Everything happened in a split second. All hell broke loose in a shit storm of tragedy.

T-BAR was the first to breach the door, followed by Trip, Cy, Slate, and Arctic. They raised their pistols, taking aim at Trent as he fired into King's back point-blank. Each of King's teammates fired at Trent, but he managed to squeeze off two more rounds before he crumpled to the ground.

"I'm hit!" Trip yelled through gritted teeth. He fell to the side holding his right thigh, applying pressure as blood seeped through his black pants and onto the concrete beneath him.

"I'm hit!" Cy brought his hand to his neck where crimson blood oozed between his fingers.

Slate ran for King. "Get my fucking med bag!" He whipped off his face mask and tore at the fabric of King's shirt, ripping it down his back, exposing a bleeding entry wound to the left of his spine. Slate applied pressure with one hand, and with the other reached into his cargo pocket and pulled out a packaged roll of clot cloth.

"Where's that fucking bag!" he roared, and ripped the sterile packaging with his teeth. He unrolled a large swath of gauze from the roll, applying it to the bleeding wound on King's back. He pushed the gauze hard and deep into King's wound, packing it tight, but King didn't stir, sending Slate's warning bells screaming. His adrenaline soared to new heights as he waited for his kit. *Come on King, Fuckin' move!*

"King! King! Come on buddy...talk to me!" Slate yelled to his friend, mentor, and boss, but no response came. His hands were covered in King's blood. The sticky, warm, and viscous wetness coated them.

He looked up to see Trip using a tourniquet he'd pulled from his pocket, wrapping it around his upper thigh. T was bent over Cy, lying on his back with his hand clutching the left side of his neck. T applied pressure on top of Cy's hand with his own.

"SITREP!" Slate called out, waiting for Arctic to get back.

"Through and through." Trip seethed.

"Just a graze," T reported to the room.

Slate was about to yell again, but Arctic rounded the door with the medkit in hand. Arctic didn't stop running until he slid onto his knees next to Slate.

"What do you need?" Arctic was hyper-focused on helping King.

"More gauze."

Arctic dug into the medkit and pulled out another roll, ripped open the package, and unrolled it in the process. Handing it to Slate, he held pressure on the blood-soaked gauze already packed into King's bleeding wound.

Slate checked for a pulse on King. "No pulse. We need to turn him over."

"He's got a spinal wound," Arctic pointed out.

"It'll be damned," Slate said, "We need to get him rolled." Just as in the field, medical attention had to be addressed on the direst of wounds and triaged as such. Even with King having a bullet close to his spine, they needed to take the chance to roll him so they could start to revive him.

Slowly and carefully, they rolled him to his back. Slate tore the front of King's tee hoping to find an exit wound but came up empty.

"Fuck! No exit," Slate told no one in particular.

T finished wrapping Cypher's neck and was working on wrapping Trip's thigh when Cy came up beside them. "What can I do?"

Both Slate and Arctic were working on King. Slate frantically rubbed his knuckles against King's sternum trying to elicit a response.

Nothing.

Slate checked for a pulse.

None.

Slate started chest compressions as Arctic held King's head and breathed for him.

"Make the call." Arctic's voice was steady, addressing Cy.

"On it." Cy pulled a burner phone from his pocket and dialed.

T rushed over, and before he could ask, Arctic directed him, "Get on Chet. Make sure he hasn't figured out a way to get gone." T turned on his heels and sprinted out of the room.

Trip limped over, carrying himself without assistance, and stood sentry, ready to help if asked.

"You good, man?" Arctic asked without looking up.

"Five-by-five." Trip replied, though the excruciating pain could be heard in this voice.

Slate spoke with heavy breaths while he continued compressions on King, "We need to get him moved, now."

King's color was blanching and Slate was deep in his blood, even though the clotting cloth was drenched.

Cy pocketed his phone. "Clean-up crew ETA, one-zero mikes."

"In the clear?" Arctic asked Cy.

"Accepted."

"Expecting us?"

"Roger," Cy answered again.

"Let's move, boys."

$\approx$

Mary kept her eyes closed even as she fought to fall asleep. Bile churned in her stomach, and she just couldn't shake the imminent feeling of doom plaguing her. *Is it always going to be like this each time he leaves?* The thought crossed Mary's mind. *It's just because it's the first time.* She tried to reassure herself this was normal but couldn't pass the belief it was just a case of missing King. She replayed the conversation she and Ember had before they turned into bed.

"I'd like a guarantee they'll be okay, but I know that can't come from King or any of the guys." Mary sat back, wedging herself in the corner of the couch and rubbing her thumb over her cell phone as if it would soothe the words King sent about going dark.

"Can't promise anything. But, if it makes it easier, they're a great team and have each other's six."

Always a first time. The words echoed in Mary's mind, but she didn't voice them out loud, not wanting to jinx the guys or their mission.

Both Ember and Mary sat in silence, neither needing to say what they were feeling. Each knew the other was processing the fact that the guys were willingly putting themself in danger and willing to accept the consequences of what each mission could ultimately bring.

"There has to be a little bit of crazy to be a special forces operator, don't you think?" The words spilled from Mary's mouth before she could think better about the question.

Ember threw her head back and let out a chortle. "Can't get any crazier than that bunch." Her laughter died a bit, "But, in all seriousness, what you may perceive as crazy, we in the Army see as courage...as fortitude."

She readjusted in the oversized armchair, bringing her feet underneath herself. "I guess resilience is a better term. Each soldier has to have a certain degree of brazenness and a bit of ego. It's mandatory if you're going to win. Being a little egotistical isn't a bad thing, but that needs to be there to know you're better than the enemy, otherwise you're no good to yourself or your team."

Mary thought about that and knew Ember was right. "Did Slate say where they were headed?" Mary knew she shouldn't ask, but this was all new to her and she couldn't keep the question from surfacing. She quickly second-guessed herself. "No. Don't answer that." Mary held up her hand. "Sorry. I shouldn't have asked."

Ember smiled, "Don't be sorry. No, he didn't say. And, even if he could, he wouldn't, because he knows I'd be scouring the internet and every news website and broadcast while he was gone. Believe me. Not knowing is a blessing in itself."

Mary pondered that. Knowing where King was would ease her mind in the short-term, but in the long run, it didn't matter if she knew. It wouldn't make missing him any easier. Wouldn't make the time apart any shorter. And, it would drive her crazy if she heard bad reports on the news about the country he was in, and then she'd spend her time worrying if he didn't return right away. It *was* a blessing, better she didn't know.

"The first time is always the hardest." Ember tried to reassure Mary. "I remember the first time Eli got deployed."

Mary had to mentally keep track of the guy's names and their monikers. She called them by their silly nicknames. They could be used interchangeably, she guessed, but only Ember ever called Slate by his given name, Eli.

"It was right after he joined...right out of high school. I just about worried myself to an ulcer thinking of all the terrible things that could happen or go wrong while he was away. It was the longest and worst nine months of my life. Then, when he was back stateside for a couple of weeks to visit his momma and see my folks, he was distant and I only got to see him a few days between my college class schedule, before he returned to his base and deployed again." Ember recessed herself into the memory, pulling out of current space and time. "It was really awful." The words were almost whispered.

Both women sat there, not adding to the conversation, reflecting on their own circumstances.

Mary broke first. "I can't imagine if anything happened to King." The words choked her. "I mean, we've only gotten to know each other, and it's been such a short time, but..." she blushed and couldn't keep the smile from her face.

"You love him." Ember's statement caught Mary off-guard. "If what you told me about your little truck extravaganza and oohlala has King feeling the same, you're in good hands."

Ember's description of what went down in King's truck made Mary double over in laughter. So much, that tears gathered in the corners of her eyes. Ember joined in.

When the two recovered, Ember's words soothed Mary's soul. "I'm happy for you. King deserves to have a good woman by his side. He's a damn good man." She sobered, "And, if his happiness is as happy as your happiness, that's all I can wish for him."

The two sat and talked a bit more about the guys and the friend-ships Ember had built with each of them, then the night came to a close.

"Gonna head to bed." Ember stood and stretched, her jammas raised at the waist, and her fit and tone slender frame showed beneath them.

Mary hoped her curves wouldn't protrude from her clothing, not that her disheveled garments after King's truck hadn't shown her too-curvy figure.

"Help yourself to anything to eat and keep the tableside lamp on when you head to bed." She pointed to the lamp beside the couch.

"Thanks." Mary didn't know how much sleep she'd be getting. Although she told herself not to worry about King and the boys, the pit in her stomach wouldn't make sleep an easy feat.

Which led her to this moment. She tossed and turned, readjusted her blankets, and fluffed her pillow, all in defeat. Sleep wasn't coming.

She looked to the nightstand. Three-thirty am. A new sense of dread rose in her stomach. *He's all right. You can't keep thinking the worst. He's got his team at his back. Everything's going to be okay.* The pep talk did nothing to soothe her harried nerves. She knew if she continued on this path, the bile would chew an ulcer in her stomach by morning's light.

Stop! Just stop! Her chastisement went unheeded. Anxiety flooded her veins. She knew something was wrong. This was more than just missing King. She knew it deep in her bones, to the depths of her soul, that something was amiss.

King had become her soulmate, somehow it happened even in the short time they'd gotten to know each other. Something was desperately wrong with her soul, which could only mean that King's soul was hurting, too.

She couldn't ignore it. She had to tell someone. *Ember?* But, what could she do? She had to know someone from her time in the Army. She was a former Ranger. *Didn't they have ties to secretive shit?*

"I've gotta get him help." Mary said the words out loud, not only to soothe her own soul but to give herself a sense of purpose. A mission of sorts.

Throwing the covers back, she was about to roll out of bed and head to Ember's room, when her door burst open.

"King's hurt."

Mary froze.

"Lakeview Hospital. Get dressed."

And in that very instant, Mary felt her soul die. Not because the dread she felt moments ago was now numb in her chest. Not because of blinding fear. But because in the depths of her soul, she felt...nothing.

No dread. No sorrow. Just the cold, stealing hollows of death.

CHAPTER 18

Mary was wishing Ember would push the pedal to the floor and get to the hospital in NASCAR fashion. She was pushing the speed limit by fifteen miles per hour, but it wasn't fast enough for Mary.

"We'll get there. But, we need to get there in one piece." Ember reached over and squeezed Mary's hand, reading the thoughts that were racing through her mind.

Mary knew she was right. If they got pulled over, it would just hinder the time they were making. Ember would get her to King as fast as she could safely drive. She just had to be patient and calm her nerves, and the wild thoughts circling her mind of everything that could be wrong. King would still be there whether they made it to him in forty minutes, the same as if it took them an hour.

"I know." Mary bit her thumbnail, then turned to watch the darkness pass by the passenger's window. "Did Slate give any more information than you're telling me?" Mary hated to call her new friend out, but she needed to know what was at stake and didn't want to be blindsided when she got to the hospital. "Please, Em, give it to me straight."

Ember didn't take her eyes from the road, and her words were terse. "I've given you all I know, and I wouldn't hold back." Ember seemed slighted that Mary doubted her honesty. An awkward silence fell over the car. Her tone softened. "All he said was that King was hurt, and we needed to get to the hospital, pronto." A moment of reflection painted Ember's face, and she continued, "One thing about me, Mary, I'm a straight shooter. I don't mince words, and I don't hold back. I'm not holding out on you, 'cuz that'd be a shitty thing to do to a friend. You know all I know."

It gave Mary a bit of ease knowing Ember wasn't holding out. But, it did give her pause at the fact that Slate didn't give any more information. If everything was all right, and it was something minor, wouldn't Slate have reassured Ember over the phone and told her to take her time getting to the hospital? He added the word, "pronto," so that gave a sense of urgency to the situation. And, that thought put Mary on edge again, and the vicious cycle of worry started all over.

Ember pulled into the visitors' parking garage closest to the emergency room entrance, and practically had the key out of the ignition before the car came to a stop. Mary knew Ember was trying not to show her nerves, but her efficiency when they left the house and the manner in which she was exiting the car, told Mary she was just as worried as she was.

The sliding glass doors were barely open as Mary squeezed herself through the entrance of the ER department, practically barging herself into the hospital. Ember was on her heels, just as hurried to get to King. They both scurried their way towards the admitting desk.

With every step, her mind kept a rhythm. *King. King. Get to King.* The cadence sounded-off in her head, each step taking her closer to him.

They arrived at the triage desk in a rush, and both their voices came out more in a demand than a general inquiry.

"Henry Clark?" Mary rolled out King's name in one word.

"Where's King?" Ember didn't use his given name.

The woman behind the desk gave them an incredulous look. "Excuse me?"

Both women began to speak over each other again.

"I'm here for Henry Clark."

"Where's King...Henry...at?" Ember muddled.

The faux pa caused a hint of a grin to come over both their faces.

Mary took a cleansing breath and addressed the woman behind the desk once more. "We're here for Henry Edward Clark. Can you tell us where he is? What condition he's in?" Mary knew the woman wouldn't and couldn't give any details, but in her worried state, she asked anyway.

The woman paused, eying both of them warily. She was the

poster child for resting-bitch-face down to a T. She didn't respond right away.

Mary nervously shifted her weight from one foot to the other. If the bitch wasn't going to answer her in the next five seconds, Mary couldn't be held accountable for her actions, meaning jumping over the desk and holding her in a chokehold until she relented and gave up the pertinent information.

Four…three…two, on your marks…one.

"You can have a seat in the waiting room. The," she paused, "*others*, are waiting as well." She addressed Mary, "And," she put an emphasis on the single word, "I'm not at liberty to give out *any* information on *any* patients, no matter who you are."

Her bitchy tone sparked ire in Mary's soul. *Who does this bitch think she is? Couldn't she explain herself nicely?*

Mary despised her tone and was ready to beat her ass if she gave one more condescending word.

Sensing Mary's volatile demeanor, Ember chimed in, "Thank you. We'll take a seat."

She took Mary by the elbow and started to pull her away from the desk, but Mary stayed rooted in place just wishing the woman would spout off one more fucking word.

"Come on, Mare, let's sit." Ember tugged a bit harder than necessary and rocked Mary to the side, causing her to sidestep and follow her into the seating area. Mary's feet may have moved, but the stink-eye she was throwing marked the registration woman as if it were a tattoo.

"Mary, come on."

The lady broke eye contact first and looked away, giving Mary a settling sense of victory.

Around the corner from the desk, both Ember and Mary stopped cold in their tracks. All four men—T-BAR, Cy, Arctic, and Trip, somber and clad in black, rose at their arrival, except Slate, who was staring down blankly at his clasped hands, elbows resting on his thighs and a bewildered look of devastation on his face.

When he sensed the other guy's movement, he raised his head and met Mary's eyes. His sorrowed and anguished face told Mary everything she didn't want to know.

The hope that King would be all right vanished when she lowered her gaze to Slate's hands, reddened with what Mary could only assume was blood. King's blood. His black shirt held a large, darkened stain.

Oh, God!

Slate rose and reluctantly made his way over to Mary. All the guys held stock still when he stood front and center. Mary asked without words if King was okay.

Slate's eyes brimmed with tears. A few broke free and streamed down his cheeks. He wiped at them unconsciously, smearing King's dried blood across his face. As if noticing for the first time he was doused in King's crimson, and Mary was staring at his hands, he lowered them, stuffing them into his cargo pockets. He then slowly and faintly shook his head side to side.

It was the answer Mary dreaded since the moment Ember burst into her room. The answer that tormented her on the drive to the hospital. And, it was the answer she wouldn't let herself believe, but the proof was right in front of her in Slate's eyes and on his hands.

Mary felt her legs tremble and her knees buckle when a flush rose in her body from her core to her head. The room tipped and whirled at Slate's next words. "I'm so sorry."

"*Noooo!*" Mary bent forward, grasping Slate's arms, staying clear of touching his stained hands. He steadied her while tears bathed her face and crushed her soul. The other half of which was no longer there. It shattered into a million pieces, never to be made whole again.

King was gone.

～

A putrid odor wafted across Mary's senses, and she turned her head to get away from the foul smell.

"Mary?"

She heard her name but she couldn't rid herself of the smell. It wafted again.

"She's coming around," the voice said. "Mary, open your eyes for us. Mary? Come on, Mare, open up."

Mare. No one called her Mare except King and the new bunch of friends she'd gotten to know. She fluttered her eyes open, squinting at the fluorescent lighting glaring from the ceiling fixtures.

"Good job, Mare...just open those eyes for us." The voice was Arctic's.

"Sit her up." Trip's voice was distant, and Mary realized he was talking about her.

She felt a set of hands pulling her arms as well as pushing her to a sitting position. Her eyes fluttered a bit more and she opened them letting things come into focus.

"What happened?" The groggy feeling sent her head into a fog. She was sitting on the floor of the waiting area.

"You passed out, but Slate caught you."

Slate. King's blood. Heartache. It all came rushing back to her.

The nurse with the smelling salts retreated and the guys gathered around her.

Mary tried to stand. "I need to see him." She pushed at the hands that were trying to restrain her. "Let me up." She spat the words.

"Mary. Catch your bearings before you stand." T was holding her bicep. She tugged her arm, but he didn't let go.

"I said let me up." This time she just about yelled the words.

"Okay, okay, just let us help you stand."

Mary was determined to get her ass off the floor and make her way to King. She needed to see him. Hold him. Whether he was here or on the other side, she needed to see him one last time.

Mary raised her knees and pushed herself up while T and Cy helped her. The woozy feeling filled her head once more, and she was grateful the guys had a firm grip on her, or she would've definitely landed back on her ass.

"Thank you," she said to the guys.

Grasping her bearings, the heartache returned and she trembled. Looking around, she saw Ember, then T... then Arctic, Trip, and Cy. "Where's Slate?"

The guys eyed each other and Cy answered, "He'll be back." His eyes dodged Mary's. "He's...in the bathroom."

At the completion of Cy's response, Slate emerged from a hallway to the left. He didn't say anything, but Mary's eyes dropped to his hands. They were washed and no longer bore the stains of King's blood. He kept his distance from her and hung near the rear of the group.

Mary repeated, "I need to see him."

"Maybe sit for a moment?" Ember steered her to an open chair. She didn't want to sit, she wanted to get to King. When Ember took the seat, she hesitantly sat too.

A nurse came into the waiting area and offered Mary a small glass of orange juice. "Here, hun, drink this to get 'cha feelin' better."

Mary took it and tried a small sip. "Thank you."

Taking in the small group, the woman offered, "Would y'all want to go to a private room?" At the nods and "Yes, pleases" that came from the guys, she made her way across the area with all seven of the group following.

Slate stayed clear of Mary, once again following at the back of the bunch.

Mary walked on trembling legs. Her body felt like a limp noodle, and if it weren't for T and Cypher guiding her, she would've crumbled to the ground. Every nerve in her body was firing. Besides her legs, her hands quaked along with her arms. The ache in her heart was marked with a frantic beat. Everything felt surreal. She wasn't in this space or time.

They entered a smaller room, but big enough to fit the weary group. It was moderately lit, giving it a low-key, austere vibe. It was fitting for the mood.

The nurse strode over to a coffee pot, flipped a switch, and the gurgle of the brewer came to life. "If y'all need anything, give me a holler. I'll be at the front desk."

Mary appreciated her soothing manner and gentle tone compared to resting-bitch-face nurse. When she was about to leave Slate stopped her, stepped into the hallway, and they had a side conversation. Their voices were too low to carry into the room, but Mary didn't care what they were talking about. She just didn't have it in her.

T escorted Mary to a three-cushion sofa and plunked her down. She didn't have the energy to resist or argue, she just wanted to get some answers. She wanted to see King. She didn't want to be there. She wanted this all to be a dream.

Slate reentered the room and the darkened stain on his shirt reminded her that this was truly reality. He may have washed his hands, but that was most likely King's blood drenching into his shirt. Mary wanted him to rid himself of it, change into a new shirt, but she also, in an eerie way, wanted to touch it, because it was all she would have left of King.

Ember stayed at Slate's side. They didn't talk but they held hands.

Cy sat to one side of Mary, and that was when she noticed he had a bandage around his neck. Hearing her inhale, Cy said, "Just a nick. Nothing to worry about."

Mary doubted that by the amount of blood that'd seeped through the white gauze. It looked bad to her.

Arctic was on her other side. He too had a stain on his shirt, but

Mary didn't say anything. She didn't care. All she wanted was someone to tell her what the hell was going on.

Trip sat in a lone chair across the room, and Mary noticed he wore a pair of doctor's scrub pants. She hadn't seen him walk in the hallway, but she did see he had limped into the room on a pair of crutches and now had his leg stretched out in front of him. It was all too much.

"Can you tell me what happened?" It was a plea, and the first thing out of her mouth. "Where's King? Why are you guys here? Aren't you supposed to be halfway around the world saving people?"

All the guys eyed each other and gauged how much they wanted to tell her. Slate turned to shut the door. There was no doubt Mary was going to be on the edge of hysterics when the news came out.

Arctic took the lead. With his head bowed, he spoke towards Mary's direction but couldn't bear to look her in the eye.

"King's in surgery—"

King's in surgery. Mary heard the words and she instantly felt the weight of dread lift. That was good news! The worst she was thinking hadn't happened. He wasn't dead. The doctors were making him better, fixing anything wrong. She inwardly sighed in relief.

"Mary, are you listening?" Arctic's voice pulled her from her thoughts. She nodded her head giving him her full attention.

"King was shot. He—"

Oh, fuck! Shot.

"He's all right, though...right?" Mary's voice heightened with anticipation and hope.

Arctic gritted his teeth and the hollow of his cheeks flexed.

Mary waited.

She looked around the room and none of the guys made eye contact. She turned back to Arctic. He was rubbing his hand across his upper lip and lower jawline.

"What aren't you telling me?"

When he didn't reply, she stated the question again, this time with force and vigor. "What aren't you telling me!"

Arctic answered, "Mare, King..." his voice cracked, and he cleared his throat, then swallowed to regain his composure, "King was DOA—"

"DOA?"

Arctic was clearly having a difficult time explaining. He closed his eyes and clenched his teeth, swallowing hard to gain self-control.

"He, I'm sorry Mare, he was dead when we brought him in." For the first time, he met her eyes and shook his head. "I'm so sorry, Mary." He placed his hand momentarily on her knee before he abruptly stood, paced across the floor, and stared blankly down at the countertop by the coffee maker.

Mary heard a whoosh of breath before she realized it was her own. "I..." she stammered, "I, don't understand. He's in surgery." She glanced at the remaining men around her. "You said he was in surgery." Her thoughts were stunted, and she had solitary focus. *He's in surgery.*

Mary heard a sob come from across the room and looked. Ember was weeping into Slate's chest while he stood rigid, almost robotically, consoling her. Mary's gaze swept across the room again, and each man had the same grave, somber look on his face, marred with anger and anguish.

Mary wasn't gauging what was happening.

"I... I don't understand." Mary was like a broken record, repeating and skipping, unable to move past this point in time. When no one offered any further news, she continued, "What? How? What...happened?" She could barely string a sentence together.

Cy took over where Arctic had stopped. He grasped her petite hand in his and Mary reciprocated, clinging on to it as if it was a lifeline.

"Mare. I'm not sure how much of this you want to know."

She wanted everything. Every minute detail.

"I want honesty, Cy."

He nodded and steeled himself. "King was shot in the back...at close range. He lost a lot of blood." Cy knew it was better to get all the information out in the open, and then they could discuss and dissect any questions once it was all said. "When we got to him, he had no pulse."

"Got to him? You weren't with him?" Then, Mary's eyes widened, slowly grasping what Cy was telling her. "But the doctors? He's in surgery. That's what you said."

She spoke in Arctic's direction but turned back to Cy. "They don't do surgery on people with no pulse." Her mind was working hard. "You helped him...they got him going? He's alive, though. Right?" Her thoughts were jumbled, and she rambled out her questions.

Cy shook his head, and once again, Mary's heart sank.

She stood before Cy could continue. "No. You're wrong." She

spoke with a slow calm, shaking her head. "No. You're not right." She continued shaking her head, matching Cy's bewildered state. "He's going to be okay." She nodded her head as if agreeing with herself. Her eyes darted around the room searching for somebody, anybody, any one of the guys to be nodding in agreement with her. When she found none, she turned again to Cy. "Tell me, please, Cy! Tell me he's going to be okay." It was a whispered plea.

"Wish I could, Mare." Cy looked crushed to be telling her. "Slate did all he could, but he—" He shook his head and swallowed back the lump in his throat.

Mary's eyes swung to Slate who was still methodically consoling and rubbing Ember's back. He didn't look away but held her gaze.

"You didn't save him?"

Slate's hand stilled.

"You didn't save your friend?" Mary's voice was loud, almost shrill. She turned to each one of King's teammates. "I thought you had each other's six? Isn't that what you always say?"

"Mary." Ember came over to Mary and held open her arms to console her. "Mare—"

"No! Don't touch me." She turned away and then glared back at the guys. "Why didn't you watch out for him? Why didn't you have him covered?" Her voice was loud in the small room. When no one answered, she shouted. "You all should have watched him!"

She sobbed into her hands, and Ember tentatively put her arms around her. Mary wailed into Ember's shoulder, barely supporting herself.

One by one, she felt a hand touch her arm, then her back, then her other arm. She cried uncontrollably. Opening her eyes, she was huddled in the embrace of all King's brothers.

Trip spoke next, "I don't know if he's going to be alright, but Mare, he's in surgery. The ER doctors were probably able to resuscitate him. When we got him here…" His voice sobered. "He's critical. They said they'd try, but they don't know how much they can do. But, Slate tried."

Mary's head came up and pinned Slate. She felt a strain of guilt come over her. She'd gone off the deep end and accused him of not saving his friend.

Slate read her thoughts, and though he should have been pissed at her tirade, he simply gave her a stiff smile.

"I'm sorry," she croaked out the words, feeling masses of guilt blanket her, "I shouldn't—"

Slate shut her down with his embrace. "I don't want to hear it, Mary. No need."

"But, I—"

"No need, Mare."

She turned to the rest of the group. Before she could apologize to them, the same replies came. No need to apologize. Mary couldn't believe the guys weren't pissed at her accusations. She'd been taken into their fold and was beyond grateful.

There was a knock on the half-open door which drew everyone's attention. The boisterous woman from the front desk entered, holding bottles of water, an orange juice, and what looked like granola bars.

She approached Mary. "Here, Sugar," she held out the juice to her.

Mary took it and burst into tears again at the usage of the same term of endearment that King called her. Slate cradled her deeper into his side.

The lady handed the remaining waters out to the other guys and Ember. "Can I get you anything else? Blankets? Pillows? Those chairs recline," she pointed to the utilitarian-looking chairs against the far wall. "Wish it were better accommodations for y'all."

A round of, "thank yous," and "they'll do," came from the guys. T requested pillows and blankets for everyone and the nurse left to get the bedding.

Mary sat on the couch and tried to open her juice bottle, but her hands were still shaky. At her second failed attempt, Cy took it from her and cracked the seal, then handed it back with the top slightly screwed back on. Arctic took the seat beside her and gave her a stilted smile that didn't meet his eyes.

She took a shallow sip then replaced the cap. "Thanks," she motioned to Cy with the bottle, then lifted questioning eyes to him. "Where were you guys? Why aren't you out of the country?" She picked at the bottle's label, "Who did this to him?"

Cy didn't want to divulge too much information. Mary was on-edge as it was, and if she knew it was her brother who fired the fatal shot into King, she'd slip into hysterics she may not recover from. Better they wait to see King's outcome before laying that news on her.

The clean-up crew would take care of the scene and would make sure Chet's recollection of tonight's events were "reworked," so he would conveniently forget to mention any of the men of Hellforce.

He would conveniently "forget," if he wanted to see the morning light. If word ever got out, he didn't stick to his cover story, he would be conveniently removed. The clean-up crew took their job dead seriously.

She fiddled with the bottle cap, waiting for Cy to answer her questions, but it was Arctic who jumped in, "We sometimes work stateside." Which was true.

The alphabets sometimes did have them work stateside, but just like any other job they did for the government, they weren't backed and would legally be held accountable, as such. It was one of the reasons King hated to work for a multitude of government agencies. They'd let their asses swing in the wind if they were ever arrested or foiled by foreign or local governments.

If you wore the flag of the US Army and did their bidding in a sanctioned war, you were deemed a hero. If you did their bidding as a contractor, the minute shit went sideways or things went harried, the spooks scurried and vanished like the cockroaches they were.

Arctic knew they were safe at this hospital. Tex worked his voodoo, and as far as needing to have a no-questions-asked medical facility, he had connections. His cast was far and wide. Stateside and abroad.

Usually, any GSW coming into a medical facility would have to be reported to local law enforcement, and the hounds of hell would be on them looking for an explanation as to the *who, what, where, when,* and *why,* of what happened.

Even though they weren't in Hellforce's home turf, Arctic knew when Cy made the call from the scene, Tex had "the crew" jump into action and had things arranged by the time they got to Lakeside Hospital with King.

No one asked questions, and no one even gave them a second glance when five bloodied men, clad in black, pulled up to the emergency room entrance with King in the back of a nondescript, windowless van. They took no names and asked no questions. Trip got his leg sutured, and Cy got his neck examined and rebandaged, and no one was the wiser.

Arctic was second in charge after King. They'd started Hellforce together after they were both medically retired from the Army, but even he asked no questions when it came to King's and Tex's connections.

If King didn't make it through this, Arctic would take over Hellforce, be it with a heavy heart, but he would keep things going.

Measures were put in place for any and all information to be divulged to him in such a situation as this. King and he spoke about it now and then, but never in more depth than a passing manner, not wanting to jinx the company or invite unwanted juju. He always told himself he would continue if the worst would happen, but at this moment, he didn't know if he would have the resilience to forge ahead or persevere in the wake if he lost his best friend. It would be a long night, but hopefully, by the grace of God, come morning King would pull through.

Mary's hand rested on Arctic's knee, "I know you can't tell me much, if anything, but I hope you got the son-of-a-bitch that did this to him. I hope you had no mercy." Mary's face was serious and held no folly.

The room went uncomfortably silent. If she noticed, she didn't say anything, and no man gave any further answers to her questions or her statement. Time would tell the story soon enough, but first, they had to see if King would make it through surgery, let alone the night.

CHAPTER 19

Morning came, and King made it through surgery but was clinging to life in the ICU. The bullet had missed his spine but collapsed his lung and nicked his heart within a millimeter.

Since the bullet had come from King's own 9mm pistol it was a hollow-point which was designed to open and flower upon entry, expand to three times its size, and cause maximum damage to any tissue or organs it came in contact with. It was standard-issue ammo for any mission they were on.

Taking down a target in one shot was the goal. *One-and-done* as they called it. In their profession, this was key. But King probably never imagined he'd be shot with his own gun, let alone the ammunition and grain he personally selected for his firearm.

Luckily, it wasn't a one-and-done. The surgeons were able to remove the bullet and repair the damage, but it was up to King to pull through. He received another blood transfusion after the surgery, topping off the four he had throughout the surgery itself. Doctors had a lot to repair, and he was lucky to be alive. But, his team knew King was one tough son-of-a-bitch and wasn't going to let a little lead keep him down. At least they hoped not. He was holding on by a thread, and his team waited with bated breath for more news.

In the process of the fight, King took hellacious blunt force trauma to his right testicle and it had ruptured. At the time, when the guys had gotten to him, they had no idea he had suffered the injury. They were focused on the visible injuries. The doctors were able to repair the damage, and he didn't have to have an orchiectomy.

The King's jewels were literally saved. Each of his teammates hoped the same was in the cards for King himself.

"Here, drink this." T held a tall cup out to Mary as he took a seat next to her on the pleather-covered couch.

She took it and looked at him skeptically. "What is it?" Smelling it, she wrinkled her nose. "What is it, and where did you get it?" The smell wasn't putrid, but it was off-putting.

"It's a vanilla protein shake, and I got it from the cafeteria. I saw you picking at your muffin this morning. If you want to be strong when King wakes up, you need to keep your strength up."

"The cafeteria has protein shakes?" She was still skeptical, and her voice held no surprise.

"They do, and drink up." T waited for her to take a sip, and he couldn't hide his smile at her antics as she made a dismaying face when she took a small drink.

"Fantastic!" She said in a mocking tone, choking back the gritty drink.

Mary had no appetite. She'd barely kept water down. Her nerves were frazzled and her stomach was on a constant churn. Knowing King made it through surgery and was in recovery was a godsend, but the true miracle was the fact that there should be no rational reason he was alive. How in the world he'd only taken one bullet, and the bullet had missed his spine and only nicked his heart, was a prayer that only God knew the answer to.

She wasn't tempting fate by asking why or how it was possible, she just knew she was grateful for the skills of the doctors and staff, and to whatever guardian may have been at King's side.

The team all stayed in the private waiting room the entire night. Trip and Mary took the recliners, and Ember took the couch. The rest of the guys claimed sleep where they lay, but not much sleep was had. Lord knew they'd slept in worse places, but everyone's mind was on King.

In the morning, they were all tight-lipped, and Mary sensed there was more going on than what they were able, or willing, to tell her. But, she didn't care. Her only concern was to see King open his gorgeous sapphire eyes, and then she could finally breathe easy. Until then, she would sit vigil at his bedside as soon as she was allowed to see him.

A light knock came at the door and the kind night nurse from earlier, Doris, came in with a box of donuts. "Figured y'all could use a little snack." She placed the box on the small table next to the counter with the coffee pot, then emptied the few ounces of coffee residue into the sink and proceeded to brew a new pot.

"Let me help you with that." Slate reached for the coffee in the cabinet above the coffee maker and flipped the reservoir open on top of the brewer.

"Child," she said in her Texas twang, "I know how to make coffee and don't need none of your help. I do this every day, work and home." She took out the used coffee filter and replaced it with a new one, loading it with enough grounds to make the devil dance. "Boy, I've been making java before you were in diapers." She eyed Slate from head to toe and then back up again, "And, believe you me, if I was thirty years younger, I'd have invited y'all into the on-call room." Her boisterous laugh was contagious.

T walked over and gave her a wink, laying on his slight British accent a bit heavy, "Never been known to turn a good-looking woman down. This bull needs tamin'." He patted his rock-hard chest and abs, purposely flexing his pecs beneath the tight-fitting black shirt, and playfully flirted with her despite the grim circumstances that brought them there.

Doris planted her hand on her jutted hip, took a *long* gazing look over T, giving him a once-over. Then, with a wavered nod of her head she said, "Lawd, Momma wouldn't want you to saddle what you couldn't handle to ride."

She patted T on the chest and made her way out of the room as a low, rousing sound came from the guys. Everyone knew T was a player, and to see him get turned down flat, even in a playful, no-harm flirting way, was *gold* for the guys.

Unfazed, T walked over to the donut box and bit into an apple fritter. "She'll be back," he said with a chuckle.

Mary doubted these guys ever ate a donut in their lives, considering their toned and muscled physique, so when all the guys dug right in, she was surprised.

Cy came over with a chocolate glazed cream-filled donut, half of which he'd eaten in one bite, and offered her a jelly-filled. "It's raspberry," he said around the mouthful of donut. He handed it to her resting on a napkin. Waiting for her to take a bite, he stood sentry in front of her.

She gladly took the donut over the protein shake T-BAR had

given her, so she put the shake on the end table and daintily took a bite of the donut. "Mmmm, it's good. Thanks."

"A mouse would get a bigger nibble than that. Mare, you need to eat." Cy's tone was kind and concerned, but weighty.

She took a bigger bite, even knowing she had no appetite, but when the sweetness of the filling hit her taste buds, her stomach let out a loud rumble.

Cy gave a wide grin and chuckled, his green eyes behind his glasses almost disappearing when his grin turned into a wide smile. "Guess your tummy knows when it's hungry."

Tummy. It was comical to hear the six-foot, one-hundred-ninety-pound, badass operator use the word tummy. "Thanks, Cy." Mary took another bite and, again, her taste buds sang. Pointing to the protein shake, she peered around Cy to see if T was within hearing distance and whispered, "Any way this could disappear and become a mug of coffee?"

Cy picked up the shake and downed it in two gulps. He set down the tall cup and smiled, protein mustache and all. The vanilla froth clung to his upper lip hair and made his dark brown beard stand out. Mary wiped her hand across her top lip to clue him in that the evidence was showing. He cupped his mouth and wiped away the proof, just as T came up behind him.

"Looks like you drank all your shake. Good, huh?" He eyed Mary with wariness.

She didn't want to lie, so she just shrugged her shoulders and gave him a passive smile. Cy didn't rat her out, but stood there nonchalantly, not a care in the world.

"I'll get you a mug of coffee to go with that donut." He gestured to the pastry and napkin still in her hand. T was about to turn to go to the coffee pot, when he stopped and wiped at the corner of Cypher's upper lip, "Missed a spot." Then, he strode over and grabbed a mug, and Slate filled it for him.

"Fuck, man's got the ears of a bat." Cy laughed and rubbed at the spot T wiped.

It sent Mary into a bit of laughter, which felt good after the hellish night and uncertain morning. She sobered in mid-laugh.

"Mare?" Cy questioned.

She inhaled deeply, letting the air expand her lungs and let out the breath in a forced manner. "I shouldn't be laughing at a time like this." She picked at the edge of the napkin holding the donut, "Just doesn't feel right."

T returned with her coffee. "Fuck that noise!"

Mary startled at his brash response, and at the fact that he heard her across the room. It was a small space, but not that small. His hearing was phenomenal.

"Do you know how often we laugh when we're on a mission?"

Mary shrugged.

"A lot. Not exactly when we're executing, but on recon and waiting, there's plenty of dumb shit these boneheads do that makes for a good laugh."

"Says the guy with the nick of T-BAR." Cy deadpanned.

"Fuck. Off." T laughed.

Curious, Mary asked, "Yeah, so what does T-BAR mean, anyway?" Mary set the donut down on the end table and cradled the coffee mug in her hands and took a cautious sip.

Arctic and Slate joined the huddle, while Trip and Ember stayed in the recliners next to the couch.

T glared at all his brothers around him, waiting to see who would be the asshole that was going to unmask his moniker.

"T-B-A-R: That Boy Ain't Right!" Ember called out from her chair.

T looked at her in disbelief.

"What? You always say I'm one of the team, therefore I have the right to call you out. I've got Army and Hellforce blood rights." Ember looked proud of herself.

"Wait, what? What does—" Mary was mentally trying to decipher the acronym that was his moniker. "Ohhhh." A gleeful grin raised her mouth.

"Believe me...it fits him to a T... pun intended." Trip chimed in.

"Look who's a chatty Cathy." T gave him a pointed stare, his normally hard eyes didn't hide his jovial side.

"Come on man, you've earned that nick fair and square. Given us plenty of fodder to rib you with it."

Mary watched in fascination, momentarily forgetting about the awful reason they were sitting in the hospital waiting room, as the guys gave example after example of how T earned his moniker.

"'Member that time we needed to get into that quarry mine, and there was only one way in and one way out?" All the guys groaned as Arctic retold the story. "We're all hunkered down trying to figure out how we're going to get in. King looks around, 'Hey, where's Junior?'"

"Junior?"

"Long story." T cut in before anyone could answer.

"So, we can hear him on comms but have no clue where he is." Arctic pointed to T, "MacGyver here flagged down a passing truck that had cages stuffed full of chickens. I mean like ten chickens in a two-foot-by-three-foot cage, it was awful. Chickens just about pecked one another to death before they even made it to the market." Arctic shook his head at the gruesome memory. "Anyway, he paid the driver a couple hundred bucks for four cages of chickens, mind you, that's forty chickens, give or take a few.

"So, we're all sittin' recon, up on this rock bluff above the quarry, 'bout fifty meters from the main gate, close enough that no one really needed binos to see the activity of the gate. We want to get in, but we need to wait until the gatekeeper and his buddy trade shifts to give us a thirty- to forty-second lull so we can get in while they're going over whatever they go over.

"Anyway, we're down, outta sight, tucked away, no one the wiser, right, when we see this damn fool creeping beside a makeshift pile of stacked, rocky boulders,"

Arctic mimicked the next part of the story, "And, we see him, arms stretched like Christ himself, the Redeemer over Rio de Janeiro, a cage wedged against each side of his ribs, the other two in each hand, and he's white-knucklin' the outer cages from the top, using their leverage to keep the others pinned to his sides, as the chickens inside the cages are freaked the fuck out, and are flappin' all their feathers off, trying to understand what this idiot is doing with them."

Mary laughed at the story, and the way Arctic tramped in place, miming T-BAR with his arms outstretched, carrying cages. T just sat, taking the ribbing his brother was laying on him.

"So, this genius gets over the mound of smaller rocks and wedges himself between the gate shack and the stack of boulders. Mind you, the guards are less than ten yards from him, and these chickens are flappin'. I don't know why, they weren't clucking, but T does a power squat, lowers all four cages to the ground, then dismantles the cages so the front panel opens, and floods the quarry with chickens."

Arctic was laughing so hard along with the rest of the guys, Mary couldn't help but laugh at what she imagined the scene to be like. "So, these chickens see the Pearly Gates open, and they're *gone*! Chickens look like the cartoon Roadrunner. All of these chickens, beating off any remaining feathers they have left on them. Oh, man!

They spread out into that quarry quicker than a ten-dollar hooker. They were in and out in a flash!"

"Well, it worked didn't it?" T smart-mouthed his team. At the team's raised laughter, he added, "Yes, it did, and fuck you very much!" and then gave them all a grandstand middle finger.

Slate was roaring, "Those jackholes were chasing those chickens, trying to figure out where in the hell they came from, and why the hell they were flocking the quarry. Every time they'd get within grabbing distance trying to capture one, those chickens would flop and fight, rear up in flight with claws forward, and peck the ever-living shit outta them."

"They probably wanted to catch them so they would have lunch." Cy's quip made the team erupt again with roaring laughter.

"But, the worst part of the story. After we get the job done in the quarry, MacGyver rendezvoused back to our location to EXFIL," Trip stopped mid-sentence and dry heaved for emphasis, and pinned Mary's attention, "You ever smell chicken shit? Have ya? It's awful!"

Arctic, Cy, and Slate couldn't contain their laughter at the memory before Trip even told it, and Mary joined in too, not knowing what was to come.

"T gets in the chopper, has to literally crawl across our laps as we get in, and even with the open space, the entire lift back to the FOB, King had chicken shit all over his camos, and it was about the only time I've seen him retch and dry heave for nearly half an hour, all over the putrid smell of chicken shit."

Although everyone should have been laughing after the story, everybody sobered at the mention of King, bringing back into focus the reason they were all here. The room went from side-splitting laughter to quiet as a church mouse in an instant.

For the next couple of hours, everyone busied themselves. None of the guys had their personal cells on them, so they resorted to watching the small wall-mounted TV, reading outdated magazines or random medical journals, and the pamphlets that lined the small wall caddy detailing the various ailments and diseases no one wanted to read about.

"You'd think they'd at least give us an update." Mary groused.

"At least a head's up, even if nothing's changed, would be nice."

Ember and Slate were watching YouTube videos on her phone, sitting together in the recliner, with his hand on her knee as she sat sideways across his lap. Ember spoke without lifting her head from the screen. "Maybe we should ask?"

Arctic stood and stretched, tossing the remote to T who was stretched out on the couch with his legs dangling over the end of the armrest, his six-foot-four frame too long for the three cushions beneath him. "Hittin' the head. Anyone need anything from the vending machine or the cafeteria?"

The list was long, so Mary wrote everything on the back of the "Everything You Need to Know about Diabetes" pamphlet, which was ironic since half the crap they wanted would give someone high blood pressure or diabetes.

Trip rose from the recliner with a groan. His leg was throbbing, but he didn't want to take anything stronger than a Tylenol or Aleve for the pain.

Slate looked over from the recliner he was in. "You gonna need to ice that."

Trip hobbled to the coffee pot to refill his mug and make a fresh pot. The guys were caffeine junkies at the office, but they'd never consumed this much in one sitting, even during planning and debriefing an op. "Outta go-juice," he held up the empty container. "Can you see if the desk has decaf?"

Decaf was the Holy Grail of swear words. *Never* was decaf allowed at HQ, and it was blasphemous to even utter the word in the presence of other operators.

"Yeah, see if they have something that will stop me from jittering like a crack addict. My nerves are wicked." Cy held up his hand and everyone zoned in, his hand quaked and shuttered enough that everyone had a view from their vantage point.

"Damn, man! Drink some water," T replied.

Trip grabbed one from the mini-fridge below the counter of the coffee pot and tossed it to Cy. "Head's up."

Cy swiped it out of the air without a problem, even with his shaky hands.

Arctic picked up the list of junk food and headed to the door, which almost knocked him straight in the face.

The day-nurse entered. "Oh, excuse me, I'm so sorry," she said sincerely.

Arctic took a step back and allowed her the rest of the way in. He didn't leave, wanting to hear if there was news about his best friend. He hoped for the best but braced for the worse.

The cute brunette addressed the room, but since Arctic was closest, her attention was drawn to him. "Mr. Clark is ready for visitors."

Everyone perked up at the news.

"Is he awake?"

"Is he talking?"

"How's his prognosis?"

Everyone started asking questions at once. Usually when on missions, King was point, and he did the talking and doled out commands. Without him at the helm, the guys seemed out of order. Arctic was the youngest of the group, but since Hellforce was his and King's concept, it was natural for him to instruct and coordinate the guys.

Arctic took the lead. "Let the lady speak," he said to the group, "please, continue."

"Well, to answer the questions, Mr. Clark is still sedated, and will continue to be for the next few days, so he's not talking or alert yet."

Arctic liked that she added the word, "yet" to her assessment. It gave him a sliver of hope that King would be coming around when the doctors thought the time was right.

She went on, "He can have two visitors for ten minutes each. We ask that you keep it to ten minutes, so he doesn't get overwhelmed. Sometimes unconscious patients absorb their surroundings, so we want to keep him as calm as possible." She took in a breath then asked, "Who'll be going first?"

She was prepared for everyone to want to see their friend first, so it surprised her when the man at the coffee pot said, "His fiancée and his best friend will be first."

Arctic looked over at Trip, and Trip gave him a chin lift, which Arctic graciously tipped his head to. With the mysterious visitor's clearance they had at the hospital, they probably didn't have to play the fiancée card, but it was always a golden ticket in sticky situations. King played it when Mary was in the hospital, so it only seemed fitting to play it in reverse.

Mary stood at Arctic's side and he ushered her through the doorway gently, his hand on the small of her back. Mary was grateful to have these men supporting her. She didn't think she could handle this on her own. Then again, she'd find a way, come hell or high water. She needed King like she needed air, which was alarming because only a month ago, she didn't even know him. How she'd fallen was a mystery to her, but she fell hard.

They walked down a long corridor and took several turns until they came to the ICU. The letters, INTENSIVE CARE UNIT, screamed out at her. Every step took her closer to her reality. King was hurt. Badly. But, he was a fighter, and this battle was one of the toughest he'd fought.

"Mary?" Arctic's voice pulled her to the present. "We can go in whenever you're ready."

She liked the fact that Arctic was giving her the lead. He'd taken command and control over the last ten hours, but now, instead of forcing her, he was letting her go when she was ready.

"Thank you, Cole."

His given name coming from her abruptly stunned him. "Why'd you call me that?" He was soft-spoken because of their surroundings, but he was still in the commanding position.

"'Cuz you're Arctic when your men need you as you're leading in the field or on one of your, 'saving the world from evil, gloom and doom' missions. But now, you're going to be with your friend." She drew in a breath and lightly squeezed his bicep, giving him comfort she knew he wouldn't ask for. "You need to be Cole when you're with him. He needs to know his friend is with him, not the squad leader, or whatever you call it."

Arctic cleared his throat, "Team lead, that's the term." He should be comforting Mary at the moment, not the other way around. He knew at that moment that Mary was the girl for his friend. She would be the new addition to the team, not because she worked for Hellforce, but because she loved his best friend. And, by the way, King uncharacteristically blathered on and on about her, he knew the sentiment was the same.

Arctic knew he'd never find someone as worthy as Mary, so he'd have to live vicariously through his friends. He knew they'd all find their "one" someday, but he knew it would never be in the cards for him. Broken family, foster kid, unlovable, loner. Fucked-up. That was his MO.

"Cole?" Mary's squeeze on his arm once more brought him front and center. "I'm ready."

She was ready, but he had to steel his nerves. He was about to see his friend, his mentor. The man who was ten feet tall and bullet-proof, confined to a hospital bed. The one who took him under his wing as a newbie when he first joined the Army at eighteen. He may be the youngest of the Hellforce team, but it was King who built him into the man he was today all those years ago. He owed him everything.

Seeing King was sure to bring up memories and nightmares he'd long ago buried. Months in the rehab center at Walter Reed Medical, where they'd both rebuilt themselves, relearning everything about themselves, before being medically discharged from the Army. It was where Hellforce was born. "Two cripples with a dream," as King always put it. And, what a dream it had become.

"Cole? Are you all right?"

He snapped back to reality and saw that Mary was barely holding herself together. He didn't know if he could do this, but he knew he would force himself so Mary could see King. "Yeah, I'm ready."

And, with a gentle hand on her lower back, Arctic and Mary entered the room where King clung to life.

CHAPTER 20

Seeing King helpless was more than Mary could handle. She sat at his bedside while the others rotated in and out. King could only have two visitors at a time, but the guys let her stay at his side, as one-by-one, they each took turns to see their brother.

After each made his rounds a few times, Ember drove them back to Hellforce so they could get their vehicles and make a quick pitstop home to shower and change. Slate and Arctic were still in their blood-laden shirts, and Trip was still sporting the green cotton scrub pants after his were cut off in the ER when he got his leg wound sutured.

Ember knew they'd feel better being refreshed and refueled.

Everyone should've been taking a break, pulling themselves together and getting some sleep, but Mary knew they'd be back as soon as humanly possible. She told them to return after they rested for a few hours, but not one of them wanted to leave his brother behind. Each said he'd be back within the hour.

She rested her head on the edge of King's mattress, and the incessant beeping of his vitals was a lullaby to her heart. Each beep meant King was still there, and each beep told her he was still in the fight to stay with her.

Mary opened her eyes and saw that evening had fallen beyond King's window. Purple and orange hues painted the sky. She'd fallen asleep at his bedside. She tried to sit up but the awkwardness of her sleeping position made her back feel like it was in a vice grip.

"Hey."

Mary peered over the top of King to the other side of his bed. She saw Ember sitting next to it caressing King's hand. Mary still had his other hand in hers, but the coolness of his skin made it feel as if it was made of wax. It felt nothing like the hands she'd become familiar with. The ones that caressed her face and ran down her arm or brushed her cheek and her breast. She wanted to feel those hands in hers, but for now, this would do. King was still here.

"What time is it?" Mary groaned as she straightened in her chair.

"Nine p.m."

"Nine!" The shock had her sitting up. "Oh, my...I must've...I fell asleep." She yawned so wide, Ember saw every molar in her mouth. Mary tugged at her shirt trying to smooth out any wrinkles.

Ember chuckled at her disheveled state. "Well, you've been here for seventeen hours.

They both watched King's still form. He looked older, even though the crevices of his slight wrinkles around his eyes and forehead were smoothed, and he had a sereneness to him.

"Calmest I've ever seen him," Ember joked, then sobered. "I'd do anything to hear him roaring like a grizzly right now." She looked at the hand she was caressing. "I need claws, not paws." She chuckled then looked over at Mary who was looking up at the monitors.

"Ya know, I keep looking at the numbers like they're going to tell me something. I have no idea what they are, or what they represent, I don't know if high numbers are good or bad, and I don't know if they're showing improvement or decline. All I know is I can hear each heartbeat, and that's all I need. As long as I still hear that, I know he's still with us."

A silence fell between them, each lost in their own thoughts.

Ember's thumb was rubbing over King's when she said, "I don't think I'd be here right now if it weren't for him." She paused in reflection, but then went on. "After I got out of the Army, I tried to reacclimate, but I was...lost for a bit. I..." she cleared her throat, "I'm proud of my service to my country, and I'd do it again, but I did a lot...um, I did some things that I, ya know, couldn't talk about with anyone. Some, because of security reasons, but the other stuff...a person who never served wouldn't understand." She spoke as if Mary wasn't there, eyes honed in on King's hand in hers.

"Didn't you have any friends to fall back on?" Ember seemed to be a jovial, outgoing person, and Mary could see her as a social butterfly. She fit in with the guys and was like one of their team. She and Ember hit it off right off the bat when they'd met.

Ember huffed a chuckle, "I don't really have many friends." Then she reiterated, "I mean, I have plenty of "friends" who are acquaintances, people I met in college, and the others I served with, but as I got out, they just moved on, which is usually how it goes if you don't stay in the same location. I came back to Texas, they stayed in North Carolina. I only have two really close friends."

That truth seemed hard to believe, but Mary knew she wasn't playing a "poor-me" card for sympathy. She'd guess there were layers to Ember that Mary didn't know yet.

"Slate?"

Ember nodded, "Yeah, and my college roommate, Maven."

"Couldn't you've talked to them?"

"No, not really. Elijah," his name came out on a smile, "Slate, he was working with the guys at Fort Hood while I was based in North Carolina. So, the timing was off. And, then he started at Hellforce. And my college friend, Maven is a riot, but I never wanted to...taint her spirit with my...'ventures,' and then there's operational security and all."

"Isn't your dad ex-military?"

"We're never "ex" military." Ember chuckled on an exhale.

"What do you call it, then?" Mary was genuinely interested.

"We're referred to as former military. It's always ingrained in who we are, in everything we do. My dad, I love my dad, but I couldn't tell him at first. He tried to get me to open up, but he's my dad. And, to him, I'm his baby girl...and, I just couldn't let him know all the things..." her voice cracked in a whisper, "...I'd witnessed. So, I became my own island."

The room weighed heavy, and no one spoke for a minute or two.

"So, King?"

Ember bobbed her head. "Yeah. When Eli realized I was messed up, he tried to get me to open up, but it was the same as my dad. I didn't want to load him down with my...stuff. I knew he and the guys were under a lot of stress. They were gone a lot at first, and I didn't want to add to his burden."

Mary nodded.

"Eli and the guys got together for a cookout, just random blow-off time after one of their excursions, and I tagged along. King clocked me as soon as we showed up. Like a sixth sense or something. Every time I looked up, he had me in his sights. It was off-putting, and I didn't know if I should've come along or if he had a problem with me. So, I stayed clear of him, which was hard, because he's such a big lug."

That made them both smile.

"I was coming out of the bathroom and damn-near ran right into a wall of all that was King. Scared the ever-living shit out of me."

"I can imagine." Mary was invested in the story, giving her a momentary reprieve from her worry. "How'd that go?"

"Ends up, he hit the nail on the head. Straight out asked me if I was suffering from PTSD, which I immediately took offense to. Then, he checked off all the things I was experiencing, and I was astonished at his accuracy. Pegged me to a T. I was actually pissed that he cornered me. I mean, I went to the cookout to unwind, have a few hours of normalcy, and here's this guy I just met, basically calling me out, and naturally, I recoiled. He handed me his card and did the whole cliche, 'call me' then walked away. What a fucker!" Ember giggled. "I wanted to tear it up and throw it in his face, but he was out of range before I could do it."

"Did you keep the card?"

"I left it on the kitchen island on my way out the door, but then at the last minute, I thought better of it and pocketed it. Which in all honesty, was literally my lifesaver." She twitched her lip to the side and bit it, trying not to let her emotion mask her face. Then, leaning forward, she clasped King's limp hand between both of hers and slowly rubbed it as if trying to warm it.

"Had a complete breakdown that night. Like full-blown, rocking in a corner, freaked out of my soul meltdown. I had a complete mind-fuck." She spoke to King's hand and continued to rub it. "The brain does stupid shit when it's fighting to survive between delusion and reality. Tells you things that are completely fucked in the sane world. I saw how well the guys were doing after their stint in the service, how none of them seemed to be affected. Which only goes to show, you can't always trust outward appearances. Everyone's got demons. I was hiding behind a veil and didn't even know it."

The moment hung between them, and it was a bit before she continued. Her rubbing of his hand slowed, and she stared at King's face. Her mouth pulled to the side once more, and she tongued her cheek, then ran her tongue over her teeth behind pursed lips. Mary stayed quiet, letting her work through the emotions of the painful memory.

"Went to my nightstand, grabbed my nine..."

Mary drew in a breath.

"Swallowed it and pulled the trigger." A lone tear fell from Ember's eye. Mary watched it fall onto her shirt when she made no effort to swipe at it. It was followed by another. "Fucking gun jammed." She shook her head. "For the life of me, I don't understand it. I never had a jam in that gun before or since."

Mary couldn't believe the story. Ember, the fun, outgoing girl she knew, had demons that no one would ever imagine. No one would ever know her pain.

"A jammed gun is a soldier's worst nightmare. It means death on the battlefield. Never in my life have I ever been more grateful for a malfunction."

Her tears had stopped, but the anguish on her face was palpable. Mary's already-battered heart wept for her.

"It was a moment of clarity. It's like the darkness was instantly sobered within me. I was so fucked up. I didn't know who to call. It was three in the morning. I knew I could call my dad or Eli; they would've been there in an instant, but I was too ashamed. I couldn't face them." She swallowed hard, the bobbing of her throat was visible even in the dimness of the room.

"King." It wasn't a question.

Ember nodded slightly. "I dug his card from my jeans next to my bed. My shaking hands were barely able to hold it, let alone dial."

"He came?"

"In a flash. Didn't ask any questions. Just told him I needed him, and he was at my door. Don't know how he knew where I lived, but he was there in a blink."

She didn't lay out any details, and that was fine with Mary. She didn't need to know. But, she knew that King did what King did. No questions. No explanations. Ember was right when she told Mary that first day at Hellforce that King was a teddy bear. He wore the mask of a grizzly, but those who loved him knew the truth. But, Mary knew why he wore the persona. She doubted that he could put the fear of God into someone with hearts, rainbows, and flowers.

"He stayed the entire night. Listened when I spoke, and when I didn't. Never interrupted or schooled me, but only spoke when he needed to answer or coax me to go on. Next day, he got me into the VA. It's a wonder how he pulled that off, 'cuz, fuck, it takes months to get an appointment. When I got there, I froze in my car. Embarrassment and mind-fucking stilted me from going in. I was frozen with fear sitting in my car staring at the entrance."

"What'd you do?"

A slow grin rose on one side of her face, and she held King in her sights. "I called grizzly."

Mary let out a breathy laugh, as Ember's grin turned into a full-fledged smile.

"Yup. Stayed on the phone with me, even though neither of us spoke. I just needed that lifeline. To hear him in silence on the other end kept the demons at bay." The memory chilled her, and she again rubbed small circles into King's hand. "Next thing 1 know, there's a tapping at my window. Looked over and all I could see was a mammoth chest as wide as my window. I rolled it down, phone still held to my ear. His was still at his ear, too. He never hung up until he knew I was in his presence. I don't remember getting out of the car, but he walked me into the building."

"Did he say anything?"

"Nope. Just guided me with a hand on my back and his hand in mine."

"He held your hand." Mary knew that was pure King. Guiding with one hand, comforting with the other.

Ember nodded her head. "All the way into the building. All the while in the elevator, straight to the reception desk. He never broke his hold." She tightened her grip on his hand between hers. "When we got to the desk, we were told the doctor was running late. He steered me to the waiting area where I filled out shit tons of paper-work. I wasn't called back until three hours past my appointment time. He waited silently the whole time. Didn't try to fill the silence with small talk or mindless drivel. Just supported me.

"When it was finally my turn, I freaked when they said I needed to go in alone." Ember's head shook. "It's stupid really. I didn't know King from Adam. I had no ties to him, no built friendship, but I needed him like I was starving for air. It's completely irrational, but rational isn't an option when you're in the middle of a mind fuck. But, the doctor was adamant."

"What happened? Did he sit outside the room and wait?"

"Nope."

"Nope!" Her curt response stunned Mary. "What'd he do?" Her voice raised a few octaves.

"After a few choice words which he didn't hold back, that I'm sure all the waiting room...hell maybe the entire floor heard, with one hand on my back, the other in my hand, he marched my ass right out of the VA."

"Really!"

"God's honest truth."

"Where'd you go? Back to your car?"

"Nope. There was no way I could drive with my meltdown paralyzing me. He put me in his truck and we drove."

"Where? To Hellforce? Did he tell you where he was going?"

Ember shook her head. "No."

"So you just drove? Not knowing where he was taking you?"

"Middle of a meltdown, the brain doesn't rationalize, so yeah. Didn't ask. He didn't say."

Mary closed her jaw and waited for her to continue.

"We drove up to this house, looked like a cottage straight out of a kid's fairy tale. Cobblestone facade. Sloped roof. Ivy creeping up the front. Damn near plucked from the pages of a book. He opened my door, guided me up the walkway right to the front door, and rang the bell."

Mary couldn't wait to hear what was next. She was so engrossed in the story, everything else faded for the moment.

"Guy answered. Looked like an average person, nothing alarming or characteristic about him. Neither said a thing, but the guy stepped aside and we went in. He led us to a side room. When we entered, I knew where we were."

Mary raised her brows, not wanting to interrupt.

"He had a black comfortable-looking leather couch, with a coffee table separating two leather chairs. It had an air of therapist all around."

"Did you freak?" The tone was low.

"Nope. King led me to the couch and we sat. He tightened his grip on my hand and never let go through my whole session."

"The guy was a therapist?"

"Yup. Turns out he's a good friend of King's."

"But, he didn't call while he was driving?"

Ember shook her head, and her gaze once more fell on King. "I don't know how he did it, or why he did it, or how it happened, but...he's King. And, that's all I needed to know."

Mary set her eyes on King, unmoving, and she wished he'd open his eyes. She knew the anesthesia from the surgery had probably worn off and that the doctors were keeping him sedated for pain management, but she really wanted to see him. Even if only for a second.

His still form unsettled her. King was stoic, a man who used few words and made a commanding presence, but his current state was counter to his personality, and she just wished he'd wake and be...King.

"Sat through the next three sessions. I didn't ask him. Just showed up on appointment day and drove me to the fairytale house. By my fourth session, I told him I could go myself, and he granted the request...almost."

"Almost?"

"When I walked out after my two-hour session, his truck was parked behind mine next to the curb. He was behind the wheel but never got out. I remember I gave him a chin lift, he returned it, and then pulled away from the curb like it was the most natural thing in the world. It was crazy."

"Did it bother you? Was he overstepping?"

"Not in the least. I needed him there the first few times, which was weird, 'cuz I couldn't even tell my dad, or Eli, my closest friend in the world, or Maven, what I was going through, but yet, here I was, blathering my deepest, darkest secrets in front of a man I didn't know, and a doctor I never met. Looking back, it's a miracle I took King's card." She quieted, "I owe him everything."

Unbeknownst to the group, that sentiment ran deep within each person that night. Each had their own personal story of King and his outreach, kindness, and life-changing story thanks to the man that was hanging on to life. He'd made a difference in all their lives, and each one would say the same if asked...they owed King everything.

≈

It was three days before King was brought out from under sedation, but when the day came, every teammate and the girls were there. Each wanting to see with their own eyes that King was going to be okay.

With their "clearance" that Mary didn't understand, protocol was broken and they were all allowed into his ICU room, which was a tight squeeze with man muscles and testosterone bursting at the seams of the room. Mary and Ember eyed each other when the nurses seemed giddy and flirtatious when they'd enter.

Mary could almost bet they were drawing lots at the nurse's station to see who the lucky one would be to give King his first sponge bath. That wasn't happening. Over her dead body. She wanted a male nurse...and one who was as straight as the day was long, to be the only one to sponge her man.

Before they were allowed into the room, King's breathing tube was removed and some of the equipment was wheeled out. He looked better without the tube taped to his face and without the whirling of the ventilator. It brought a sense of peace to her.

Baby steps.

It would take baby steps to get him back to himself. She knew it wouldn't be easy, and King would definitely not be an easy patient, but she had to keep telling herself, *baby steps.*

"If you talk to him, it'll bring him around quicker," Dr. Metsler addressed the room. "Just don't overwhelm him. Keep it gentle and tranquil, peaceful. We need him to stay calm."

Mary wanted to laugh because he definitely didn't know his audience. There was nothing tranquil or peaceful about the men who took up every square inch of the room. Each man would battle the hounds of hell, walk through fire, and fight to the death for one of their own.

T was on the opposite side of the bed from Mary, and he spoke first. "King, get the fuck up!" A rousing bout of laughter came from the guys, and the doctor wasn't pleased or amused. Ember elbowed him in the ribs and glared at him as if to say, "Don't get us kicked out." T looked aggrieved at being elbowed and didn't see what was wrong with his frank approach.

Arctic was next to Mary, and he went next, speaking in a much gentler voice than T. "King, we're all here with you. We need you to wake up."

Everyone waited to see if he'd stir. When nothing happened, Cy spoke from the end of the bed. "King, buddy, need you to open those eyes." He lightly grabbed King's big toe covered by the blanket and gave it a little wobble. King didn't respond.

Mary held his hand and took her turn. Running her hand up and down the length of his arm, she said, "King, it's Mary, can you hear me?" She paused hoping he'd wake, then continued, "Need you to wake up. We've been waiting for you."

Everyone watched, almost sure that he'd hear Mary's sweet voice and pop his eyes wide open. Sadly, nothing of the sort happened.

Everyone took turns trying to wake him to no avail. Dr. Metsler said it would take a while, but to just keep doing what they were doing. Though he gave T a disapproving look when he left.

And, so it went.

They all talked directly to him at first, making sure to say his name and direct their voice to him. Eventually, the tone in the room turned to chatter amongst themselves, while they continued to talk to him as well. About a half an hour later, King began to stir. The room came to a standstill and everyone watched and waited.

Mary didn't know what to expect. Would he slowly wake up? Would his eyes pop open like in a drama series? Would he wake and then fall asleep again? Only time would tell.

At first, he made subtle movements like he was in the middle of a dream. Then, slowly he became more agitated, shifting as if his dream had turned haunted. The nurse came in periodically to check his progress and his vitals, and encouraged the group to continue to talk to him. So, they did.

"King, it's Trip. Come on buddy, we're all here waiting. Gotta get up so you can holler at me." It was a known fact that Trip constantly angered King. Not in a vengeful way, but Trip was the prankster, the icebreaker when things got heated, and a constant pain in King's ass, and the others loved it. King took it good-heartedly, but when he reached his threshold, he let Trip, and everyone else, know it. "Remember when I put food coloring in your coffee? That was gold!"

King didn't react, but Mary knew everyone remembered that day by the burst of laughter from the guys.

Chatter continued, and King stirred more and more. After another ninety minutes, he finally woke. Mary cried, and she didn't miss the others swiping at their faces when King looked around the room, questioning what had happened.

It was a glorious day.

CHAPTER 21

It was Tuesday afternoon, four days since King awakened, a week since the shooting, and King was struggling through another round of physical therapy. It wasn't that it was hard, rather it was frustrating, He was a former Delta operator for Christ sakes. Taking a deep breath and holding it for a count of five shouldn't have been that difficult. Expanding his lung capacity was this morning's task.

Now, he was working on ventilating his lungs, blowing into a spirometer, trying to get the ball to hover at a level higher than the day before. Mary kept reminding him to take it slow, but he wanted to get the fuck out of the hospital and back to work. He was thankful beyond measure she was at his side, but today, her chipper attitude was grating on his nerves.

"Why don't we take a break and come back to this in a bit? I know you can do it. It'll just take time." Mary cajoled.

He didn't know what did it, but something set him off. "I fucking know I can do it, Mare. It's a fucking breathing exercise. But, this," he pointed to the spirometer on the table in front of him, "this, is a fucking joke!" He batted the plastic meter so hard, it flew across the room, hitting the wall.

Mary jumped at his sudden outburst. King was on edge the last few days, and she tried to make it better, but it seemed the more she tried, the more irritated he became.

"I need to get the fuck out of here and back to my routine. The world doesn't stop turning just because I had a little setback."

A little setback? Was he fucking high? She knew she probably should've kept her mouth shut, but she couldn't stand his attitude. She was trying to help. "Even when you get home, you're going to have to take some time off to heal. Doctor says you shouldn't go back to work for at least a month. You're kidding yourself if you think you'll be able to do half the things you did before the month is up."

Wrong. Thing. To. Say. Irritation became anger, anger became rage, rage became a boiling point. King flew!

"What the fuck do you know, Mary? Are you a doctor? Did you somehow, overnight, become a fucking expert?"

His words stung. She knew he was frustrated and angry, but that gave him no right to take it out on her. She wanted him to stop, but he continued, "I know my body, I know my limits."

"That's before some asshole almost put a bullet in your lung and heart."

Mary didn't know the details of what went down that night. She didn't know it was her own brother who fired the shot that almost killed him, and King made it crystal fucking clear to the team that she wasn't to be told.

Each time she asked, the guys said they couldn't tell her. She wanted to ask King but was afraid it'd upset him. She wished he'd confide in her. Until then, she could only let her imagination run wild. Not knowing would be something she'd have to come to grips with if a relationship between them was going to work.

King came to his senses. His anger settled when Mary rose from the chair and reached for her purse. "I'm sorry, Sugar. I was totally out of line."

She pushed the chair back against the wall and folded the blanket that had covered her the previous night.

"Mare...I'm sorry, Mare." His eyes pleaded with her but she didn't see because she was avoiding eye contact with him. "Mare," the plea was now in his voice, "please look at me, Mary. Sugar, please."

She couldn't look at him. She knew if she did, the tears stinging the back of her eyes would burst like a dam. She wouldn't let him see her cry. He didn't deserve her tears.

"Mary, baby...Mare, I'm sorry." He tossed the coverings to the side and swung his legs off the bed attempting to stand.

"Don't." The single word sliced her tongue, and King stayed put on the edge of his bed. "Never, *ever* take that tone with me. Ever.

Don't you *ever* insult me. I may not be a big bad soldier, I may not be as smart as you, but don't you *ever* insult my intelligence."

King felt the lash of every word, and he'd take it because he deserved it. "Mare—"

"Don't!" She held up a staying hand. "I can't be with you right now. I don't want to be with you right now."

King's blood ran cold.

"I can't even look at you right now." Her words held venom, but they also held hurt and sorrow.

He did that. He put that there. She was just trying to help and be his support, and he'd been a dick. No. He'd been a complete asshole. He tried once more, "Please, Mare."

She turned and reached for the door. With her hand resting on the pull, she left him parting words. "I know you're hurting. I know this is hard, and I know you're finding it difficult to come to grips with limitations because you've never let anything stop you. I can't do it for you, and I can't make it easier, but I can and was willing to be your cheerleader."

Was. Why is she using past tense?

"When you can get your head out of your ass, stop acting like a baby throwing a tantrum and you're ready to get back to work, I'm ready to be back at your side. Until then, have a pity party, feel sorry for yourself, get it all out. Then, you get your big boy pants on, and we'll move past this."

He thought she was done, but he was mistaken.

"Until then, I'll be waiting for you." Without another word, she opened the door and walked out.

And he let her.

She didn't let the tears fall as she walked the long hallway to the elevator. Nor did she let them fall on the long descent down to the ground floor. They were held at bay when she went through the rotating door and across the parking lot to her VW Beetle, Sophie, that Slate and Ember brought to the parking lot yesterday morning. She held her head high and kept moving forward.

One foot in front of the other.

The same as she'd done every day since her father died, her mother got sick, and the man she loved almost died.

However, the river of tears washed down her face as she sobbed behind the wheel. All the sorrow, all the anger, and all the hurt, all the uncertainty she'd been hiding came out. She cried until she couldn't cry anymore. She let it all out. There was a time for sorrow, a time to grieve, and she gave that to herself.

When no more tears fell and her hiccupping sobs diminished, she wiped her nose and wetness from her eyes, put on her big girl panties, and headed home. It was time to face a new day. One foot in front of the other.

~

The house smelled musty and old, boarded up, and of something rotting. It was an unfamiliar scent, and Mary wrinkled her nose at the odor.

Growing up in the house, her mother always had something cooking on the stove or baking in the oven, and the aromas were heaven-sent. Even after Mary moved out on her own, whenever she returned the smells of her childhood met her at the door. And, when she moved back in to care for her mom, they often baked together on her mom's good days, and the familiarity was all around her. But, since her mom left, and Mary was working two jobs, the house had become just that, a house.

It no longer bore the characteristics of a home.

It was a place to sleep, shower, and shit, which was a fitting example of what she was experiencing now. No warm aromas. No childhood memories. Just a means to an end.

She looked around and the house was still a disaster. She hadn't returned since the break-in, so things were in a sad state, and she inwardly sighed. She was still reeling from King's outburst but wanted to run back to his room and hope everything would be better. But, she knew it wouldn't be and maybe a moment apart was what she needed. Time to recoup, reevaluate.

She walked over to her mother's china cabinet and stepped over the shattered china strewn across the hardwood floor. *Why so much disaster? Why would someone stoop to such a low as to break the china if they weren't going to steal it?* It didn't make sense to her.

Mary made her way to the kitchen and the smell hit her. She pulled back a gag. The room smelled of rotting food. The garbage hadn't been taken out, and when she opened the refrigerator the stench wafted out, overtaking her senses.

"Good Lord!" She said with her hand pinned over her mouth and nose.

Trent mustn't have returned since the day of the break-in. It wasn't uncommon for Trent to disappear for weeks on end and then come barreling in when he was out of money. She wondered when he'd be on the doorstep, pandering to her. Just thinking about it made her blood boil.

The loving brother she knew became dead to her the first time he struck her, and the day of the break-in was the final straw. She had an inkling that Trent had something to do with it, but every time she wanted to ask King if he knew anything, the timing wasn't right. He had to focus on his recovery, and she didn't want to have him focused on anything except his health.

Anger rose within her. Trent was emotionally dead to her. She felt nothing but hatred towards him. He was no longer her brother if he could be so cruel and callous towards her.

And, if he was involved in any way, that would also mean he had taken the safe and hocked her parents' things. The thought was almost too painful to fathom.

And couple that with all the times he'd hurt her in the past—the fists, the kicks, and the punches—all the times she had to go to medical clinics in different cities, and how she had to hide and lie about her bruises and injuries at the diner and women's shelter.

And, that was the irony. She helped women get away from the very situations she herself was stuck in. She noted the hypocrisy.

Trent had hurt her for the last time. She wouldn't take him back when he came begging for a place to stay. She wouldn't give in when he begged her for money. He was absolutely dead to her, and she felt no remorse for having such an abhorrent thought. The brother she knew and loved no longer lived.

She formulated a plan. She couldn't confront King and upset him, but as soon as she'd see Cy, she would ask him for a favor and see if he could find out anything he could about her brother. Where he'd been, who he was running with, and where he was now. Finding her brother may be the only way of getting her Grandmother's and father's rings back.

Cy was a computer genius, and according to Ember, he could crack anything, hence his name, Cypher. His original moniker was Cyber Cipher, and the guys eventually shortened it to Cypher, combining the two words. He could possibly give her answers.

She donned a pair of yellow rubber gloves from beneath the sink and grabbed the roll of garbage bags, tore one from the pack, and set out to clear out the refrigerator and throw the rotting food away. It was as good as any place to start the clean-up.

Looking around, she felt discouraged. It would take her the better part of the week to get everything cleaned up. Obviously, the guys wouldn't be working at HQ, so there was no need for her to be at the office. She'd take the time off to get what was left of the house back into order. It was going to be one hell of a job.

~

It turned out, cleaning was very therapeutic. After her last trip outside to the garbage cans, she set out to scrub the refrigerator. She scrubbed the daylights out of it. The monotonous work set her mind thinking, and of course, naturally, her thoughts turned to King.

After he'd fully awakened and came out of sedation, he was oblivious to what had happened. The guys were cryptic, and their explanation of why he was there was downright clinical. Mary sensed they didn't want to talk in front of her, so she and Ember went to the cafeteria to have a bite to eat. Only the vending machines were open, but at least they were able to get a cold sandwich and a hot cup of coffee.

An hour later, they returned to the room and King was on a warpath. She could hear raised voices coming from his room, and it wasn't the cool and collected, serene environment the doctor insisted on earlier.

She and Ember entered and the room went silent. The guys went stock still, and Mary couldn't help but know they'd interrupted something important.

King was closed down and shut everyone out. Dr. Metsler came in shortly after the room hushed, and everything felt strained. Mary thought once King woke, there would be a jubilee. It was the furthest thing from the truth.

The doctor asked King if he wanted privacy when discussing his condition.

"There's nothing you will tell me that my men won't know. I can either repeat everything you have to tell me, or you can just say it now and get it over with."

All the team nodded at King's declaration, and Dr. Metsler went into the explanation of the gunshot wound, what it penetrated, what it missed, and what he had to repair. Mary was sickened at the thought of how close he'd come to dying. The pang of anxiety piqued once more. Venom ran through her veins, and she hoped that whoever was responsible died a slow and painful death at the hands of the team around her.

She found herself wondering which of these warriors had the pleasure to drain the life out of whoever tried to kill King. It didn't matter. All that mattered was justice was served. There would be no trial or mercy for the bastard. Mary oddly took comfort in the thought.

When he finished explaining the gunshot wound, the doctor turned to King's groin injury, a ruptured testicle. King vividly recalled the moment before he passed out. How the guy had latched on and tortured his jewels, and then he had no memory after he'd blacked out.

But, for the record, King's balls hurt. It was one of the first things he realized when he became lucid. *Why does my dick hurt?* The question was relentless in his mind. He wanted to lift the covers and examine the culprit, but with Ember and Mary at his bedside, he had to hold off the reveal.

Now, hearing Dr. Metsler describe the trauma to his boys, one: made him want to throw up and then pass out, and two: it raised a whole new shitstorm of questions about this entire fiasco.

Dr. Metsler explained that the trauma to his testicle was repaired, and King was one lucky son of a gun to have an injury that didn't require an orchiectomy. King blanched when the doc explained that they didn't have to remove the testicle, but King would have to be careful not to re-injure himself in the coming weeks before he was fully healed.

Mary thought he would have a litany of questions about his heart and lungs, questions about the stint of his recovery, so his first question out of the gate set her back as it did the rest of the group.

"What about kids?" King's question was direct. "Am I still able to have kids?"

Wow. The question brought tears to Mary's eyes, and the others in the room went mum.

"That'll be a bridge we'll cross after you make a full recovery." Dr. Metsler made no promises he couldn't keep.

"Not good enough." King sat up a little taller in bed, wincing as he strained to readjust himself. "I want answers. Run tests, give me a cup to fill. Whatever you need to do, do it. I want to know."

"We'll have to wait and see. After the injury heals, we'll do a semen analysis and perform a sperm count to give you the proper fertility rating. If a test is done now, it could rupture or compromise the repair, and then you would be in a worse state than you may be in right now."

Nobody thought King would put such an emphasis on procreating. Maybe Mary was reading into his line of questioning too hard. Maybe it wasn't about procreation at all. It was every man's worst nightmare to damage the family jewels, so maybe King's adverse reaction was just that...the thought of no longer having the means to procreate would lessen his manhood and resign him to cashing in his man card. Was that the reasoning behind his intense interest in his ability to produce offspring?

After Dr. Metsler left, King ordered everyone out of his room. No visitors, no one gawking at him. The team chalked it up to him not wanting anyone to see him as vulnerable.

After he ordered them out, they all stayed. He fired all of them on the spot, but still, it didn't make a lick of difference.

In fact, it pleased the guys when Ember put her hand on her hip and told him she didn't work for him, so it didn't mean a damn thing if he fired her. Case closed. She was staying. Mary was on Team Ember and wouldn't leave either.

The guys stayed until nightfall, then retreated to their homes. But, they left on their own terms, not because King ranted and raved, but because they were afraid he'd tear a stitch or have a heart attack each time he raved. Mary stayed at his side though he grumped about it, but she wasn't leaving him.

Before she knew it, she had the kitchen back to an almost normal state. She'd scrubbed the fridge and stove, gotten rid of all the broken kitchenware, and she was finishing sweeping the floor before she mopped it. It was just one room of many, but it was a start.

Though the effect of cleaning had the exact opposite effect of what she wanted. Instead of clearing her mind of King, it only allowed her mind to wander and bombard her with more memories and thoughts of him. She'd need to put her mind into action on something else. The last thing she wanted to think about was King. But why then was he the first thing on her mind?

~

He was an asshole. Plain and simple, no doubt about it, he was an ass! Why he exploded and chased her away had him kicking himself. His temper got the best of him, and he spouted off without thinking.

Granted, he had a lot on his mind, but it was no excuse. Mare had left, and he didn't know when she would return. He dialed her number for the hundredth time but couldn't hit the send button. He needed to give her time. *He* needed time.

What if it came down to him never being able to father children? God, the thought alone shot daggers of pain within him.

He never thought he would meet someone he'd fall in love with, let alone want to have children with. The thought was as staggering as it was frightening. But, he'd found Mary.

He couldn't explain how it happened, but she was *the one*. He was crazy in love with this sexy, beautiful, intelligent, fun-loving woman, and he knew he wanted to make her his, for life. But, all his anxiety heightened at the news that he may not be able to have kids.

Unlike him, Mary was still young. Not that he was ancient at almost ten years older than her, but before she came into his life, he'd come to peace and reconciled that by the time he hit forty, he'd live a solitary life.

And, *if* he did find someone after that milestone number, she would most likely be the same age as him and wouldn't be inclined to have children.

But Mary was vibrant and spry. Would she want him if he wasn't able to give her a family? Would he be enough for her to be content? No.

He wouldn't and couldn't do that to her. Mary deserved every great thing available to her in this world. He wouldn't rob her of the joy of motherhood. Even though they could adopt, she would never be round with his child, and he wouldn't take that from her. He wouldn't rob her of natural motherhood.

The other thing that needled his gut was that most likely by morning, she'd be notified that her brother's body was found in a drug-ridden neighborhood, known to Los Caballeros Rojos, the biggest local cartel in the area, and he was "killed by a drug deal gone wrong." The *"crew"* would make sure Trent's body was found, so Mary would have closure. If Trent just disappeared, it would be hell on her for the rest of her days wondering what happened to him, and it would eat her alive. He'd need to get a hold of the crew to make sure everything was taken care of. He didn't need any surprises.

He'd also contact Cypher and go over any news or chatter found on Chet. King knew the crew would take care of Chet as well, and if he was smart, he wouldn't be talking to anybody.

But, that was the thing—Chet was far from smart, so King would get a tail on him to keep him from blabbing. King believed in the old adage, "Keep your friends close, but your enemies closer."

CHAPTER 22

After her initial cleaning spree, Mary went back to Ember's to regroup and get away from the heaviness of the house and King's outburst. She needed to take a break from the drama surrounding her life. When she got to her temporary oasis, Slate and Cy were there with Ember.

Cy. Just the person she wanted to see. Though she would feel awkward, she would ask him if he could help her track her brother. Hopefully, Cy could help her make sense of it all. He was a nice guy. He was pleasant. And he was hot but in a nerdy sort of way.

He had brains and brawn.

His short brown hair had that sexy, mussed look up top, and his light green eyes behind his glasses rounded out the complete package. Though he wasn't as thick in mass as some of the others, he had a chiseled tone that was drool-worthy. Not that Mary was wanting, but she *was* a woman, after all.

She set her purse down on the entry table and toed off her shoes, pushing them to the side against the wall with her foot.

"How's King?" Ember was the one to ask, though the others looked eager to know how their boss was doing.

Settling down on the open seat on the couch, Mary closed her eyes and inhaled a deep breath.

"That good, huh?" Slate asked.

Mary nodded. "He's not too happy with his physical therapy. He's frustrated and being a complete jack-hole."

The group chuckled at the description.

"I know he doesn't want to be there. I know he's not used to limitations, but he took a bullet for God's sake. The man has to realize he's not invincible and needs to slow down." Mary stood, went into the kitchen, and grabbed a beer from the fridge. Twisting the cap off as she came back to the living room, she tossed it onto the coffee table and took a long pull from the bottle before she continued. "He's acting like he has a paper cut and can just walk it off. I mean, what is it with you alpha males and your need to completely disregard your health? And why can't you just admit when shit's fucked-up?" She addressed the two guys and then plopped down on the couch and took another pull.

"We're alpha males?" Cy quipped to Slate. He stretched both his arms along the back of the couch and relaxed into the cushion, "Think I'll be updating my resume."

Mary glared at him with humor in her eyes.

Slate flexed his pecs and then his biceps, kissing the bulging muscle stretched beneath his black tee, then winked at Ember.

"God, you two are such dorks!" Ember rolled her eyes.

"Anywho—" Mary reiterated, "King had a massive tantrum at his PT exercises this morning and blew up at me when all I was doing was trying to help and be supportive." She went on to explain King's meltdown and what he said to her.

Neither Cy nor Slate looked surprised, and Ember looked pissed.

"What a jerk!" Ember rolled her eyes.

"I know. Exactly my thoughts." Mary replied to Ember's reaction.

Both guys stayed quiet, not adding to the current conversation.

Mary leaned forward towards the coffee table and set the bottle on a coaster. "*I* don't understand why *he* can't understand *he* needs to slow down and take time to heal."

Cy and Slate chuckled.

"And this is funny how?" Mary questioned.

Both men looked at each other while continuing to smile. "He's Delta." Slate said in a manner as if it were obvious that everyone should know.

"And?" Mary waited.

"And, what?" Slate truly looked puzzled.

"He's Deltaaaa...?" She held on to the last syllable accentuating her question.

"Yup." Both Cy and Slate replied.

"That's not an answer." Mary was getting flustered.

"Then, state your question." Slate came back.

At this point in the conversation, even Mary was unsure as to what the original question was. Then continued, "How does, 'He's Delta,' answer the question of him not understanding he needs to slow down and get well?"

Slate shook his head in bewilderment, "*Beeecause* he's *Delllta*." He prolonged the words as if schooling an imbecile.

Cy laughed at the unintentional banter between Slate and Mary.

Ember came to the rescue and put the vying back and forth out of its misery. "Mare, because he's special forces he puts himself into an entirely unique class of survivors. He's trained to work hard and survive harder. Normal everyday injuries, aches, and pains don't stop the elite forces. They suck it up and continue on. 'Embrace the suck!' as they say."

Mary was about to lay into her friend, whom she thought was her ally, but just turned traitor. "A gunshot that almost killed him isn't an everyday injury."

"Not saying he's right, but I'm just clarifying what Slate was trying to say."

"Trying to say? I think I said it perfectly clear." Slate was ribbing Ember.

She locked icy eyes on him then turned the conversation back to Mary. "King's not one that's used to sitting around waiting for things to get better. He's always been the one to make things better. It's gotta be frustrating for him to not be in control. He's the boss. He's point. He's the lead, the one that controls the uncontrollable. So, I can understand him being irritated, but he shouldn't have taken it out on you." Ember sat back in the overstuffed chair and brought her feet under herself.

"True," Cy added. "King's never idle, so this has got to be killing him."

Though Mary was still pissed at his outburst at her, she had a tinge of regret leaving him earlier. Being angry didn't give him license to yell at her, but he did try to apologize. She was so mad and hurt she didn't even want to be in the same room with him. But maybe she should have stepped back and seen it from his point of view before leaving.

"Give him some time. I'm sure he'll come to his senses." Ember reassured her friend. "If not, I can gladly pay him a visit for you and set him straight." Ember looked hopeful, but Mary knew that wasn't going to happen.

"Thanks, but I don't think that'll be necessary."

"He'll come around," Cy reassured her.

"Yeah, he's just having a hard time. The last time he was out of commission was when he and Arctic…" Slate's voice softened, "…was when they lost their team."

Mary's eyes widened. "What? What happened?"

The other three looked sullen.

"His team was ambushed leaving a Forward Operating Base in Afghanistan." Cy cleared his throat, "Only King and Arctic survived." Cy didn't want to get into details, because it wasn't his story to tell. If Mary wanted to know, needed answers, she'd have to get them directly from King.

The room grew somber. Mary hadn't known about the accident.

"The burns on his arm?" Mary subtly asked the question as to why King's forearms were disfigured under his tatted sleeve. He rubbed them absently when he was worried or agitated. It was his tell.

Cy and Slate both nodded.

"After they recovered, King opened Hellforce. Four years later, long story short, here we are." Cy bit the inside of his cheek, reflecting in his memories.

No one said anything or continued the conversation, but the room was heavy.

"Think I'll fire up the grill." Slate clapped his hands together and stood.

Ember stood as well, "I'll get the steaks out of the marinade and bring them out to you."

They both went to the kitchen, and Cy got up to leave.

"Cy?" Mary's voice was hesitant.

"Yeah?"

"I was wondering if I could ask you for a favor?" She was hoping he'd say yes, but then again, there was the chance he wouldn't want to get wrapped up in her fucked-up family mayhem. Maybe he'd leave it to King to help her find Trent so she could find her family heirlooms.

"What'cha need, Mare?"

Mary kept her eyes on her clasped hands, wringing them, and then she looked up at Cy. "I was wondering if you could do your, 'cyber thing' and help me find my brother?"

Oh, fuck! Cy remained quiet. He didn't let his thoughts conform to his expression.

Mary continued, "I went back to the house today and tried to clean up the mess." She halted at the thought of cleaning the rest of the house. It overwhelmed her. "It was in the same shitty state as when I left. I looked around, even downstairs, and there's no sign of Trent being back there, and I haven't heard hide nor hair of him."

Cy shifted his weight nonchalantly and kept his focus on Mary.

When he said nothing, Mary felt she needed to give him more. "I don't care where Trent is. I've come to the realization that he could fall off the face of the earth for all I care."

Cy inwardly cringed at her callous remark and hoped she meant what she was saying.

"After the past year and a half, how he abused me, and I said nothing," Mary reflected and let out a shuddering breath, "I guess I'm just as much at fault for letting it continue to happen. I should have—"

"Don't you dare make excuses for that piece of shit brother of yours." Cy was instantly pissed, and he couldn't let her think for a minute she was at fault for her asshole brother. "Anyone that hurts a woman, lays one finger on them, should die a slow and painful death." Cy inwardly cringed again at his choice of words, not letting it show, but the one thing he couldn't stomach was the abuse of a woman or a child.

Mary was surprised to see the change in Cy. He was normally the calm one of the group, so to see him riled startled her.

Mary let the abuse topic fall to the wayside. She didn't want to discuss it. She was embarrassed that she'd allowed it, no matter what Cy or any of the group said. She should have called the cops after the first time he hit her. She knew all the blame lay with her brother, but it was a can of worms she didn't want to open. It would take time for her to hash it out and to come to grips with it and lose the guilt.

"Anyway, I was wondering if you could try and track him down. Not so I can talk to him," she added, "but, I thought if I could find him, I could possibly find what he did with my grandmother and father's rings. I'm almost certain he had something to do with the robbery."

Mary thought back to when she spoke with Ranger Daxton Chambers and he surmised the break-in looked staged and set up. It was too ransacked and destroyed to be a run-of-the-mill robbery. "I really don't think he would stoop that low, but," she paused and wrung her hands again, "he's not the same person anymore, and I'm afraid, and I really think he could have it in him to come back and hurt me again. I don't want him in my life anymore."

Mary thought of contacting the Ranger and getting a restraining order against Trent, but they would need to find him to serve him. That's where Cy's "magic" skills could come in handy.

Cy knew that Trent wouldn't be coming back into her life and would never lay another finger on her again. Those days were gone. *Fuck! What should I say to her?* He didn't want to lie and say he'd look into it, but he also didn't want to be the one to tell her about the demise of her brother and the circumstances leading up to it. King gave strict orders for the guys to keep that info locked down.

Mary waited patiently. "If I need to, I can hire you guys to take the case...to find Trent."

Oh, shit! He was between a rock and a hard place.

"Fuck that!" His words were sharp, so he softened his tone. "No way would we take this as a case."

Mary's face fell.

Cy went on to clarify, "King would never take something on as a *case* for any of us. That's not how we work." Knowing Trent was dead, and that her brother put the bullet into King and wounded him, Cy's next words made it hard to swallow. "I'll see what I can do." It was the only answer he could give her at the moment. He didn't lie. He didn't commit to finding him, and he didn't placate her with empty promises. He felt like shit, but his answer would have to do for now.

Mary's grin made her look hopeful. "Thanks, Cy. I'm glad I can count on you to help me find him and hopefully lead to finding our family's things. I know King and you all don't like him, but I know you'll do the right thing when we find him and just leave it to the authorities to punish him."

Cy stiffened his lips, trying hard not to blurt out the truth. He stayed stoic.

"You're good men, Cy."

Oh, no. this was going to be a shit show.

~

King paced the hospital floor, pissed and worried about Mary's request. Cy had stopped by the hospital after supper and gave King the 4-1-1 on Mary's plea to find her brother. He knew it was just a matter of time before the truth would be known. By all accounts, he was surprised the police hadn't contacted her yet. He spoke to Tex and knew things were at work in the system.

He ran his hands down his face and stroked the length of his beard, which was longer than normal since he'd been laid up the past week. "You didn't tell her anything?" King admonished.

Cypher gave King a harsh look, saying what didn't need to be said, "No, King. I didn't say anything. I told her I'd see what I could do."

"Good, good," King said with a nod.

"I didn't make any promises or lead her in any direction that would make her ask questions."

King paced back to the window and looked out into the blackened abyss of night. "God, I hate this. I feel like I'm lying to her. If not outright, at least by omission."

"No, King. She hasn't asked you anything. If anyone is misconstruing facts, it's me. She can't be mad at you when the truth comes to light. If she's gotta be mad at anyone, the team will take the fall."

King didn't want to lay any of this at the feet of his men.

"After all, it wasn't you that took him down." The words were matter-of-fact from Cy, not holding any reserved measure or judgment.

King knew his team put the fatal shots into Trent, but they wouldn't have had to if he would've trusted them and not barricaded himself in the warehouse room. So many things about that night were so fucked-up.

King never went vigilante. He was so driven by the haunting thoughts of what Mary had gone through at the hands of her brother that rage, anger, and lust for blood justice blinded his judgment. What started as a plan for a simple interrogation, led to an all-out fucking nightmare. King vowed to himself that he would never, ever, seek revenge for vigilante justice again, no matter the circumstances. He had let his training and judgment be blinded by his emotions. He was a better man than his choices and ultimate decisions that night.

"Did she say anything else? Ask any more questions?" King questioned Cypher as he paced the floor, the ache in his groin constant whenever he moved.

"Nope. Just asked if I could help find the whereabouts of her brother."

Damn it! He hadn't even thought of the fact that she would ask

Cy for help. He sat on the edge of his bed wanting to know every detail of the situation.

"Left it vague and open." Cy had his arms crossed over his muscled chest, a posture he struck often.

"Thanks for keeping me in the loop," King groaned out a breath. "Word is, I should be sprung from this joint tomorrow or the day after. If things aren't disclosed by the police, I'm going to have to tell her." It was a conversation King would dread having with Mary, but he couldn't leave her in the dark any longer.

Cy gave him a nod. Looking at his watch, he said, "I'm gonna get going. Let me know what the doc says, when he decides to let you leave."

"I'll do that."

"And, another thing," Cy paused with his hand on the door pull, "don't be such a dick next time Mary tries to help."

King pursed his lips.

"If I had a woman that cared for me as much as Mary cares for you, I'd snatch that up in a heartbeat." He threw King a chin lift, which King returned, and he left the room.

King strode back to the window and felt a rush of regret come over him. He hadn't called or texted Mary since she left, nor had he heard from her in either form. Swallowing his pride and guilt, he picked up his cell and began typing.

KING: *I'm a dick.*

Instantly the dots started to bounce in response to his message. King held his breath waiting for her reply.

MARY: *Yes, you are.*

King smiled down at her candid words. The dots bounced again, and he waited.

MARY: *But, I guess if you're a dick, then I'm a bitch for walking out on you. I'm sorry. I should've stayed.*

KING: *No need to disparage yourself. It was unfair of me to take out my anger on you.*

KING: *Please, forgive me?*

MARY: *Only if you do the same for me.*

King knew she did nothing to forgive. She was right to leave in the midst of his outrage. But, reluctantly, he agreed.

KING: *Ok.*

MARY: *You're just agreeing so I'll forgive you.*

King's smile broadened. She knew him too well.

KING: *Pleading the fifth.*

Mary sent an angry emoji face, followed by a series of random hearts, so he knew all was forgiven.

KING: *Doc says I may be leaving tomorrow.*

As soon as he hit the send button, he waited for the dots to bounce, but instead, his phone instantly rang with Mary's ringtone, which made his already huge smile grow even larger. He sent up a silent thank you and answered. "I miss you, Sugar!"

He could hear the smile in Mary's voice. "Miss you too, babe. I'm so sorry I walked out."

King wanted to move forward. "No need for apologies. Just promise me you'll never walk out on me again."

"I promise."

"And, I promise never to take out my anger on you. I was wrong, Mare."

"You were upset, and I should've been more patient."

"We could go round and round with this, so let's just agree we both fucked up." King wanted to end the apologies.

"Agreed."

"Although, I'm adding the caveat that I'm most likely going to fuck up in the future...a lot, so I'm going to have to get this groveling thing down for next time."

Mary liked that he was lightening the mood between them. They'd both fucked up, and it was done and over with. Both were sorry, and both knew they handled things in a stupid manner. "You're coming home tomorrow?"

The hope in her voice almost brought him to his knees.

"Either tomorrow or the next. Doc said I'd be his first stop in the morning, so I'll find out then." King hoped with everything in him that he'd be allowed to leave. If he'd have to stay any longer than the next two days, he'd sign the AMA and leave the hospital against medical advice. He knew Mary and the gang wouldn't like it, and most likely give him a heap of shit about it, but he was going stir crazy. He wanted to be back home, back to the office, back into his routine.

"I'll be there in the morning." Mary was asking, without asking, for permission to come.

"I wouldn't want it any other way, Sug.'"

Mary's heart beamed at his endearment. "Anything I can bring you?"

King rattled off a few things he'd like, namely a change of

clothes. He sent off a text to Arctic in the midst of their conversation and got an instant reply.

"Arctic will meet you in the morning at my place and give you a key."

Mary didn't know where "his place" was. "And what, per se, is the address of said place?"

King laughed at her etiquette. "I'll send you the address. Give me a sec." He sent off a text while she was still on the phone. "You got it?"

Mary checked her messages and one new notification appeared. She opened it and then opened the map app, locating his place.

"Whoa! You live right down the road from HQ!" It was more of a surprised shock than a question.

"Surprised?" King was unsure of her reaction and drew out the word.

"Well, yeah, I guess."

"You pictured me in a glorious penthouse in the sky or a shithole fleabag apartment on the wrong side of the tracks?" He was teasing her at her astonishment but could hear her sigh in amusement. "I have a modest, four-bedroom house...on eighty-five acres."

"Eighty-five acres!" Mary's shrill surprise made King pull the phone from his ear. He waited.

"Wow! That's a lot of land."

King didn't know if now was a good time to tell her that his land joined the additional two hundred acres Hellforce sat on. She'd toured the outdoor range and the mocked-up raid houses, so she knew Hellforce sat on a large spread of land. He assumed she'd figure out his land butted up to HQ when she drove to his house in the morning.

"Arctic will meet you there. Eight a.m. all right?"

Mary agreed. "You're not afraid I'm going to go through your medicine chest or look in your nightstand...or maybe raid your underwear drawer?"

King threw his head back and barked out a laugh that made his chest ache. "Sugar, you can peruse my medicine cabinet, you'll find nothing strange. I'm a boxer-brief man, not a tidy-whitey man, and if you look through my nightstand, you won't find anything astounding—"

"No Playboy or lewd magazines?"

"Not even a pin-up. I think I have an expired box of condoms and a bottle of lube in the top drawer, but other than that, nada."

Mary wondered why his condoms were expired. Had it been that long since he'd had sex or brought a woman back to his place? That set her face into a deepened frown at the thought of another woman being with King. Then the image was swept away with the thought of a bottle of lube.

"Lube?" The word popped out before she could call it back. She settled her head in her hand and squeezed her eyes shut. *What the fuck, Mary?* She chastised herself.

King chuckled on the other end of the phone. "Yeah, Mare...lube."

She was still hating that her inner voice trumped her outer voice when King continued.

"When I get you in my bed, and you're naked and writhing under me, and I'm ready to take you, believe me, you'll be thanking your lucky stars that it's in the drawer."

She went speechless. All the images King described came alive in her head. She wanted him. She yearned for a glimpse of him. His touch. His kiss. His hands roaming her body. She clenched her thighs together and felt herself pulse.

"Mare?"

"Yeah."

"You thinking of me?"

"Uh-huh."

"You thinking of us?"

She gulped, "Yeah."

"You embarrassed?"

"Kinda."

"Why?"

She didn't know how to answer that. She was thirty years old and could certainly have an adult conversation about things regarding sex. Yet, she was acting like a grade-schooler who just found out boys have penises. *Or is it peni...peniseses?*

"Mare?"

"Um-huh." She broke from her thought of penis verbiage.

"You want it to happen?"

Mary wanted it. God, did she want it. She craved it. But, another thought entered her mind and it had her stalling on the line.

"Mare. Where'd you go?"

It was as if he were reading her mind through the phone. "I'm here."

"I know, but what's running through your mind that's got you clamming up?"

The thought of why he'd be needing that lube, and lots of it, ran through her mind. If King were anywhere close to the size she'd felt that night in his truck, she was screwed. And, it was the "screw" that had her wincing.

"Sugar, what's wrong."

Should she tell him? Was this the right time to have this discussion? Maybe now was good, since she wouldn't have to look him in the eye, and he wouldn't see her embarrassment.

"Talk to me, Mary."

"Lube." Again, she hated herself. *Adult words, Mary. Adult words.*

"Okay?" His confusion was palpable. "What about it?"

"We're going to need...a lot of it. And, I mean, a lot."

Understanding dawned on King. "Mary?"

"Yeah."

"Are you afraid I'm going to hurt you?"

She knew King would never intentionally hurt her, but she knew the loss of her virginity was going to hurt. Especially if he was well-endowed. *Should I tell him I'm still a virgin?* She squashed the thought before it even got a chance to form. She went about it on a different kind of track. "So... you're kinda porn-worthy, and I'm kinda...not."

Her description made King want to burst out laughing, but instead, he let out a deep chuckle. He didn't want to embarrass her even more than she already was. "Porn-worthy?"

She laughed too. "Um...yeah? Have you seen yourself?"

What was his answer supposed to be to that? "Yeah, Sug'. I know I'm big."

"Understatement of the century."

King never really thought about his size. He was a big man, therefore...he had big parts. It never dawned on him, until now, that it may impose a problem.

"Mare?"

"Yeah."

"Don't worry about it."

Don't worry about it. Ha! "You aren't the one that's going to be skewered."

That made him laugh. "Skewered? That's...new."

He continued to laugh, and it relaxed her. If they could make light of the subject, maybe it would ease her embarrassment.

"King?"

"Yeah, Babe?"

"I want it to happen. Correction, I *really* want this to happen." She paused a moment. "I want to be with you."

"I am with you."

Mary guffawed. "You know what I mean."

"Then, just say it."

Mary inhaled a strong breath, hoping it would build her inner strength. "I want you to fuck me." She startled at the crudeness of her words. *Fuck? Why did you say fuck?*

"Not happening, Sugar."

What? "What?"

"I won't fuck you."

Her brows furrowed.

"When I get you under me, and after exploring every inch of you, Sugar, I'm going to make sweet, long, passionate love to you. No fucking. No rush. No skipping anything to get to 'the fun parts', 'cuz every inch of you, Babe, is going to be the fun parts."

Mary was putty on the other end of the line. She was damp and aching for him. No doubt she would be thinking of him tonight beneath her sheets...and panties.

"Mare?"

"Uh-huh."

"You wet?"

"Um-hmm."

Her throaty, short mewling answers had him hard as a rock. He could pound nails with the hard-on jetting beneath his hospital gown. He just prayed the night nurse wouldn't be making her rounds soon.

He glanced at the clock and saw it was pushing ten-thirty. "Think it's time for bed."

"Um...I think so too," she said, followed by a yawn.

"Sugar?"

"Yeah."

"I—" He wanted to say it, needed to say it, but the first time he said it wasn't going to be over the phone, where he couldn't look into the depths of her green eyes and pray for her to return the sentiment. "I... hope you sleep well." King closed his eyes.

Mary was silent as if waiting, then answered, "You too." Then, she added, "King?"

"Yeah, Babe?"

"I lo— I'll see you in the morning." The sentiment was on the tip of her tongue, she yearned to tell him, yet she stifled herself.

"Bye."

"Bye."

King ended the call and swore to himself. He couldn't wait to be with Mary, but for now, he had to deal with his raging hard-on, so he headed for a long, cold shower in the en suite bathroom of his hospital room.

~

Mary set the phone down next to her pillow and swore at herself. Why didn't she broach the subject? The white elephant was in the room. King would've probably thought she's an idiot, being a virgin at her age. *Will he be repulsed? Not want to touch me? Ugh! Maybe he'll think it's enduring, sweet even.*

She closed her eyes. *God, I'm going to need that* whole *bottle of lube!* Though she knew, once she caught a glimpse of what King was packing, even an entire bottle wasn't going to soothe her. The thought made her laugh and she relaxed onto her back, settled into the feather pillow, and pulled the covers under her arms.

Staring at the ceiling, her mind wandered to King and all the tantalizing things he would do to her. Her hand crept under the blankets and skimmed her inner thigh. The thought of King's hand roaming her body struck a shiver down her spine, and she brought her hand to rest just below her belly button. She circled her navel with two slow passes.

King.

The thought had her swallowing, hard. Her fingers delved beneath her lace panties, skimming through her short, trimmed curls, lowering until she felt the wetness coating her hand. She pressed in and a moan slipped from her lips. She had to be quiet, keep her keening to a minimum. And, she did just that, as images of King filled her mind, and she brought herself to ecstasy with one touch, one thrust, one man. *King.*

CHAPTER 23

"Awe, Mare, come here. Don't cry."

King pulled Mary into his arms and cradled her while she held the miniature glass ballerina figurine with the frilly pink tutu her mother kept on top of her dresser. She'd given it to her when she was seven and was in beginner's ballet. Her father spotted the figurine at the local gift shop where the two were shopping for Mother's Day. Mary's mother loved the figurine and said she'd always see her little girl when she looked at it. Mary always thought it was silly when her mom would reminisce every time she'd dust or pick it up, but now, seeing it broken in two sent splinters into Mary's heart.

"I'll glue it back together for you. You'll still have it." King took the two broken, chipped pieces and tried to line up the cracks to see if it could be salvaged. "We'll fix it, Mare."

Mary looked around her mother's room and the devastation overwhelmed her. Mary wiped her swollen, reddened eyes with the heels of her palms. "It makes no sense." She picked up what was left of an old cigar box and sniffed again when she saw her father's baseball card collection. "At least these are still here." She looked through the cards and placed them back into the box with the wrecked lid. "Why?" she asked again.

King tread lightly. "Sometimes people get desperate. Sometimes there's no rhyme or reason." He felt the tinge of anger bubble but tamped it down. He would tell Mary the truth tonight, at his place. He didn't want to tell her Trent was responsible for the ruin all around her. But, it was time. It'd been two weeks.

The police hadn't contacted her yet, though King knew the detectives had discovered Trent's body the day after the shooting. Even though it was a neighboring county, he didn't know what was holding them up. Identification shouldn't have taken so long. King had all the bases covered with Tex, but still, the time frame was making him a bit nervous.

Ember walked in with a roll of trash bags, followed by T and Trip, who was still walking with a slight limp. "Got the living room back in order, and the dining room is pretty much cleared out," Ember said lightly.

The team came together and pitched in to help clean the house. They were making progress, but each guy knew Trent was responsible for every broken item they picked up, and it was eating them alive not to say something in the midst of cleaning.

T touched the sleeve of Mary's shirt, "We're going to head downstairs. Is there anything you need?"

Everyone knew Mary wouldn't want to go into her brother's room. She made a few remarks hinting towards the fact that she hoped Trent didn't show up while they were cleaning, and the guys all felt the gravity of her statement. Each guy knew there would be no visit.

Mary shook her head and thanked everyone again for their help. "I know you probably have better things to do than this, but I really do appreciate the help." She wiped her nose with her sleeve.

A round of, "no problem" and "it's cool" came from the group. T-BAR, Slate, Arctic, and Cy headed for the basement, while Ember and Trip stayed in the bedroom with King and Mary. King bent to pick up an overturned armoire when Mary let out a yelp.

"Uh-uh! Stop!" She was pointing an outstretched finger at King as if scolding a disobedient dog.

King stopped mid-bend.

"No way, mister! Doctor's orders."

King had been discharged three days prior. Dr. Metsler wanted him to stay one more day, but when King said he was leaving come hell or high water, the doc said he would release him on one condition—that King promise he'd take it easy for the rest of the week and not do anything too strenuous. Everyone was skeptical, but knowing Mary would be staying with him at his house, and not at Ember's, they knew Mary would keep him in line.

"Not happening!" She looked to Trip and Ember who jumped in place and took over lifting the heavy cherrywood wardrobe.

"Mare—"

"Nope, don't want to hear it." Mary put up a staying hand.

"It's not even that heavy," he muttered under his breath.

King heard Ember and Trip chuckling from behind him. They didn't hide their joy and humor.

Mary unrolled a trash bag and handed it to King, "You can fill this."

King took the bag and slightly shook his head, muttering something inaudible. He swore, if Trip made one wise-ass remark, Hellforce would be paying for a new set of dentures for his friend.

Trip kept quiet but bent to pick up a paper doily at his feet. "Here, boss. Gotcha covered."

King was not amused.

Ember couldn't hold back and let out a side-splitting laugh, and Mary snickered at King's obvious disdain for his teammate.

"You're fucking fired!" King threw a scorned glare at Trip, but in normal Trip fashion, he smiled his full, radiant smile and laid on the charm that had so many ladies' panties dropping at his feet. King wasn't charmed in the least.

"King, stop wallowing and hire your teammate back. There's plenty of things to get done," Mary playfully mocked. Seeing that her spirits were somewhat restored, King set to picking up the broken and littered items that weren't salvageable. Trip and Ember righted the other dresser against the far wall.

Time seemed to stand still cleaning her mother's room. It seemed every item she picked up had a memory tied to it. She salvaged what she could and parted with the rest. Having everyone there helped move things along, and the house was getting straightened and cleaned quicker than she could do on her own. It would be ready for the sales market. The real estate market was booming, so she knew a quick sale was possible. But, to get a quick sale, the house first had to be cleaned. She was ready for a fresh start. A new place to call home.

Arctic appeared at the bedroom door, his demeanor passive to Mary, but the instant King made eye contact with him, he knew something was amiss. "Can I talk to you, boss?"

King straightened, "Sure."

"In private." Arctic's voice held no warning, but King knew better.

He handed the almost full trash bag to Mary and headed towards the doorway.

"Trip." Arctic's voice summoned him also.

Both men headed out of the bedroom.

Mary stood, dumbfounded, and turned to Ember. "What'd you think that's about?"

Ember shrugged. "Maybe they got called out for something unplanned or unexpected?"

Mary's heart fell. Would they leave without King? It would kill him if he had to watch his men leave and he stayed behind.

"Or, maybe they have something that needs all their heads? Something Arctic can't discuss in front of us, or can't make a decision on, without the boss's input?"

Maybe that was it. She felt a little better. "No one has eaten yet, I should get some lunch together." Since there was nothing left in the house, they decided to run to the local delicatessen and get some sandwiches. "You know what they eat? You know them better than me."

"Usually anything red meat and potatoes, so any triple meat sandwiches and potato salads will probably suit them fine." She shot Slate a text, letting him know they were leaving and would be back shortly.

Mary grabbed her purse and they headed to Ember's car.

≈

"What the fuck!" King muttered under his breath.

"Guess he was dumber than we thought." Trip said.

"Or had a death wish." Cy returned.

T let out a whistle as the others let out similar expletives. All six men looked down at the opened lockbox on Trent's bed, a box which held fifty little sealed bags of small, bluish-white crystals. Also, inside the box was a small black card, about the size of a business card. No name, no contact, just an insignia they all knew well. A chess knight bathed in crimson red.

King shook his head in disbelief, "He was either selling for them—"

"Or stealing from them." Trip finished King's exact thoughts.

Slate rubbed the back of his neck and added, "Or possibly both."

"Los Caballeros Rojos. The Red Knights. Fuck!" King ran his hand down his face and groomed out his beard after seeing the card. "This just made it a game-changer. If he was selling, and now he disappeared, they are going to think he split with the stash.

And, if they found his body, they're going to be looking for the stash."

King uttered another *fuck* under his breath. The warehouse where they left Trent's body was Rojos turf. Their playground. It was dumb fucking luck. They knew it was gang turf, but now knowing Trent was involved with the gang had King edged. "We gotta get Mary and Ember out, now. It's not safe here for them."

"They just left. Went to get lunch." Slate looked up from his phone showing them the text.

Another barrage of curses came from King. "As soon as they're back, we leave. No telling when, or if, someone'll come around looking for this." He pointed to the box. "Wipe it down and put it back where you found it."

Cy nodded and T added, "Yeah, 'cuz that's the best hiding spot...no one ever knows to look under the bed, right?"

The rest of the guys shook their heads in disbelief that Trent would have the lamest hiding spot. Either he was that dense, or he had a death wish. Either way, his judgment was utterly lacking. Once everything was put away, they righted the furniture and finished cleaning up the mess. King made a few phone calls and they all headed upstairs.

All six men sat in the living room waiting for Ember and Mary to return. The room was awkwardly silent.

"Something doesn't add up." King's deep baritone filled the room.

Five heads turned towards him.

"The police did a thorough sweep when they came through after the alleged robbery. You telling me they didn't look under the bed?"

All the guys looked puzzled in agreement.

"That'd be odd if they didn't," Cy remarked.

"Yeah, that'd be a rookie mistake, and I don't see that happening," Arctic added.

Slate was the next to add to the conversation, "But, they did have shit-for-brains Meyers running the show."

King agreed, then added, "Yeah, but even Meyers isn't that incompetent. Believe me, he'd love to find anything that could give him brown-nose-brownie-points with his superiors. He probably scoured this place looking for anything he could find. Especially knowing Trent's history and having him on his radar."

T added to the round of speculations, "True, he'd love to find something to cement him and justify his status of detective."

"*Dick*-tective!" Trip uttered, making the others laugh.

"The word is mum for the moment with Mary. Not until we can figure out what's going on. She has a lot on her plate, so let it lay low for now." King warned the guys.

A sharp and terse knock sounded, and they all turned in the direction of the front door. King rose along with the others and headed into the dining room to the door. Looking through the side glass and seeing two uniformed officers, he went on high alert. He cautiously signaled to his team, "authorities," and unbolted the deadbolt then addressed the two men on the porch.

"Can I help you?" King stood with his hand bracketing the door, while his bulk filled the doorway. *Dick*-tective Meyer and another officer King wasn't familiar with, stood before him.

"Mary Jones." It was more of a statement than anything, and Meyers held a smug, cocky look on his face when seeing King. The douche even flashed his badge. *What a dick move.*

King hated Meyers. The two had butted heads in the past and again on the day of the alleged robbery. "She's not available." King's countenance didn't change.

"And, you are?" The officer behind Meyers questioned, being nothing short of an arrogant prick. Instantly, King disliked him, too.

"This is Rambo," Meyers told the officer, whose name was Graves, by the tag on his uniform. Meyers thought he was humorous, but King didn't give him any fodder.

He addressed the officer over Meyers' head, purposely, since King dwarfed Meyers by five inches. "Henry Clark." Flat. Crisp. Short and sweet.

"This is a matter of urgency," Meyers replied, shifting his weight. "When will you be expecting her—"

A Texas Ranger SUV pulled up behind the police cruiser in front of the house. Two men got out, one put on his traditional Stetson, then both came up onto the porch.

"Afternoon, gentlemen," the Ranger addressed the two men at the door. His tone was terse but directed at the men before King. "Meyers, this isn't your call."

"My case, Chambers." Meyers bit back.

"My jurisdiction." Dax responded, "Ya know, Texas and all."

"It's federal now, Meyers." The man who spoke wore an FBI jacket.

"Didn't know you were on this, Livingston." Meyers was pissed he was outranked.

"Nice to see you, Cruz." King gave him a nod.

"You too, King." FBI Special Agent Cruz Livingston replied.

King stood sentry in the doorway backed by his five teammates. Everyone was curious about the discussion between law enforcement when Ember's car pulled into the driveway. Meyers turned back to King as if asking, "Is that her?" without saying as much.

King gave no response. He was sure he knew why these men were paying the visit but gave away nothing.

The women got out of the car, Mary rounding the rear, both looking curious. They'd obviously seen the patrol cruiser and SUV parked at the curbside and now saw the officers at the door.

Mary was the first to approach, "Can I help you?"

"Mary Jones." Ranger Chambers and Detective Meyers said in unison. Meyers threw a fierce look at Chambers. Chambers addressed her with courtesy, while Meyer was questioning her identity.

Mary acknowledged hesitantly, "Yes."

Cruz spoke up next, ignoring the stare-off between Dax and Meyers. "I'm Special Agent Cruz Livingston, and this is Ranger Dax Chambers. May we have a word?"

Mary climbed the four steps up to the porch, followed by Ember. "Sure...yes, of course." She fumbled nervously with the packages she was holding.

"Please, come in," she said. She went to enter and stopped when King didn't move. He took the packages from her.

"Only necessary personnel." King stared directly at Meyers and Officer Graves behind him.

Mary looked lost and out of place, so King pulled her past him and guided her into the protection of his teammates behind him, followed by the same with Ember, then stood solid in the doorway.

Daxton stepped closer to the door and sidestepped Meyers. "Jurisdiction."

When Meyers stayed planted, Agent Livingston was a bit more forceful. "Turn around, Meyers. If you can't make that happen, I'm sure your chief will." With that said, Meyers stood his ground for a split second, then turned and bounded down the porch steps.

King stepped outside the doorway, leaving the entry to Dax and Cruz, all the while keeping his stare on Meyers. Meyers returned his glare. King wasn't backing down. Meyers' "small-man-syndrome" got the best of him, and he stomped back to his cruiser. King watched him and caught his eye before he opened his door. King stood unwavering. Meyers caved and disappeared into the driver's seat. King watched and waited until Meyers and Graves drove away before reentering Mary's house. He knew this was going to be hard on Mary.

Trent would re-emerge but not in the way she'd anticipated. King knew a shitstorm was just on the horizon.

～

"I'm sorry, Ms. Jones." Dax's voice was firm but sympathetic.

All five Hellforce teammates stood around Mary, as she was told that her brother's body was found in war-torn gang turf on the west side. King sat next to her ready to comfort her when she crashed. But, oddly, she didn't. She sat frozen, eyes searching in disbelief, but she didn't scream or wail.

"Are you sure?" Mary's voice wavered but didn't crack.

"Identification was made this morning," Cruz told her.

This morning? King knew it may have taken a bit to identify Trent, but it seemed odd that it would've taken so long. It was two weeks since the shooting. Trent was left with no form of identification. No phone. No wallet. It wasn't The Crew's first rodeo. They worked in the shadows; hid in the night. Black ops securities used them when things needed to appear in a certain light, or out of it. When a crime scene needed to cease to exist, when witnesses needed to see nothing and when collateral damage had to be leveled to a minimum. King wasn't the only security entity to use The Crew. They were well-known in his circle of business. They did the job, did it flawlessly, and "didn't exist." A win-win for all involved.

A lone tear escaped Mary's eye, and she quickly brushed it away. "I haven't seen him in a while, but it's not unlike him to disappear for long periods. He—" She looked lost, almost lonely, yet exasperated. A myriad of emotions washed over her face. More tears began to fall, and she couldn't wipe them away fast enough before they fell from her cheeks.

King felt awful. It was because of him she was going through this. He did this to her. He put that anguish on her face. He was to blame for each tear that welled and fell. *Fuck! Why did I push the boundaries?*

As if sensing him breaking, Arctic put a hand on King's shoulder and squeezed with unusual force as he reached across him, making it seem as if he were using him for balance, and handed Mary a handkerchief. The squeeze was in warning, the handkerchief was in kindness.

King got the message and was thankful for his friend's warning pulling him from the brink. He couldn't crack. He was also thankful for his friend's kindness towards Mary.

Who carries a handkerchief nowadays? King was distracted, which was very unlike him. He had to focus, stop letting his mind wander into unnecessary qualms.

"Do you know...is there—" Mary's eyes were on Dax and Cruz, but her stare went right through them, "Do you know who did this?"

King stiffened for a millisecond but returned his posture to normal. Guilt ate at him. Not only was he keeping the truth from Mary, but also from his friends, Dax and Cruz. He knew his team was feeling the same way without having to glance at any of them. He knew his men.

"We have no witnesses, but word on the street is it was Los Caballeros Rojos. We have an informant that said the gang has claimed credit."

Mary's eyes widened.

Agent Livingston continued. "We have an open investigation into a major meth ring operated by the Rojos gang and unfortunately, your brother was a key player in the activity."

She couldn't believe what she was hearing. *Trent was in a gang? Not just any gang, but the most prevalent gang in the area.* She couldn't wrap her head around it.

"Are you sure?" It seemed like a stupid question to ask, but she was at a loss.

"Yes, ma'am," Dax answered. "He was just initiating, and word on the street is, he was skimming from the top."

Mary's brow furrowed.

He continued, "Whenever a new member is brought into the fold, they're always tested and tempted. Most new initiates know they're being tested, monitored, and tried, and it's not until later they try to cut, for either their own use or their own side profit, but unfortunately—" he cleared his throat, "unfortunately, your brother fell to the temptation. I'm sorry." Both men truly looked pained to be passing on the discovery of the investigation.

King was floored. *Holy shit! Trent was embroiled deeper than they'd imagined.* In all reality, it was just a matter of time before the cartel would have taken Trent out themselves. Nobody stole from the Caballeros Rojos and lived to tell about it. And, the gang was taking credit for his murder in order to show other members what happens to those that cheat and steal from them, even though they didn't have a single thing to do with his death. Anything to show dominance and keep things tight. Trent had signed his demise the minute he made the choice to fuck the cartel.

The truth did nothing to ease the guilt King was laying on himself. He would have to come clean with Mary if a relationship between them was going to work and flourish. He couldn't keep something like this from her. The thought soured his stomach.

Two scenarios were in his future. One: she would hate him and leave him, or two: she would somehow come to grips with the fact that it was Trent who put the bullet in King and tried to kill him. So, it was either kill or be killed, and his team executed the former.

Ranger Chambers and Agent Cruz went through the standard procedure of the investigation and questions, answering, as well as asking. Mary answered all she could and vice versa.

"We can instruct the Medical Examiner to release your brother to the funeral director of your choice."

Mary raised her eyes to King, asking what to do.

"We'll let you know what she decides."

That seemed to soothe her, and she was about to stand as the pair rose, but they halted her.

"We'll see ourselves out."

Mary nodded and King stayed seated but shook both their hands. They walked to the front door, Cy and Slate following behind them.

Both men handed their cards to Cy. "Please give her these. If she has any questions, tell her not to hesitate to contact us. Again, our condolences to her."

He took the cards and nodded. Slate held out a hand and shook both gentlemen's, as did Cy. They left, and Slate shut the door, then they both returned to the living room.

Mary had a range of emotions running across her face. She was physically in the present, but her mind was miles away. All six waited. Ember sat on the other side of her, adding her support. No one spoke. They just let Mary process what she'd just learned.

Her brother was dead.

≈

The news of Trent's death hit her hard. She felt a pit of regret from her earlier thoughts of not caring if she ever saw him again.

Now, she never would.

The finality of that reality crashed over her. Her words ate at her. It was one thing for her to *say* her brother was dead to her, but another to find out he *was* dead. She folded her arms across her stomach and leaned forward, trying to dull the ache that settled deep in her gut. Trent was dead. She knew she should cry. Knew she should wail. Something. But oddly, none of those emotions flooded her.

Shock, that must be it, I'm in shock. The thought flitted through her mind as she tried to rationalize and process the current, new reality: Her brother was dead.

King's hand settled on her leg, startling her. "Whoa, Sugar," his voice was smooth and gentle, "it's just me."

She turned to him and saw the concern in his eyes.

Again, she got lost in her thoughts. Things didn't make sense. If Trent could abuse her for so long, join a gang, steal from a prevalent drug cartel, what else was he capable of doing? Trent always ran in a rough circle of friends. If he was attempting to initiate into the Rojos gang, surely his friends would do the same. Trent never did things solo.

She spoke to no one in particular, "I know he's bad, hangs out with bad people, but a drug deal gone wrong? With only Trent at the scene? Doesn't add up. I know he could do petty larceny, even could have had something to do with robbing me and pawning the safe, but why would he do a major drug deal or sell by himself? It's not like him. He never runs solo. Why wouldn't there be more than just his body found? There's got to be something else." She stared blankly through her clasped hands. "This just doesn't make sense."

She was processing out loud, and the guys let her work through her emotions and thoughts. "He's always gotten into some form of trouble, scams, even stole from my parents when he was a teenager. He always made bad choices. I know he's dabbled in minor drugs, marijuana, even steroids back in high school, but he would've never been involved with a ring this big, with a drug cartel." She shook her head, "He's dumb, but dumb enough to get involved in something that big or that risky? He has street smarts, maybe he would peddle for a small gang, but a cartel?"

A lone tear streaked down her face. King read Mary as she sorted things out. He knew there was something else bothering her besides her brother's death. "Something else is bothering you, what is it?"

"I don't know. Something in my gut tells me this is wrong. If he was selling for the gang, where's his friends? He may have stolen from me, may have been involved in the robbery, but if he's selling why would he...plan...a robbery?" She was disjointed, but it was good she was verbalizing instead of internalizing her emotions and thoughts.

Then she said the one thing no one in the room wanted to hear. "I know my brother isn't a good person, but did he deserve to be killed?"

King looked around the room of his teammates. Each one held the posture of an operator. No one was relaxed. They all were on edge, just as he was. Meeting their eyes, he took measure, calculating his next move. Each man's composure granted him his next decision.

"Mare, if there's more information, do you really need to know?"

"Of course, but what more is there to know? We know where he is." She hitched, "he's...dead."

King took in a deep breath, holding it a bit longer than normal, then let it out, controlling and centering himself. He clarified, "There *is* more."

Mary's eyes widened.

"I know you *want* to know, but Mary, do you *need* to know?"

King's cryptic words were throwing her all over the map. Of course, she wanted to know. If there was more to her brother than the authorities already told her, she wanted and needed to know.

"Tell me." Her gaze hadn't left him.

King looked to the guys to get a final blessing to tell her. When they nodded, he braced to tell Mary the truth. Come what may, she deserved to know.

"We tracked Trent and his friend Chet to a pawn shop a couple of weeks back. He was pawning your family rings."

Though Mary knew in her gut that Trent was responsible for the break-in, it still shocked her to hear it was true.

"He set up an alibi and had his friends case the house and do the robbery. According to his friend, Chet, Trent thought there was cash and jewelry in the safe. They staged the house as a break-in. You weren't supposed to be here. You were caught unexpectedly in their plan."

Mary sat frozen. King wasn't sure if she was hearing him.

"Mare?"

She unconsciously touched her head where she had been hit during the robbery. "He was selling our things? From the safe? Are you sure?"

King nodded. "The safe was in the car at the pawnshop. We tracked him and 'detained' him and his friend at the shop."

Her eyes widened with the reality that King was responsible. "What did you do?" Her barely-audible words hit him with the same force as if she'd shouted them.

King swallowed. "We needed to find out who else was involved, and who hurt you that morning."

"You went after Trent?"

The question rocked King. "You asked for mercy...and I... the plan was supposed to be simple." King was stammering, not able to articulate his thoughts. "I wanted the names of those involved. Those that hurt you."

"What did you do?" Mary closed her eyes.

"We *removed* them from the pawnshop."

"We?" Mary looked around at the men standing around her. No one flinched at her scrutiny.

"We. All of you." She turned back to King and he nodded.

He chose not to use tactical descriptions and gave her the briefest of information, but enough that she would understand. "We secured them, took them to a secure location then separated them from each other." King was flustered. Hearing a generic description wasn't painting the picture he wanted. *How could he make her understand? How could he let her know his state of mind? Did he want her to know his state of mind?*

"Mary, I needed to find out why he hurt you in the past. How he could put his fists, and scars, and bruises on you. How he could hospitalize his own sister. His same flesh and blood. I needed to know who was aiding him in the robbery."

Mary was trying to process everything. "A couple of weeks ago." Her mind raced. Then, the switch clicked. Her breath hitched. "Did he do this to you?" She pointed to King's chest, her hand hovering over his heart.

He didn't answer.

"Oh, my God...he *did* this to you. My brother—" It wasn't a question, it was a knowing. "Trent—" Her stomach dropped. She wanted to vomit.

She turned to Cy with realization shining in her eyes, "Did he do this?" She pointed to the healing scar on his neck. "And Trip?" She turned to him, "Did he do—" She pointed to his leg.

Mary was on overload. She was volatile like glycerin. Nobody wanted her rattled. Her response was predictable. She knew the truth.

"Oh—" she was panting, looking at nothing, playing her thoughts back through her mind. "Oh, my God." She turned to King. "Did you —" She couldn't form the words. "Did you—" she swallowed, "Trent?"

Slate spoke. "It wasn't King. We had no choice, Mary."

She whirled in his direction, "No choice?"

She wasn't panicked or angered to the point of delirium; she was in self-preservation mode. Her head was on a swivel and whirled back to King.

King wasn't a remorseful man, but when he spoke, his words were doused. "I tried to show him mercy, Mare...I did. I unarmed myself...I tried...with mercy, like you asked, I tried. In the robbery, I almost lost you, Mare. Until I was overpowered...He had my gun..." King tried to remain stoic but panic was creeping in. "I was rendered—"

"Did he do this to you?"

King answered with a single nod.

"And, you—"

"Mare, it wasn't King. It was either *we* pull the trigger, or *your brother* pulls the trigger... on *him*." Slate motioned to King.

Mary didn't look at Slate. She didn't take her eyes off King. The emotional dam broke, and she sobbed, bringing her hands to her face, then leaned into King, her head to his chest over his heart, and she sobbed. And he let her, wrapping his strong arms around her.

King knew each man was breaking, watching Mary in misery, but knew they felt no remorse. They were a team. Brothers. Each would die for the other. No doubt. So, the only pain they were feeling was for Mary and not for taking the life of her brother.

Mary pushed her head further into his chest. Her ear pushed against him.

"Mare, I'm so sor—"

"Shhhh…" She stayed planted against him. For over a minute, she didn't move.

"Mary—"

"Shhhh...give me this."

"What?"

"This. Every beat. I need to hear this." She hiccupped a little sniff. "I need to hear that you're still with me. You're still alive."

King's arms tightened. He was alive. He had his woman in his arms. His life in his arms.

"Mare. Your brother—"

"Tried to take you from me."

"I know, but—"

"Henry. Don't."

He was taken aback.

"I don't want to know. Not right now. I just need this moment."

King didn't move. Didn't say a thing and neither did his team.

Ember stood and went to Slate, pulling him into an embrace. She knew the gravity of taking another human life. In battle, it was justified, but the implication wasn't lessened. The stain was left on the soul. So, even in defense, the mark was still bitter.

After a minute, the group started to disperse, giving King and Mary the time they needed alone.

King wasn't sure how long they sat together with Mary burrowed in his arms, but it was what she needed. What he needed. What they needed.

Time would tell if she'd have a reckoning, and if she would truly come to grips with what had happened. She may leave him, and that scared the ever-living shit out of him. She would ask questions. He would answer. She would need time to grieve. Time to hurt. Time to hate. She would need time to heal. Through it all, he would give her what she needed and be at her side.

"King?"

"Yeah, Sugar."

"I don't want to be here."

"Okay, Mare."

"Please, take me home."

He paused. She was home.

"Ember's?"

"No."

He knew what she was saying, but needed to hear her say it.

"Where, Sug'?"

"Your home."

He placed a kiss on top of her head and she pulled back. Looking into her eyes, he searched for any depth of hatred or resentment...blame. It wasn't there.

She rose, then pulled his hand as he stood. She wrapped herself in his arms again, never wanting to leave his protection. Looking up at him, her eyes were clear. "I need to leave. Take me home."

"Anything you need, Mare."

He pulled his key fob from his pocket and he went in search of his team.

Soon, they left, heading for home.

CHAPTER 24

The next six weeks were a rollercoaster of emotions for Mary. Rebecca's Hope, the local women's shelter where Mary once worked, came and picked up the furniture and household goods from her mother's house. The guys loaded up certain pieces Mary wanted to keep, her mother's china cabinet and her grandmother's antique grandfather clock and such, and brought them to King's place. They also packed up keepsakes and mementos she wanted and got the house ready to be put on the market and got a quick sale.

Mary made it a point to visit her mother more often, but still, her mother had no recollection of her own daughter, which piled onto the sadness she was already feeling. King turned in the box he found in Trent's room to Ranger Chambers, who would get it to Special Agent Livingston at the FBI. Trent's involvement with the gang only solidified the alibi Hellforce and The Crew put in place.

Tex was given a marker that King knew he'd never cash and the case was now closed.

Since then, a myriad of emotions poured through Mary, and King could only stand by and be her support when she needed it. She volleyed from deep, gut-wrenching sadness at the loss of her brother, to extreme anger and rage that he was the one responsible for putting a near-fatal bullet into the man she was falling in love with.

If she was completely honest, she had already fallen but just hadn't told him yet. She felt like a schoolgirl waiting for her crush to break first and admit he "liked" her. It was more than obvious he liked her.

Hell, she was living with him, working with him, spending the nights cradled in his arms, but that was it. No one professed their undying love, and they weren't having sex.

Oh, there were heavy make-out sessions, and once or twice they'd come close to stripping each other naked and jumping one another, but King was always the first to step back. She knew he was giving her time to process everything that happened. He told her, even though they'd sprinted off the starting blocks full force into a relationship, he wanted her to heal her soul before they started a new chapter, one he knew he would never be able to walk away from once they took the next step.

Mary wanted to leap to the next step. She'd gotten close, but life seemed to get in the way. The team left on a few jobs—short stints, saving the world from hell and chaos was her guess, so the opportunity was always lost once she thought they'd finally reached the pinnacle and juncture to move forward.

She wasn't having it any longer. If the opportunity wasn't comin' knockin', then she'd march straight to its door and let herself in, guns a-blazin'.

Tonight was that night. King was taking her for an early supper and when they got home, she'd pounce. No more waiting around.

∼

"You wanna catch a movie?" King looked over from the driver's seat of his truck, taking his eyes off the road for a second, to take in Mary seated beside him.

She was absolutely stunning.

Her hair was pulled up into a messy bun, with rogue tendrils that had escaped its confines, and she wore a white gauzy top with a fitted tank underneath showing the luscious curves of her breasts. She matched it with the tightest pair of black jeans King had ever seen. They were painted on her, but she filled them out with a rounded ass and killer legs he'd dreamt about night after night.

Although, he wanted to wrap her in a turtleneck and baggy sweatpants when he saw a few men ogling her from the bar when they walked through the supper club. He had to inwardly smile and congratulate himself when he saw their faces fall as they spotted him noticing their stares. One glaring, pissed-off look from King was all it took for them to turn on their barstools and shrink into their drinks.

He was satisfied with their quick retreat, but Mary slapped him across his broad chest when she saw him giving death stares to anyone who happened to get within her view. He played dumb, but Mary gave him her own evil-eye-death-stare that had him curbing his alpha vibe.

"No. No movie tonight. I was hoping we could turn in early." Mary had no intention to turn in early. There would be no sleeping on tonight's agenda.

King shrugged. "Okay. Maybe another night." He brought their grasped hands to his lips, then settled it back in place, just the way he always did when they drove.

Mary squirmed in her seat, hoping he didn't notice as she envisioned what the night would entail. She'd bought a new matching lace bra and panty set that she'd slipped into after her shower before they left for supper. She couldn't wait to see his reaction.

It was so sheer that her nipples almost pierced between the intricate lace pattern, and the thong was nothing more than a scrap of wadded dental floss. She groomed, shaved, scrubbed, and exfoliated every inch of herself. She hoped her painstaking routine didn't go for naught.

"Everything okay?" King spared another glance.

Shit! Did I miss the conversation while lost in thought? "What?"

King gave a chuckle, "You seem a million miles away and you're fidgeting."

She calmed herself. "I'm fine, just thinking...just a bit antsy, I guess."

"Antsy? Care to share?"

God, no! "No. Nothing in particular." She was glad when he let it go and they drove the rest of the way home hand-in-hand, listening to the radio with King humming and singing along in his sexy, panty-melting, smooth baritone. As if she wasn't antsy before, his crooning did it to her now.

When King unlocked the door, she hardly gave him time to disarm the alarm and relock before she wrapped him in her arms and planted a kiss on his lips.

"Well," he pulled her close, "I'll take this over a movie any night."

He deepened the kiss and within minutes, they were in the throes of passion. Things escalated quickly, the same as the last few nights that ended in disappointment for Mary.

Feeling him growing hard, she ran a hand over his length, squeezing the bulge beneath her palm and stroking him to the tip. His jeans were tightening and he moaned, then broke their kiss when he caught a breath.

"Sugar," King murmured in a playful tone, then bowed his head to the side of hers, "Whad'ya doin'?" She could hear the uptick in his breathing.

"Playing." Mary purposely used a raspy voice.

The groan was low in her ear, and she stroked him again.

"Mare. You play with fire, you may get burned."

She smiled to herself because King hadn't pulled away like usual. "Maybe I'm a pyromaniac?" She kept her voice heady.

"Sug', I don't think—"

"My panties are so small, they're barely there."

King froze.

"I'm wearing a new lace bra that hardly contains my breasts, with a matching almost non-existent thong."

His groan again was lower and more feral than ever.

"And, I shaved. Bare."

That's all the motivation he needed. He hitched her up and her legs encircled his waist. He carried her to his bedroom and kicked the door shut with his booted foot.

King pulled open the top drawer and took out a foil packet and a bottle of lube, setting them both on the mattress beside the pillow.

Mary swallowed. "That's not from the expired ones, is it?"

King smirked, "Nope. New box."

"A whole box?"

"Yup."

"Good—"

King's eyes widened.

She caught her faux pas, "Oh...no... I mean, 'good,' 'cuz it's not expired...not that you have a whole box," she stammered, "but, yeah, I'm glad you got a whole box because that means more than one time—" she couldn't stop herself from rambling. Even though she wanted this more than anything, she was nervous as hell.

She looked at the condom again. "Wow! Magnum...Holy shit! That's going to tear—" The thought slipped out vocally and she slapped a hand over her mouth. She was mortified.

King let out a raspy laugh and wrapped his arms around her waist. He caught her mouth as her breath hitched, and he took full advantage of the moment, sweeping his tongue in deep.

Forgetting her ramblings, she relented and gave him control, wrapping and twisting her tongue with his. She moaned into his kiss when he pulled her hair tie, allowing her hair to cascade down her back. But before it unraveled, King had it fisted around his hand, using it to control the arch of her neck and dictate the movements of her head.

He fucked her with his tongue, spearing it in and out, and Mary only grew wetter wondering if his dick was as talented as his tongue.

God, she hoped so.

He broke from her lips then trailed a tattoo of kisses down her jaw, tugging her fisted hair to the side, giving him access to her exposed flesh. King bathed her neck, kissing down to the hollow of her shoulder and up the other side, pulling her hair in the opposite direction to nibble at her ear. She could hear the carnality of his breathing with every tantalizing nip and bite.

King controlled her, pulling her into him so close there was no room between them. One hand dominated her hair and the other pushed her lower back into him, wedging his thigh between hers to give her balance.

The pressure ground into her pussy, and the tiny scrap of her underwear rubbed against her clit. The friction was as arousing as it was painful. Mary never knew pain could be so pleasurable. She felt each heartbeat rush and pulse between her legs as her excitement was pushed to its limits.

With every brush of his hand up her spine and the deepening of his kiss, she felt herself dampen. He added more pressure and his rock-hard length pushed against her. Her heartbeat pulsed deep within her inner walls. She ground deeper and let out a mewing cry muffled by their kiss. It was wild; sinfully carnal. King froze, broke the kiss, and stepped back.

An instant ache pierced her core with his absence. "Did I do something wrong?" Her voice was airy.

"No. No," King closed his eyes, ran his hands through his slightly greying hair then down his short, peppered beard, and willed patience into submission. "We gotta slow this down."

Mary could hear the frustration in his voice.

"This first time, isn't going to be rushed, isn't going to be a frantic lay." His eyes softened along with his tone, "I want to worship you, Mare."

If Mary's heart was ever going to melt, it did at that very moment.

He regained his composure and stepped back into her, bringing his hands reverently to the sides of her face. He gently placed his lips over hers. It was a sensual kiss, so different from a moment ago, bred from love, not lust. It wasn't deep or heady, but spoke from the depths of his heart to her soul.

"I love you, Mary." His words were a prayer to her, like angels' wings brushing across her heart. He loved her with every piece of his being. It was the first time he uttered the words; ever. Never to another. Only to her. The sheen in his eyes glistened, and she knew his heartfelt words were true.

"I love you too, King."

He pulled back, but not enough to break their embrace. "I'm not telling you so you have to say it back…I just want you to know how I feel." A smile crept across her lips, and he brushed his thumb across the apple of her cheek. "I fell in love with you the first time I saw you, Mare."

Mary's look of love and longing fell into confusion, "The first time you saw me, I was swearing like a sailor in a coffee house."

"Yes. Exactly."

Mary stared at him.

"I knew I had an interview coming later that day, and when I heard you yelling that the next interviewer could, 'fuck off and kiss your ass,' I thought I'd love it if you were the one to come into my office. And even crazier, for the first time in my life, I admitted to myself that I'd love to have a woman like you by my side."

"But, you looked horrified."

He shook his head, "I was in 'horrified-awe.' You were bold and brash, not to mention gorgeous, and had a take-no-fucks attitude, something that is almost impossible to pull off without being a bitch, and you were owning it. To tell the truth, my heart fluttered as you flew out the door, and I kicked myself for not getting your name and number."

Mary stood dumbfounded.

"Honest to God, Mare. I fell in love with you without even knowing your name."

Mary blushed from head to toe, and he took advantage of the moment.

"I never knew I could love someone so deeply." He grazed against the crest of her ear, running his tongue down the edge of her velvet skin, then sucked the lobe gently, adding a nip, just the way she liked it.

Mary sucked in a breath and moaned when he trailed kisses down the length of her neck to her collarbone.

"You drive me wild, Sugar. Absolutely insane. I want to do so many things to you. Sexy things, passionate things...filthy things."

She shuddered. Would he do the things she fantasized about? The things she'd imagined while taking her own pleasure? She squeezed her thighs around his.

"Are you thinking of the one-hundred-and-one things I'm going to do to you, Mare?"

"King—"

"Shhh, Sugar. Let me take this. Nothing you need to do."

Mary wanted it all. Every. Single. Thing. If King's cock was as big as what was pressing into her body, she was in trouble. She shuddered again.

"I got you, Mare. Don't worry about a thing."

"I'm...I'm," she couldn't get the words out. *What if King was horrified and stopped? What if he thinks I'm ridiculous? What if he won't take me?* She panicked.

King continued his assault, ravishing her. "Mare—"

"I'mavirgin." Mary blurted the sentence out in one word.

His kisses stopped.

Fuck! She waited.

He froze. Along with time itself.

He slowly pulled back and stood to his full height, which she couldn't interpret as a good or bad thing. Towering over her with his six-foot-two frame, Mary felt small even though she stood only seven inches shorter.

"Are you mad?" Her voice wavered.

King's blank face morphed with confusion, "Mad?"

She built a bit of courage, praying he wouldn't call off the night of debauchery. She wanted every sensual thing he'd give her. "I'm untouched," she corrected herself, "well, not untouched...I mean, I've touched myself, but not by a man. Sometimes at night, or in the shower, I—"

"Not. Another. Word."

His reaction shocked her. *Oh, shit!* He was mad. By the way his jaw tightened and body went rigid, oh yeah, the news of her virginity had him stewing.

Mary stayed silent trying to get her heart out of her stomach. She instantly regretted saying anything. *Why the fuck did you have to tell him? You could have faked it.*

Total. Lie.

She knew there was no chance in hell that she could fake it. By the size of him, it was going to be like trying to get a Saint Bernard through a doggy door. The thought had her wincing, but also her core clenching. She craved it more than before. His cock was impressive, and she knew she'd scream at his first thrust.

King scrubbed his hands down his face.

"King, I'm sor—"

"Not another word, Mare."

She closed her mouth.

His eyes hardened, and the hollows of his cheeks flexed. "If I thought I was on the edge a minute ago, fuck, Sug', I'm about to blow in my pants. Honest to God, I'm going to spill a gallon of cum down the front of my drawers."

"A gallon?" The words popped out on a laugh, and she wanted to call them back.

"Yup. 'Cuz my blue balls just went into overdrive and ramped up a thousand-fold."

"So... are we still gonna, ya know—"

His eyes clouded with confusion. "Absolutely. Why would you think otherwise?"

She shrugged, glancing away, not meeting his eyes.

"You think I wouldn't want you 'cuz you've never been with anyone? Fuck, Mare, I can't even tell you what it means that you chose me to be your first. To have you untouched."

She nodded, still not meeting his stare. "Well, not touched by anyone but myself..."

The menacing growl had her eyes meeting him.

"Damn...that's the sexiest thing I've ever heard, Mare. One, you're untouched, and two, you touch yourself."

She pinkened.

"You do that often?"

She shrugged again, embarrassment heightening.

"Tell me, Mare," he pulled her close; she instantly melted. "Do you think of me when you touch your sweet pussy?" His lips brushed her ear, his hot breath skimming across her skin. "In your mind, are your fingers mine? Do I bring you to your knees in your fantasies?"

Mary took in a sharp breath. Hearing him talk dirty did things to her...naughty, sensual things that had her clenching her thighs again.

"Uh-uh-uh," he pushed his leg between hers. "Keep yourself open and wanting. Don't purge the ache. Tell me, Mare, what do I do to you in your dreams?" He leaned farther into her, one hand on her waist, the other cupping the nape of her neck. He came millimeters from her ear, never touching, but the wisps of his breath made her panties drenched. The minuscule thong would never hold back the dam waiting to explode.

"You think of me when you run your hands over your slick folds?"

One kiss below her ear.

"Is it me," he switched sides, "when you push your fingers into yourself?"

Another kiss.

"Do I push in slow, or do I claim my keep? Do I tease and play, or do I thrust in deep to the hilt and make you quiver with each curl of my finger?"

Her clit ached with every filthy word and thought.

His lips crested her ear, and she let him take what he wanted.

She held her breath.

"Tell me, is it just your fingers, or do you use toys?"

"Um, just my fing—"

He groaned and nipped and she moaned.

"Do you make that noise when I plunge deep? Am I taking you only with my fingers, or am I taking you with my mouth, too?"

Mary panted at the images bombarding her. His questions kept coming, keeping her on edge.

"Do I bring you to climax? Or, do you stave off your orgasm and prolong the ache, so I can devour you all over again?"

She tried to close her legs, but he wedged his leg deeper.

"No, don't close, Mare," He pushed harder against her. She was practically straddling his massive thigh like a saddle. "Gonna make you deny it, work for it. Make it worth it in the end."

Mary swore she was going to leave a wet mark on his jeans. Taking no shame, she ground down. Hard.

"Do I set you off, Sug'?" He squeezed her breast over her shirt. "Do I make you want to touch yourself right now?"

Did he ever! The ache was sinful. Wicked in its desire to be tortured, touched, and teased.

"I need you to touch me, King."

"Not yet, Mare. Not until you're naked, and I see your glistening pretty cunt."

The word Mary usually found abhorrent, now spurred her on.

"Touch me, please." Her hands clutched and fisted his tee.

"Uh-uh. Why would I want to do that when I have you practically riding me now? I can feel your sweet heat pulsing against me. Gonna make you cum with just my words and my innocent touches."

His touches were anything but innocent. His hand was painfully kneading her breast, the other was hitching her ass into his thigh. His dick pressed hard against her stomach. His mouth roamed her neck. She was going to die!

"I'm going to take you places you've never been; make you feel things you've never imagined. You want to cum, Mare?"

His desperation overcame her. She was practically writhing on his leg. She shook her head yes, and moaned when he squeezed and held her breast. Oddly, the sudden bite of pain and ache made her ecstasy soar.

"Tell me, Sug', how bad do you want it?"

"Bad!" She got the word out between pants. "Please!"

"You begging me, Mare?"

"Yes."

"Ask me to make you cum."

"Please, King, make...mak—"

"What, Mare?"

"Please, make me cum!"

King bit down on her neck, pinched the nub of her jetted nipple, then pushed his thigh and erect cock hard against her throbbing pussy.

Mary screamed. Tightened. Shuddered. Collapsed.

She held herself rigid against his body. Her pussy spasmed while she clamped her legs around his so hard, she was no longer standing. She was twisted in erotic pleasure, her orgasm crashing down on her. The dam flooded between her legs, and her fisted hands held tight to his tee.

She heard nothing but her heartbeat in her ears. *Whoosh. Whoosh...Whoosh.* The white noise pulsed. King flexed his thigh and she humped against him, squeezing harder. He balanced her over his leg. She was putty. He lowered her to the ground, making sure she could stand but still in his arms.

She came back to herself and so did her embarrassment. "Oh, my God...I can't believe I just did that." She spoke into his chest, muffling her words, hiding her shame.

"You are absolutely beautiful, Sugar." King kissed the top of her head.

"What?" Mary still spoke to his tee.

"Look at me, Mare." He waited until she reluctantly lifted her head and stared at his mouth. "Eyes up here, Mare."

She met his stare.

"I have never had someone cum with just my words."

The thought of him being intimate with anyone else bit her with jealousy.

"No one's ever been worth my words." King read her. "I have a past, Mare, obviously, but it has never been more than a hump and dump. Nothing as beautiful as this."

"Hump and dump?"

"Yeah. No bar hog wants anything but a quick toss in the sack. No promises. No feelings. Just a quick orgasm, and then goodbye."

Mary's eyes fell.

King pulled into his trademark half-smirk. "Don't go hiding from me, Mare." He tipped her chin with his knuckles. "Mary, I love you." His hand brushed a tendril of hair from her face. "You are so beautiful when you let go and let me lead you." He lowered his head to take her lips. "Thank you." His lips brushed hers, as his words rushed over her.

Once. Twice.

He lowered over her. Nothing was ever this perfect.

"I need you, Mare."

"I need you, too." Her words were breathy.

Those four words were all he needed to let him know that Mary Peyton Jones was going to be the last woman he'd ever claim. She was his.

She was his *One*.

King lifted the hem of her shirt, pausing as if asking for permission to continue. Mary nodded with barely a bob of her head, and he drew it up her body and over her head, tossing it to the floor where they stood, then did the same with her underlying tank top. His hands reverently roamed up and down the sides of her torso. His eyes met hers then dropped to her breasts, covered in a pale pink, lacy bra. He cupped her, gently grazing his thumb over her large pert nipple, barely confined beneath the intricate lace.

"They're large," Mary stated the obvious, looking down at his hand covering her left breast.

"They're perfect." King ran his other hand alongside the other breast and cupped its weight, letting the heft settle in his palm.

Mary looked down again, "I heard more than a handful is a waste." She wavered nervously.

"Whoever said that is an idiot." King continued to explore over the top of the lace. "These are absolutely the most perfect breasts."

She followed his hands and swallowed, feeling her nerves rise in tandem with her arousal.

King let his hands drop to the waistband of her jeans and popped open the button with one flick of his fingers, then widened the zipper, pulling apart each side of the fabric.

"Shimmy." He directed.

She complied.

He pushed the jeans down her wide hips and over her luscious ass as she wiggled back and forth. Gravity did the rest of the work and the material fell to the ground. She stepped out of the pooling material, awkward in her undressed state.

King took both her hands in his and stepped back, admiring her in her lacey bra and minuscule thong. The scrap of fabric barely covered her pubic mound and hid her bareness beneath. The tuft of hair she left above her clit was minuscule as well.

King dropped one hand to her panties, running his fingers alongside the front patch of the thong, then dipped beneath it with an upward draw. He rubbed the backside of his finger over the barely-there curls. "You trim yourself?" He knew the answer; she'd told him earlier, and now his finger was roaming over the evidence.

Mary blushed, and a flush ran over her exposed chest. She looked everywhere except at him. "Yes." Her answer was whisper-soft. She was embarrassed because she knew her thong didn't hold her wetness, and her arousal was smeared between her thighs. She knew she'd be mortified if his finger delved any lower.

And as if reading her thoughts, King's finger dipped lower, caressing the moistened folds of her pussy. She felt the burn of embarrassment flush over her, and she pulled her thighs together.

"Mare," King's words were terse and commanding, "open."

She released the pressure, freeing his hand, and waited.

His fingers rubbed the velvet skin of her bare, swollen lips but never ventured between them. He only rolled the length of them with a slow, agonizing brush. "And, you shaved. You're bare."

Her flush deepened again into a crimson hue and she shuddered as his finger continued to explore.

"Yes." The word was so breathy it was almost inaudible.

He freed his finger then pushed against her hip with his palm, guiding her. "Twirl." He held up his other arm holding her hand, allowing her to pass underneath, as she spun in a slow, graceful spin, parading herself for his eyes.

"Absolutely gorgeous." King stopped her and she stood before him once more. He bent, taking her lips.

Mary was the first to pull back. "Um...I think one of us is over-dressed."

King pulled back farther without loosening their hold, "Definitely you." His lips curled into a smile, and Mary held him with a stare, memorizing the moment.

"Strip, mister!" Her order was met with King's smile widening.

"Are you ordering me around?"

"Can't let you have all the fun. Now, strip."

He stepped back and bent down without preamble or grace and unlaced his boots, toeing them off and removing his socks as well. He pulled his black tee over his head with one pull to the back of the collar, discarding it where he stood, then disrobed himself of his jeans. It was done in silence and with precision. When he was done, he stood before her in just his boxer briefs.

Mary took in his masculine form, a sculpted mass of muscles. "That was quick."

King scrunched his face and shook his head. "Not something any man wants to hear."

Mary huffed in laughter. "You gave no striptease, either." She brought her hands to her hips.

She was sexy as hell. His little vixen with her hand on her jetted hip. "Didn't know you wanted a show." King pulled her into himself.

"Well, a little show would've been nice."

He slowly shook his head no, bringing his hands to the sides of her face. He was as gentle as he was demanding. His head lowered and he buried his face in her ample cleavage, his beard tickling her against her skin. He lightly bit the swell of her breast and she threw her head back with a moan. They were heavy and large, but unbelievably perky. They sat high and round on her chest, parting barely with a natural curve of her chest. "God, you have amazing tits." He nipped at the other swell. "I gotta feast."

Before she knew it, he unclasped the front of her bra and her tits spilled out.

King let out a feral groan and latched onto her nipple. He wasn't subtle. He was ravenous. He bit the sensitive nub, suckling and pulling it between his teeth. He didn't let the other starve. He rolled and pinched the offered nub with his fingers. Mary let out a small screech and he backed off, but just enough to make the sting linger as he sucked and played.

"Sweet mother of Jesus." King was still in her cleavage, pushing her side boobs together and nestling his face. He pulled back, said nothing, but stepped into her, causing her to step back in retreat.

He didn't stop.

He kept coming.

She kept retreating until the back of her calves hit the bed. Her eyes widened as he continued towards her, stalking her. Then in one swift motion, he lowered her to the mattress behind her. If Mary didn't know him better, his piercing eyes would have scared her, but instead, she knew it was nothing but a lustful hunger. She was on her back, her ass barely on the edge of the bed. She pushed her weight to scooch farther up, when King's wide, roughened hand came down across her belly, pushing her into the mattress and halting her from going anywhere.

Mary startled, freezing in place. King went down to his knees and settled himself between her splayed legs. Without words, he pushed his fingers beneath the strings of lace on her hips and slowly pulled the thong down her legs, freeing it from its delectable confines. Mary watched him with bated breath. It amazed her how he could switch from eager and hungry to slow and sensual in a heartbeat.

He pulled the minuscule lace over her knees and down her calves, and finally off her feet. He lifted her thong so she could see, and a sly smile of accomplishment drew across his face. Dropping them, he wasted no time. He pushed her inner thighs apart, and a blush consumed her.

She was splaying herself bare, ass halfway off the mattress, exposing her most intimate parts to King. It was unnerving but at the same time, it excited her.

King would be her first. *Her only.* The thought settled her. It should've frightened her, but it did the opposite. Their relationship was new but felt so right.

A breath across her clit summoned her attention.

∾

King blew across her glistening folds and hitched her legs over his shoulders, spreading her wide.

God, she's beautiful.

With his thumbs, he parted her folds to the sides, exposing her pinkened flesh to the cool air.

Pink. Delicate. Untouched.

The latter pleased him, yet scared him to his core. Mary sucked in a breath and it made him smile. She was his. He wasn't wasting time. He pulled back the hood of her clit, exposing the swollen nub.

The first swipe of his flattened tongue zinged with her tangy taste. *Heaven.* A second pass, and he tightened his tongue on the upstroke, catching her hardened clit with the tip.

Mary jolted, bringing her ass off the bed, which spurred him on. He held her down with a palm across her mound, spanning the entire width of her belly, and held her in place.

Lapping a few more times, he licked her with flat, long strokes. He felt his dick harden and lengthen even more, and the head breached his waistband. Still holding her in bliss, licking her mercilessly, he reached down and pushed the head back into his briefs. His fingers passed over the top, smearing his precum weeping from the tip. He prayed for forbearance. He didn't want to blow. When he came, it was going to be inside her, with her writhing on his cock while her convulsing muscles orgasmed and milked every last drop of cum out of him.

He pulsed. *Shit!*

He wrapped his hand around his shaft at the base and squeezed. Christ, it was like steel, long and hard, jutting out from within his boxers. *Sweet Christ.* If she had him on edge with just the taste of her pussy, he was fucked! He had to hurry this along. No more sweet. He wanted to make her explode.

While he flicked her clit with his tongue, he pushed a finger into her sheath. *Fuck!* She was tight and wet, but he pushed against its resistance, sliding deep. Mary moaned, and it almost did him in. He pushed until he was seated and then slowly dragged out.

Repeating the motion a few times, he sped up the strokes while nipping at her swollen lips. Her essences and nectar were in his beard, and he could smell her arousal. *Sweet Jesus!* She smelled and tasted divine!

Mary squirmed.

He added a second finger, curling them up against the rough edges of her G-spot. He could tell by her racing breath she was close. He sped up, his fingers milking her juices while her wetness sounded in the quiet room. He lapped at her and drank her in as if he were dying of thirst.

"Mare, I want you to cum." He spoke without lifting his head too far from his feast. She panted with urgency. "Cum for me, Sugar. I want you to cum on my tongue." He dove back in, buried his fingers to the hilt, curling and strumming repeatedly against her G-spot.

She gave one last moan and a mewling cry, then released herself onto his face.

A geyser exploded in front of him as he sucked her clit and bit down lightly.

She yelled his name, hanging onto it with her cry, fisting the comforter beneath her.

King had never had a woman go off like Mary. Free and uninhibited. No fake moan or sultry winces. No, it was all her. Real and exhilarating. Before she could come down from ecstasy, he picked her up, the weight of a feather, and hitched her farther up onto the bed.

She was loose and sated, barely comprehending what was happening. He planted a kiss on her lips, her scent still tangled in his beard, but she didn't protest. She opened for his kiss. It was short but sweet.

"Welcome back." King's smile curled his lips.

"Hi." It was all Mary could utter. Her eyes were heavy, and she slowly blinked him into her vision.

"You good?"

"Yeah."

"More?"

"What?"

"Are you done, or would you like more?"

The question had her alert and she pushed to her elbows, making King pull back before she knocked him in the head.

"Are you crazy?"

King arched an eyebrow.

"If you think you're going to get me all worked up and twitterpated, and then we're done, you got another thing coming."

"Twitterpated?"

Mary gave him a mock frown. "That's what you're focusing on?"

King loved when she got feisty. "You have the cutest little crease on the bridge of your nose when you get all riled up." He traced it with his finger.

"King!"

"Mare." He mocked back.

She huffed at him and flopped back against the mattress. "I'm fully naked in your bed, and you want to talk about facial creases? Which, I will warn you, cute or not, no woman wants to be told they have creases on their face."

"It's adorable."

Mary pinned him with a glare.

"As are you." He gave her another quick kiss that morphed into carnal lust.

"You ready, Mare? All joking aside, if you're not ready, or you changed your mind, I'll understand."

She incredulously tilted her head. "So if I said, 'Thanks for the one and done,' and rolled over and went to sleep, you'd be fine with that?" Mary stared at him skeptically.

"Yes."

"Yes?" She huffed out the word with disbelief.

"Yes. Not saying I'd be pleased, but I'd understand. I'd have to rub one out in a cold shower, but I'd be okay."

Mary belted out a laugh, and King loved how her tits jiggled and bounced with her laughter. She settled back and wrapped her arms around his neck, pulling him down onto the tits he adored. "I wouldn't be that cruel."

"You're running the show, Sug'."

"Well, then I say, the show must go on!"

King melted her with one more quick kiss, then stood. Mary's eyes roamed his body. He peeled off his boxer briefs, shucking them to the ground, and stepped out of them. His erection jutted away from his body, hanging heavy and thick. He palmed the shaft and gave it a few tugs.

Mary's gaze was plastered to his fist. He jerked it a few more times, then squeezed the base, when she absently licked her lips.

His words broke her reverie. "Not right now, Sugar." Her eyes lifted to his and met the eagerness in his own. "If your lips and tongue even crest my cock, I'm going to explode in a monstrous cum."

He palmed himself, squeezing at the base again, at the thought of her sucking his cock, her eyes peering up at him through heavy lashes, as his length disappeared between her red, pursed lips—

King let out a groan at the thoughts his mind was conjuring. His head lifted to the ceiling as he concentrated on not coming. He squeezed his base harder. "Fuck, Mare. I'm not gonna last a second inside you."

"Then get over here and we'll see if I can hold you at bay."

"No, Mare."

"Who's running the show?" She put a commanding tone into the question.

King knew he was a goner. "Mare, I'm almost forty."

She furrowed her brow, and that adorable crease made another appearance. This time he held his tongue.

"If I cum, I don't get an instant erection. I'm old. Anatomy 101. Age, plus libido, plus hand job, equals temporary impotence. No matter what you've seen in porn, or read in those shirtless men romance books—which are just girl porn, may I say—at my age, the only instant hard-on after release is with Viagra."

Mary opened her mouth to say something.

King cut her off, "And, don't even think that I'd be taking those little blue pills. I may be aging, but I'm not dead."

That had Mary in stitches when she rolled up onto her knees, balancing upright, and pulled King's forearms, causing him to reluctantly stumble closer to her. Her tits, ass, and curves were like a goddess'.

Without words, Mary grasped his shaft, gently pulling and pushing the length in her hand. King let out the lowest groan she'd ever heard. Her name was attached to the end of the moan.

"Marrrrre."

"Shhhh. Let me explore."

King never thought he'd use calculus or trigonometry after graduating high school, but he thanked the gods he could run calculations because it was the only thing that saved him from falling over the edge. He had a good mind to write a check to the mathematics department at his alma mater.

"Sugar…"

When Mary didn't say anything, but only cupped his balls,

feeling the weight in her palm, King bit the inside of his cheek, almost drawing blood.

"Let me explore...I've never seen a live naked man before."

"Are you perusing dead naked men?" King had to use humor as a diversion to distract himself from giving in to her. The way she was circling his cockhead with her thumb, it was like she was playing with an Atari joystick.

She let out a chuckle, "No... only you, big boy."

His head lifted to the ceiling once more when she pulled on his sack.

"Easy, Mare. Remember, those are fragile. They've been through enough trauma." Which was the least he could say.

When he finally did get to check out the boys in the hospital, he almost passed out when he lifted his hospital gown. His nutsack was swollen to the size of a grapefruit and was bandaged after the surgery, but he could see the exposed skin was a blackened, plum-purple color. It made him queasy and lightheaded. He couldn't look at it for days, and every time he thought about it, it put him in a tailspin.

The thought of his battered balls distracted him and tamped down his excitement for the moment. He thought he'd be able to stave off exploding in her hand. That was, until he felt her delicate lips wrap around him, engulfing his head, and she pushed her throat down his hardened shaft.

Lord and baby Jesus!

She was going to kill him. He saw stars! "Mare!"

She gave a sultry hum in response and he felt it reverberate to the base that had his balls tingling.

Oh. Fuck! He sucked in a breath, holding it for good measure.

She rose and bobbed, taking him halfway, and he felt himself bump into the back of her throat, while she used a hand to stroke his remaining unsuckled length. With the other, she cupped his balls. He gathered her hair in his fist, which was an awful idea because he could see her taking him in.

"Mare, God, Sugar." His words were incoherent. Hell, he could've been speaking Latin for all he knew. His intelligence was dimming. All the blood was rushing from one head to the other.

She was bent before him, still on the bed, with her luscious, rounded ass in the air, bobbing on his cock in front of him. The sight—she was absolutely stunning.

She bobbed at a quickening pace, and he knew he wasn't going to last. He felt his balls tighten and pull up, the base of his spine tingled.

"Mare...Mare, babe— I'm going to cum."

He pulled her off just as the first spurt erupted out of the tip and landed in her cleavage. He wanted to throw his head back and relish in the glory, but seeing his ropes of cum jet and land on the flushed skin of her gorgeous breasts, was breathtaking. A sight he would never unsee.

With a final groan, she pumped him until he was dry, then used his length to spread his seed across her chest. She wasn't lying; she wanted to explore.

King braced himself with his knees against the mattress and used her shoulders for balance. He knew if he let go, he'd fall to the floor. He was at a loss as Mary watched his cum coat her. When she had enough, King took himself in hand and smacked his softening cock in the V of her cleavage, making Mary smile and peer up at him with submissive eyes. *Fuck!* It was enough to make him want to harden again, but at his age, it took a little more time for round two.

"Mare—"

"You like?" she asked in a playful tone.

King just shook his head, "No words, Sugar. There are absolutely no words."

She smiled as if satisfied with herself.

"I'll go get you a towel."

She sat back on her heels and waited. King went to the en suite bathroom and grabbed a washcloth, wet it with warm water, and turned to head back to the bedroom. What he saw snapped his libido to attention.

Mary was running a finger over the top of her left breast, pulling it through his jets of cum, then dragging down into the valley of her cleavage and swirling it over the opposite mound.

King grabbed the door jamb to keep himself upright. But, when she swept two fingers into his release and brought it to her outstretched tongue, he thought he was going to drop another load where he stood.

The sight of his untouched, innocent woman lapping at his cum made him hard, and he started to stiffen. Looking down, he wouldn't have believed it was possible if he weren't the one experiencing it.

When Mary saw him come back into the room, she dropped her hand and reddened with an all-over flush.

King stood before her with the washcloth in hand. He took his finger, mimicking her earlier curiosity, and she watched as he dragged it over her breast, down the valley, and swirled the opposite mound, then lifted his finger to her mouth. She peered up at him with those same submissive, heavy-lidded eyes, and sucked his finger into her mouth. If he wasn't hardening before, he sure as hell was now. Straight-up, solid erection.

Mary's eyes widened and she smirked, pointing to his bobbing dick. "Thought that was only possible in porn and girl-porn novels?"

King smirked back "Chapter two." He fell forward and caged her as she flopped back.

"You ready, Sugar?"

"Absolutely."

He wiped her breasts, tossed the washcloth, then claimed her with an all-consuming kiss.

CHAPTER 25

King hovered over Mary, inches from her lips, feeling every breath she exhaled. "I love you, Mary." His voice was deep and sincere. He suspended his weight on his elbows, his bent knees and legs carried his weight below. Her legs were spread open before him and draped over each of his massive thighs.

"I love you, too."

King placed a light kiss on her lips, then made his way down to her breasts, taking in one of her pert nubs and pinching the other. She had gorgeous tits and he loved the feel of them in his mouth. Sucking hard, she moaned and he pulled back with a pop.

He sat back, propping himself up on his heels, and reached for the lube and condom he'd left at the head of the bed next to the pillow. He set the lube aside, but within reach. Ripping the foil packet with his teeth, he placed the rubber on the head of his cock, pinched the tip, and rolled it down his length.

Mary watched with rapt fascination. *This is really going to happen.*

Noticing she was holding her breath, King smiled and reminded her, "Breathe, Sugar."

She drew in a deep breath and exhaled settling her nerves.

"Good, girl," He reached between her legs and ran his finger through her folds, testing if she was ready. She was wet, almost soaked, but he didn't want to take any chances. The last thing he wanted to do was hurt her.

She was a virgin, and with his size, he knew she'd have some pain. Anything he could do to minimize it, he would do. He grabbed the bottle of silicone-based lube, flipped open the cap, and squirted a bit onto his fingers, then ran them through her already-wet pussy, coating her well. He squeezed a little more onto his palm, then ran his hand down his length and back up again. He capped the bottle and set it aside.

Wiping his hand on the sheet, he noticed his hands were shaking. *WTF?* He was former Delta Force, yet the thought of taking Mary was overwhelming him.

Breathe, Henry. The reminder steadied him. Meeting Mary's eyes, he asked, "Ready?"

She nodded and took in a deep breath...and held it.

King cocked an eyebrow.

Reading him, she exhaled.

"Good girl. I want you to relax, don't worry about a thing. I gotcha."

"Relax." If the situation was anything but what it was, she would've laughed. Instead, she just nodded.

"Love you, Sugar."

"Love you, too."

"Pull your knees back towards yourself." She did as he said, lifting her heels off the bed, and he guided them into place, widening them enough to accommodate him. She was splayed open as wide as she could, open to his mass and he came forward, settling between her.

Guiding his cock, he placed the head at her entrance and slowly pushed into her. Watching himself disappear inside her was the most beautiful thing he'd ever witnessed; a moment that would be seared into his memory for eternity. She sucked in a breath, tightening around him, and he froze.

"You okay?"

Mary blew out the air in her lungs, "Yeah, I'm good." She panted a few times then controlled her breathing and wrangled in her nerves.

King waited, holding himself in place.

"I'm good...I'm good. Maybe don't go slow. Maybe it won't hurt if it's quicker." She panted some more.

Fuck! No way in hell! "Not gonna happen, Baby." King knew he had to go slow, had to read her every tell and watch for signs he wasn't causing too much pain. He was barely inside her, just a couple inches past the tip, and she was already panting.

Shit. He retreated a bit. She relaxed. Then, he pushed in again, watching her as he slid in farther. She was tightening around him again. He knew it was a natural reflex, but it wasn't helping. He stopped pushing.

"Mare?"

Her eyes were screwed shut but popped open at the call of her name.

"Need you to relax."

She opened her mouth—

"Breathe, Sugar."

She loosely closed her eyes and took in a couple deep breaths. He felt her loosen around him.

"Good job, Sug.'"

Again, he pushed in, a little quicker and deeper than before, and made good headway. Then he felt it.

A tear.

Fuck! Before he could stop, she let out a cry and winced, squeezing her thighs against him.

"Oh, God! Oh, God. Wait, wait, wait, King—" Her hands were fisted into the comforter. "Oh, God...please, wait—"

King panicked and started to pull out. "Mare—"

"Stop!" She didn't want to lose him, "I'm good...I'm good."

He froze, but by her reaction, he knew she was anything but good. "Mare—"

"I'm fine, I'm fine." She blew out a breath. She didn't know if the pep talk was for her benefit or his. The lancing scream of pain that heated and burned inside her was being stretched beyond its limits. Right then and there, she vowed to herself that she would never have sex again. This was anything but enjoyable.

Breathe. Breathe.

It was all she could do to keep from crying out. She took in a few measured breaths, waited a moment, and the pain began to dissipate. The lightning blaze eased into a slight sting, and then to a twinge of a dull ache.

Breathe. Breathe.

It was working. She felt herself relaxing...well, as much as she could.

King held still, hating himself at the moment. Mary was in agony. Agony he caused and he could do nothing about it. *Fuck!*

Her eyes were clamped shut. "Okay. Okay...I'm good."

"Mare."

She opened her eyes to see the torment on King's face. What was supposed to be a beautiful moment, a sacred moment, was anything but. She swore she saw wetness in his eyes.

Now that the ache was bearable, she smiled up at him, "Baby, really, I'm good."

He shook his head but said nothing.

"Babe...King, look at me...I'm. Good."

He held still, not wanting to cause her any more pain.

"King." She reached for him, bringing him into her arms as he came forward. "Babe, I'm good." She coaxed him, not wanting him to berate himself. Pulling him to herself, she took his lips with hers. She was kissing him, but in a moment, he wasn't kissing her back.

"God. Sorry, Sugar." He whispered the words to her.

Mary shook her head, "No, don't be sorry. Every girl...this happens." Then, her snark came out, "God's honest truth, I'm better. You're half in... or half out...so, I need you to take me. I'm runnin' the show...so, I say, make me fly." She pushed her hips into him, gaining an inch of ground.

He smiled against her lips, "My pleasure." He placed one more kiss on her silky lips, then pushed in slowly, working in and out, to the hilt.

They were one.

A perfect union.

Where one started and the other began was beauty in the making. King reveled in the thought. *One.*

He pulled out and pushed back in, waiting for Mary to show some sign of resistance. But, when none came, he repeated the motion, this time pulling back to the tip and pushing deep to the root. Still, she didn't wince.

Closing his eyes, not letting his tears fall, he thanked God for the woman lying beneath him and he quickened the pace, showing her with every stroke what she meant to him.

She was his *One.* The one he'd love until his dying breath.

It was glorious. Magnificent. Mind-blowing. Breathtaking. No word could quite describe what she was feeling. With her arms wrapped around him, King's slight weight settling atop her, he gave her sensations she could never imagine, sensations that weren't of this world. He'd transported her to a place where just the two of them existed and time stood still. *Heaven.*

At first, she panicked. *Why in the world would anyone want to have sex?* It was crucifying. God, she couldn't imagine why anyone would willingly put themselves through it. Every woman must be a masochist to find pleasure in that excruciating pain. *Why?*

But now, the breathtaking she'd experienced at first, was not the breathtaking she was experiencing now. With every stroke, King brought her closer to euphoria. He brought wholeness to her. To them.

They were one.

Two souls joined: one and the same.

She knew at that moment, there would never be another. He was *it* for her.

He was her *One*. The one she'd love until her dying day.

King's increasing pace set her on a wave of pleasure. He had his head buried in her hair, kissing a path that scorched her skin. *Would she ever get enough of him?* She hoped not. He wasn't rough, but he made his presence known with each jarring thrust. He was on a mission, and she was riding the wave. And, for as vocal as he was before, he was surprisingly quiet.

She writhed beneath him, giving as good as she got, thrusting against him, meeting him with the meshing of their pubic hair. Her inner muscles grasping and resisting with each of his thrusts. They were keeping a rhythm. She was cresting a wave and started to shiver.

"King..."

"I gotcha, Baby." The words were muffled in her hair.

"Oh, my God...oh—King." Her words caught on every breath. Set between the rhythm.

He sat up, cradling her legs and draping them over his massive forearms, bracing himself with his hands, pushing them into the mattress beside each of her shoulders. She was practically bent in half. Her ass was off the sheets. He angled her pelvis and rammed straight down, deep within her.

Holy. Fuck! He was huge and hitting something. Whatever he was hitting was like nothing she'd ever felt, sending ecstasy through her. Tension built and she huffed a breath with every powerful shove of his cock. *Fuck!* She grasped his shoulders, digging her short nails into his flesh.

"Oh...Oh...O—"

"Let it happen, Baby. Don't resist it." King's voice dropped an octave and was sinfully commanding. "I want to feel you cum around my cock."

There was no slow. There was no gentle. Wetness leaked from her, and she knew not because she felt it, but by the sloppy, wet suctioning sounds filling the room between the slapping of their flesh. It was carnal and aroused her more, spurring her on. She zoned into it.

"You want it, Mare?" His tone mesmerized her. "Take it. Feel it," He burrowed deeper. "Claim it." One more deep plunge. "Cum for me, Baby."

At his command, she lost it.

"Kinnnngggg!" She wailed his name and sailed over the precipice into euphoria, clinging to his mountainous frame.

He didn't let up until she sailed. He held deep, pushing with pressure against her clit as she quaked and quivered, orgasming around him. He hadn't cum, but he was going to let her writhe and hump against him until her orgasm stilled.

Seeing her in the throes of her first penetrative orgasm was glorious. Like the heavens opened and the angels sang. She was more than angelic; she was ethereal. He lowered her hips and felt her juices coat his balls. Her thighs were drenched, and he knew the sheets were going to be soaked through when they got done.

He kept his strokes small while she came down from her high. He didn't want to break the rhythm he'd set before, but he wanted to let her recover.

She melted into the bed. Her body weighed a thousand pounds, and she couldn't lift her arms. They'd fallen from King's shoulders and were flopped awkwardly beside her, weighted and unmovable. Her breaths evened out, and she felt the heaviness of King leaning over her.

She opened one eye, the lid defying her efforts. King appeared in her view and she greeted him with a satisfied smile. He smiled back and kissed her. She didn't kiss back. She was satiated. She wanted to lay in bliss forever. King nuzzled her neck and she allowed him room. He peppered kisses up its length from her collarbone to her ear.

"You're absolutely gorgeous."

She couldn't reply but widened her smile.

She wanted to sleep, but he was rousing her with nips at her lobe.

"Baby...I'm so tired."

"Not done yet." He thrust deep within her, and it sparked a jolt that had her squirming. "Feel that, Mare? That's me. I'm going to take you, hard. Is that what you want?"

He was asking permission, but she didn't think it mattered. He was pumping slowly, but hard enough to jar his words.

"Tell me, Mare."

The spark turned into a fire, that turned into a blaze, ending in a raging inferno. "Take me, King!"

She thought he would hammer home, but it was just the opposite. With force, he rocked and pushed, bringing her along with him. She met him thrust for thrust until she couldn't keep pace.

"Say it, Mare," he demanded, "I gotta hear it." He was almost frantic.

Her tits bounced, swayed, and parted with every upward jolt. She knew what he wanted, but she teased, "What?" God, she was on the edge again. Her climax was about to crash over.

His eyes hardened. He knew what she was doing, "Say. It. Mare." Each word was emphasized with a merciless, driving plunge.

She couldn't hold back. She wanted to ride the orgasm with him. Her eyes were plastered to his, open, wanting to see him lose it. "I love you!"

He rocketed. She shattered. And, it was the most beautiful thing she'd ever witnessed. His head flew back and his body tensed. Every muscle was visible. The sinews twisted in his stiffened arms. His hardened abs thrust forward, holding himself deep. Mary felt him pulse repeatedly and for a moment, she wished she could feel his ropes of cum christening her insides.

He broke. Dissolved. Raptured. Every feeling the antithesis of the description. His heart was slamming against his chest and he fell forward, barely holding his weight above Mary. He'd never, ever experienced an orgasm of this epic proportion. It was all her. The woman he loved. Whole-heartedly. His *One*.

"Um, King? Kinda crushing me."

He pushed up onto his forearm, still inside her, and he could feel her muscles twitching, milking him. "I love you, Mare."

"I love you, too."

He held her gaze, "Forever."

"Forever."

Their lips met, sweet and sensual at the same time. They lingered in bliss together.

"Gotta take care of this condom." He pulled out and felt her wetness coat him once more. He loved it.

"Be right back." King strode to the bathroom. Mary watched his hardened ass disappear into the darkened room, and he flipped on the light.

Curiosity got the best of her, and she watched him take the condom off. He tied off the end and tossed it in the trash can.

He washed and dried himself at the sink, then came back into the room with a warm washcloth.

"Spread."

"Bossy."

"I'm going to clean you."

Uh-uh! Even though less than an hour ago he'd had his mouth on her pussy, deep down and dirty with it up close up and personal, and he'd touched, played, and fucked it, she felt embarrassed to spread for him. With only the side table lamp casting a glow, he noticed her blush.

"Embarrassed? Really?"

She wanted to crawl under the blankets and hide.

He didn't ask. He pulled her knee to the side, far enough to give him ample room, and settled the cloth against her, holding it in place.

Mary sighed in contentment.

He wanted to care for her. He knew he was rough. Rougher than he'd planned, and she needed pampering. Come morning, she would most likely be hurting. Wiping at her folds, he saw the loss of her innocence on the washcloth and blanket. As off-putting as that would be to some, he had an animalistic, caveman sense of claiming. Her virginity was his. He would mark her in time, coat her with his seed, but for now, she'd marked him, and he would take the claim.

She languidly lay in his bed, almost asleep. King tossed the cloth onto the floor next to the one he'd used earlier and turned off the lamp. Darkness filled the room. Moonlight bathed her body, and her beauty radiated in the darkness. He once again counted his blessings.

Rolling her to her side, he pulled the mussed comforter and sheet from under her. He settled in behind her, his chest to her back, then pulled the blanket over them and wrapped his arms around her, as they did every night. Though this time, they were skin to skin, completely bare. His hand splayed her ribs, pulling her to him, and perched beneath her heavy tits.

He didn't know if she was sleeping, but when he kissed below her ear, he whispered. "I love you, Mary. You're my *One*. My forever."

She made a throaty sigh and adjusted herself to mold to his body, absently clutching his hand below her breasts.

Before he drifted off to sleep, she mewled the sweetest thing to ever hit his ears, "Love you, Henry."

He was home. And in bliss. Sweet, unadulterated bliss.

CHAPTER 26

The next week went by in a blur. King and the guys left on a mission at the end of the week, and Mary and Ember spent girl's night watching chick flicks, eating junk food, and indulging in lots of ice cream. Needless to say, King insisted Mary stay with Ember until he returned, and in Mary-fashion, she dug her heels in, in defiance.

"I don't need a babysitter while you're gone." Mary wasn't happy with her man. She was sitting across from him at his desk and was going to settle this before she left for lunch.

"Did I say, a babysitter? No, I just need you to stay at Ember's 'til I return."

"Which is the exact same as a babysitter!"

King pinched the bridge of his nose between his eyes, staving off the headache he felt coming on. "Mare, Sugar—"

"Don't Sugar me. I know you're just setting up to sweet talk me, but it won't work."

King held his tongue instead of telling her that his sweet-talking worked wonders in the bedroom last night when he had her on all fours, and in the shower this morning against the tiled wall, but he knew he had to pick his battles. He didn't need Mary riled up like a wet hornet.

"I'll be perfectly fine at your place. Hell, you got more security than Fort Knox."

It was true. King had security cameras at every juncture and angle recording every inch of his property. With his location, there was rarely a drifter, but if there was, it meant they were either utterly lost so far from town, or they were there for nefarious reasons. So, being out in the middle of nowhere, he wasn't taking his chances.

"Our place."

"What?"

"You said, 'your place,' meaning my place, but it's our place."

Mary closed her eyes and shook her head. He was trying to throw her off track. "Whatever. The point being, I don't need to have Ember at my side twenty-four-seven now that things have settled down."

King couldn't make her see reason. She was so green, which was one of the many things he loved about her. She always saw the best in people and gave them the benefit of the doubt. But, seeing the worst of society, in every corner of the earth, made King know that a lot of people were inherently bad no matter where they came from.

It wasn't class, or race, or wealth; if people thought they could get away with it, they didn't care what law they broke or who they hurt, as long as they got what they wanted, it was fair game to them.

"Sug'—Mary, please, listen to me. Just because things have settled down doesn't mean you're not in danger."

"I could get hit by a bus, or killed in a car accident," she waved her hands frantically, stating her point, "or fall, trip, and break my neck, yet you still let me out of the house...when are you going to order me to stay indoors?"

He tightened his jaw, biting on his molars to stay silent, letting her get her rant over with and off her chest.

She stood and crossed the office to the window, then turned back to face him. "Really, King, you can't expect me to stay at Ember's every time you leave. I was fine staying there when you left, when I first moved into your place—"

"*Our* place—"

Mary threw daggers with her eyes. "But I'm not going to stay there this time."

King didn't know how to make her see reason, and he knew arguing this out would be a losing battle for both of them, so he decided to table it for now. He rose from his chair, crossing the room to her side. "Mare, why don't we get lunch, and we'll discuss this later?" He went to pull her into an embrace, but she crossed her arms over her chest.

"Doesn't matter if we discuss it now or later, I'm not giving in on this."

King made an indistinguishable sound and walked to the door. If she was going to be stubborn, so was he.

"Where are you going?"

"Lunch."

"But, we didn't finish this."

King pinned her with a hard stare. "No sense to continue talking. Neither of us is going to be satisfied with the outcome. I'm getting lunch, and I'll be back in an hour. Are you coming?"

She stayed rooted in place.

"Suit yourself."

She watched him exit the office and stood there stewing. *Big lug!* When would he stop being so overprotective? She laughed at herself because she knew the answer before she finished the thought. The answer was never! She turned and stared out the window, mulling over her anger at him.

"Is it safe to enter?"

She turned, and Trip was in the doorway.

"Were we that loud?" Mary winced.

"Do bears shit in the woods?" Trip quipped and walked over to where she was standing.

Mary shook her head at his response. Leave it to Trip to be able to make her laugh when she was pissed. "Can you believe him?"

Trip stayed quiet.

Arms still crossed, she dropped her gaze on him, trying to elicit a response.

Trip raised his hands in surrender.

"I know you have an opinion, and I know you're never one to hold back your thoughts, so tell me what you think." Mary waited.

Rubbing at his short beard and scratching at his temple, he contemplated his next thought. "Don't want to overstep my bounds, and it may not be my place, but I think you need to humor him and give him this."

Mary let out a huff. "Do you realize how unreasonable it is for him to have me followed twenty-four-seven while you all are gone? I mean, Ember has a business to run, and I'm sure she has better things to do than sit around guarding me from King's imagination." She threw up her hands in disgust and shifted her weight to the other foot. "Chet hasn't surfaced and my brother—" she let the sentence trail off.

Trip sucked up the stab of guilt he always suffered whenever thinking of her brother. Though he wouldn't make a different decision with King's life in the balance, he felt a pang of sorrow in his heart for Mary.

Mary's voice softened. "Anyway, the threat," she put the word in air quotes, "is no longer, so there's no reasoning to his argument."

He rubbed his beard again, a sign he was going to say something she would vehemently disagree with. "Not completely true, Mary," he measured his words, "Adrian Wheeler is still in the wind, and there's no telling if Los Caballeros Rojos is a threat or not."

She knew her brother's friend, Adrian, was still nowhere to be found. He, along with Chet, carried out the staged robbery, and he was the one responsible for her injuries that day. King was searching for him and had feelers out to all his contacts, but it was as if he'd dropped off the face of the earth. He was MIA.

If King's contacts couldn't track him, either he was so deep undercover and hadn't surfaced since the shooting, or he was dead. And, as for the Rojos gang, as far as King knew, there was no tangible information they were a threat, or if they even knew Trent had a sister. But, it wasn't a chance he'd take.

Trip continued, "Mary, just please, humor him, and stay with Ember."

She started to protest, but he cut her off.

"He has a million-and-one things he's thinking about and executing when we're out in the bowels of hell. Not only is he trying to keep himself alive, but also the other five of us. He's good at blocking out everything and staying solely on the task at hand, but we all know you're constantly on his mind. If he has to worry about your safety, our safety, his safety, and the safety of the mission, that's not an equation that ends in good odds."

"So, what, am I supposed to stay under Ember's wing for the rest of my life?" Her statement surprised her, and she knew Trip didn't miss it by the smile that rose on his face. She was in it with King for the long haul. She wanted forever.

"He'll relent...eventually. It's just going to take him time—"

"It's been months, Trip."

"I know, I know, but he'll come around."

"And, if he doesn't?"

Trip thought about it and answered, "Make you a deal. If he's still irrational after six more months, the guys and I will stage an intervention."

"And, if he fires all of you?"

Trip laughed, knowing that wouldn't be a stretch of the imagination. King had fired each one of the guys at least 1,487 times since they'd come to Hellforce. Going without saying, Trip being fired more often than most.

"If he doesn't let up, then we'll boycott and picket until he comes to his senses...or I'll Ex-Lax his coffee each day. Either way, he's shit out of luck." Mary chuckled, knowing if anyone would do something to get under King's skin, it would undoubtedly be Trip. "He will come around, Mare, it's just that he loves you and doesn't want anything to happen to you." He pinched the apple of her cheek. "And, anyway, you're adorable, so I can see why."

She laughed at his weird sense of reasoning. He was always making her and the others laugh, breaking the tension with something funny, though she wondered if he used humor to hide something deeper, something no one knew about.

"Fine." Mary exhaled the word.

"Oh, shit!"

"What?"

"I know when a woman says *fine*, that means you're *fucked*!"

"So, not true!" Trip nodded his head, even at her denial. Mary rolled her eyes, "Whatever."

"That's another live one!" Trip turned towards the door, "I'm out of here before you start mansplaining to me about how all men are responsible for keeping all women down." He was joking, but Mary picked up the box of tissues on the table next to her and hurled it at him as he left.

"Oh, shit! She's on a roll!" She could hear him yelling with humor all the way down the corridor. She shook her head at his antics and thought about what he'd said. She could humor King for a little bit longer, though it'd kill her. But if it went on any longer, she'd really put her foot down.

"Pass the popcorn." Ember was sipping her soda from the Krazy Straw that looped twice before ending at her lips. She had shown up at King's place earlier that week, as was Mary's compromise with him, that she'd stay with Ember as long as she could stay at his place. Ember was game since she wouldn't have to drive Mary from her house to Hellforce and then back into town to her gun range. Hellforce was right down the street from King's place, so she could just drop Mary off and head straight into town. It was a win-win for everyone.

Mary passed her the bucket and grabbed for the bag of Twizzlers between them. "Ya know, I could watch *The Notebook* on a never-ending loop and never get sick of it."

Ember furrowed her brows, "Really?"

"Yeah, I mean, it's the perfect love story. It has everything a girl could want. Lust, love, romance, drama. It's every girl's fantasy."

"They die in the end."

"True, but they die together." Mary nodded as if to punctuate her point.

"You're so weird." Ember popped a few kernels in her mouth. "So, you think you and King will end up like Noah and Ellie?"

Mary smiled at the thought. She and King together until old age, madly in love. "In the end, yeah, but not all the in-between stuff. I don't want to do a breakup, or drama, misunderstandings, or any of that bullshit..."

"So, you just want to skip to the 'dying in bed' part?"

Mary nodded, pulling the Twizzler from the bag and biting the end. "Yeah, basically."

"Totally weird."

"What about you and Slate?"

Ember scrunched her face. "What? No way. I told you, we're just friends."

"You say that, but you can't tell me you've never thought about it."

In all honesty, Ember never had. "No. God, he's practically my brother. We've had this conversation already, Mary."

Mary leveled her with a mocking lift of her eyes, "Paaaa-lease!" She pointed the bitten end of the licorice at her, "You can't tell me you *never* thought about what it would be like to scream out his name?"

"Ewww...that's really gross! Eli and I grew up together. I don't see him like that."

"So, the fact that he's drop-dead gorgeous, has the most mesmer-izing eyes on the planet, is hot, smart, kind, ripped with abs to die for—"

"Wow, sounds like *you* want to date him. Shit, tell King to hit the road and jump Eli." Ember was joking, making Mary roll her eyes again.

"Come on Em, he follows you like a lost kitten—"

"No he doesn't," she paused, "he just cares for me, that's all. I'm like his little sister."

"Well, then buckle up, hun, 'cuz there's 'bout to be some incest comin' your way!"

Ember scoffed and threw a handful of popcorn at Mary. "Whatever, let's just watch the elderly couple perish in bed and call it a night." It was only a little after eight-thirty, but Mary knew Ember turned in early to be at her range by five in the morning.

"Now who's the weird one?"

They both cackled in laughter and turned back to the movie.

"You know the book doesn't end like—"

The television went black, as did the rest of the house.

"What the fuck!" Mary belted. "Power's out."

"Stay here." Ember made her way to the side table and pulled King's Glock from the drawer. Racking the slide, she went to the shelf hanging on the wall and moved the vase of flowers to the center.

"What are you do—"

Immediately, the lower half of the shelf dropped open, revealing another handgun, answering Mary's unfinished question. Ember knew of all King's hidey holes for irons around his house.

"Here, take this." She handed the gun to Mary.

Mary took it with hesitation. "Um, Annie Oakley, why are we armed? The power's out."

"Weather's perfect, no windstorms, rain, or lightning. Something's not right." The hair on Ember's neck was standing straight up, and she knew from her time in the Army that was never a good sign. It usually meant shit was going to hit the fan, and seeing as they were sitting ducks out in the middle of nowhere, she wasn't taking any chances.

Mary grasped the pistol, her nerves rattling. "Em, maybe we should just call the power company?"

Staying in the shadows, Ember peered out the front window, using the jamb as cover.

"Why didn't the generator kick in?" Mary knew Ember probably didn't know, but her nerves were ramping up, and the darkness had her on edge.

Ember turned to make her way to King's security room to check the camera feeds when glass shattered from the bay window and a flash of blinding light exploded. A concussion bang went off, rendering both women unresponsive.

Booted feet came into view as Mary rolled to her side. "Nighty night," a voice said and she inhaled deep in shock and panic as a cloth came over her face. The struggle was short-lived, and the fight was drained as darkness enveloped her.

The wheels touched down just before nine, and the guys couldn't wait to unload their gear, shower, and head home.

Five days in a godforsaken shithole of a country most couldn't find on a map had them thankful for being back stateside. The debrief would be short; the mission went off without a hitch and there wasn't much they needed to go over. It would be a short end to the long night, and then a few days of R&R for the guys.

King couldn't wait to have Mary in his arms. He knew she'd rake him over the coals for making her stay with Ember, but at least she'd agreed when he compromised and they stayed at their place. King had peace of mind with the security of their home. No one would get past his cameras and cybersecurity fences.

Slate walked beside him as they crossed the tarmac.

"Gonna pick up Ember after you shower?" King spoke while he walked, heading to the lot where his truck was parked.

"Yeah, figured I'd drive her into town so you can get your fill of 'Mary-time!'"

King shot him a glare but the corners of his lips gave him away. Not letting Slate get the best of him, he schooled him. "Just about as much as you want your 'Ember-time.'"

Slate didn't retort.

"It doesn't go unmentioned that your place is clear across town from hers, and it'll take you twice as long to get home if you drive her."

Still, Slate was mum.

"Are you going to tell her?"

Slate pursed his lips then rubbed the back of his neck, a tell of his that King knew. A tell that said he was nervous or uncomfortable. "Don't go there, King." His tone was terse, but King continued as if he hadn't spoken.

"Don't know why you're letting it linger. You like her. You've known her forever. Her family adores you. Her *dad* adores you!"

King was pointing out all the things that didn't need to be pointed out.

"Exactly." He rubbed his neck again. "All the more reason to stay away from her."

"That doesn't even make sense."

"You wouldn't understand."

King stopped and faced his teammate. "No. no, you're right. I don't know what it's like to have a lifelong friend, someone who knows me inside and out better than I know myself, knows all my quirks and bad habits but still likes me anyway. I just found that in Mary, and it'll be a cold day in hell before I'd ever give that up. I thought I'd go the rest of my life and never have that, but thank God I found her, and thank God she's woman enough to have me."

Slate looked away.

"Telling you, Slate, not as your boss or teammate, but as your friend, grab onto that while you can, before it's too late. Before you see her with someone else, falling in love and walking down the aisle on her daddy's arm."

The thought made Slate burn within.

"Don't wait. You want to see her with someone else's babies—"

"Enough!" Slate's anger had bubbled, and he knew King was working for his reaction.

"Telling you friend, we both know her, we both love her, although in different ways, and we both want what's best for her. Grab her, and don't let her get away."

"Whatever, King. Just because you're in love and seeing romance at every turn, doesn't mean the rest of us have it in the cards." He continued walking, leaving King behind him. He wouldn't admit to King that he was absolutely right. He'd loved Ember for as long as he could remember.

Yeah, he grew up with her, he loved her family, they loved him and her father treated him like his very own son. They were family. But, that was the reason he could never tell Ember how he truly felt. Because that's exactly how she saw him...as family.

She'd given him that message loud and clear before he ditched a full-ride four-year scholarship and enlisted in the Army.

The guys pulled out of the parking lot and headed to HQ. Dusk was falling and the hues of orange had turned to dark purple. The full harvest moon illuminated everything. Night was falling and the weather was calm.

King couldn't wait to see Mary. Using the truck's Bluetooth, he dialed Mary's phone. It rang until sending him to voicemail. Finding it odd she didn't answer, he tried the house's landline. It, too, went unanswered.

King's hackles rose, and he had to tamp them down, knowing Mary was probably busy and would accuse him of overreacting when he got home. He dialed Slate.

"Mary not answering?" Slate's voice was stern.

"No. Wh—"

"Neither is Ember."

His hackles rose higher along with his worried temper. "Tried the landline, but it went unanswered, too."

"Did the same for me." Slate didn't want to sound any false alarms, but it wasn't like Ember to not answer his calls, especially when he returned from a job. She waited for his call and would answer day or night. He palmed his neck, "King?"

He didn't answer, just fell into operator mode. "Gonna swing past the house before going to the office."

Slate agreed. "Good call, I'll follow."

The parade of trucks ventured towards headquarters, each of the guys following, as King led them down the country road from town to Hellforce. Something didn't sit right in his gut, and for once, he hoped like hell he was overreacting.

∾

"Wake up, bitch!" Mary felt a slap to her face, and the sting of pain radiated along her cheek to her temple. "Open your eyes, we got some fun for you."

She felt a haze come over her, and her head throbbed. She opened one eye, fogged with confusion.

"Wake up sleeping beauty...let's play."

Mary's eyes popped open when she didn't recognize the voice. Although the room was dark, she didn't recognize the man leaning over her. His breath was horrendous, and his clothes were unkempt. The stale smell of body odor wafted from him, and Mary recoiled when he loomed above her.

"Daddy's got a big surprise in store for you."

His laugh scorched her. *What was happening? Why am I in the master suite?*

"Don't hog all the fun." Another man's voice came from outside the room.

Instantly, Mary recognized the voice. Chet Richardson. *Oh, fuck!* A rush of adrenaline dumped into Mary's veins. A panic set in, and she wanted to scream, but the tape across her mouth held the shriek in.

What do I do? She searched her mind but came up blank. A tug on her elbow had her standing. One minute she was lying on the ground, the next she was being pulled upright. The bite at her wrists told her that her hands were taped behind her back. Her ankles were bound as well. *Fuck!* She was in deep shit! *Ember!* She was with Ember. *Had she gotten away? Is she bound, too?* Before she could look around to find her, a scream came from the living room.

"She fuckin' bit me!" The crack of a slap followed Chet's outburst.

Mary realized Ember was in the other room with him.

"Bring the bitch in here. She can watch the fun we'll have with this one, then we can play with her."

A shiver iced down Mary's spine. *What are they going to do?* God, Almighty, she knew exactly what they were going to do! She prayed with all that was in her, somehow, she'd be able to escape or get free.

Ember appeared at the bedroom door, arms stuck behind her back, feet bound, dragged by Chet. Even though it was dark, Mary could see her split lip bleeding. Ember had a look of death seething from her eyes. Mary knew Ember could kill a man with her bare hands, but that point was moot, seeing as she didn't have her hands free, or feet for that matter. She couldn't fight back or escape.

Panic welled again, and regret pooled in her mind. Why had she been so stubborn and not heeded King's warning? She traded intellect for stupidity, and boldness for demise.

Chet pushed Ember to the ground and she fell with a thud. "Watch it, you motherfucker!" Ember cursed him which earned her a kick to the stomach. She cradled as much as she could, but Mary saw the pain cross her face.

"Shut her up." The man holding Mary tossed Chet a roll of duct tape.

Chet grabbed it and straddled himself over Ember's chest. Ember spit on him, and he backhanded her, smearing the blood from her lip across her jaw. "Fucking cunt!" He tore off a length of tape and slapped it across her mouth. "Spit now, bitch!

Ember's eyes bore through him. Mary had never seen the happy-go-lucky woman enraged, and Mary could only imagine this was the face she'd worn in battle. She wished with all her might that Ember would free herself and kill both the scumbags.

A jolt to Mary's arm had her attention on the man holding her upright. "Time for us to get acquainted."

Mary stiffened when the man licked a path up the side of her face. *Please, please, please, King, where are you? Please help me!*

She knew he was thousands of miles away, across the globe, but she threw her prayer up to the universe and hoped he'd hear it.

"Adrian, I want the first go at her."

Adrian! Oh, God, this is Adrian Wheeler. It all came back to her. He was the one she'd seen going through her brother's things when she walked into his room the day of the robbery. He must've been the one who hit her and knocked her unconscious. *Oh, shit!*

A wicked laugh came from him, "Ah, light dawns?" Mary closed her eyes and hoped this was all a bad nightmare, and she would wake up in King's arms. He grasped her jaw and squeezed her cheeks. "Look at me, bitch." He waited for Mary to open her eyes. He angled her head so she was forced to look him in the eye. "The party's just starting." Adrian shoved her towards the bed and let her fall with a push. She was on her side and stayed that way, too scared to move an inch.

The moonlight bathed her through the window. With its brightness, Mary was able to see what was happening around her.

Chet chimed in again with his unanswered demand from before. "I get her first. You can have the biter."

Adrian set eyes on Ember, now propped up against the wall by the closet shooting death at the two men. "Don't matter to me...I like my women feisty!" He walked over to her and bent down to eye level, "I'm gonna rock your—Ouuu, *fuck!*"

Before he could finish the sentence, Ember rammed her head straight in his face.

Adrian reared back, holding his nose, blood gushing from his cupped hand. He stumbled back, but recovered, and kicked her as hard as he could.

Mary heard her winces and yells even with her mouth covered.

Adrian kicked at her mercilessly as Ember tucked herself in a ball, trying to protect herself as best she could. Chet ran over and stopped the torment, pushing him away from her sheltered body.

"You'll pay for that, bitch, when my dick's up your ass!" Adrian yelled over Chet's shoulder, "And, your friend will pay for it, too!"

Oh, God. They're going to rape us. Mary went from panic to frantic.

Chet examined his friend's nose. "It's not broken. Just lots of blood." Adrian wiped at it, smearing blood across his knuckles.

Mary looked at Ember's crumpled body. She wasn't moving. Maybe she was just passed out or playing possum, but Adrian got a few kicks to her head. Mary prayed she was just unconscious and not dead.

There were times in her life she was scared, but they were child's play compared to now. She was scared out of her mind, absolutely petrified! Chet was leering over her, and she wasn't sure what his next move would be. She tried to think of any way to get out of the situation, but her mind drew a blank. She'd seen Ember head-butt Adrian, but she was too scared to try anything like that.

"You're ol' man fucked with the wrong crowd. Did me a favor cutting your idiot, fuck of a brother out of the fray, out of my way. God bless him for that. But, when his guys fucked with me, taking a pound of flesh...well, sweetheart, I'm going to take back my pound right here."

Mary screamed beneath the tape, terrified and crying.

"Scream all you want, bitch...G.I. Joe ain't going to save you. And, anyway, I like screamers."

Chet drew a knife, from where Mary didn't have a clue, and trailed it down the side of her face, "Say we have a little fun before the pleasure begins?"

Mary turned her head, pushing her face into the mattress as far as possible to get away from his touch.

"Maybe cut into these beauties?" He spoke while running the knife over the swell of her breasts.

She stared up at him, helpless to do anything. "Let's see what you're hiding under here." Without warning, he ripped her sleep shirt from the V-collar, all the way down the front.

Mary screamed beneath the tape, squirming under Chet. She was still wearing a bra, so she wasn't completely exposed to him, but the terror overtook her. She started to cry. Rivers of tears welled and pooled, falling in streams over her temples.

He grabbed her face and she winced. "Oooh, yeah, you like that."

Mary cried harder, and it was hard to catch her breath only breathing through her nose. She turned her head, trying to get away from him. Opening her eyes, she saw Adrian leaning over Ember.

King! Her single thought was a prayer.

∼

King drove down his desolate road and spotted a car pulled to the shoulder. Slowing, he noticed no one was inside. The hood wasn't open and there were no signs of distress. Stopping his truck, he put it in PARK and got out, leaving the driver's door open.

Five other trucks came to a halt, then his five brothers gathered around him, on alert and scanning the surrounding area. Under the light of the full moon, King walked to the front of the car, placing his hand on the hood. The surface was cool. T-BAR reached through the passenger's window and pulled the hood release.

"Keys still in the ignition," T stated. "Seems weird someone would break down and not take their keys when they left?"

King unlatched the hood, hovering his hand over the engine block, then touching it. His blood boiled, and he knew it wasn't good.

"Block's still warm. Someone's been here at least thirty minutes, no longer than an hour ago."

Each man's demeanor morphed to operator mode. Gone were the carefree brothers, and in their place stood six pissed-off warriors ready to kick ass and take names.

King looked down the road to the distance of his home. The house sat dark. The yard light and perimeter lights that came on at dusk were dark as well. Something was definitely wrong. Worry and fury spiked in his veins. "Grab your gear, boys. Plates and pistols."

Each of the guys carried sidearms outside of work so they set to the trucks and donned their vests, KABARs, and other gear. Gathering at the front of King's truck, they waited for his command.

"One truck; we'll stop by the underbrush, fifty meters from the house. Cy, you take point Slate, you're with us, T take the patio deck, Trip, Arctic, you take the back. Smooth, easy, no shots unless fired upon. Don your comms and keep them open."

Each man was replaying the shitshow that happened at the warehouse. None of them wanted a repeat of that night. King wasn't out for blood, wouldn't go vigilante again, but they could see it in his eyes, he wouldn't hold back if Mary were in danger.

King drew his phone from his pocket and dialed 9-1-1, reporting he had a possible disturbance at his home. He knew he and the boys would get to the scene before the authorities, but also knew he'd need the official personnel of law enforcement there when whatever had his hackles up was dealt with. Pocketing the phone, King finished laying out the plan then headed for the driver's seat.

Five men settled into the bed, ready to wage hell on whoever was stupid enough to be waiting at his house.

～

Coming across the driveway and ducking into the portico of the front door, King tested the handle, "Fuck! It's locked," he said in a low tone that didn't carry farther than the distance of Cy and Slate.

Slate stepped out from under the cover of the porch stoop and surveyed the front of the house on the other side of the door. "Window's breached!" The front bay window was completely shattered. The glass was gone, pushed in from the outside; no glass was scattered outside of it.

All three swore under their breath. King spoke into his comm, alerting the others of the damage. "Breach in front. Must've entered through the window. Stand down 'til notice." He kept the comms open, so each man could hear, and unlocked the door, not wanting to alert whoever may be inside.

Cy was first to enter, pistol drawn, scanning the room, while Slate covered him from behind. King entered after him when Cy signaled with a sign of "all clear." Slowly, the three moved as one, passing through the front room and making their way to the back of the house. Cy held up a fist and they stopped in the hallway when they heard a voice.

"Let's see what you're hiding under here...oooh, yeah, you like that."

King's blood ran cold when a muffled scream came from within. Instantly, all three men were moving, entering the room in a flash.

With the element of surprise on their side, Cy entered first, followed by Slate, then King. What should have been mass chaos was executed precisely with precision. Cy holstered and came up behind the man who had his back to the door, hovered over the bed, and had him pinned to the ground, knee on his back and his head pushed into the ground before the guy knew anyone was even there.

Also holstered, Slate honed in on the man crouched by the closet. When the guy turned, looking over his shoulder at the last second, Slate palmed him in the face, stunning him as he reeled back then tackled him to the floor. Both takedowns happened in seconds.

King bypassed his teammates subduing the men on the ground and rushed to the bed. What he saw had him crazed.

In the moon's light, Mary laid wide-eyed and terrified, staring up at him, bound and gagged, as if he were about to jump her.

He had to soothe her. "Mare, Mare...Babe...Mary, it's me, it's King!" She flailed and shook, closing her eyes and screaming beneath the tape. The sounds ruptured his soul. The terrified screams were muffled but still blood-curdling. King lifted his night vision goggles and held his hands to the sides of her face. "Mary... look at me, I got you." Still, she fought with everything in her. He reached down and tore the tape from her mouth, knowing it would hurt, but hoping it would stun her enough and she'd stop, coming to her senses.

"Mare, Sugar...Mare look at me. I got you, Baby. Sugar—"

Mary stilled but was still incoherent. Her face, cupped by King, was held in place, but her eyes darted back and forth, trying to make sense of her surroundings.

He brought his face close to hers, within inches, and made her see him. "I gotcha, Mare. Look at me, Sugar. You're safe. I gotcha...shhhh."

His coaxing went on as she settled and returned to herself. Her body still shook, but this time because of her nerves and not a frantic scramble to get away from him.

Sirens screamed in the distance and came to a blaring halt.

"King?" Rivers still streamed from her eyes.

"Yeah, baby, it's me, you're safe." He leaned over her and planted a kiss on her forehead wishing with all that was holy that he could spare her any more terror.

"Oh...Kin—" she didn't finish his name before she sobbed with a hiccup.

T-BAR entered the room, still bathed in darkness, after clearing the rest of the house and finding no others. On T's heels, Trip and Arctic entered with the sheriff and deputy, firearms drawn and raised, but the two hung back in the hallway when the room was overcrowded and let law enforcement control the scene. T bypassed Slate and immediately went to Ember, crumpled against the floorboards by the closet, performing first aid on her unconscious body.

Checking for a pulse, the sheriff kept his hand on her neck, as he pulled his radio secured to his shoulder and called for backup and an ambulance.

At King's feet, Cy had his knee planted deep into Chet's spine, Chet's left arm pulled high and tight behind his shoulder blades, while his right arm was pinned beneath his own body's weight. Chet moaned and whined at the unbearable pain and pressure Cy inflicted. Served the cocksucker right. With the downward force, Chet was immovable and rendered useless.

Holstering his sidearm, the rookie deputy, one Cy didn't recognize, knelt across from Cy and removed his handcuffs from his utility belt. He cuffed Chet's left wrist, as Cy lifted the pressure off Chet's back and stood so the deputy could cuff the other wrist pinned underneath.

In a rookie mistake, the deputy hadn't applied enough weight to hold Chet down but instead rolled him to dislodge Chet's arm.

Mayhem erupted and shit hit the fan, setting two events into motion.

In all of a split second, Chet rolled to his back, swinging his now freed arm across the deputy's chest, knocking him off-balance and sending him backwards as he scrambled for purchase. In one fluid motion, Chet reached for the deputy's gun but the deputy caught his wrist mid-draw. Seeing the two grappling, Cy lunged for the fight, as did Slate. But before they could come to the deputy's rescue, King un-holstered and sent two rounds straight into Chet; double-tap to the forehead.

Adrian, now abandoned by Slate, took his one and only chance. He lunged for T, whose back was turned assisting Ember. He pulled the Sig P226 strapped to T's thigh. T-BAR spun, but before Adrian slid it from its Kydex holster, Slate was over him. He fired a round followed by a second, copycatting King's shot, and sent Adrian to his maker with a keyhole between the eyes.

The sheriff spun at the sight of Adrian's move, drew his weapon and fired two rounds into Adrian, the shots in tandem with Slate's. Arctic and Trip barged into the room to join the melee but didn't fire.

The concussive blasts left everyone's ears ringing, and the room filled with the smell of burnt gunpowder and sulfur.

Mary shrieked at the consecutive blasts and King was immediately hovering over her before he re-holstered. "Shhh...it's alright, I got you, Sugar."

King picked her up, wanting to remove her from the scene of their room, and carried her to the living room where he settled her on his lap. Cradling her in his arms, they both sobbed together.

"It's...it's Chet," Mary got out between cries. "Adrian...too."

Hearing her heartbreaking cry, it took everything within himself not to jump off the couch and put more rounds into the two motherfuckers. Mary was more important than his need for revenge, and he knew the sheriff and his team would hold him back. Besides, even if he could, he wouldn't leave Mary alone while he did bidding. "I know, Sugar. They'll never hurt you again."

As T, Arctic, and Trip filed past them on the couch, King addressed Arctic. "Stay with Mary."

Mary froze, clutching at his vest.

"I need to cover you, Mare."

It hadn't occurred to Mary that her breasts encased in a lacy, sheer bra were exposed to the men around her, though they were averting their eyes.

Before she could further protest, Arctic had his friend covered, "No. Stay there, boss."

Arctic pulled the throw blanket from the back of the couch and laid it over Mary.

A moment passed between them, and King knew his brothers would always have Mary's back. She was his, so she was theirs.

Mary burrowed deep into King's chest, and he thanked God he was able to get to her before the unthinkable happened.

"Ember?" Mary jolted upright and almost clocked him in the chin. "She's hurt, I gotta—"

"Shhh, Sugar...Slate and Cy got her." The last thing he wanted was Mary returning to that room. Hell, King had the mind to burn the damn thing down, because he was never letting her go in there again.

"But, she's—"

King pushed her back to his chest, settling her in place. "She's in good hands, Mare." Which was true, but by the sounds coming over the comms, King knew shit was flying.

Slate was losing his shit. He came barreling through the front room at a brisk pace, knuckles dripping with blood, with Cy on his heels leading him out the front door. The entire team knew Ember meant the world to him, so when he realized she was hurt, they all heard him over comms as he wailed away, sending his fists through the wall, taking every ounce of frustration out that he couldn't take out on Adrian's already cooling corpse. Cy let him have his pound of flesh, if only in drywall, but stopped him before he inflicted too much damage on himself.

King heard the ambulance sirens along with more deputy backup, and again, he thanked the heavens and universe for the woman he held in his arms.

CHAPTER 27

Moans of pleasure fell from her mouth as she flung her head back and writhed against him, leading to her third explosive orgasm of the night.

King had come home from HQ dressed in a navy-blue suit and a red silk tie, something Mary knew meant he'd been in meetings with 'big brass' all day. His demeanor was grumpy, as expected, and there was one way she knew she could bring him out of his stupor. She'd left work early to prepare herself to greet him at the door.

"Hey, big boy!"

King looked up from taking his keys out of the lock and groaned with sexual prowess. He immediately ditched his jacket in the entrance and was taking off his cufflinks as he beelined towards her.

Mary's excitement heightened at the look of animalistic lust in his eyes. She was wearing a white see-through babydoll teddy with a matching white thong that covered not much of anything. And besides her silver, strappy heels that wound up her ankles, she was bare. When he reached her, she was expecting him to grab her close and kiss the hell out of her. Instead, with a dip of his shoulder, he hoisted her up and over his shoulder, stalking off towards the master suite, and Mary squealed with delight!

Almost three weeks had passed since Chet and Adrian broke into King's place. Cy had offered his home to them while he stayed with Slate until King decided what he wanted to do with his place. He wanted to torch it, but Mary said he was being utterly ridiculous and put him in his place, arguing that he was being an irrational idiot. He'd thought about selling it, and again, Mary put the kibosh on that idea. She told him under no circumstances was she letting the two assholes keep her from *their* house. King almost lost it, becoming a puddle of mush, when she'd finally addressed the house as theirs.

At first, Mary couldn't go into the master suite, and she panicked every time she saw the space. They spent their nights in the guest bedroom, but by the week's end, she'd forced herself to come to grips with what happened and decided enough was enough. King wanted to get a new bed, but Mary said no. She wanted to keep the bed; the bed where they became one. King was leery, but Mary said they had to re-christen it.

Which was what led to her three monstrous orgasms of the night, as she rode King unabashed, slamming down on him relentlessly. He grabbed her hips, thrusting up into her and guiding her back down onto his cock.

"Fuck, Baby, you're fucking gorgeous!" King watched as her tits bounced with every downward pitch she took. Her nipples were perked, the buttoned nubs begging to be touched. He obliged by tweaking first one, then the other, and she screeched at the sting and moaned when he released the reddened tips. A ripple of her inner muscles told King she was on the edge of another orgasm. She let out a sultry moan, and King closed his eyes. Never had he been with a woman who could make him cum with just a moan. He'd been on the edge through her last two orgasms, and he couldn't hold back much longer.

"I'm close baby, gonna need you to cum." He gripped her hips so hard and thrust up into her, he knew she'd have bruises from his fingers in the morning, something he knew she didn't mind.

He'd caught her examining the evidence of his holds before, and when he'd profusely apologized, she set him straight, telling him she loved to be branded by his love holds. He'd never held back after that.

"King, oh, fuck, Baby..." her voice was sultry and raspy, as she hammered home. "I'm gonna...fuck, I'm going to...King," she held back her ecstasy as long as she could. "Oh, fuck...*Kinnnggg*!"And, with the wail of his name, she shattered with an ear-piercing scream announcing her orgasm, clenching around his cock so hard, he shot off immediately. She milked him as he thrust deep and held her planted on his dick. Mary collapsed on top of him, panting, her breasts plastered to his chest, while he groaned into the crook of her neck.

Adding an afterglow, he bit her collar bone, prolonging her orgasm.

Heaven.

Absolute perfection.

There were no other words to explain what having Mary in their bed, in his arms, in his life, meant to him. They were perfect together. She evened him out. She was soft to his harsh, mellow to his temper...love to his hardened heart. They were the perfect union, and he knew what he needed to do. It was time.

He kissed her temple tenderly and spoke into her sated body, "Sugar, I gotta take care of this condom." He kissed her again, not moving her from his chest.

"Uh-uh." Her sleep-laden response made him smile.

"Baby, really, we're gonna have a mess if I don't get this thing off...then, one of us is gonna have to sleep in the wet spot."

"I don't mind."

He chuckled at her response. He loved how relaxed she got after sex. "You say that now, but you won't be saying that when your hip is stuck to the sheet."

They'd never had unprotected sex, so it was never his seed that caused any uncomfortable, post-sex sleep. The only wet spots they'd had were from when she'd come undone and wet the sheets when she came.

Reluctantly, she'd rolled off him, King guiding her to her side of the bed. She kept her eyes closed, savoring the post-orgasmic bliss.

She felt King rustling beside her and cocked one eye open. "You're disturbing my euphoria." When he didn't get out of bed and head to the bathroom as usual, she turned her head in his direction.

He rolled to his side and removed the condom, tying the end and dropping it off the side of the bed.

"What are you doing?" She was confused because it was his regular MO to head to the bathroom, clean himself, and return with a warm washcloth to pamper her.

He dug around in the bedside drawer then shut it. Thinking he was digging for another condom, she mock-complained in protest, "King, I thought you were coming up on forty and couldn't go multiple rounds without an intermission."

He laughed, then rolled to his side, spooning her from behind. Nestling his head on her shoulder, he began to speak. "I never thought it was in the stars for me to find the love of my life." Mary settled into him. "Even from a young age, after losing my brother, I knew I was going to be a career military guy and never imagined myself settling down. And after joining and making it to Rangers, then to Delta, I didn't feel I needed to have a woman to feel whole." He paused, collecting his thoughts, and Mary didn't fill the silence.

"Becoming Delta Force was the love of my life. I loved my job. It was my mistress in every way. Never once did I entertain the idea of stopping. I was on top of my game. Peak of my career. Time went on, and I got older with each passing year...never realizing what I was passing up in my thirties."

He kissed her ear, grounding himself in his reverie. "After the IED sidelined me, I spent months stewing, thinking it was all for naught since my military career was ended. I'd never last as a desk jockey, and I wasn't going to stay in just to milk out the next years without medically retiring. I thought maybe God was punishing me, and the physical recovery was just as tormenting as the mental recovery. It was really lonely. No visitors." He corrected, "I mean, my folks came but couldn't stay for long."

He chuckled, "I had Arctic, but he was as cranky a son-of-a-bitch as me, so we weren't the best company to each other."

King laughed at the distant memory of his time in the hospital with his best friend. "Then, when I got out, time passed, I'd realized I needed what I always denied I wanted. It was sobering, as it was shocking. I didn't want the bar scene, I didn't want the one-nighters. But, I didn't want to be alone. I'd all but given up hope that I could find someone...ya know...my *One*."

His voice thickened, "Starting Hellforce was the best thing I've ever done in life, Mare...because it brought me to you."

Mary hitched, and he could feel her smile radiate throughout her as she hugged his arm tighter around her waist.

"The stars aligned, and there you were." His voice cracked, "Not a day goes by, Mary, that I don't thank the heavens for you. I never knew I wasn't whole without you by my side. And, I can't imagine going a day without you in my life."

She thought she heard a tremor in his voice.

"I love you, Mary."

"I love you, too. I don't ever want to go another day in my life without you, Henry."

It was his name on her lips that sealed him. *Henry.* She didn't say it often, which made each time she did all that more incredible.

"Marry me, Mare."

His words shocked her. *Did he just say what I think he said?* The question didn't even have time to settle in her mind before King reached over her shoulder and held a ring between his fingers.

"Marry me Mary, say you'll be my wife."

Her chin began to quiver and she couldn't take a breath. She could hardly see through the tears in her eyes when she zoned in on the ring he held in front of her.

Her grandmother's ring.

King kissed the back of her head. "You make me whole, Mare. We both know how short life can be. We've survived to know how true that is."

He started to get nervous when she didn't speak or reach for the ring.

Panic welled within him, "I know it's soon, but I know it's right."

She didn't reply.

"If it's the ring...if you want a new one...one that's new and yours, not...um, not used."

"Yes!" She turned in one motion to face him, plastering him with a kiss that morphed into a deep, passionate one.

He could taste the saltiness of her tears as they mingled with his own, catching on their lips when he deepened their kiss. He was the first to pull back. "Yes?"

"Yes!"

He brought the ring to her. "We can get a new—"

"No! Oh, My God, King, no... you got my grandmother's ring." More tears flooded her cheeks and soaked into their shared pillow. In the time since the robbery, the warehouse, King's near-death experience, and then the break-in with Mary and Ember, she'd never asked about the ring.

King had taken it to a jeweler and made sure everything was secured and got it looked over and cleaned. It still held its antique charm but glistened like never before.

"I thought I'd never see it again. I didn't even think to ask you if you found it." Disbelief overcame her.

"Will you marry me?" He held the ring between them.

A thousand years could go by, and she'd never get over the love she felt for the man beside her. Things may not always be roses, but she knew that they could weather whatever came their way. Through the storm, he'd shelter her, and through the grief, she'd nurture him. They'd ride out the hard times and revel in the good times. Through it all, they'd persevere.

Smiling through her tears she answered, "Yes, King! A thousand times, *yes!*"

They both waded through a myriad of tears and kisses. Then, with shaking hands, King slipped the princess-cut diamond onto her left finger, then kissed the ring.

"Always and forever, Sugar…"

"Always and forever," she repeated.

≈

Six men stood in a Vegas wedding chapel, one, more nervous than the others.

"Breathe, Big Guy." Arctic's voice came from beside him.

"Easier said than done," King quipped.

"It's going to be great." Cy encouraged him, "You've been waiting for this moment since you first laid eyes on her."

It was a little bit of a stretch of the truth, but for the most part, it wasn't far off. The preacher came forward, smiling at King.

"Last-ditch effort to duck out, King! Now's your chance," Trip said from the row of men, letting out a breath when Slate elbowed him in the gut and gave him a glare. "What?" Trip rubbed his abs and straightened out.

"Your soon-to-be-bride is going to be gorgeous!" The pastor remarked. "Are you ready?"

King rubbed his sweaty palms on his thighs, tamping down his nerves, "Ready as I've ever been."

With that, the pastor cued his wife, who'd come through the doors at the back of the chapel and started the wedding music.

≈

"You look absolutely stunning, Mare!"

Mary watched in the mirror as Ember fixed her veil, pulling it into place. "You make such a beautiful bride."

Ember's voice broke, and Mary started to tear up. "No, no, no… none of that!" She retrieved the box of tissues from the vanity and handed one to Mary. "Don't want to ruin your makeup."

Mary dabbed at the corners of her eyes. "Thanks, Em."

Ember took the tissue and threw it away.

"I just want to say, thank you, for being here."

"Oh, my God, you don't have to say that. I wouldn't be anywhere else."

"It's just, with my mom not being here…" she started to well again, and Ember handed her another tissue.

"I'm honored that you wanted me as your maid of honor."

"Well, you are my only friend, so it was slim pickings." Mary laughed.

Ember put her hands on her hips, "So, I was the winner by default?"

Mary mocked, "Yeah…basically."

Both women burst out laughing, and it lightened the mood and settled her nerves.

"In all seriousness, Em, thank you."

"I love you, Mare." Ember loosely wrapped her arms around her friend.

"Love you, too."

"Are we just about ready?" A woman in her late sixties came fluttering into the room and stopped dead in her tracks. "Aw, look at you! Such a gorgeous bride!" She shook her head in admiration and circled Mary, fluffing out the crinoline tulle around the skirt of her dress. "You've got one lucky man waiting for you."

Mary and King had settled on a quick jaunt to Vegas to tie the knot. With minimal family, they didn't want to do the extravagant wedding ceremony but wanted to be able to share their wedding with the people who were closest to them. The ones they considered family, even if it wasn't by blood. The only stipulation, Mary had insisted they be married by a pastor. She didn't want any Elvis impersonators or fly-by-night Justice of the Peace, she wanted their marriage to be sealed.

King remarked how he couldn't wait to undress her in a white wedding gown, so when they arrived yesterday, Mary and Ember ventured out to get dresses. She didn't set out to do the whole "poufy-gown thing," but when she saw the gorgeous Cinderella gown, she knew it was what she wanted. Ember agreed and cried when Mary tried it on, letting Mary know it was the one she wanted. If it made Ember cry, she couldn't imagine King's reaction when he saw her.

Ember was wearing a strapless, floor-length Merlot wine-colored gown. Her hair was up in a sexy twist and she looked absolutely stunning. Both she and Mary donned a pair of Tiffany-blue

Converse beneath their dresses, going for comfort over heels. The guys were dressing in their blues, and Mary couldn't wait to set eyes on King. She'd never seen him in uniform. Her libido was set on high alert just thinking of him. They'd all agreed not to dress until they got to the chapel, so the anticipation of seeing him was piquing.

"I'll let the others know you're ready." The pastor's wife hurried out the door into the adjoining chapel.

The music began to play, and that was their cue to start the show.

"Ready?" Ember handed Mary her bouquet of red roses.

"Ready." Mary sucked in a breath, and the biggest smile ever settled across her face.

"Let's go get you hitched!" Ember grabbed her smaller bouquet of white roses and disappeared through the double doors.

The ceremony was over, and the group of friends sat in the small dining area of the casino-hotel. King and Mary were so engrossed in each other, it was as if no one else existed around them. The group didn't mind and mingled the conversation between themselves.

King stared into his bride's eyes. *God, she's beautiful!* He just about died when he saw her walking down the aisle. She was absolutely stunning. As many times as he'd imagined her walking towards him, he'd never envisioned anything like what he saw. She took his breath away. It wasn't the dress, which he couldn't wait to tear off of her, and it wasn't her hair or makeup; it was just...her. Her pure, natural beauty. Every bit of her excitement and love radiated out of her. Now, sitting next to her with his ring on her finger, he couldn't imagine anything more perfect in the world.

King stood, lifted his glass, and waited for the conversation to die down. When all eyes were on him, he took in the faces around him. "Y'all know I'm not grandiose, so I'll keep this short," he cleared his throat, "but, besides Mary, there's no other group of people I'd rather have spent this day with. You're more than teammates or employees...and friends," he held onto Ember's eyes a little longer on that note, "you're family. And like family, y'all I know I'm a grumpy son-of-a-bitch—"

"That's an understatement," Trip interjected, making everyone laugh.

King gave him a mocking glare, then continued, turning to Mary, "You keep me grounded, you see the best in me, even when I can't, and others don't. You never know what kind of bear you'll wake up to."

"Paws or claws," Mary said, winking at him, causing him to smile.

"Yes, definitely more claws than paws." He let out a breathy laugh. "But you love either side of me, and God only knows why." Mary sent him a kiss. "But, in all seriousness, I never thought I'd find someone to settle down with, let alone, fall in love with. And, this posse will testify to that." Heads nodded around the table. "But, you not only keep me grounded, but you also took this ragtag, motley group under your wing."

"Shit, she's a saint!" Slate cut in.

"That she is!" King agreed, then addressed the table, "But, I wouldn't want to have any other ragtags or motleys next to me. Thank you all for celebrating this day with us." He turned to his bride, "Whatever comes our way, I'll love you for eternity."

Everyone clapped then started dinging their forks and spoons against their glasses.

King pulled Mary up from her chair, locked his lips over hers, and dipped her low, making the sultry kiss weaken her knees.

Hoots and hollers came from those around them, and after a minute they finally came up for air.

Still standing, King cleared their chairs and took Mary by the hand.

"Going to try your luck on the casino floor?" Arctic asked the happy couple.

"It's not the casino floor where he'll be getting lucky," Trip added to the conversation. The table erupted with laughter, Mary blushed, and King threw his cloth napkin at him.

"Any of you assholes disturb our room tonight, it better be 'cuz one of you is missing or dead." King scribbled his signature on the bill and turned to scoop up his bride, hoisting her up, and headed out of the restaurant. Mary screeched at the sudden movement, and in a cloud of white tulle, thrown over his shoulder, she waved at the group as they all catcalled and whooped.

"Well, on that note, I'm heading to the blackjack tables." T stood.

"We're going to go for a stroll on Fremont Street and see the lights." Slate grabbed Ember's hand, and she grabbed her clutch from the table. "Gonna take in the glitz and glam of the city. Anyone else want to join us?" She waited to see if there were any takers and didn't see Slate visually beat down each of his teammates who dared to accept her offer. "No...no one?" Ember waited patiently as Cy, Trip and Arctic declined. "To each their own, I guess."

Slate was eager to leave. "We'll meet you guys down here for breakfast." With a chin lift, he bid farewell to his brothers and left with Ember in tow.

"How long until they hit the wedding chapel?" Arctic asked the remaining two.

"Maybe they'll be like Ross and Rachel and have a drunken nuptial, and by morning they'll be hitched, too," Trip joked.

Cy stood, drinking down the last of his Scotch, then set the empty glass down on the table. "Anyone up for a show? Burlesque...tantalizing vixens?"

"Scantily dressed women, classy yet bare...I'm in!"

"Feathers and boas hiding perky tits and ass. Lead the way!"

Both Arctic and Trip drank down their drinks, and the three ventured off into the streets of the Vegas strip.

~

T-BAR raked in his winnings of the last three hours at the blackjack table and was feeling pretty good about his odds so far. His night in Vegas was off to a great start, and he had a feeling his luck was just starting. He'd just keep getting luckier as the night wore on. He figured he'd quit while he was ahead and try his luck at the roulette tables.

Pushing away from the table, he stood and checked his text messages, phone in one hand, drink in the other. Cy had messaged they were catching a show and would be at the Golden Nugget afterward. Seeing it'd been a few hours since they'd all split, he figured he'd meet up with the group and see where the night took them.

One minute he was typing out a text, and the next, his drink splashed over the front of his white button-down shirt.

"Son-of-a-bitch!" The words were out of his mouth before he could call them back. Hands outstretched in disbelief, and keeping any further liquid from spilling, his eyes stared at the amber stain of whiskey bleeding into his chest.

"Oh, my God...I am so sorry!"

The most angelic voice T had ever heard came from the woman patting down his chest, as if the stain would magically disappear with a wipe from the daintiest hands he'd ever seen. His eyes cast up and his surroundings faded.

A girl...no, a woman, stood before him with cascading locks of midnight black hair, waves of which hung over her shoulders, cupping her small but full breasts, and framing her beautiful face. She had a pout of thick, plump lips that had T absently licking his own, and her green eyes were mesmerizing below her perfectly manicured arched brows. T had seen a lot of attractive women in his life—hell, he'd attracted them like moths to a flame without even trying, but none of them had him dazed, with his palms instantly sweating and his voice stolen.

"Oh, my...I'm such an idiot," she dabbed at his chest again and T-BAR hated that she'd disparage herself. She glanced up at the ceiling, wildly looking around, then frantically wiped at him again. "Fuck, my father's going to kill me..." the words were uttered under her breath but had T alarmed. She absently wiped at his slacks, not even noticing if she rubbed him any harder, she'd have him raging in her hand in a heartbeat. "I'm sorry—"

T grabbed her wrist to stop her from patting him into an erection. "Doll, don't worry about it. It's completely my fault; I'm usually always aware of my surroundings." His accent laid soft on the pet name that popped out.

At his term of endearment, she stopped patting him and raised her gorgeous eyes to meet his. Her lashes were thick and long, but T knew, undoubtedly, they weren't false. He'd seen over-made, pancake-face-makeup women and knew natural beauty when he saw it. She was all real. She had a tinge of eye makeup and a hint of lip-gloss, but other than that, nothing hid her untouched glamor.

Noticing he still had a hold of her wrist, he suddenly let go of it. She stared at his hand as if missing its grasp. She took a twenty out of her purse and handed it to him, "Here, take this for your dry cleaning. If the shirt's completely ruined, I think I have another twenty—" she dug into her small purse again, retrieving a second bill and held them both out to him.

T stared at her outstretched hand, wondering what the fuck she was doing.

"Here, take it." She shook the bills at him, "I don't have anything bigger, it looks like an expensive shirt...God, I'm so sorry!" She apologized again, scanning the ceiling once more.

T looked up, trying to figure out what she was looking at, but only noticed the security bubbles affixed to the ceiling.

"Just fuck it," she pushed the bills back into her purse, "Let's go to the haberdashery and get you a new one. I know a great one right in the hotel." She bolted from where they stood as if the hounds of hell were at her heels, and T unwittingly followed behind her.

Her ass. Was. Fine! T was an ass man. He loved a fine set of tits, but nothing spurred him on more than to have his hands grabbing onto a woman's ass as she rode him or he rode her from behind. Either way, the sway of her ass in her flowing, thigh-high wrap dress, had him groaning and willing his hardening cock from growing. Not helping, was how her legs went on for miles in the dainty, aqua-colored stilettos she wore.

Though she was tall for a woman—he'd guessed about five-eight —her heels put her just below eye-level with his six-four. Usually, he preferred shorter women, someone his height could dominate, but something about this raven beauty had him following her, without question, at a quick pace.

Entering the lobby and then following the wide corridor, they both walked in silence. T was never short on words, especially when it came to women, but at the moment, he couldn't come up with a single thing to say.

"Here we are." She entered a men's apparel store, beelining for a rack of shirts. "Pick out whatever you want, I've got it covered."

He stood dumbfounded, not even sure as to what was happening. When he didn't move, she rummaged through the rack, pulling out a shirt and holding it against him but far enough away that it wouldn't be stained from the one he had on. "That looks like it's the right size." She eyed the sleeves and then settled her hand on his muscled biceps. Feeling a jolt, she pulled away.

How she had pulled out the exact size, especially when T was broader than most men, had him surprised.

"Is this all right?"

T looked at the shirt and nodded his head. She sauntered to the register, biting off the price tag with her teeth and handing it to the gentleman behind the desk.

"Here, change in the fitting rooms. If you need it tailored, we can get that done, too."

What the fuck is happening?

She shooed him towards the changing room, when he stopped in his tracks.

"Um, miss...I'm sorry, what..." he couldn't get his thoughts in order, "I don't need to change, and I don't need a new shirt."

She looked defeated, "Oh, shit, I'm sorry...I—"

"And, quit apologizing."

She was taken aback and winced at his commanding tone, taking a step back.

When he saw her wince, he softened his tone. "It's all good. Really, I'm good."

Relaxing, she bit her thumbnail, "But, I already took the tag off, so...um, you got a new shirt." She turned to the clerk, who stood silently watching their exchange, "Put this on my tab."

Whoa! No way was he having her pay for his shirt. "Doll, you're not paying for this," he held up the shirt she'd shoved in his hands. *Why does she have a tab?* His thought was cut short when she went on.

Stopping him with a staying hand, she continued, "No, I insist." She set the clerk with a look, and he immediately scanned the lone tag and entered it into the computer.

"Yes, miss. Anything else, miss?" His voice was sweeter than sin as if he were bowing to royalty, and T didn't like it.

Pinning T with a stare, she pushed, "You need to try that on, to see if it needs tailoring."

T looked down at the shirt, as if in bizarro world, still trying to figure how he'd gotten there, then shrugged. "I'm sure it'll fit. I'll just go change in my room."

She bit her nail again, something T found sinfully attractive, and she relented.

"Can I wrap the shirt for you, sir?" The clerk said it more for the lady's benefit than for his.

"No, that's okay. I'll just be heading up to my room."

Again, she bit at the same nail, then dropped her hand when she noticed he'd caught her.

An awkward moment passed between them, then T held up the shirt, "Thanks, for...this." He was out of sorts and pursed his lips. "Um, thanks." He turned to leave the store, and she watched him go. Before he was a few steps out into the grand corridor, he stopped, trying to figure his direction to the nearest elevator bank.

"What wing are you in?"

He closed his eyes at the sound of her voice from behind, hoping the sweet sound of it wouldn't have his cock jumping to attention. He turned, and she was smiling a small smile at him. She seemed shy, yet bold at the same time. Normally he hated clingy and needy women, but she was neither. She seemed to just be looking out for his well-being. T pulled his room card from his pocket and examined it, turning it over with one hand. "Um, west wing, I think."

She came up, took the card from his hand, and studied it. "Oh, yeah, this is…West wing, tower, which means you have the best view of the strip from the center of the floor."

T didn't like anyone knowing where his room was located. He wasn't paranoid, but he kept his privacy close to the vest. Chalk it up to his time in the military.

She started towards a bank of elevators, then looked over her shoulder when she noticed he wasn't following. As if drawn by some magnetic field, he was behind her in a few strides, standing next to her, as they waited for the car to arrive. She slid his key card into the elevator panel. The bell dinged, and she entered when the doors opened, and dutifully, he followed.

"I'm on the twentieth," she answered, without him asking what the hell she was doing.

"Twentieth? Top floor, penthouse?" T let out a whistle.

As if embarrassed, she looked down at the floor.

"You're either a high roller, or you know someone in the mob." He laughed at his own joke but sobered when she didn't laugh along. He noticed her wide-eyed reaction in the mirrored doors. In fact, she seemed nervous, looking anywhere besides him. He immediately felt like an ass.

Fuck! He chastised himself. *What is it with this woman that has me falling all over myself?* Usually, he was smooth as silk when it came to women.

"I'm sorry, that was utterly rude of me," he apologized.

She shrugged it off, "No, no, please, don't apologize."

It seemed the entire time since they'd met, someone had been apologizing.

The elevator arrived at the nineteenth floor and the doors parted.

"Guess this is me," T uncharacteristically stammered.

She gave him a flattened smirk, "Guess it is."

Standing longer and prolonging the awkwardness, he lifted a hand to her, not knowing what else to say, so he threw her the lame gesture.

She raised her hand, giving him a small wave of her fingers.

He stepped off onto his floor, then watched as the doors drew closed.

Shit, damn and fuck!

T sighed to himself then scrubbed the stubble of his beard. Staring down at the now-wrinkled shirt in his hand and shaking his head, he regretted not asking her out for a drink, seeing as she was partially responsible for spilling his first one. The thought had him huffing out a chuckle. *Shoulda, woulda, coulda.*

Regret wasn't his forte, so he started for his room when the ding of the elevator stopped him in his tracks. Turning, he saw the doors part and there she stood, twisting her hands. Not saying a word, she stepped off the elevator and gave him the same flattened smile as before.

T didn't miss a beat. "Would you care to join me for a drink?"

Taking in a breath, she glanced at the ceiling and then smiled back at him. "I'd love to, especially since I cut your last drink short." She pointed to the stained shirt he was still wearing.

T laughed, finding it incredibly sexy she found humor in the same joke he'd thought of moments ago. He nodded in agreement, then walked back to her and took a few steps towards the elevator. When he reached to push the button to call the car, she grabbed his wrist, much like he'd done to her earlier.

T stopped himself before he reacted, and would have had her facedown on the ground in any other circumstance.

Sensing him tense, she loosened her grip, then dropped his hand. "I was hoping we could get a drink in your room." She was trying to come off more bold than normal. T could tell by the racing pulse in her neck, unobscured by her hair pulled away over her shoulder. She brought her thumb to her mouth, perching the polished nail between her teeth.

T felt his dick twitch. Without hesitation he lowered her hand from her face, freeing her abused thumb, and led her down the hallway to his room.

"By the way, I'm T."

"T?"

"Yeah, it's a nickname," he said while inserting his key card, opening the door, and ushering her into the room.

She nodded, "Well, if you're T, then I'm A."

And with that, the door closed behind them.

EPILOGUE

SLATE, CHILDHOOD

Five-year-old Elijah sat on the hard, uncomfortable folding chair, looking at all the people milling around the room. Some of the people he knew, but most weren't familiar. His mother sat next to him with a tissue in her hand, occasionally dabbing at her eyes and blowing her nose, while people came near to talk to her in low voices or hug her in an embrace.

Elijah didn't know what was happening. This morning, his mom dressed him in his Sunday church clothes and told him he had to be a good boy. She clipped his tie to his white shirt and told him she loved him more than anything in the world, then kissed him on top of his head.

All the faces around him were sad, and the mood was sad too. He watched a man and woman walk to the front of the room and stop next to the brown wooden box where his daddy was sleeping. He hadn't seen his daddy come home after work like usual, and he hadn't been home in a few days, so Eli didn't know why his dad was sleeping here, and why everyone was watching him sleep. On the end of the box was a big flag. Maybe it was there like a blanket in case his daddy got cold. He knew his daddy was a brave policeman, and someday, he wanted to grow up to be brave just like him.

Eli swung his legs back and forth on the chair and pulled at his collar, wishing he'd be going home soon and could change into his play clothes. He couldn't wait to play in his new sandbox and line his army men up on the wooden sides.

"Elijah, come have a seat." His mother dabbed her eyes again and walked to the front of the room, then patted the cushioned couch seat beside her. Eli followed, not liking how the room had suddenly gone quiet and everyone was staring at him and his mom.

The church preacher stood at the front of the room by his daddy and said some really nice things about him. It wasn't like normal, like at church, when he heard stories of Jonah and the Whale, or about the animals on the ark. It didn't make sense to him, but he remembered his mom telling him to be a good boy, so he didn't ask any questions.

The preacher talked for a long time, and it was hard for Eli not to fidget. Daddy always told him to pay attention when they were at church, so he thought his daddy would want him to sit still and listen now.

"We have to go say goodbye now." His mother blew her nose and her eyes were red and filled with tears. She grabbed him by the hand, and they went and stood next to the brown box. Eli could hear people crying behind him and it made him sad that others were sad. The pastor stood next to his mom and put his arm around her shoulder. His mom leaned close to the box and kissed her hand then put it on Daddy's. She started to cry, and the pastor led her back to the couch.

Eli stood on his tip-toes and looked over the edge of the box. His daddy didn't move or sit up, or say, "Hi, bud," then lift him up to wrestle or read stories like he did when Eli would wake in the morning and sneak into his parents' room. His daddy sometimes pretended to be sleeping and would swoop him up and tickle him until he laughed so hard his belly ached. He wished his daddy would do that now.

Eli reached for his daddy's hand and when he touched it, he jolted back. It was cold. Really cold.

"Eli, son, go have a seat next to your mother." The pastor helped him back to his seat. He couldn't get rid of the icky feeling he had in his stomach. Something wasn't right, but he didn't know what it was.

"Can we go home, Momma?" Eli didn't want to be there anymore.

"Yes, sweet boy, in a minute." His mom wrapped her arms

around him, and he settled into her side. Soon he'd be home, and when the sun went down, his Daddy would come through the door like normal. He couldn't wait to see his Daddy come home.

Find out more about little Eli by picking up the next book in the Hellforce Security: Alpha Team Series, Saving Emmy

ACKNOWLEDGMENTS

First, and foremost, I have to thank Susan Stoker for allowing me to play in the Aces Special Forces Operations Alpha world and giving me the opportunity to hobnob with your amazing characters. Though fiction in the world of literature, these characters have become real and cherished by your readers, and I hope I've done them justice. Thank you for your words of advice and encouragement. Writing in your Stoker Universe has been an adventure, and I am forever grateful for the experience.

To Riley Edwards, I thank you (and apologize) for the endless lists of questions I bombarded you with, on an almost daily basis. Words are immeasurable for my gratitude for the insightful advice you always lend. It sounds cliche, but is ever true, I could not have done this without you. You've taken an unknown, untried, newbie author under your wing, mentored me, guided me, and supported me before I got through my first manuscript. And, even when I didn't believe in myself, you gave me the encouragement to succeed and a kick in the pants when needed. I will forever be grateful for your support, and I hope to one day be able to return the favor to a newbie.

To my "Smutties," yes, you know who you are! This dream envisioned, first as a practical joke, blossomed into an unimaginable dream come true for me. I couldn't have done any of this without your love and never-ending support. Becky, you are literally my life-line on speed-dial and video chat, 24/7, to *every* crazy and unimaginable question I could throw at you: from medical opinions, to coffee bar menus, down to the choice of a character's underwear color. Thank you, a million times over, for not unfriending me...or calling the authorities. Anne, many times you have talked me off a ledge when I wanted to give up, pack up, and never wanted to write another word in a manuscript. Your push and encouragement kept me afloat in desperate times and for that, I am forever thankful. Jo, your mad reading skills are a gift to me, and I am honored that you take to heart my written words to heart and grace them with your intellect. You've encouraged me from the start to chase the dream, grab it, and never let go. You're a force to be reckoned with, my Cyclone Jo. So, to each of you, there are no words that can express my gratitude. Words are inadequate. Hellforce would not exist if not for this group of Smuts! I know I've driven each one of you bonkers at one time or another, but you kept me grounded, going, moving forward, AND gave a dose of cold hard truth when needed. Though miles of land and even oceans divide us, you've woven a dream come true for me. I love you all with the depths of my heart.

To Anna, Lynne and Nicole thank you for letting me invade your Messenger and FaceTime with my overload of every question that this newbie author could fathom. You are a gem in my host of treasures, and I am unbelievably grateful for your time, understanding, and patience. It takes a village!

Rebecca, I am humbled by your gift of editing and the eye of an eagle. Without you, literally, none of this would be a reality. It would be a love-lust romance buried in the files of a computer. You know my depths of gratitude, and I will never forget the gift you have bestowed upon me. My words are short, but my gratitude is unending.

Lori, thank you for gracing the cover with the prime cut of alpha meat! Your artistic eye makes it look easy, but I know with my vision of romantic eye-candy, most likely had you rolling your eyes and wondering how you got roped into making King a reality. Forever, I am humbly grateful.

And, finally, TO THE READERS: Thank you for taking a chance on me, a new author, and this first series book. Thank you for giving me a few hours of your precious time. You don't know how much your support means to a newbie, and I'm honored that you chose to join the pages of Hellforce.

Love, peace, and hugs,

Rayne

ALSO BY RAYNE LEWIS

Hellforce Security: Alpha Team

Justice for Mary

Saving Emmy

ABOUT THE AUTHOR

Rayne Lewis is a lover of all things books. On an ideal weekend, you'll find her curled up in a comfy chair, cup of tea brewed, binge reading a good series. She loves a happily-ever-after romance and also a good "who-done-it" mystery. Baking is a passion and her favorite sweet is her Mandarin orange-pineapple cake (or anything that'll curb her sweet tooth). Though a novice, sewing is a hobby. When she isn't in the kitchen, she enjoys evening walks with her husband and spending time with their furry doggo at the dog park. She's a Midwestern girl and loves her family.

There are many more books in this fan fiction world than listed here, for an up-to-date list go to www.AcesPress.com

You can also visit our Amazon page at:
http://www.amazon.com/author/operationalpha

Desiree Holt: Protecting Maddie
Kathy Ivan: Saving Sarah
Kris Jacen, Be With Me
Jesse Jacobson: Protecting Honor
Silver James: Rescue Moon
Becca Jameson: Saving Sofia
Kate Kinsley: Protecting Ava
Rayne Lewis: Justice for Mary
Heather Long: Securing Arizona
Gennita Low: No Protection
Kirsten Lynn: Joining Forces for Jesse
Margaret Madigan: Bang for the Buck
Trish McCallan: Hero Under Fire
Kimberly McGath: The Predecessor
Rachel McNeely: The SEAL's Surprise Baby
KD Michaels: Saving Laura
Lynn Michaels: Rescuing Kyle
Olivia Michaels: Protecting Harper
Wren Michaels: The Fox & The Hound
Annie Miller: Securing Willow
Kat Mizera: Protecting Bobbi
Keira Montclair, Wolf and the Wild Scots
Mary B Moore: Force Protection
LeTeisha Newton: Protecting Butterfly
Angela Nicole: Protecting the Donna
MJ Nightingale: Protecting Beauty
Sarah O'Rourke: Saving Liberty
Victoria Paige: Reclaiming Izabel
Anne L. Parks: Mason
Debra Parmley: Protecting Pippa
Lainey Reese: Protecting New York
KeKe Renée: Protecting Bria
TL Reeve and Michele Ryan: Extracting Mateo
Elena M. Reyes: Keeping Ava
Deanna L. Rowley: Saving Veronica
Angela Rush: Charlotte
Rose Smith: Saving Satin
Jenika Snow: Protecting Lily
Lynne St. James: SEAL's Spitfire
Dee Stewart: Conner

Harley Stone: Rescuing Mercy
Sarah Stone: Shielding Grace
Jen Talty: Burning Desire
Reina Torres, Rescuing Hi'ilani
Savvi V: Loving Lex
Megan Vernon: Protecting Us
LJ Vickery: Circus Comes to Town
Rachel Young: Because of Marissa
R. C. Wynne: Shadows Renewed

Delta Team Three Series
Lori Ryan: Nori's Delta
Becca Jameson: Destiny's Delta
Lynne St James, Gwen's Delta
Elle James: Ivy's Delta
Riley Edwards: Hope's Delta

Police and Fire: Operation Alpha World
Freya Barker: Burning for Autumn
B.P. Beth: Scott
Jane Blythe: Salvaging Marigold
Julia Bright, Justice for Amber
Anna Brooks, Guarding Georgia
KaLyn Cooper: Justice for Gwen
Aspen Drake: Sheltering Emma
Emily Gray: Shelter for Allegra
Alexa Gregory: Backdraft
Deanndra Hall: Shelter for Sharla
Barb Han: Kace
EM Hayes: Gambling for Ashleigh
India Kells: Shadow Killer
CM Steele: Guarding Hope
Reina Torres: Justice for Sloane
Aubree Valentine, Justice for Danielle
Maddie Wade: Finding English
Stacey Wilk: Stage Fright
Laine Vess: Justice for Lauren

Tarpley VFD Series
Silver James, Fighting for Elena

Deanndra Hall, Fighting for Carly
Haven Rose, Fighting for Calliope
MJ Nightingale, Fighting for Jemma
TL Reeve, Fighting for Brittney
Nicole Flockton, Fighting for Nadia

As you know, this book included at least one character from Susan Stoker's books. To check out more, see below.

SEAL Team Hawaii Series
Finding Elodie
Finding Lexie (Aug 2021)
Finding Kenna (Oct 2021)
Finding Monica (TBA)
Finding Carly (TBA)
Finding Ashlyn (TBA)
Finding Jodelle (TBA)

Eagle Point Search & Rescue
Searching for Lilly (Mar 2022)
Searching for Bristol (Jun 2022)
Searching for Elsie (Nov 2022)
Searching for Caryn (TBA)
Searching for Finley (TBA)
Searching for Heather (TBA)
Searching for Khloe (TBA)

Delta Team Two Series
Shielding Gillian
Shielding Kinley
Shielding Aspen
Shielding Jayme
Shielding Riley
Shielding Devyn (May 2021)
Shielding Ember (Sept 2021)
Shielding Sierra (Jan 2022)

SEAL of Protection: Legacy Series
Securing Caite (FREE!)
Securing Brenae (novella)
Securing Sidney
Securing Piper
Securing Zoey
Securing Avery
Securing Kalee
Securing Jane

Delta Force Heroes Series

Rescuing Rayne (FREE!)
Rescuing Aimee (novella)
Rescuing Emily
Rescuing Harley
Marrying Emily (novella)
Rescuing Kassie
Rescuing Bryn
Rescuing Casey
Rescuing Sadie (novella)
Rescuing Wendy
Rescuing Mary
Rescuing Macie (novella)
Rescuing Annie (Feb 2022)

Badge of Honor: Texas Heroes Series

Justice for Mackenzie (FREE!)
Justice for Mickie
Justice for Corrie
Justice for Laine (novella)
Shelter for Elizabeth
Justice for Boone
Shelter for Adeline
Shelter for Sophie
Justice for Erin
Justice for Milena
Shelter for Blythe
Justice for Hope
Shelter for Quinn
Shelter for Koren
Shelter for Penelope

SEAL of Protection Series

Protecting Caroline (FREE!)
Protecting Alabama
Protecting Fiona
Marrying Caroline (novella)
Protecting Summer
Protecting Cheyenne
Protecting Jessyka
Protecting Julie (novella)

Protecting Melody
Protecting the Future
Protecting Kiera (novella)
Protecting Alabama's Kids (novella)
Protecting Dakota

New York Times, USA Today and *Wall Street Journal* Bestselling Author Susan Stoker has a heart as big as the state of Tennessee where she lives, but this all American girl has also spent the last fourteen years living in Missouri, California, Colorado, Indiana, and Texas. She's married to a retired Army man who now gets to follow *her* around the country.

www.stokeraces.com
www.AcesPress.com
susan@stokeraces.com